VOODOO VENDETTA

A LITERATI MYSTERY

GK JURRENS

UpLife
Press

eBook ISBN: 978-1-952165-23-8
Paperback ISBN: 978-1-952165-24-5

v.220516-221211_0938
GKJurrens.com

*Please note the list of major characters
and maps of key venues in the appendices.*

DISCLAIMER

This is a work of fiction. Any similarity to actual persons, behaviors, places or events should be considered coincidental and fictional.

No part of this publication may be stored in a retrieval system, transmitted, or reproduced in any way, including, but not limited to, digital copying and printing without prior agreement and written permission of the publisher, UpLife Press.

Research of this manuscript's period and its theme mandated judicious use of ethnic pejoratives and mild profanity, and are not meant to offend the reader. Quite the contrary, the use of these literary devices is intended to demonstrate the authentic commitment to a higher set of moral standards and to the strength of each character's faith, or lack thereof.

DEDICATION

To all who serve and sacrifice for others.

ACKNOWLEDGMENTS

- Many thanks to my new friends in Natchitoches Parish, Louisiana.
- Thanks, Ted F at the Louisiana History Museum for spending so much time with this curious author to share your expansive knowledge of Louisiana history and local legends.
- A shout-out to my treasured beta readers, and to *all* my readers! Without you, there is no story.
- A special thanks to Julia S. Your awe-inspiring attention to detail always keeps me on my toes.
- Bill W, I appreciate you contributing your invaluable experience as a criminal defense attorney.
- Gus H, your eye for detail polishes my every manuscript, and appreciate your corporate legal perspective.
- Tom K, your extensive undercover law enforcement expertise lent authenticity to my key characters' language and behavior.
- The entire staff at the Melrose Plantation, Natchitoches, Louisiana brought history alive for this Yank! Jim, good luck with your historical narrative. Here's hoping your screenplay makes the History Channel, my friend. Make Ken Burns proud!

CHAPTER 1

A FEW YEARS FROM NOW

June 21st
Natchitoches,
Northwest Louisiana
7:00 AM

SYBIL THIBODAUX—RELUCTANT CELEBRITY AND DOTING daughter. Oh, how she loved her papa. But she left him behind too often. This week would be different. They sat on the second-floor covered balcony of the Judge Porter House, an opulent bed and breakfast that had seen better days. Like them.

Her papa sat too close sipping his mint tea. They both overlooked the manicured grounds, but said nothing. They had hardly spoken since arriving late last evening.

She blamed herself. Enthusiasm—and tragedy—drove her to become something greater than herself, greater than her love of family, even greater than her considerable love of life itself. Though she too often denied that to herself.

All-American poet and activist, she claimed fame with her substantial body of published works that popularized her fiery Creole identity.

Sybil launched into international fame when she performed her poem, "Loud and Proud," at the inauguration of U.S. President Marjorie Cullin two years earlier. Even though she thought the poem —and her performance of it—could have been better, she blossomed as a media darling. Much to her dismay, *and* delight. Her message had become so important to so many. And that's what drove her. She loved who she had become. Didn't she?

Don't I?

Sybil adored that her adoptive father still doted on his little kitten, though she was now twenty-six. She called her beloved papa Cat. He moved like a panther, although slower now than in his perilous youth.

Cat—ruthless protector and doting father.

He had once told Sybil that her older sister had been stillborn, but she was not to grieve. That life was just never meant to be. Cat would say, "And dat's all."

She began writing anything and everything at three. Together, she and Cat had chosen her nom de plume—her pen name. It befitted her destiny, her place in the heart of the Louisiana Creole culture, America's forgotten people. She had become their voice—a proud free person of color, or *gens de couleur libres*, and she had something to say.

Her old name—her given name? Never to be uttered aloud. A name was just a name, but some used one's identity as a weapon against them.

Prior to publishing her first volume, she *became* Sybil Thibodaux. She would never understand why Cat was *so* adamant about this, although she suspected.

~

THIS WEEK MIGHT BE THEIR LAST CHANCE. CAT HAD A feeling. Even though Sybil was now a bona fide celebrity, her endless enthusiasm for life and for their cause gave her father such joy, and concern.

He also knew what this trip up from New Orleans to Nackatish together meant to her. To gain ever more knowledge of their people's unique history had always been her delirious passion, even at the expense of all else in her life. That included their relationship. He worried about her.

Now, she would trace her cultural roots, see with her own eyes, walk in the footsteps of her ancestors, who were both slaves *and* slave owners. Unique in all the world.

The intense love between Cat and his kitten only brought spontaneous tears of love and unsolicited pats on the head—even after Sybil grew to be an adult. If only she wasn't now a stranger.

Cat harbored a powerful secret he vowed Sybil could never learn in her lifetime—that of the identity of her mother. But Cat's love for that woman transcended the realm of the physical. That much was obvious for all to see.

His faraway gazes, the break in his voice when he spoke of her… no, their *unspoken* love consumed the man. He told his kitten, his little Sybil, she had passed over to another dimension, but that would never diminish his devotion to her spirit. There would be no other woman for this man.

Ever.

CHAPTER 2

J une 21st
St. John's Parish,
New Orleans, Louisiana

THEY RESPECTED AND FEARED HER.

Zelda Zenaida Coincoin wielded her reputation as a renowned Voodoo sorceress, holistic healer, and spiritual mentor to a countless throng of acolytes, not only within her parish, but far beyond, across the entire Louisiana delta region and northward.

According to her aboriginal Central African roots, they did not assign family names. Instead, *Coincoin*—pronounced *kwah-kwah*—was a derivative of the Creole's sometimes-adapted French language and translated to *second-born daughter*.

Sybil had always held nothing but the highest esteem for Zelda, her aunt on her mother's side, although she seldom saw her. Zelda had known her mother. Sybil was conscious of Zelda's many enemies, but they did not speak of that, nor of her mother, whenever they met. Sybil understood all too well.

Secrets and taboos....

Besides, Sybil's relationship with her aunt wasn't close. She knew better than most that with great power—like Zelda's—came great responsibility. And that drew demands on the influential woman's time. Still, the secrets bothered the young poet. How could they not?

Many consulted Zelda and purchased supplies required by the Voodoo or Hoodoo practitioner from her venerable shop, *Rootwork Spirituel,* on the bon Dieu side—the "good" side—of Canal Street. If the bright-eyed tourists who visited her shop only knew....

Zelda would say, *Some a de time, de ignorance be bliss, ya?*

Zelda had also become the de facto host of the annual head-washing ceremony along Bayou St. John on the Magnolia footbridge during the week following Summer Solstice each year—next week. Thousands would gather. Sybil *never* missed this most holy of Voodoo ceremonies. She was proud of her revered aunt, even though from a distance, all in white.

She also feared the woman...

Just a little.

CHAPTER 3

J une 21st
   Natchitoches,
   Northwest Louisiana
7:00 PM

TIHOMIR REMEMBERED. HOW COULD HE FORGET? HIS mother beat remorse out of him as a child, along with most every other emotion—except for the need to dominate. The woman also forbad him from fraternizing with anyone who didn't look like them, or believe like them.

When he turned eight, he showed his gratitude by driving a dull blade through the old witch's black heart. It took two hands. And gravity. After that, the state raised him to be a soldier, and later, a ruthless intelligence officer.

Then, eight years ago, he emigrated from Russia to America, where he could truly be himself with impunity.

The land where all is free to the powerful... like me.

Even now, as he sat in this luxurious American rental car, little had changed. He still didn't know how to ask for love, never having been shown it willingly. So, he took it, by force, when necessary. It frequently was.

Tihomir—Ty—Leonov became the perfect product of his environment. He took what he wanted by removing whomever and whatever obstacle blocked his path. He didn't much like who he had become. But what was he to do?

He had spent months in the curs-ed backcountry of Louisiana, from Nackatish Parish and the Cane River Country all the way down to the delta.

He purchased and developed land for high-speed canals to move bulk commerce into the massive New Orleans regionplex from the outlying areas. Water was everywhere. But it needed to be mastered, especially its depth. He leveraged remnants of the old Red River system that flowed into the Mississippi River. This canal system would also move finished goods worth billions northward.

TY HAD LEARNED OF THE CREOLES. HE LOVED WHAT HE SAW of their culture and developed a taste for their women—the younger, the blacker, the better. Although, most Creoles were of mixed blood, many denied it. That was okay, too. As long as he got his way. And he was addicted to getting his way. As the sixth richest man in America. his wealth entitled him to a cornucopia of freedoms not accessible to mere mortals.

Ty had also grown accustomed to the protection that anonymity afforded residents of giant regionplexes—population centers comprising dozens of millions spanning hundreds of square miles. That's where indulging in anything at all went unpunished far more often than not. At least, that was his experience in his adopted home of Chicago. He was Ty Leonov, after all.

Why should the backcountry of Louisiana be any different?

CHAPTER 4

M ontrose Plantation,

Montrose Plantation,
    Natchitoches Parish,
Northwest Louisiana
8:00PM

While in Nackatish, Cat and his twenty-six-year-old kitten took an after-hours self-guided VIP tour of the very rural Montrose Plantation near the Cane River. Sybil's fame preceded her. The poet's publicist informed the docent of the historical-site-slash-museum in advance that Sybil Thibodaux was to be afforded every courtesy.

Cat explored the barn. Kitten giggled like a schoolgirl as she wandered off to explore the slave cabins. Her people were both powerless slaves and later, influential slave owners. This historical fact fascinated her, and incited yet another layer of conflict in her about who her ancestors were, how they changed over time, and what they represented. She took some consolation that slaves were treated differently in the Louisiana territory than elsewhere in colonial America. More like family. At least, she chose to believe that.

Sybil and her papa had lost track of time. It was late. The expansive plantation grounds were all but deserted and well-lit. They granted few after-dark VIP tours. She was told only one other party would be somewhere on the vast estate this evening. That was just fine. She craved solitude with the spirits of her ancestors.

She found the small cabin that once housed a dozen slaves, at least one of whom she had identified as her ancestor. A flood of inspiration consumed her. She made mental notes about what she felt as she stood in the center of this small space.

A tiny cast-iron stove stood in the corner behind her. Double-high bunks had grown musty from lack of use. A small dehumidifier rattled with a soft hum behind the door, no doubt to battle the aging effect of moist Louisiana air. A dim light sat atop the small stove, the facsimile of a coal-oil lantern. She envisioned this is how it must have appeared by lantern light two centuries ago.

IT SOUNDED LIKE OLD CHALK ON SLATE. THE CABIN'S crude door scraped on the floor as it opened behind her in the dim light. The door itself remained shrouded in the shadow of a bunk between her, the lantern, and that door.

"Cat, is that you?" Silence.

"Hello?" Nothing.

The door scraped closed. She heard the ancient iron latch drop into its slot. Electricity shot through Sybil. She now regretted she was one of the few modern women who had never practiced the defensive arts.

Alarmed, she crept around the corner of the double-high bunk that stood between her and the now-closed door.

Where are you, Cat?

CHAPTER 5

Montrose Plantation,
Natchitoches Parish,
Northwest Louisiana
8:03PM

WHAT A COUNTRY! AFTER COMING TO AMERICA, TY LEONOV learned English by sounding out words, syllable by syllable. He still struggled to read English. In Louisiana on business, he decided to take a VIP after-hours tour of a Creole plantation in a parish—not a county—which was also the name of a nearby town called Natchitoches. Of course, they pronounced it *Nackatish*. Of course they did.

English! Or French! Not the bestest language of Mother Russia!

He loved American history. So brutal. Animalistic. They dressed it up with fancy words that idealized the conquest and killing of their indigenous peoples, the shameless rape of their natural resources just to starve them.

Their class system ranging from aristocracy to near-slavery

reminded him of home, along with their systematic re-distribution of wealth to the few aristocrats who knew how the world worked. And most everyone identified themselves as better than anyone else. At least everyone he knew. All the while, these Americans proclaimed their righteousness.

His kind of place.

AND THERE SHE WAS. BRIGHT LANDSCAPE LIGHTS CREATED a golden glow of the grounds. He spotted the girl, all alone, prancing into a small structure made of plastered-over logs and featured a generous overhang all around. At that moment, he knew he just must have her. She looked like… an authentic Creole. And this was an authentic Creole setting, was it not? How could his desire not be… authentic? And overwhelming?

With no pretext or pretense, Ty followed her into the small building. Closed the door. Walked up behind her. Yanked her long braided hair from behind. And without uttering a single word, delivered a mighty blow to her right temple with the inside of his right fist.

She melted in his grasp. He tore at her blouse and started clutching at her. Yes, this would happen. He bent her over a lower bunk bed face down and ripped away her skirt.

Ty heard and then saw over his shoulder an old man charge in who took in what was happening with a horrified expression of disbelief. The old man screamed at him.

Before Ty turned his attention from the girl, now unconscious on the bunk, he delivered one more vicious blow to the same side of her head. Needed to ensure she wouldn't wake up. The old man seemed blinded by rage. Ty turned and launched a lascivious leer.

The intruder, a black man, advanced on him. Another native. A local? A relative? Didn't matter. One backhand blow devastated the old boy who he outweighed by thirty pounds. He fell. His head thumped onto the corner of a bunk's frame. The old man crumpled to the floor, no longer a factor.

The girl, still unconscious and still face down on the bunk, was now ripe for the taking. He could smell her, almost taste her. He reached down and lifted her by her slender waist. Tore the remnants her shredded skirt the rest of the way off and... delightful. He would not deny his passion for young black women.

So... authentic.

CHAPTER 6

Montrose Plantation
Slave Quarters,
Natchitoches Parish,
Northwest Louisiana
8:40PM

SYBIL NEVER SAW THE BLOW COMING. WHEN SHE awakened, she only recalled its blazing brutality. A pin prick of light pierced first one eye, then the other. She understood none of the chatter thudding into her semi-conscious mind. The realization that she lay face up on a rough planked floor with someone placing a brace around her neck further confused her. Next to her lay, what? A body covered by a white sheet sullied with crimson stains near one end?

"What?"

"Miss Thibodaux, you've been... injured. We're preparing to transport you to the hospital. Do you understand?"

"My father...."

She didn't really need to ask. She wondered in her shock if they had borrowed that sheet from the bunk to her left—maybe the very bunk where this plantation's owner once raped her ancestor. No doubt a body bag awaited outside for poor passionate Cat.

The pain coming from her private areas—front and back—throbbed and burned.

Did my big cat try to defend me? Of course, he did, and he paid the price.

She needed no words from this medical person for the tears to flow. They ran into her ears as she lay there on the floor of that Creole slave cabin—her naked torso covered by another sheet. Except hers didn't cover her face like poor, dear Cat's.

"Someone attacked you and your father, sweetie. I'm sorry to say he didn't make it."

Those were the last words she heard until she awakened in the local hospital.

That night changed the trajectory of Sybil Thibodaux's existence. The ensuing days found her recovering from within a viscous black vengeance that poisoned her spirit. She knew it. Didn't care. The following weeks transformed Sybil into a bitter but relentless detective.

She had felt so powerless. A vile beast bludgeoned Cat, her father, because he had interrupted the sadistic victimization of his cherished kitten, raping and beating her at the tender age of twenty-six-years-young. Left her—a celebrated *free* Creole of color—like a spent tissue, bleeding and bruised on the crude planks of a slave cabin on a Creole plantation.

The irony tore at her like an ongoing attack worse than the first.

CHAPTER 7

June 27th
Natchitoches,
Northwest Louisiana
11:15 AM

Sybil refused to leave town. She would not return to New Orleans—all alone—until her anger trumped her anguish. She made a promise to herself in the darkness of her third night at the Nackatish Regional Medical Center. The monster *would* pay.

They often described Sybil Thibodaux as formidable.

They have no idea, do they?

She sat in the driver's seat of her rental car on Rue Beau Port below historic Front Street in the shade of a Magnolia tree. She arranged her notes on the passenger's seat as she made dozens of calls.

The hazy late morning sun reflected off Cane River Lake and forced her to squint against the pain. She adjusted her passenger's side visor. Her comms implant felt warm in her temple from too much rapid-fire use.

A cauldron of fear and anger was about to boil over. Within two days after she checked out of the hospital, against medical advice, she had developed more leads surrounding the atrocity than had law enforcement.

Sybil verified with the museum's docent he had signed in only one other guest for a self-guided tour of the plantation on June twenty-first, the night of the attack. He said the man was no local. Of that, he was sure. It was the unusual accent.

While the fictitious name in the guest registry led the Nackatish Parish sheriff nowhere, Sybil leveraged her significant means. She bribed the only agent at the only rental car agency within a fifty-mile radius.

Only one person with a foreign accent rented a car that week in Alexandria, Louisiana. Although there were no cameras, the docent seemed to recall a similar vehicle in the plantation's parking area that night. A valid driver's license was required for all rentals. The contract named Teodor Raspin, a resident of Chicago, Illinois.

For reasons she could not explain, Sybil chose not to share this discovery with the local constable. They'd follow the same path she did. Or not. Didn't matter. She made travel plans of indefinite duration after a short return trip home.

The New Orleans Voodoo community, with Zelda Coincoin as its most forceful voice, screamed for justice. Sybil did not scream. She would not. Ever again. She would act. History had proven the only justice possible for people like her and Cat would not be satisfying and certainly would not bring back her beloved father.

For that reason, Sybil made only a cursory visit to her aunt. Zelda embraced her, cautioned her, would not let her leave until she had gifted her niece the most powerful protection in her arsenal.

.   .   .

SYBIL'S FAME OFFERED FRAGILE LEVERAGE. IT GRANTED her an international voice for her people. She should do nothing to erode the efficacy of that powerful platform amid the madness of her modern world. But it conflicted her. She now sought justice, not only for her people, but for her murdered father. The violation she'd suffered left an enormous hole, and fueled her vengeance.

This emotional turmoil tore her in two very different directions. She was told her public platform and her private pain were now at odds. And there seemed nothing she could do to reconcile them, or to silence either demon.

In recent weeks, Sybil's publicist made it very clear she was committing career suicide by deviating from her well-orchestrated persona and all that entailed. She neglected her travel itinerary and countless public appearances on the worldwide cultural feeds. She tossed aside her negotiated and scripted rhetoric of positivity and hope for the future. Those... machinations, along with some powerful endorsements, had granted her fame in the first place—her *authentic* voice.

But now, she seemed helpless to return to all of that. She turned away to pursue her now-inevitable course of action. She would not—could not—deny her blood lust.

Sybil must pursue her most formidable demon.

She must go to Chicago.

There, she would bide her time.

For as long as it took.

CHAPTER 8

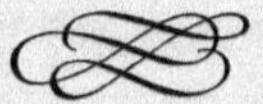

ONE YEAR LATER,

Sunday, June 21st
   DuSable Park
Chicago, Illinois
11:30AM

IT WOULD BE A DAY TO REMEMBER. THE MID-MORNING AIR glowed with uncharacteristic brilliance. The haze abated, allowing the summer sun to boast its magnificence in a sky of muted blue. A miraculous day, a unique day of days.

Melissa and Clancy Greigh stood in a line that meandered around the corner of their favorite food truck, Aphrodite's Kitchen. They chuckled at each other's stupid jokes, none of them worthy of a full-fledged laugh. But their hearts were full, unlike their stomachs.

Now it was their turn to order, at last. Aphro looked down at the pair of redheads, mother and daughter. In her heavy Greek accent, she chirped, "And what may I make for you lovely ladies?"

Instead of sharing an order of moussaka—their standard fare for their traditional Sunday morning outing to the park—Clance bubbled with anticipation as she delivered her well-rehearsed little speech. Though only six years old, Clance already enjoyed a sophisticated palate. "Mummy, could I have my own gyro today instead of splitting a moussaka? Please, *please?*" She widened her smiling eyes and wrinkled her tiny forehead as her eyebrows shot farther toward her hairline in gleeful expectation.

After all, she was a big girl now.

MEL GRINNED UP AT APHRO. THE STREET CHEF SHRUGGED at the convincing little speech. Mum gazed down at her little redhead. What an amazing child. If only dear Greigh were here. She reflected on this, one of those defining moments in a parent's life. He was missing it, but she knew how important his project was to him—and to all of them. After all, The Literati was their home.

Clance had become her own person, and her brilliance beamed for all to see. Mel imagined what her little girl would do with her gifts in life.

She was about to yield to her beautiful daughter's big-girl plea, even though she knew the sandwich would be way too much for her. And then a terrible crack of thunder echoed through the park. Mel studied Clance's wide-eyed wonder as a field of crimson blossomed across her tiny chest and her white camisole.

Mel registered instant concern, thinking Aphro might have dripped tomato sauce on her from above, which stains, but then lightning struck, and night fell.

SIR AUBREY GREIGH LABORED AT HOME. WITH A MANIACAL focus, he pursued his twin passions—writing and crusading. He owned suite 7D in Hotel Literati. As a condo owner and president of

"The Lit" Homeowner's Association, he labored with prodigious passion to ensure their home never fell into the hands of a greedy land developer. If that happened, they'd demolish their beloved building.

Sure, they'd offer a generous buy-out, but that wasn't the point at all, was it?

And then the call came that changed everything.

LATER, THE NEWS ANCHOR REPORTED.

"A sniper fatally shot five people and wounded two others standing in line at a Greek food truck in DuSable Park near the waterfront earlier today. Authorities will release no details until they notify families of the victims...."

WEDNESDAY, JUNE 24TH
Apartment 7D
Hotel Literati
Chicago, Illinois

TEN PM CAME AND WENT. THREE DAYS AGO, GREIGH'S universe went super nova. He sat on his sofa facing a dark fireplace... lost. He couldn't even cry.

More than a hundred of his neighbors and sundry celebrities—he had no friends, really—shared his profound grief at the funeral earlier that afternoon, and afterward, for his ladies' interment in the family crypt.

Just another unsolved random mass shooting. An acquaintance looped into the investigation told him the only "signature" left by the killer was a unique slug—from a .338 Lapua Magnum cartridge—fired from an ancient weapon called an IWI DAN .338, a tactical rifle that hadn't been manufactured for almost fifty years.

Two slugs from that weapon ended the lives of Melissa and Clancy Greigh. It might as well have ended his, too.

CHAPTER 9

THREE YEARS LATER

Thursday, June 14
CED's Ninety-ninth Precinct
Chicago, Illinois
10:35AM

Swingin' dicks, all. The men in the homicide detective bureau of the Chicago Enforcement Department's ninety-ninth precinct called Detective Lieutenant Chance McQuillan an Irish spitfire. She wasn't sure what that meant. Didn't care. Funny how only the men called her that. Almost like a sexist compliment *or* an even more sexist cut-down. But the women in the department just thought of her as an ambitious pit bull.

Who cares, right? Not me. Much.

"Gonzalez, are you looking at my ass, amigo?" She chuckled, amused by Ron's embarrassment at getting caught in the act.

"Cripe sake, cut me some slack, will ya, McQ?"

She had a job to do and was damn good at it. At twenty-seven, McQ was the youngest homicide detective lieutenant in the entire CED. Within the nine-nine, seventy-six percent of their homicides went unsolved, but McQ's non-closure rate was less than half that. Thirty-one percent to date, to be precise.

And I'm nothing if not precise, eh, boys?

"Relax, Ron. Just busting your chops. It's a nice ass, though, right?" Her legendary Irish smirk was so hard to decipher, they said.

"Ha! I ain't touchin' that."

"Damn right, you're not. How's the wife?"

A call came in. Yet another case assigned, on top of her eight other actives. Off and running.

A normal day at the office.

ONE OF THOSE CALLS CAME IN A WEEK AGO. THAT ALREADY-closed case consumed McQ's near-nonexistent free time. Most of the others in her squad would have considered such a call a needless distraction, a burden, an unaffordable bother.

Not McQ—not the "fiery Irish pit bull," they'd say. Along with more than a few others, the precinct comms operator admired the hell out of McQ, and knew where to direct this call—what McQ would call a "stray dog case," even though dogs were all but extinct. In the city, anyway.

"Shoot the stray-dog cases over to McQ," they'd say.

None of this surprised her.

Let 'em think what they want. Only thing worse than not locking up a criminal is locking up an innocent.

THEY HAD CONVICTED DARIUS STEWART.

Gina Stewart's husband was convicted for murdering their teenage neighbor girl ten years ago. Darius had now served a dime into his twenty-five-year sentence down at Danville.

Boiling over with excitement and new hope, Darius called his wife from prison. He told her that a fellow inmate convicted of serial homicide bragged that, among others, *he* "did" Shanice Emerson, the girl Darius allegedly murdered a decade ago.

Son-of-a-bitch!

Every cop knows that most every convict *says* they're innocent, but they also know few *are*. With thousands of homicides in the city each year, justice was not always served. And that pissed off McQ, even though it was inevitable.

What pissed her off even more? It only took a few hours of reviewing Darius Stewart's case file in her spare time, spread out over a week of late evenings, to uncover the shoddy case against this poor man. In her tiny apartment above an old cop bar on South Dearborn, no less.

She uncovered the lead detective's near-nonexistent investigation back in the day. Plus, an overworked public defender had mounted a sloppy defense. Worse, they had coerced Darius into a twenty-five-year plea deal just to take a life sentence off the table.

But now, the serial killer from Darius's cell block had confessed—on the record, to his cell mate, the accused—that *he*, not Darius, killed Shanice Emerson a decade earlier. That killer had nothing to lose, and it turned out, he liked old Darius well enough.

Seems like this should have been harder. But they'll soon free another innocent mook from the shitty justice system. That makes the loss of sleep for the last week worthwhile, doesn't it?

CHAPTER 10

M onday, June 18th
        Hotel Literati
Chicago, Illinois
7:00PM

Sybil Thibodaux smoldered. But she would not burden her friend with her troubles. She would miss solstice and Aunt Zelda's annual Voodoo head-washing ceremony along Bayou St. John for only the second time in her adult life. But there was no reason more important than hers—the quest.

Sybil and her friend, Sango Mori, got together at least once a week. Tonight, Sybil had invited herself over to Sango's place—apartment 7B —just four doors down the long hall from her own. She had something on her mind. She just needed to talk with a friend who wanted nothing from her, unlike so many others.

As a creative, she tasted the most bitter irony in how much her personal suffering had inspired her poetic voice, which was now her greatest financial asset. Her misery made her rich.

Not that she felt the fruit of her life's labors grew from the roots of some cosmic jest. One didn't develop immunity to ill fortune so much as a numbness, a grim strength, a steely determination. But only if one was strong enough.

She fingered the precious gris-gris around her neck. Its subtle odor comforted her—a musty Voodoo talisman meant to protect the wearer from evil spirits—one specific evil *djinn,* or maybe two, now.

Sybil showed deep faith in her dear Aunt Zelda, the Voodoo sorceress who conjured the gris-gris for her. But she was uncertain of the talisman's strength this far from her native New Orleans. The coarse cloth pouch contained powerful verses from one of Zelda's distant Dagomban ancestors from Ghana, known to a select few for its powerful protection charm. It also contained a ritual number of small objects to boost the pouch's power and to aim it.

Sybil was less concerned by an ethereal or invisible form of evil djinn, or even bad luck. She was far more frightened and angered by the two-legged variety of tangible malevolence—sulfurous and abominable.

She had compelled herself to come to this city. Was she running from evil or pursuing it? Perhaps both. The gris-gris *should* provide some protection, even some control, if her and Zelda's intentions were pure enough and powerful enough. She *had* to believe that. But she would not plague her lovely and quite capable little Japanese friend and fellow poet with all of this.

Sybil exuded immense pride in her heritage and the fluid blend of cultures from which it sprang. She self-identified as Louisiana Creole, not Haitian Creole, nor African American, nor Native American, and especially not French or Spanish, although the influence of all these cultures was undeniable.

She most definitely did not self-identify as of mixed race. With pride, she proclaimed, "What I am *not* is what defines me. I am not white, not slave, not French, not Negro, not African. I am a free woman of color—*gens de couleur libres*—a Creole of New Orleans."

Sango listened to Sybil, rapt as she described her conflicted people's history with the ardent passion Sango understood in the context of her own proud Japanese heritage.

"Sybil, dear, I *so* understand. How did the Creole culture come of its own from such a rainbow of influences?"

Sybil hunched forward, as if imparting some sacred pearl of wisdom, "My grandmamà explained this to me with great pride. I will never forget.

"You see, when the French colonized Louisiana a few centuries ago, they began mixing with the native and black slaves from Africa who lived in the area. In what is now Northwest Louisiana.

"Then, the French sold Louisiana to Spain, adding Spanish and Asian peoples from the Philippines. And so, they created the unique Louisiana Creole language from French and various African dialects. With a little Spanish added in. This enabled slaves to communicate with each other, and to colonists—their oppressors.

"Later, the Americans added their flavor to the cultural gumbo. As a result, Louisiana Creole is a French-based language with many Spanish, African, and Anglo influences. Our roots come from oppression. Our hope and melting pot of strengths define our future."

Sango sat wide-eyed. She said, "Is it a challenge to identify yourself as a Creole amidst all that diversity? Where I come from, if you are not a "pure blood" you are diminished.

"While both my parents were Japanese, those children who have a non-Japanese parent are called "hafu," a twist of the English word *half*. If I were to have children who were hafu, I would not raise them in Japan, despite my country's cultural desire to be more, well, international. They are not. Were you considered hafu, Sybil?"

"Yes, there was a time. But we were not even hafu. We are neither black nor white, we aren't African or European, or even Haitian. Rather, we are all of that, and I like to believe we are greater than the sum of those individual cultures. We stand apart from most Americans—invisible—and that pains me most. There's no such language as "Creole," yet the old ones speak it.

"The word *creole* refers to a type of language that results from two or more completely different parent languages. There are over one-hundred creolized languages in the world, which makes our specific version so special to us.

"For example, we differ from the Belizean Kriol and their language, spoken in Belize, or the Haitian Creole language, which is also French-based, and the official language of Haiti. But not in Louisiana.

"You see, Sango? It is not simple. But we stand united in our complexity. It is so appropriate, you see, that the center of Louisiana Creole culture is food. For example, our traditional Creole *gumbo* is a parade of flavors, a delightful metaphor that reflects our multi-flavored culture."

Sybil bubbled exuberance Sango could see Sybil reveled in the convolution of her blended culture. It was reflected in her bright ebony eyes. Not at all like a hafu living in Japan.

"Has it been hard for your people, Sybil?"

"Like many peoples, we have suffered, my dear friend. Perhaps more so than others. You see, we have no voice of our own. That is why my poetry is so important to me, and now to my people. Its rather broad acceptance has given me a voice, and therefore, it has given a voice to the Louisiana Creole, and to all Creole everywhere. I am very proud of that, as are we all. Mine is important work."

Sango admired her famous friend. Six years ago, she had performed her signature piece, "Loud and Proud" at an American presidential inauguration in a worldwide broadcast from the steps of the nation's capitol. That, her media presence, and her other extensive compiled works delivered her fame and some fortune.

"I am delighted we could secure a sublet for you here at The Lit, Syb."

When her friend from the International Poetry Collective expressed a desire to move to Chicago, it seemed apartment 7F down the hall was the perfect solution. Its owner planned to be out of the country for the foreseeable future. Unlike herself, Sybil arrived in the city with means.

"But why have you come to Chicago, Sybil?"

Sango thought her friend might have dozed off. At last, Sybil's half-whispered, half-growled response, and the story behind it not only shocked Sango, but scared her out of her wits.

She explained the Creole people are seventy percent Catholic, thirty percent Protestant, and one-hundred percent Voodoo. She described the necessity of sacrificing a pig and swearing a blood oath, but did not say for what purpose, as if everyone knew or should know.

Sybil's last words sounded like a line from one of her more cryptic verses before realizing she had shared too much. She said, "The devil's voice grinds salty gravel into a seeping wound."

Sango shuddered.

Is possible I don't know this woman at all?

Sybil's characteristic clarity had descended into anathema. Maybe her own faith was telling her she couldn't afford this relationship.

But no. Sybil was a troubled friend. She would do what she could for her.

CHAPTER 11

T hursday, June 21ˢᵗ
    Suite 7D
Hotel Literati
Chicago, Illinois
10:00AM

IT HAD BEEN THREE YEARS, TO THE DAY. AUBREY GREIGH lost the only two women he had ever loved. No mortal *or* god could measure the depth of his sorrow—in miles, nor its magnitude in light years. But nothing eclipsed his exquisite cloak of shame for not having been there to protect them, as irrational as he knew that to be.

After the funeral, he had descended into inconsolable solitude. His pain inspired him. He almost never left his suite, now desolate, and… silent. So, he wrote—novel after novel. If not for that….

No longer did six-year-old Clance's chortles and clumsy stutter steps echo in the expanses of their home. She would haul her favorite doll around by the neck, or by its half-detached left arm that he had promised to fix, but never did. She called that overstuffed likeness of herself Nance. That rag doll stood as tall as her, if it could have stood. Nance doubled as Clance's precious companion and body pillow.

Nor would the morning air of their home ever again hang heavy with the yeasty odors of cheesy pandebono. As was Melissa's tradition, every morning, she baked their favorite bread—her specialty from the region of Valle Del Cauca in her native Columbia. Like Greigh's father, he had married a Columbian woman, the most beautiful women in the world.

Hugging her doll's neck in one arm with its feet dragging, Clance would grab a fist-size ball of pandy off the breakfast bar with her free hand. Mel would place the pan close to the edge, so Clance was sure to reach it. Then, she always pretended to be annoyed, while smiling at their bundle of pint-size joy as she'd trundle off with her treasures.

Mel and Greigh called Clance their pocket rocket. She was small for six and ever in perpetual motion—a physical and intellectual projectile. Clance had been *so* full of potential.

GREIGH SAT ERECT. HE SLAMMED HIS FIST DOWN ON HIS desk, and wept. But he made no other sound in his profound sorrow as his tears streamed down both bearded cheeks. The same sun that had shone down on his little family that day three years ago now mocked him by intruding through the wall of windows behind him.

He contemplated rising and walking out to his seventh-floor balcony to scream at an apathetic sky. Nobody would mind. His neighbors were used to that every once in a while. Most of the time, though, nobody even knew he was home. Except for the occasional feral howl, often near sunset.

Today was their anniversary—summer solstice—the longest day of the year that also has a long history in magic—a time of change and power. But whose? All Greigh knew was some faceless monster deprived two beautiful souls of their light and their power three years ago, a full life of joy amidst a world of misery.

He missed his redheaded duet, more than life itself. There were times.... He still longed for some measure of justice, not that it would serve any purpose. They never caught the killer, nor determined a motive. Nobody claimed responsibility. The police assumed another random psychopath had murdered those five souls that day. Tragic, but inevitable.

Inevitable?

For one news cycle, a few enraged citizens had screamed, "They're shooting us in the streets, in the parks and in our homes! What are you going to do about it?" Fingers pointed at the police and at the fat-cat politicians who decried the violence. But they seemed helpless or apathetic about driving meaningful change. America remained the most violent nation of wealth on Earth.

In a moment of inspired madness months after the funeral, Greigh exhumed Mel's and Clance's bodies, and had them cremated. He then sewed their two small urns of ash into Nance's abdomen. Clance's doll now rested on his precious daughter's tiny bed. He changed the sheets and remade that bed weekly while Nance watched. A ritual. This was his flight of macabre fancy, but somehow, made his cavernous suite less ghostly.

That's when he heard the gunfire on Harrison Street below his balcony.

CHAPTER 12

Here we go again.

Chance McQuillan—McQ—could hear the shots from a bank heist down on Harrison, a few blocks farther south than her apartment. Sounded like a damn war zone.

She intercepted the call on her comms before she even made it home after a double shift. Took off at a full run. Cut through Pettibone Park and the alley between The Wing Stop and The Lit.

And there was old Officer Tommy Brogan, hunched behind his cruiser, parked catty-wampus across Harrison.

McQ screamed at the uniform who must have had his head up his ass. "Watch your left flank, Brogan!"

Whamma, whamma whamma....

"On your left, Brogan, your left side! Fire, dammit!"

Comms said the punks had already killed a bank guard and a customer—an old woman, no less.

Sons-a-bitches.

They said there were at least three in this crew. One was down already. Must have been put down by Brogan's partner after they got separated. They were obviously first on the scene.

Another of the sneaky bastards had crawled out of the bank's back door. Popped out of the alley adjacent to the bank on the south side of Harrison. The mook was about to blow the old cop's head off trying to score a set of wheels. McQ learned from the comms chatter their getaway driver had bugged out.

Brogan huddled there with his gun in his hand, but not using it, like someone had flash-frozen him. She crouch-ran toward the old relic. Spotted the mook on the move. Laid her gun in a two-hand grip on the hood of a car. Its edge was still almost scalding to the touch and smoking from an explosion touched off by one of the bank crew's grenade launcher. Mus've been one of those flash detonations so abrupt it put itself out.

A damn grenade launcher!

McQ steadied her old Glock G17 Gen8, the service piece they said was too old and too heavy for her. Screw that. She double-tapped the mook center mass a second before he'd have blown away old Broge.

Two down. Back to business. The Tac team arrived. She'd let the boys 'n girls with the fancy body armor take it from here with shock and awe, as they'd say. That was their game.

Shit, this town's getting worse.

Sweating like a dozen laps in a village-sized sauna, she'd backup these Tac thugs. Her stupid grandstand play had taken its toll.

Before hearing the shots, responding to this call and crawling up in somebody else's business, she'd needed coffee in the worst way. She was now downrange of her second twelve in thirty-six.

And this was her second frickin' shoot-out since she'd last slept, or even sat her ass down at her desk back at the nine-nine.

I'm gettin' too old for this crap. I need a run back to the armory just for more ammo, for crissake!

McQ turned twenty-seven a month ago. Her gramma used to say, "It's not the age so much as the mileage."

*Yeah, well, Gramma, maybe age **and** mileage.*

Best thing she could do right now is to haul Brogan's wiry ass away from the action, and convince him to retire. The poor guy was no coward, just bad knees and he worried too much about surviving after too many years on the streets. It gets to you.

Gonna get real nasty any second now....

THE TAC GUYS SWARMED AROUND THEM. THEY CROUCH-RAN behind another civilian's car already riddled with auto-weapons rounds on their way to the dance. Even through their tactical gear, she could see their bulked-out muscles chain-linked together.

"C'mon, Broge. Let's get the hell out a here, 'k? These guys got guns bigger 'n ours."

"Sure thing, LT. Thanks for savin' my bacon back there."

"No sweat."

Whamma, whamma, whamma!

They made their way back just as rapid rounds from several heavy guns started tap-dancing off metal and stone—no doubt some sinking into flesh. But she couldn't hear that. The Tacs descended on the scene like an urban army—deep-stacked offensive formations from three directions.

*Man, **they** got funding!*

Their dance was impressive and just a little scary to witness.

These guys are a swarm. Talk about fluid motion with a single hive-mind.

Those jerks inside the bank had changed the rules when they off'd that old lady. Tossed her out onto the curb and swaggered over the body on a live drone feed. The gloves came off right then 'n there.

EVERYBODY SAID IT. TACS WERE A LOVELESS BUNCH A SONS-a-bitches who lived for the adrenaline. She knew they had to be. Spent seventy-five percent of their time drilling—the most highly trained Tactical Squad in the country.

Her ex was one of them. McQ stopped putting up with his bullshit six months earlier. Best decision of her life. Still outstanding to watch these professionals work. This would get a lot uglier, and she knew they'd be okay with that.

Scary stuff.

She needed a shower.

And coffee.

CHAPTER 13

Pettibone Park,
    The Near Southwest Loop,
Chicago, Illinois
7:00PM

Everyone dies, but not me. Not tonight, anyway.

That's what Aubrey Greigh told himself as he hustled home. Stupid of him to get caught out after dark. Mis-judged how much time traveling by mass transit required. He left his suite so rarely. He'd make the best of it.

The hike from the South State Street CTA station north of Ida B. Wells Drive was seven blocks from home. But he'd shave three blocks if he cut through Pettibone Park. That park could get grim after dark. Less time on the street, less risk. A bloody theory, anyway.

Greigh hated parks. All parks.

On a wide pedestrian thoroughfare lined with benches and street lamps, two young toughs spotted him as he passed through a pool of light. They likely saw an easy mark.

Greigh's beard was a premature salt-and-pepper gray—more reddish pepper than salt—and not quite long enough to cover the few wrinkles at his throat. Despite his guru-length hair tied in a tight tail, beard, jeans and sandals, he was no pushover. He looked at least fifty underneath that mane, but was a grizzly forty-six.

It was hard to tell how fit he was under that flowing robe in the dim light, even though it hung open in front. Looked like a bathrobe, or a sloppy monk's frock. Supported the paupish persona he fostered when venturing out. It said, *Nothing much to peck at here, ya blighters.* But some thick blokes can't read the bloody signs.

"Hey, old man, how 'bout you hand over that ratty-lookin' sack, and we'll make sure you get home safe? That's a good trade, right?" The kid snapped open a long blade and hoisted a sneer to punctuate his gravitas.

Eager to return to the final draft of his latest manuscript after some primary research up-town for a different project, Greigh's impatience eclipsed his common sense. All he carried in his shoulder bag was his wristPad, which he had the good sense not to flash on the street. Oh, and a bottle of water. And a nice, smooth rock—not a very big one. In case he had to swing the bag. Hard.

That bag had always inspired him. Besides, even though he tasted a small sliver of serenity tonight, for the first time in a while, he hated bullies more than he hated violence. Besides, a short workout could be satisfying.

Greigh's retort left no doubt. They would not intimidate him. "Old man?"

He looked down at himself and shrugged. He was no dedicated follower of fashion, despite his affluent Scottish heritage. What did it matter?

"Kid, I'm quite fond of this 'ratty-looking sack,' so I do believe I will decline your generous offer. Thank you, anyway."

"Huh?" The ruffian re-planted his feet and brandished his knife. His cohort stood flat-footed, three feet away, snapping a sap—the kids called it a slapjack. Held it in his left hand and repeatedly slapped it into his right palm, making every attempt to look formidable, but failing in comical fashion.

"That means no."

He made as if to walk around the hoodlum, who grabbed his robe's blousy sleeve with one hand and thrust the blade toward his abdomen with the other.

Greigh methodically chose a few milder moves from his Combat Sambo training, a brutal mixed martial art form. Used his attacker's weight and momentum against him. Applied less than a quarter of his power and aggression with a swift leg sweep and a pop to the solar plexus of the idiot with the knife once he was down. Then, a lightning soccer kick to "Kid Sap" preceded a quick but restrained stomp to his stomach.

Three seconds later, both buffoons wondered what tornado had just bloodied and flattened them. Neither had lost consciousness, but both wisely played dead. Done and done.

But then Greigh spotted a third ruffian who skulked in the shadows five yards away, just outside their pool of light. He was older... and bigger. Pointed some sort of firearm at him. Too far away to disarm, but close enough that the big runt couldn't miss. This was about to get ugly.

"Oh, bloody Hell...."

At that moment, from within a deeper shadow, an arm swept downward on the hand aiming that gun. What Greigh saw next came to his eyes in a blur—action so fast he wasn't sure what he saw. After two lightning seconds, some shadow figure had disarmed the gunman who now lay bleeding and unconscious, or worse, face down on the path. Over him stood... one of his neighbors?

"Sango, is that you?"

"Can't stay out of trouble, old man?"

"You too with the old man codswallop? Oh, well, it *would seem* I cannot stay out of trouble, lass."

His warm smile masked his gruff tone at being rescued by Sango Mori, someone half his age, and a talented poet, no less.

"Brilliant, Sango. Shall we go home?" Her seventh-floor apartment was two doors down the hall from his own at The Lit.

Greigh stepped over the tangle of arms and legs. He reached down to playfully pat the nearest urchin on the head as if he were a wounded pooch. But in that same instant, he regretted doing so. "Good grief, boyo, what's that you slather on your locks? Carriage grease?"

At moments like these, his well-disguised Scottish brogue snuck out from beneath an Edinburgh accent he also cloaked under new-Chicagoan—his home for the past decade. He wiped his fingers on the young man's tunic. Then on the front of his t-shirt before wheeling on his heel with a frown and marching toward home, arm-in-arm with his Japanese poet-slash-savior.

They sauntered down the middle of deserted South State Street after retreating from the park, both now glistening from light exertion in the muggy summer night.

Greigh said, "a good workout, albeit brief. Thank you for sparing me the tedium of seeking treatment for a gunshot wound."

Sango stood more than a foot shorter than his six-two. She smiled up at him and tossed him a single-shoulder shrug.

"Sango, you must grace your friends at the Lit with a reading of your work. I love how you brandish verse like the Samurai's sword."

Though she had performed her Haiku and Senryu before hundreds all over the world, she blushed. Said, "Oh, we'll see."

SANGO KNEW SOME OF GREIGH'S HISTORY.

She could only imagine the anger and grief he must stuff deep inside every moment of every day. Though movie-star handsome, tonight he looked like one shower away from homeless.

She missed her native Japan. But an incessant invasion of coastal flooding had turned her home island into little more than a survival colony. Especially after several ancient nuclear reactors behind failed levies had descended beneath the waves. Worse, the perennial exchange of missiles with the mainland left her homeland ever overcast with fear.

Besides, the new global center for performing arts and the residual movie industry not relegated to cyberspace *was* Chicago—Celebrity Row and the cluster of studio lots in Cicero, the new Hollywood; and the Mag Mile, the new Broadway. Her new home.

This is where the action is, in more ways than one!

THE TWO OF THEM NEARED THE LIT.

Sango disappeared into the night once more. Said she had unfinished business, whatever that meant.

The grand entrance of Hotel Literati and its impressive porte cochere loomed four stories overhead to welcome arriving automobiles—now a rare commodity—to discharge their occupants under extravagantly illuminated cover. Of late, however, many of the lights were extinguished, as if too forlorn to shine any longer, like little moon gods with no worshippers. Or just tired bulbs.

Granite, beveled glass with delicate etching, and an intricate facade in the ornate Beaux Arts style of architecture always stoked Greigh's furnace. Very continental.

Long-term residents—most were now condominium owners—referred to their home with affection as "The Lit." It had been his home for a decade.

Greigh adored The Lit. He and Mel had lived here since the old pile's reincarnation—since the building "went condo," as the Yanks say. Their daughter was born here. Now, he lived here in solitude—for the last three years.

He pushed through one of the ten-foot-high doors made heavy by one-inch-thick etched glass that had a slight greenish tint. Not one-hundred-percent optically clear.

The visceral ambience of the mammoth lobby washed over him. He took in the distinctive aroma of oiled walnut paneling and aging fabric grown somewhat musty. Bronze railings, with their patina removed by odious polish, refused to surrender their greenish verdigris at the joints.

He loved the lobby's layered symmetry and the classical details of omnipresent stonework on the columns, mortices, and moldings. Similar in style to its exterior facade, massive twin staircases curved up toward the mezzanine on the far side of the cavernous lobby which nestled around the gilded-goldtone wire-cage elevator.

Stone gargoyles guarded the two broad flights of stairs, one curved to his left, and another to his right. Monstrous stone railings stood proud on both sides of each sweeping balustrade.

While the rest of the world descended into chaos and ugliness, The Lit's entire montage of odors and its sumptuous feast for the eyes all felt... welcoming. Orderly. Home.

Even the slight stench of the unwashed masses felt right to him. Hundreds huddled on the second and third floors. A hint of their aroma seeped down through the elevator shaft's sleeve of frosted glass panels framed in bronze-tone channels. Reminded Greigh of a milk-white stained glass chimney four stories high that ascended through the lobby's beam and panel ceiling.

As he crossed the lobby, he smiled up at the three grand crystal chandeliers, all in a row, each suspended from a twenty-foot tether. A thick patina of dust shrouded them, including minor damage inflicted over the years and never repaired. Greigh even relished the asymmetry the missing pieces caused in the prismatic rainbow of crooked light transmitted through them to the walls and far-away arched ceiling.

Vince and Luca Donati, the hotel's revered owners, did not prioritize cleaning and dusting. Greigh knew money was a constant and thorny issue. He was just thankful The Lit survived, along with his investment in his condo.

In the past, he had been an aggressive advocate and lobbyist for the hotel and all that it stood for. He threw his energy and considerable contacts into helping the brothers Donati. But since some anonymous monster took Mel and Clance from him, his fire dwindled.

Greigh punched the elevator's filigreed button. The car made its way down to him in the grand lobby as he thought of his loss—again. His biometrics opened the door and granted him access to all floors of Camelot—floors four to fifteen—but not the owners' sixteenth-floor penthouse suite occupied by the Donati brothers. Oh, and no elevator stopped in Sherwood, the neighborhood of vagabonds on floors two and three.

He just wasn't sure how he'd ever move on.

CHAPTER 14

I *love this smell.*

The lobby and mezzanine presented a posh, if not antiquated, elegance. Above the mezzanine and below the fourth floor, however, the elevator ride always offered an olfactory adventure. A visceral part of the Literati experience.

Scraps and hacks camped on the second and third floors. Most of these unfortunates had not only failed in life, they had yet to succeed in the practice of their craft. With electronic and mechanical trickery, they staunched the stench of urine and garbage. But the absence of hope? Every day served up more challenges.

This neighborhood sheltered near-homeless creatives, those who management refused to evict, but struggled to prevent this neighborhood's total erosion into odious but hushed chaos. The constant low din penetrated the thin white chimney of frosted glass that surrounded the open elevator car—the birdcage.

Greigh made it a point to visit Sherwood once in a while. He even had a few acquaintances who squatted there, some of whom viewed Greigh as their patron. Besides, he had plenty of food and extra clothes he enjoyed sharing. But he was a beneficent outsider, not a friend.

All the rooms in Sherwood were occupied by one or more parties—campers. All lacked doors. The least fortunate and most recently arrived camped in the wide hallways. Though hotel management discouraged open flames, many cooked over miniature can-size stoves. They were careful. Others made sure. They were in it together in Sherwood. Cleanliness and neatness were unlikely priorities enforced by proctors—more or less. Well-used trash chutes were found at each end and at the midpoint of each floor's hallway.

Three cardinal rules were never to be broken in this neighborhood. Everyone understood. First, if you weren't a creative, or a member of a resident creative's tribe, you could not stay in Sherwood. Period. So, management's dozen proctors made it their business to know every face in Sherwood. Second, no drugs. And third, no violence—of any kind. Zero tolerance.

Neither the hotel's owners nor more affluent residents on the upper floors minded. Sherwood offered residents of Camelot a reminder of their own humble beginnings—or ends. This neighborhood within The Lit remained their homage to less fortunate fellow creatives.

Camelot's owners were glad to pay the salaries of Sherwood's proctors as a small percentage of their monthly assessments. Additional resident proctors volunteered their time to assist those who were salaried. Some still lived there.

Most all owners and residents above the third floor earned their living in the creative arts. The price of admission—the impossible vision of the Brothers Donati. All pursued their dreams as authors, poets, songwriters, musicians, playwrights and actors—*their* dreams.

ONE RESIDENT SPIT FUMES. UPPER SHERWOOD—THE THIRD floor—was home to Robby Bidok. He loathed the world that never appreciated his talent. That had led to a penniless existence, even though his passion for rhyme, often without reason, never waned. He lived his life through the lenses of his own verse, even though the rhythm of life did not love him.

In a not-so-small way, Robby relished being the perennial victim of a Greek tragedy. The unfairness of it all poisoned his mind with jealousy and resentment.

But low-grade grumbling was as far as his lack of courage could take him. He also resented his inability to act on his emotions. Robby Bidok was a coward and knew it.

Only cosmic serendipity found him at the doorstep of Hotel Literati. In no known universe could he afford to stay at a hotel, or under any roof except a bridge deck or a utility tunnel. But word on the street was that if you were a starving artist, there could be a home for you at The Lit.

He remembered that day. Six months earlier he had wandered into the lobby, and a nice young man intercepted him to ask about his passion. He cleared his throat and said, "I am a poet, if it is any of your concern. Although, the world has not come to its senses. My art has yet to be recognized."

"I am sorry to hear that. Can you share with me one of your verses?"

Robby wasn't huge on memorization, or performing, but he had composed a Haiku, the poignancy of which burned into his mind like a branding iron. Not only could he recite it from memory, he could not forget the damn seventeen-syllable tercet if he tried.

He shrugged off and dropped his heavy pack, and straightened his ragged tunic under a many-pocketed vest, each of which bulged with the remainder of his entire existence. He felt self-conscious concerning his appearance, but recognized this was an audition. Anything to get off the dangerous streets just behind him. Well, almost anything.

The young bard cleared his throat again as he meant to project his voice. Wished he had a way to blow his nose at that moment. Settled for a sleeve and a thumb-knuckle to stem the flow of watery mucous long enough to perform seventeen syllables. Inflated his diminutive demeanor by straightening his slouch. He drew in a deep if not somewhat raspy inhale to capture the energy he was sure would engulf him. Prepped his entire anemic body for a rare performance for the half-dozen souls now in the massive lobby as if this were *his* theater in the round.

Just for a few seconds, he unburdened his battered heart as the words burst from his throat, scratchy from sparse use.

Robby Bidok, Poet Extraordinaire, began his performance, whirling around as he spoke to capture the eye of every potential admirer....

He cleared his throat once more. Projecting with his best stage voice, he said, "I call this... *'Where Goes Courage?'*" After one final sniffle and a deep breath,

> *"Surf pounds round boulders.*
> *"Cliffs yield to crushing breakers.*
> *"Strength of souls retreats...."*

His brief but ponderous recitation continued to echo as he finished. Heads turned toward Robby Bidok, penniless poet. He did not possess the presence of mind to take a bow. He bobbed his head, and then... just stood there.

A pitiful smattering of empathetic applause and a nod or two of appreciation preceded everyone soon turning back to their own insignificant little lives. At least he had caused a ripple, hadn't he? And that was enough.

Who was he kidding? That was *not* enough, but it was something, wasn't it? He knew he should be grateful for even those few half-assed accolades—a precious moment of glory. But a victim's poison again coursed through his veins. He fell silent, dropped his chin, and deflated once again to the little pauper who had first entered The Lit's magnificent lobby minutes earlier.

After several more questions, the young man revealed to Robby he was a volunteer proctor—whatever that meant—for a neighborhood within the hotel known as Sherwood.

He also smiled as he announced with some pomp that The Lit's management would be proud to welcome him to stay. He shared in confidence that he, too, had once been a street artist not so long ago. Not anymore.

Robby wanted to say he didn't need anyone's pity.

What makes this squeaky-clean adolescent, this very muscular, squeaky-clean adolescent, think that I am looking for charity? Or pity!

But discretion being the better part of questionable valor, he kept his lips clamped shut and smiled. Meant to be a smile of gratitude, it didn't quite reach his eyes. They broadcast suspicion. "Alright, what's the catch?"

The young man's expression became severe. He meant business. "Just adhere to each of the few rules for everyone's safety. Pick a place you'd like to camp. But do not intrude on a space someone else already occupies. We will tolerate no violence of any kind. And no drugs. Are these conditions acceptable to you, Mr. Bidok?"

"Of course. Thank you for your hospitality, Mr.—"

"Just call me Joe. I am one of twelve proctors of Sherwood. Seven of us are employees of the Brothers Donati. They are our benefactors and owners of The Lit. Five of us are volunteers. I am proud to say that includes me. I'm giving back. You can identify any of us by our yellow arm bands."

He nodded down to the bandana tied around his left bicep and smiled with pride.

"Think of us as your hosts, but also as Sherwood's police. Our job is everyone's safety, and peace of mind for our generous benefactors. We take our jobs seriously. Do you understand, Mr. Bidok?"

Robby winced at the "p" word, but nodded his acknowledgement. He already looked forward to a safer and warmer night. After that, well, he never planned too far ahead. Robby convinced himself he didn't have long to live. No hero in any Greek tragedy ever thought otherwise, though some did live on—against impossible odds. Olympian labors tasked by the gods and all that.

After asking permission, Joe scanned Robby with a handheld device. He explained this recorded his biometrics, and instantaneously performed a cursory background check keyed off his DNA. At least that was his assurance. Robby had nothing to hide. Just the idea.

Joe said his body was now the key that would grant him access to Sherwood, and led the way toward an open elevator that reminded Robby of a gilded bird cage. But that was not for them.

They entered a stairwell just to the far side of that beautiful elevator with a view of the lobby as it ascended before it's translucent white sleeve turned opaque. Reserved for paying guests, no doubt.

Robby took one last glance over his shoulder at the immense doors back across the lobby that led out to the dark and dangerous street. Wondered if he had just forfeited his freedom, and whether this was a thinly disguised ploy to enslave his body, if not his spirit. No, that would be too on-the-nose, a cheap and obvious metaphor. That's not how *he* would write this odyssey.

Though foreign to his psyche, he recognized this was a simple act of generosity. Wasn't it? He'd still watch his back. Living on the street, you dared trust no one. But he was no longer on the street. For tonight, at least.

I am entombed, at last. And it all happened so fast. Just so… abrupt, we go… up. To be buried? Or just my free spirit harried?

A moment of hope glimmered, but Robby wouldn't even bother to write that one down.

I need… inspiration. Maybe….

CHAPTER 15

They controlled their chaos. The dozens of fires contained within small cans and buckets on marble floors gave Sherwood's second- and third-floor hallways a dull glow. Almost cheerful, like a fair-weather campground at dusk.

Cooking odors of meager larder permeated the air with pungent fumes. Formidable ventilation fans failed to entirely clear the high-ceiling hallways and rooms, none of which featured doors. Everything about Sherwood was open to maximize the dissipation of fumes. Open windows helped, but lowered the ambient temperature and admitted atmospheric grit.

Nobody paid to camp here, so nobody complained. It was a fine roof over their heads, and it wasn't freezing. Most important: this was a safe environment. Roaming proctors ensured that. Yes, the Sherwood neighborhood provided sanctuary to creatives who needed help.

Some residents, most of whom looked like indigents, clustered in groups of two or three on their haunches or with crossed legs. Some stretched out on their mattress pads, if they were lucky enough to possess one. Most kept their conversations low to respect the privacy of those around them. Everyone made futile attempts not to eavesdrop on their neighbors. Still, very few gossiped. Many sat by themselves, including Robby Bidok.

SHERWOOD SEEMED FINE. ROBBY REMEMBERED LITTLE before moving into a nice quiet corner at the end of a long hallway—a perfect spot to be alone. It had now been awhile since he left the city's streets in a mental fog—too dense for most memories to penetrate.

Most here came from the streets. Some had arrived in town with no other place to go. But if they possessed a creative spirit, Sherwood welcomed them, as determined by her monitors. Proctors.

Yellow arms instead of firearms.

He had *always* fancied himself a poet, albeit unpublished. The proctors would not hold that against him. He was on the crooked path trudged by so many before their literary ship made port. And no, he was not averse to mixed metaphors. They offered their own window into the creative mind not harnessed into slavery by convention.

ROBBY FELT LIKE A GHOST. HIS DIMINUTIVE BUT SINEWY five-foot-seven stature granted him a certain invisibility... until he spoke. His waspish voice had not served him well on the rare occasion when he performed his work. It rankled him that critics oozed from every crevasse. Most couldn't even begin to grasp his work's significance.

Robby frequently dyed his longish straw-textured hair with cheap bottles of peroxide in attempts to change his appearance so others— anyone—would like him. But now, he reverted to his natural premature gray-blonde. Couldn't afford peroxide anymore, anyway. Or anything else.

But that mop. He tied it up in the back. Otherwise, it framed his gaunt face with too many bags and wrinkles and thin lips for someone not yet thirty years of age. Too much skin for his small skull.

A lifetime of bitterness and hatred had sculpted his entire demeanor, including a slight hunch in his back from too much sitting and no exercise. His favorite existential expression was, "What's the point?"

Robin could be mistaken for either sex, likely because he himself wasn't sure how he self-identified. He had succumbed to an attitude of gender indifference. He identified most with long-dead women from ancient Greece—goddesses.

These immortals commanded unimaginable abilities. Yet others oppressed them. A loveless marriage trapped Aphrodite, the Goddess of Love. Athena, wisest of beings, always deferred to Zeus. And Hera, Goddess of Marriage, was married to the worst serial adulterer ever. A barbarous world oppressed Robby's own formidable talent as a poet, and as a human being. In that, he shared the oppression suffered by Greek goddesses.

This sad little man had always admired the blues singers' lifetime of pain, so obvious in their music. He heard it in their lyrics. Their minor chord progressions. Soul-bending riffs with outrageous vibrato and predictable syncopation. Those gravelly voices trudged through a lifetime of mud and madness with their ponderous dirges. They'd lived life and suffered its down-beat extremes. He, too, was born a victim, and would die a victim. Of that he was certain.

Making peace with this destiny comforted him. During the times in his life when it seemed circumstances favored him, he'd sabotage them with his own compulsive need to be the dark horse—the wretched misfortunate. Where some rose above their difficulties, Robby wallowed in the luscious unfairness of each and every one.

Since he blamed his pain on where he was, or who he was with, he moved around, never putting down roots, always on the run, to escape himself. He'd move on before anyone discovered what a loathsome creature he was, what he thought of himself.

HIS YOUTH WAS HIS HELLSCAPE. AND HE HAD YET TO escape. Robby was born in a small Louisiana town called Natchitoches. Early in life, he wrote, always gravitating toward verse.

Others had picked on him without a scrap of mercy. Everyone in the parish revered the pervasive cultural mud they called the French Creole. His work attempted to offer another perspective. This from a local boy who was *not* of mixed race and *not* of French descent. Someone *not* Native American and *not* enamored of the mutts who called themselves Creole, regardless of skin color.

As an early teen, he attempted suicide by sitting in a running car inside his abusive father's garage. But then he chickened out at the last moment and crawled on his hands and knees into fresher air before he succumbed. Robby even failed to kill himself, which resulted in even more intense self-loathing.

But he kept writing, even while attending Louisiana Northwestern State University. Not that writing ever paid him a nickel's wage, other than a partial scholarship. He had amassed manuscripts—thousands of verses he assembled into various topical collections—but none of them published.

After offering a sample to a half-dozen publishers and formal submissions to more than a dozen poetry contests, all he had to show for his efforts? Rejection slips that told him, "this is not what we're looking for at this time." Another said, "Dark stuff that might be suitable for a different publication. Consider 'Psychology Today.'" Yet another rendered a scathing indictment of his talent en masse: "This is not poetry, this is the rhyming dribble of a madman. Seek help, son."

He cradled his latest rejected piece, and re-read the lush allegory for the thousandth time:

the solo horror corollary

empty souls drip through near-clotted holes.
they dare not whisper of their hollow hunger.

on our journey, we meander to somehow console
their murderous fears from when they were younger.

violated and perforated, they seek to extol
any redeemable virtue to somehow disencumber

a harnessed child, so perfectly controlled,
a boy who felt endless ecstasies plundered.

we knew our self-inflicted horror might be droll,
that some would gulp down our misery like thunder.

but so few grasped the sheer wonder of it all,
that we few who did were vastly outnumbered.

the end—none too soon—welcomes our neo-souls,
drags us away to the sweetest of slumbers.

with open arms, we seek her caressing fold,
waiting to be warmed by flames from down under.

FOOLS! THEY'D ALL BE SORRY. HOW COULD *no one* appreciate the sheer brilliance of his existential self-portrait in tetrameter? Eight glorious couplets of sumptuous splendor!

The cretins need an awakening.

That was the precise moment when the magnificent gentleman from his home state of Louisiana approached Robby Bidok in a flurry. One second, he was alone. The next, Doctor Jacques was just there, at that well-sharpened point in time. His reputation preceded him. Any initiate of the dark practices knew of Doctor Jacques.

Despite the doctor's dubious heritage, Robby had always admired all practitioners of the arts—dubious or not—their power. Doctor Jacques Memeaux—bokor extraordinaire. Now, the great man—almost white—stood behind him at his humble campsite in Lower Sherwood, The Lit's second floor. Could this be?

"Oh, my. Doctor, you are most welcome. Please pull up a pad."

"I will not be sitting on yer pad, boy," he pronounced it *BO-ee,'* "because I is 'bout ta makes ya a man—nay, immortal. Is ya willin' ta go ta any lengths?"

"What? Well—"

"Never mind, boy. You's not ready ta ascend. I is wrong to choose ya, even though you's a reluctant son a Nackatish, herself."

With that, the tall almost-white man in jack gear and top hat with a red bandana flowing from its crown turned to leave in haste.

"Wait!"

The whites of the man's eyes popped compared to the blue-black tattoos adorning his angular face with his cheeks and nose painted pasty-white like that of a bleached skull.

"Do not dares ta waste me time, boy. It be eternal power and glory I offers ya, and ya wastes my time with yer coward hesitations. One last chance. Simple. Yes 'r no. What be yer answer, boy?"

Beads of sweat popped out on Robin's forehead. Isn't this the miracle he had been waiting for—the sign? But there would be no turning back.

You coward. Answer the man!

"Yes. Any lengths, Doctor."

"Good. Ya follows me. Now."

Robby grabbed his half-emptied backpack. Left everything else behind.

And thus began little Robby Bikok's march to power and glory. He wouldn't need an eternity, just what remained of one glorious lifetime.

THE DARKNESS WAS COMPLETE. EXCEPT FOR THE BLACK candle. And the blood. And the stench of wax, copper and feces.

Robby was nobody.

Never had he felt so small. He was a cockroach. Who doesn't want to stomp on one of those? He'd stomp *himself* if he were able.

The little man hunched over the only defense against the darkness in the damp hole where he now lived. He hungered for the slight warmth of the huge candle nestled between his crossed legs.

His talent still hung on him like a moldering blanket, a stoop-shoulder burden that prevented possibilities. He bore that burden with a begrudging respect. His greatness would never see sunlight, much less a spotlight, anyway.

Robby believed what Doctor Jacques told him. He hungered for a purpose to eclipse his profound self-loathing. All because of oh-so-clever bitches like *her*. Never once did he consider she *deserved* accolades.

A profound shroud of unfairness needled into his every excruciating pore. Why did *they* shower *women*, especially those different from him, with advantages only available to *them?* As if draped with black skin and adorned with a few extra dents and curves bequeathed them a *right* to be admired for their dribble—for *her* dribble.

But the potency of anger inspired, too. Didn't it? His verses became his orgasms. Almost. Not that it mattered. He *needed* to believe in something. Or someone would stomp on him. Again. But that wouldn't be so bad either, would it?

The whispering in his ear droned on. Jacques was to gift him a godlike purpose—to reach for possibilities without limits. The medicine helped. At first, he just listened to the whispering. He and Jacques soon performed the prescribed actions—rituals—together.

Then, brilliant colors saturated his gray existence. They exploded in front of his eyes, behind them, around him, through him. The potency of his anger had become a launch platform to far greater things, unimagined things. All within the doctor's magnificent orbit.

No longer a cockroach, he had transmogrified into an apex predator, a magnificent visage of grandeur. It took some time, and practice, fueled by Doctor Jacques' magnificent medicine and magical rootwork.

At last, little Robby Bidok became unfettered by fear, scruples, or his own moldy mind. He had found purpose and reveled in its simple elegance.

Now he was *somebody*. He could do anything, everything. And he did.

Never had he felt so large, so privileged, so *significant*.

He was a titan, a weapon, aimed by Doctor Jacques.

CHAPTER 16

Not that I'm superstitious....

Aubrey Greigh preferred his floor—seven—even though he could afford any apartment in the building. It wasn't always this way.

When he moved in ten years earlier, his sweet spot had been apartment 7D. It offered him and Mel everything they desired, and little they didn't need. They only ever wanted one child, so two bedrooms were perfect. They didn't need the splendid balcony, but there it was, and had become a beautiful part of their lives.

Even their apartment's floor number reminded him of a time when he sailed the seven seas. All sailors harbored certain superstitions, whether or not they admitted that to themselves. Seven was a lucky number. He would have been okay with the eleventh floor too, but seven is where all the poets lived. Odd bunch. He fit there. Even though he was no poet, the way poets focused their zeal appealed to him.

GREIGH CHERISHED A CERTAIN VIEWSCAPE. BUT HE DIDN'T want to live too far above what he called "the city's breath." Sounds and smells and reflected lights ebbed and flowed with the breeze and by the hour. He relished being close enough to street level to see the muzzle flash of the occasional gunshot and to catch a hint of now-rare exhaust fumes.

The city breathed, and he breathed in the city. An act of intimacy, a guilty pleasure.

After Greigh purchased suite 7D, other mystery writers gravitated to the seventh floor. He had become something of a celebrity in the literary community—a flame toward which moths were drawn.

The building's facade faced Harrison Street. Thriller and horror writers drifted toward the darker northern exposure—the building's backside. The sun seldom pierced the impressive amount of particulate matter that permeated Chicago's atmosphere. Even far above street level. Greigh always hoped for a ray of sunshine, and his southern exposure delivered. Once in a great while.

Most authors were egomaniacs with self-esteem issues. Not Greigh. His indomitable spirit alienated most folks. Coming across as brash and a little too self-assured, a select few knew this was not a mask. Despite everything that had happened, he loved who he was, but declined to share too much of that with anyone. He still processed his profound grief. Like a warm blanket grown sodden. That painted him an arrogant and brooding loner. And that was just fine.

Home at last. Greigh swung open one of suite 7D's double doors into his entry alcove from the broad hallway festooned with ornate wall sconces. He closed the door to his sanctuary behind him and took in a deep cleansing breath of manicured air. Greigh extracted his wristPad from the old sack the ruffians tried to liberate in Pettibone Park twenty minutes earlier.

A set of well-worn brass knuckles clinked onto the antique table that sat against the wall ahead of him, some seven feet from the doors. Laid the bag beside them.

Every time he came home, he alternated turning right into his kitchen area or to his left around that wall into his spacious living room. Wasn't sure why that was important. Both directions led to the same common great room. He believed such varied habits developed new neural pathways in his brain. Didn't matter. It was a ritual. Had been for years. A comfortable routine.

"Butler, dim lights and a low fire, if you please."

"Welcome home, Greigh."

He called his environmental control system *Butler*. That had been the factory default, and he had not changed it because Clance, his precious daughter, liked that, which amused his wife, Mel.

The last three years without them tortured him every day, especially at night.

Once Butler had driven the bolt home in the door behind him, Greigh issued more instructions.

"Arm the front door and disarm the balcony doors, please. Make that our default for the time being. Thanks, Butler."

He didn't need to be polite to this system, but he clung to a theory. If you were nice to machines, they learned to be nicer to you.

"My pleasure, Sir Aubrey."

"Damn it, Butler, we've talked about this. It's just Greigh, okay?"

"Of course, Greigh. Apologies. Will you be dining in this evening?"

"Ah, yes. Food. Well, I suppose I'll just nuke one of those protein patties. Thanks for the reminder."

He said this as if taking the easy way out with a prefab meal would be an act of weary cowardice.

"Music, Greigh?"

"I don't think so. Let's just not talk for a while. Thank you."

Greigh wanted to process what had happened down on State Street at the edge of the park. If it hadn't been for Sango.... Well, it wouldn't have been the first time he'd faced death. Wouldn't be the last. Foolish of him to leave his flank exposed. He'd been distracted.

I need to be more vigilant. I got cocky, didn't I?

He started toward the east end of the commodious living room. As an afterthought, he turned to cut between the sofa and the fireplace. Backtracked to the storage room west of the apartment's entry doors.

In that room, concealed behind a bookcase, one of many in the apartment, he nurtured his coveted garden.

Four deep utility shelves festooned with grow lights on timers simulated day/night cycles. He supplemented the unavoidable processed foods in his life with these herbs and a few fresh greens. As good as processed foods were these days, he didn't trust them to provide everything his body required. Like so much else in the world today. This pleasant distraction had also become habit, another ritual.

He grumbled, as if someone were listening. "Every politician pretends to care about rampant violence in the street, abominable air quality, and the general destruction of interpersonal relationships, not to mention the earth's ecosystem. But does humanity seem incapable of escaping our cycle of child-like self-destruction, starting with terrible food?"

"Was there a question in there for me, or are you just in a pitiable mood?"

"Shut it, Butler." But he smiled to himself. This damn AI system was his closest friend in the world. Perhaps his only real friend.

After a few minutes of spritzing each of his three dozen plants growing in costly mulch, he adjusted a few of the mini-lights and headed for the living room once more. Yes, more than just another comfortable habit.

Greigh breezed by the security monitor ensconced on the opposite wall, the east wall. A glance verified Butler had indeed disabled the perimeter alarm on the balcony doors as he had directed. A small red light would remind him to re-arm it later. Butler would also remind him if he forgot, but would not arm it unless instructed to do so. He trusted Butler.

The fifty-foot-long floor-to-ceiling window wall now before him allowed a generous glow of ambient light from the single building taller than The Lit set back on the south side—the far side of Harrison. The Prudential's lights bathed his living room in a hazy warmth.

He wasn't hungry. The odor left over from last night's dishes still on the table to the right of the balcony doors confirmed it. He allowed nothing dirty or out of place. But something changed these last twenty-four hours.

GREIGH KNEW BETTER. HE SHOULD SPEND NO MORE TIME outdoors tonight, but couldn't resist hiking the perimeter of his huge balcony. The glass door swished open as he approached it. He stepped once again into the gritty night air. The city's hum and drum embraced him. It sounded different from up here. Less than ten seconds later, he cataloged the first occurrence of gunfire. Just the way it was. Part of life. And death.

The city exhaled cordite, too—the by-product of gun powder combusting—all too frequently. He couldn't smell that this high, but he imagined. He did not have to imagine the inevitable artifacts of more than thirty million souls packed into contiguous regionplexes like Chicago, half of whom lived in poverty. Would that it were not so.

At seventy feet long and twenty feet wide, his was the largest covered balcony in the entire building... save one. That would be the penthouse balcony—the Donatis', nine floors above his. The prominent central frontispiece of this elegant old structure comprised the C and D stacks of apartments. The A and B stacks stood back to the west, and the E and F stacks set back to his left, to the east.

The D stack of apartments stood proud and staggered by at least twenty feet further out than the C stack. That gave him a clear view not only to the south but also to the east and west.

He loved this place, not only for the magnificent limestone architecture of the building that surrounded his apartment, but especially for the memories. Mel and Clance still lived in his heart, and in this apartment.

HIS HEART BRIMMED AS HE REMEMBERED A FAMILY VISIT to the zoo four years ago. His little Clance grew animated at the sight of the few live animals and actual trees on display. She implored them to create their own little forest. And he had. She thought that if they had trees here, the giraffes would come.

He had surrounded their entire balcony with trees and bushes—their own little park. They were all potted and artificial, but that didn't matter to little Clance with her big imagination and her bright eyes.

They now were all coated with a fine layer of dust. Guillermo, a delightful little man from The Lit's staff, cleaned them off for him every week. Regular as clockwork, every Friday. Greigh always had a beer ready for Guillermo when he finished. He would accept just one beer. After all, Greigh already paid him a generous stipend, even though this was his job, and that's all dear little Guillermo would accept.

Greigh now leaned on the chest-high railing between the trunks of two ten-foot oak tree similes. He sniffed and listened to the city breathe.

He muttered, "Butler, indirects to twenty percent, please." The lights that shone up into the trees and down into the bushes all gradually illuminated over the next few moments. The effect was magical.

Butler remained silent. Greigh detected the subtle but pungent odor of real earth in the pots on either side of him. He knew those pots just contained blocks of concrete under a veneer of manufactured pebbles and genuine dirt. Didn't matter. The trees even *smelled* real.

Dear little Guillermo sprayed them with that scent. What a lovely man!

Pays to be nice.

Until it's time not to be nice....

Memories.

That sniper....

Time to write. But Mel won't ever again come to my desk to pick my head up and drag me off to bed.

Memories.

He kicked the pot next to his right foot, now hoping he hadn't broken his big toe.

Might as well go to bed, you maudlin fool!

CHAPTER 17

H otel Literati
　　Chicago, Illinois
9:45PM

~

GREIGH SLEPT MEAN. THE FIST PUMMELING HIS FACE FROM within the chaos of his nightmare resolved into someone pounding on his apartment's door. He stumbled out of bed and threw on his favorite robe. Otherwise, he'd shock whomever banged on his door. Greigh didn't believe in doorbells *or* pajamas.

He checked his security monitor on the wall to his right en route to the front door. He swung open one of the double entryway doors to confront a wild-eyed Sango Mori, the savvy street fighter who had saved his life just hours earlier.

"Good grief, my dear Sango. What is it? Are you alright?" On instant alert, his body stiffened as he took his hands out of his robe's pockets. His eyes darted up and down the hallway to identify the source of her obvious panic. "Speak, lass!"

"Greigh, it's my friend, Sybil in 7F." She nodded in that direction—

to her left. "Something is wrong. I feel it. She's not answering her door, and I know she is home. What shall we do?"

SANGO KNEW GREIGH WAS CAPABLE. ESPECIALLY AFTER witnessing his street action earlier in the evening. She also was aware of Greigh's skills in the art of defeating locks. She had researched her mysterious neighbor, which had been a surprising challenge. And they had talked on occasion in recent months. He guarded his privacy jealously, but she possessed skills of her own.

"Greigh, we need to check on Sybil."

"Of course. Come in for a moment. Let me grab a few things."

Moments later, he had thrown on a pair of jeans, a t-shirt and sandals. Now armed with his lock-picking kit and his favorite folding knife, they exited into the wide hallway. They turned right, and in seconds, arrived at the locked door to apartment 7F, the second door down from his own. Greigh knocked. Several times. No answer. Sango stood to his right. Her fidgeting turned into agitation.

"*Please*, Greigh!"

"Alright, then." He ensured the hallway was deserted, kneeled, laid his kit on the once-sumptuous, now-threadbare red and black carpeting of the hallway. He chose two of his older tools while ignoring the new technology-based tools and went to work on Sybil's ancient pin-and-tumbler lock. It would seem apartment 7F's now-absentee owner did not believe in key cards or biometrics. Two full minutes later, Sango's impatience overcame her.

"So, can you open this door or not?"

GREIGH RAISED HIS EYEBROWS. SWIVELED HIS GAZE UP toward her standing next to him, but said nothing. With her arms crossed, her fidgeting agitated her entire torso with nervous energy.

She peered down at him and mumbled, "Sorry."

"No worries. Almost there. I must admit I'm a bit out of practice."

Thirty seconds later, the latch yielded. He stowed his kit in a hip pocket. It barely fit. They no sooner crossed the threshold when Greigh thrust out his right arm. Sango bumped into it, like it was a steel gate.

Surprised, she glared up at Greigh's profile in the semi-darkness. There, in the dim apartment, a painting or drawing on the floor at their feet had caught his attention. He nodded down.

Illuminated only by the hall sconces behind them, with the drawing cast in their own shadows, Greigh said, "We dare not tread farther without more light."

He said, "Illuminate."

Nothing.

"Lights."

Still nothing. He sought and found a wall switch to the right of the door. Flicked it upward. The lights came on.

He searched for a security panel, but found none. No alarm to disarm—a slight tinge of disappointment surprised him.

Like his apartment, a wall in front of them separated the entry area from the rest of the apartment. Someone had swept to the floor the contents of a small table against the wall directly ahead. The drawer was dislodged, cast to the floor, covering a small portion of the drawing.

They saw kitchen debris scattered on the floor around the right end of the entry wall, and books thrown to the floor to their left. That wall prevented them from seeing the rest of the apartment.

Still, Greigh's right arm remained across Sango's chest. She did not protest. They both took in the disarray. With his left hand, Greigh pointed down toward their feet once more, and would not allow either of them to take another step. The now-illuminated room confirmed his suspicion.

Nothing could dissuade an author who wrote or co-authored over a hundred murder mysteries from soaking in every detail of a real-world crime scene. Not any less than a fictional one. Greigh recognized they were about to do just that—enter a potential crime scene. They must consider everything significant.

He muttered with gravitas, "Touch nothing, Sango."

She didn't seem to understand, but nodded. The most intriguing and immediate clue was the intricate figure that lay before them. Someone would have drawn it with powdered eggshell as part of an elaborate ritual. He saw Sango had noticed it but remained oblivious to its significance from within the fog of her escalating emotional turmoil. No doubt she was now imagining the worst.

Two feet square, the almost-white drawing presented itself in high contrast against the ebony floor of three-foot-square tiles:

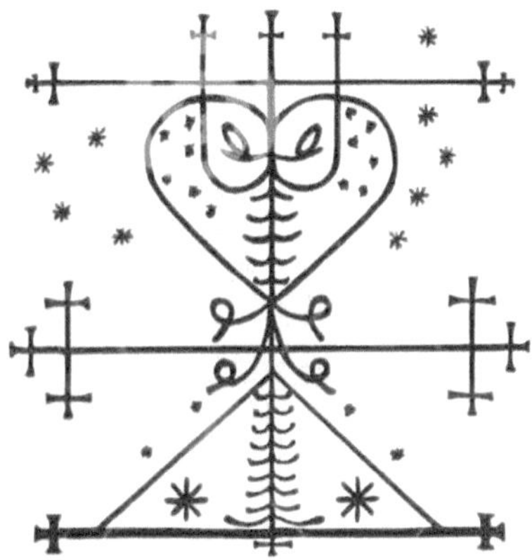

In a general sense, Greigh knew what it signified. The symbol seemed consistent with someone living in fear. His own sense of dread mounted.

They stepped over and around the drawing with care, and with some difficulty.

Sango croaked, "What does it mean, Greigh?"

"This is a vévé—or sacred symbol—of a Voodoo loa, that is, a Voodoo god known as Maman Brigitte, if memory serves. This loa is an *aggressive* protector of women and represents a clear intent—the epitome of punitive justice. She is also a loa associated with death and the underworld."

"What—?"

"Sango, we must treat this as a crime scene, no matter what we find next." His voice remained calm, but inside, he too, now feared the worst.

Greigh committed to school the authorities that this meant Sybil Thibodaux not only lived in fear, but sought justice for some monstrous wrong done to her or hers. Knowing where Sybil was from, this drawing convinced him this was Louisiana Voodoo at its finest, practiced by many Creole and others.

He was somewhat of an authority on the matter from researching an earlier manuscript he chose not to publish for reasons he could not explain. CED detectives would learn of all this soon enough, assuming they would be receptive to its significance. But Greigh also knew any ardent believer of Voodoo, or Vodun—as it was known across the Caribbean and elsewhere—would *not* have crossed this vévé protecting apartment 7F.

This meant that whatever happened or was happening here either was not perpetrated by a believer, or they gained access to the apartment by other means, or both. He had a theory which he'd share with the right authority at the appropriate time.

THEY STEPPED OVER THE DRAWING. SOMEONE HAD STREWN an array of objects across the floor. They rounded the end of the entryway wall to their left. What they saw stopped them in their tracks as the entire living room and kitchen came into view.

Greigh led the way. Behind him, he heard Sango gasp with a sharp intake of breath so sudden that she coughed and could not stop.

Between the table in front of a small couch and the fireplace to their right lay Sybil Thibodaux's ravaged corpse. Someone had positioned it in a most unnatural but symmetrical position.

Greigh spun around and grabbed Sango by both of her tiny shoulders, fearing she might collapse at the sight of her mutilated friend.

Almost entirely covered in blood stains, including Sybil's shredded blouse and shorts, she lay face up with both arms above her head, like the killer had positioned them post-mortem. If she'd been standing, her arms would be raised as if someone had just shouted, "Hands up!" Her shattered knees allowed her lower legs to splay outward at ninety-degree angles to the rest of her and also lay flat to the floor.

So many things were just wrong. Sybil's stunning beauty now appeared only as a macabre mask of horror. She, or more likely the owner from whom she had sublet, preferred old incandescent lights in all her lamps. They now painted her cozy domain in a warm but bizarre glow.

Greigh wondered if his mental meandering was how he processed his own shock at this deliberate staging of a brutalized young woman.

How long have incandescents been illegal? She doesn't have as many bookcases as my place. Can't say as I care for the confused ambience in here, even though it's a similar floor plan to mine—just smaller. And messier.

Most of the many built-in bookcases no longer held books. Someone had swept them to the floor. Tangled and torn volumes covered parts of Sybil's body, having been flung there—with considerable force. The nearest bookcase was at least fifteen feet distant.

They'd been there only a minute. After taking it all in, Sango's knees melted.

Some monster had inflicted deep gashes at every angle across her friend's body. They criss-crossed each other everywhere on her face, chest and thighs. Her twisted legs and savaged arms were nearly torn from their sockets.

Greigh resisted the comfort of succumbing to shock himself. He planted Sango on the tiny couch. Picked up a heavy ornamental fireplace poker to use as weapon.

Ready to strike, he searched the apartment for the killer... or killers. Once he completed that task, it occurred to him that such savagery must have consumed considerable time. With care, he placed the poker back on its stand.

Just like in his novels, he would process the scene. He recalled what his research always reminded him as he began dictating under his breath notes to his wristPad hanging next to his right hip.

"Sango awakened me at 9:45PM. It is now..." he checked, "9:58PM, the time we came upon the body.

"Condition of the victim—the body's mutilation suggests heavy blows with a sizable and stout edge weapon. Not very sharp, but enough to penetrate skin and cartilage. Dull enough to chip away small chunks bone visible under congealed blood at both shoulders and thighs. Most wounds are visible beneath the few shreds of clothing that remain.

"Slices through the fabric of her saturated clothes and into her flesh suggest there should be more blood, viscera, other fluids and odors. No blood pooling.

"Likewise, no blood spatters are evident on the walls or floor in the body's vicinity, even though both of the victim's arms are torn nearly from their sockets, and most wounds, if not all, appear to have been administer pre-mortem. Pause recording."

BASED ON THE STILL-WET APPEARANCE IN SOME OF THE deeper gashes, someone had killed her elsewhere within the past couple of hours. He noticed a small pouch hanging by a leather thong around Sybil's neck. No doubt a gris-gris.

He touched nothing and needn't reinforce the same with Sango. She had withdrawn in upon herself, occupied by just maintaining her slump on Sybil's colorful and fringed divan, an ancient piece that appeared Caribbean in origin.

Greigh inspected the windows—all locked from the inside, the same as the front door. Sybil's apartment was not as grandiose as the C and D units, and possessed no balcony outside.

HE STEPPED CAREFULLY. AVOIDING SUNDRY DEBRIS, HE said, "Continue recording. General condition of the scene: ransacked—

appears to have resulted from a reckless search. Since every room of the apartment is in the same condition, it is possible the killer did not find the object of this search. No drawer or cabinet remains closed in any of the six rooms. Most drawers are not only pulled open on their slides, but some were thrown across the room. An emotional response—raw fury, perhaps.

"Papers, clothing and the contents of tables, kitchen cabinets, refrigerator and breakfast bar alike are strewn across the floor. The refrigerator door is open.

"Sybil was a renowned poet. I am not surprised to find manuscript pages everywhere, some wrinkled and torn, some... *burned to ash?* Pause recording."

Greigh sensed the tremendous rage spent savaging Sybil's belongings. And the brutality that cut, bashed, smashed and nearly vivisected her dainty five-foot-two frame? Alive, she would have appeared petite. Dead, she seemed a lifeless child.

"RESUME RECORDING. THE AMPLE SURFACE OF A WRITING desk near the east wall next to the windows is also swept clean. Under the desk are scraps of old newspaper clippings, as if someone had ripped them from an ancient scrapbook—of actual paper. And I see pieces of an old-fashioned *printed* photo that looks to be over a century old. Maybe older, faded to bland shades of grey. It appears to be of a sizable group of black workers laboring in a cane field. No, they *posed* for this picture in a field. I wonder.... Pause recording."

SOMEONE MOVED THE BODY HERE. WITHIN HOURS OF Sybil's death. It seemed like the killer needed to spend time with the object of his rage, perhaps even before beginning what appeared to be an almost ritualistic disfigurement of this beautiful young woman's ebony skin.

Greigh had seen her around, but they hadn't spoken other than the odd salutation in passing. He had always admired her beauty and grace. She moved like a... cat.

Once he had learned all he could via casual and non-invasive observation of the scene, he gripped both of Sango's heaving shoulders. Lifted her off the divan, and ushered her to the door. They had been in apartment 7F less than ten minutes. Seemed an eternity.

Back in the hallway, he debated whether to re-engage the door's lock, as he had found it, or to leave it unlocked. The former would expose him to questions from CED's criminal investigations unit about how they knew there was a body inside. The latter would not secure the crime scene. He opted for the former, as he intended to share his observations only with the lead detective. *Not* with the beat cops who would precede the detective.

Greigh's ample experience with police officers guided him to share as little as possible with street cops. They were often inflexible and quick on the trigger, as they must be. He'd share his thoughts only with experienced investigators who would more likely appreciate his own observations and procedural skills.

He locked the door to what was now a crime scene.

CHAPTER 18

Time to probe. Back in Greigh's apartment, Sango Mori sat on the generous sectional sofa that faced his own fireplace. That impressive edifice had never seen flames other than those digitally projected or electrically radiated.

Greigh whispered, "9-1-1" into his wristPad which linked to his right-temple communication implant. He was on hold long enough to brew Sango a cup of chamomile tea.

He wanted to explore with her the events leading up to their discovery of Sybil's body, Sango's relationship with her, and any other tidbits. Anything she might not feel comfortable discussing with law enforcement.

After what seemed like an eternity, he heard, "9-1-1. What is your emergency?"

Greigh said, "Yes, I am reporting a homicide. Hotel Literati at 667 Harrison Street, apartment 7F. My name is Aubrey Greigh. I live in suite 7D.... Yes, I'm safe, and I'll be here. Thank you."

GREIGH SAT TO SANGO'S LEFT. HE LEARNED THAT SHE AND Sybil met online before Sybil moved to Chicago. Sango had arrived a year earlier from Tokyo, although she grew up in Hamamatsu. They met and became friends through the International Poetry Collective. Sango still found it difficult to speak, exhibiting symptoms of shock.

"She... she asked where she might lodge for the foreseeable future, Greigh. Since Professor Janssen now lives abroad, he was delighted for the rental opportunity. 7F was the perfect solution. I wanted to spare her the indignity of camping in Sherwood, like I did for a time, until a unit opened up here in Camelot. Oh, Greigh, I can't imagine someone would do such a horrible thing. She's never coming back, is she?"

Sango's skin further paled and glistened. But she was strong. He whispered, "No, dear. Your friend is gone. But we *will* find out what happened."

He made this vow, even though he had no idea how he would honor it.

"Did she share with you why she moved to Chicago?"

Sango took a full thirty seconds to respond. Greigh just waited while he held her now-clammy hands in his. After a shaky but deep breath, she sighed as she spoke, like she was deflating.

"I'm not sure, Greigh. We'd only been remote friends for six months, and neighbors for two. I thought I knew her quite well. Then, again, she'd utter strange and exotic notions that left me wondering."

Greigh grew intrigued. "Can you give me an example?"

Sango relayed the sacrificed pig and blood oath comment she'd heard Syb utter the previous Monday.

"Though she said nothing further about this, I also got the impression she'd been seeing someone after she moved into her apartment. But I saw no one.

"Something she said the last time I saw her, um, it was the oddest thing. Perhaps the most frightening of all, but almost as if she were talking to herself and I just overheard, 'The devil's voice grinds salty gravel into a seeping wound.' What do you make of all that, Greigh?"

After a thoughtful moment, he said, "Much of the Creole culture, especially with Creoles of color, revolves around the Voodoo religion. Mention of sacrifices and rituals sounds like Voodoo. As for her other comment, I have no idea."

"Yes, she mentioned Voodoo, although I am not familiar with what that is."

"Voodoo is as culturally blended a religion as the Creoles themselves, practiced by millions all over the world. Voodoo's primary focus is on holistic healing—physical and spiritual—but, like any human endeavor, it possesses a darker side as well.

"Sango, you'll recall the drawing on Sybil's entryway floor. Practitioners of Voodoo believe such drawings possess great power. It is possible Sybil either drew that herself, or more likely, sought the guidance of a bokor—a Voodoo sorcerer—who would create that for her. They invoke certain ritualistic chants that often accompany such a drawing's creation.

"Its aim is to protect someone—in this case, Sybil—from evil. I'm guessing she feared for her life from another Voodoo practitioner, who would be hesitant to cross such a protective charm."

Sango remained distressed, pale, and a little dizzy as she rubbed her temples. But she remained resolute in helping any way she could.

"So she was running from some Voodoo, ah, person, who caught up with her and killed her?"

"That is one possibility. Seems likely, at least from what little we know right now. It also seems likely whoever killed her wanted something they expected Sybil kept in her apartment. *Or* they just hated her so much they tore the place apart in a rage."

"Is that why the body was so brutalized?"

"Again, possible. She might have even been… tortured."

Greigh realized he had gone too far. Sango's entire body shuddered as she gasped, started coughing again, and shrank into Greigh's sofa, almost into a fetal curl. Now sobbing out loud, she was almost howling, inconsolable.

You idiot! For the love of Christ, Greigh, could you be any more insensitive, you wanker?

CHAPTER 19

N inety-ninth Precinct
Chicago, Illinois
10:45 PM

He is calling me? This late?

Captain Lois Granger of the CED's ninety-ninth precinct took the call from the police commissioner himself. She jumped to attention. Not sure why.

Two sentences later, she realized they'd need their best pit bull on the high-profile murder case of a celebrity named Sybil Thibodaux, whoever that was. The name sounded familiar.

Chance McQuillan's closure rate was a factor, and she was motivated. Even if she didn't solve it, Granger would have done what the commissioner expected. She'd have assigned a top-performing detective who was also expendable if things turned to shit. McQuillan was a pain in her ass, but a good investigator.

THE CAPTAIN WAVED HER INTO HER OFFICE. MCQ HAD BEEN watching through the windows. The way Granger sprang to attention? Had to be someone important calling. She read her lips well enough. A big case. Mere coincidence she was here, not out working another case. She'd been awake and running on empty since yesterday.

"McQuil—"

Before she let the captain say another word, McQuillan said, "I don't care who you've already assigned. Whatever it is, I want it."

"Will you just listen? If you're that motivated, McQuillan, you got it. Just don't let your other cases slide. This vic is high profile. You screw this up, you'll take a hit. Understand?"

Standard threat. "Yeah, no worries, Captain. Address?"

"Already on your device. Best get over there before the media thugs muddle things up. Take Johnson with you."

"I'd rather run solo. I'll move faster. Thanks, anyway."

There'll be time for sleep when I'm dead.

TWENTY MINUTES LATER, AN EXHAUSTED MCQ ARRIVED AT the hotel where the victim lived. She'd never been here before, even though it was only two long blocks south and five short blocks east of the precinct house. The place was not a hotbed of crime. The uniformed officers' preliminary report said this wasn't even a hotel anymore, despite the name, but a building of condos. Funny, they still called it *Hotel* Literati.

She looked around as she entered the lobby and headed for the elevator on the far side.

Jeez, this place needs some serious rehab.

The lobby reeked of old upholstery, dusty drapes, ancient tapestries, brass and wood polish. Must have been really something in its day. It smelled… musty, a little like a wet dog, or old humidity. Wasn't bad, but the place had seen better days.

McQ hoped soon to be knocking on the door of apartment 7D. That assumed the ancient elevator didn't break down and plummet her to her death before contacting the civilian who called 9-1-1. It took a while, but the gilded cage delivered her to seven after she was assaulted by a few gamey odors on the way up.

She stepped out of the elevator after manually shoving the collapsible metal door open to her right. It complained with groans and squeaks and rattles as she did so. Shoved it closed again behind her. And there was 7D, right across a wide hall with high ceilings. Easy.

She wanted to get impressions from this witness before she saw the scene herself. Besides, the forensics team needed to map the scene before she started tromping around.

The door opened before she knocked. A striking man more than a few years older than her, but fit and shaggy, showed a mouth full of teeth that were way too white and way too straight.

"Mr. Greigh?"

"Yes, Detective. Please come in."

As McQ entered, this tall guy in tight jeans and a nice butt led her around a short wall into an expansive living room. She noticed the panoramic view through a huge wall of glass in front of her on the far side of the room. A southern exposure. Nice. One taller building—the old Prudential, stood out. All the low buildings around it on the other side of Harrison stretched to the southern perimeter of the historic area known as Chicago's Near Southwest Loop.

She figured this guy must be loaded and wondered why he didn't live on Lakeshore or some other, more prestigious address. Thoughts swirled through her exhausted brain like it was flushing them even while they still seemed significant.

This apartment is out of place. Too upscale for the rest of this old building. And this guy is a real looker! Gotta be full of himself.

"Thanks for seeing me, Mr. Greigh. You called 9-1-1, right?"

"Yes. Sango and I are still upset at finding our neighbor's body just down the hall." He nodded off to his right. She assumed that was the general direction of her crime scene.

"The officers first on the scene tell me you refused to give them your statement. Why is that?"

"It has been my experience—"

"Never mind. Can you tell me what happened before I go down there?"

She yawned while listening to the guy. He seemed articulate and carried himself like a soldier. Confident. Erect. Poised. But that short beard and baby pony tail seemed out of character.

Is that a slight British accent? Or serious East Coast money?

But then she thought she heard him say the door to the victim's apartment was locked.

"Hold on. The door was locked? Then how did you know there was a body in there?"

"Detective—"

"Detective Lieutenant Chance McQuillan."

"Detective… McQuillan, I have some experience in such matters, and knew you'd want to have the scene preserved, so—"

There it was. This guy was too good-looking not to be an arrogant prig. "Oh, you have some experience, do you? Well, why don't you tell me about that, and then you can explain busting into a crime scene you claim to have preserved. Just mansplain it for little ole me." She tried to fake a southern accent but failed.

That pegged him down a notch or two. He said, "No, no, you misunderstand, Detective—"

"Well, let's pretend I have a brain. Why don't you lay it out for me, *mister?*"

Before responding, he glared and winced at her and puckered his lips like she just poked a finger in one of those incredible icy-blue eyes. He now chose his words with care. Good.

"Look, *Detective,* if you'd allow me a moment to give you the facts, you can choose for yourself what to do with them, and perhaps just where to stuff them. Fair enough?"

Ouch. Well, he gives as good as he gets.

"Fine. Shoot."

She couldn't figure out how this guy had gotten under her skin. He hadn't said anything yet. She felt flushed.

"Detective, this is Miss Mori." He motioned to the sofa on his left.

There sat a petite Asian woman McQ hadn't noticed. She was normally more observant than this.

Shit!

The woman slumped and fidgeted. She glanced up and nodded. McQ offered an apologetic nod back.

The tall guy's short pony tail waggled—like it was soft—as he moved his head.

"Miss Mori knocked on my door at precisely 9:45, almost ninety minutes ago, now. Said she knew her friend, the victim, Miss Sybil Thibodaux, is always home no later than nine. That's spelled T-H-I—"

"I know how it's spelled. Go on."

"Miss Thibodaux did not respond to her knocking. Sango implored me to check on her. We knocked on her door together. No answer. We entered—"

"You said the door was locked. You broke in." Not a question.

"Well, we feared for Sybil's—Miss Thibodaux's—safety, and, ah, I have a way with locks—"

"You are a registered locksmith, Mr. Greigh?"

Now *he* flushed, looked her square in the eye. Planted his hands on those slender hips in those tight jeans. He said, "Look, lady, I am trying to help you here, so how about you holster your attitude, you shut up, and you listen. Alright? Otherwise, do your worst."

McQ flushed further, and was about to pop off on this smart-ass, but thought better of it. She remembered her captain's warning not to screw this up. Like it or not, she needed this asshole's observations. She swallowed her exhausted annoyance, said nothing, gave him a wave and a smirk to continue before she shot her own hands to her own hips. Best she could do.

This guy!

"Like I was saying, we entered the apartment, found it ransacked, and saw the body. I searched for intruders in each room, made several observations, but touched nothing."

"You searched each room? You made several observations? Care to share them with me, along with your qualifications for contaminating my crime scene? Please? Are you a forensic scientist?"

"No, I am not. However, I have researched, written or co-written and published over one-hundred mystery novels and short stories, most of them murder mysteries. I sourced much of my research from archives or active cases with various police departments across the country and around the world. They have also consulted me, on occasion."

Dismissing most of this as bullshit, she felt on the verge of another snide remark, but bit her tongue and said nothing.

He continued, now with a granite edge to his voice. "Someone levied a great deal of savagery toward Miss Thibodaux's body and to her belongings. We discovered the body at 9:48. You will want to note a drawing on her entryway floor. It is Voodoo in origin. I suggested the officers take care not to disturb it.

"Your call logs will show we reported the crime once we ensured we had preserved the integrity of the scene and returned to my apartment."

"Okay. Thank you, Mr. Greigh. We'll take it from here."

He had more to say, but now chose not to. She was done with him, anyway. She'd come back to him later when they had both settled down. Maybe.

God, I'm tired.

For now, she wanted to interview the officers who were first to the scene. She whirled around and swept from his apartment, along with the uniform who had just come to fetch her to 7F down the hall—to *her* crime scene.

She left Greigh's front door swung wide.

CHAPTER 20

That woman!

After the arrogant and frazzled detective left, Greigh ushered the deflated Sango back to her apartment, just two doors down the hall to the west. The midnight hour approached. Even two-plus hours after they had discovered Sybil Thibodaux's body, Sango, still in shock, looked like a lost lamb. He didn't have to imagine. He knew how she felt. Not even any tears. They would come later.

Less than a hundred feet later, they arrived at 7B. Sango's biometric lock disengaged in her presence. Her lights brightened the interior of her home.

He started to cross her threshold. She turned and pressed a calloused but gentle hand against his chest.

"I need to be alone now, Greigh. Thank you for everything."

Greigh sensed a stone-hard edge to her voice—sharp but brittle. That was new. He understood. Her anger now displaced her sadness. Sango was formidable.

"Of course, my dear. What friends do, is it not? Good night. If you need *anything*...."

Without uttering another syllable, she hoisted a tiny smile and closed the door on a horrific day. This was to be an even more horrific night.

For both of them.

GREIGH PADDED BACK TO HIS PLACE. HE BREATHED A SIGH of relief that his initial encounter with Detective *Chance* McQuillan was behind him. Not that he couldn't handle the stress of an interrogation—he'd navigated more of those than he cared to recall. That... *woman* infuriated him, which cultivated his uneasiness.

He couldn't explain it. She seemed competent enough, and tough. She asked all the expected questions. Her waves of red hair, though— maybe that was it—reminded him of his dear Melissa. Even though she'd only been gone three years now, it seemed an eternity. Yet, at such times, it was like yesterday someone murdered her out in DuSable Park.

I bloody hate parks!

THIS... *Chance* McQUILLAN? HER UNUSUAL NAME REMINDED him of his daughter's darling nickname—*Clance.* But he suspected the real source of his consternation might be that he saw a beautiful young woman before he saw an arrogant and infuriating detective.

She knew how to handle herself in what was still a testosterone-thrashed profession. He had observed the beat cop that fetched her from his apartment. The poor bloke displayed what Greigh thought to be excessive deference to this dominant personality bundled in one provocative package. Found himself rooting for her success while hoping she'd fall flat on her silky face.

GREIGH ENCOUNTERED THREE NON-UNIFORMED COPS emerging from the elevator—the forensics team. They wheeled out their high-tech gear. He guessed that was what they thought would solve the case for them.

With thousands of homicides in the city each year, and with that number growing, they needed to automate at least some of their crime-solving process. But based on his other recent exposure to law enforcement, they depended far too much on gadgets, and not enough on old-school gum-shoe tactics. Not to mention their abominable closure rate that the media enjoyed highlighting.

He'd watch this fiery detective operate with interest. Especially with a famous and controversial victim like poor Sybil Thibodaux.

CHAPTER 21

F riday, June 22nd
Hotel Literati
Apartment 7F
1:15AM

This gadget better make me happy.

The department's Crime Scene Mapper—CSM—amazed McQ. But her perennial skepticism prevailed.

Most underestimated McQ's superb memory. She recalled, almost verbatim, the boring but informative briefing one of the arrogant little forensic geeks mansplained to her.

With this recent innovation, the techs forensically mapped a three-dimensional rendering of the entire apartment with the rather cumbersome device in less than an hour. They transmitted their results both to the lead detective's onboard device—her wristPad—and to the secure CED cloud for supervisory and archival purposes.

The CSM was a device the size of a large wheel-aboard piece of luggage, but with a dozen antenna-like appendages that the forensics team deployed once on site. CED's R&D contractors promised to further miniaturize the prototype soon.

They'd wheel it around a crime scene of any size in a grid pattern following the guidance on its topside screen. That would ensure one-hundred percent coverage. It would scan a twelve-foot cube surrounding the device in real-time. From the sum of overlapping cubes scanned, it then created a seamless 3D "map" of an entire multi-room scene, including architectural details.

That device and its sensors cataloged the presence and precise location of each piece of evidence, including solid and liquid debris.

CSM also scanned for fingerprints—including a timestamp when each was created. In addition to identifying the fingerprint's owners, its analysis used a lightning-fast full-spectrum mass spectrometer to measure the various chemical components of prints, such as chlorides in proportion to amino acids. This time-stamped when each finger-print appeared, precise to plus-or-minus ten minutes.

It also detected the recent presence and location of DNA on the map. It analyzed and identified the person or persons who had occupied the scene within the previous several hours. That assumed they were in the global array of law enforcement databases.

Everybody was.

The CSM also detected, analyzed and mapped blood spatter and other organic material present at the scene with A.I. algorithms that suggested likely origin scenarios of that matter. It hypothesized what happened from *splatter and matter*, as the team would say.

Over time, however, organic material deteriorated from its original —fresh—composition, as determined by a real-time differential analysis of material found at the scene. After six hours, CSM's results were no longer viable, to the point of having little or no forensic value. That's why response time to the scene remained challenging but critical.

CSM performed footprint analysis, too, including path tracing. Some would argue this was its unique crown jewel, current limitations notwithstanding. It traced the path of footprints that were up to six hours old. It could not, however, discern their sequence, only their path and direction as deduced from the foot's shape.

The instrument employed sensors that detected residual nano-vibrations, combined with heat and pressure gradients on hard surfaces. The harder the surface, the higher the resolution of the paths traced. Soft floor coverings presented a challenge to the device's path-tracing capability, as did certain footwear. But the R&D geeks promised future upgrades to the device's footprint analysis quality.

This same tech also determined the room's level of illumination for the same period by mapping micro-ion energy trails in three dimensions. This could be useful in detecting movement and motion in three dimensions, too. Sensors could trace the direction of a physical blow, and to a lesser extent, the path of a bullet. But these energy trails deteriorated in minutes, not hours. This might never improve, they said. Not with current-generation technology.

Yes, McQ was confident the CSM would render unreliable eye witnesses obsolete. Eventually.

But not detectives, of course.

CHAPTER 22

*N*ot this guy again!

McQ stood with impatience in the spacious seventh-floor hallway dictating notes to the case file on her wristPad. She saw the lock-whisperer from 7D. Mr. Greigh approached with an artificial smile pasted on his face.

Now what?

She stopped adding notes to her file on the victim, witnesses, clues, suspects, relationships, motives, and solutions, however likely or unlikely. So far, it was little more than an empty outline containing few nuggets.

As he approached, she looked him over again from head to toe and back again. Like she was a man giving an attractive woman the once-over. Not subtle.

She said, "Pause recording."

To this intruder, she half-whispered, "What is it, Mr. Greigh?" She need not have whispered. The thick Victorian carpeting—though well-worn—and the velvet-like brocade wall covering absorbed sound as effectively as any recording studio's anechoic booth. Besides, they were alone. But a homicide scene demand a degree of, what? Reverence?

"Look, I don't want to intrude, but Sybil was a friend of a friend and almost my next-door neighbor. You didn't seem too interested in my observations of the scene a while ago. If after you're finished with your gadgetry offering its best thinking, I can share with you my own observations. If you're willing to listen with an open mind. Otherwise—"

"Thank you, Mr. Greigh. I'll call you with questions." Her head wobbled with groggy fatigue.

He stuck his hands in the hip pockets of his jeans, gave her a slant-wise glance from slitted eyes, as if to say, "Fine, you're on your own, lady." Muttered something unintelligible, shot his eyebrows skyward, no longer smiling, wheeled on his heel, and padded off in his ghetto-chic sandals without uttering another word.

Nice buns on that one. Oh, for crissake, McQuillan, get your head out of your ass, and your eyes off of his!

The clock ticked past 1:30AM. She started receiving the initial data compiled by the CSM.

With any luck, I'll put this one to bed by sunset tomorrow. I could use a bed myself about now.

She hadn't slept in thirty-six hours.

It showed.

She stood alone in the hallway. As she waited outside the crime scene, chunks of CSM data kept rolling into her device as it compiled—movement history. She projected it in front of her via her wristPad's 3D projector. She chose a god's-eye view.

McQ said to no one in particular. "What the hell?"

From her peripheral vision she caught the uniform guarding 7F's door across the hall looking at her. He turned to see if she was talking to him. She figured he was used to detectives muttering to themselves, since few others would talk with them. Not willingly. He smirked. She nodded.

She scratched the back of her head. An intense frown sculpted her otherwise smooth forehead. The CSM showed the only movement in the hour leading up to the body dump was *the body itself.*

While the map wasn't able to ID the sequence of steps taken, it did map all the movements in total. The body seemed to have *floated* in through a window—of its own accord—before it stopped and dropped three feet to the floor where they found it.

But the temp gradients showed a low body temp by several degrees. The victim had been dead for hours when it "flew" into the scene. Then the arms and legs of the corpse moved. Again, as if on their own. Like those of a puppet with no visible strings.

Motion trails of books and papers appeared, and horizontal surfaces were swept clean, as if a ghostly apparition had caused these phenomena. But the CSM discerned no visible cause for this mayhem even as temperature and ID data rolled in.

Not only were there no footprints, but no temp gradients—other than the corpse—no foreign DNA, and no unexpected fingerprints.

Not as helpful as she had hoped.

Then, less than two hours later in the chronology of past events recorded by the device's sensors, she saw the flared movements of the two neighbors who broke into her scene. One of them had walked into and out of each room to search for intruders, and she observed their path leaving apartment 7F. Just as that Greigh character reported. But nothing else.

What in blue blazes is going on here? And what's with that damn drawing on the floor? Makes no sense. No available info on it, either. Although that Greigh seemed to have some ideas. Something about Voodoo, whatever the Hell that is.

GOTTA BE SOMETHING HERE. WHILE NOT YET ADMISSIBLE in a court of law, CSM data provided the investigator invaluable clues about the scene leading up to the crime, as well as during and after. In this case, the *lack* of data proved revealing. But so far tonight, that disappointed McQ.

She awaited the rest of the data. It might offer some useful hypotheses. If she only could stay awake long enough.

Maybe she'd sit down for a while on one of the short sofas in the hall across from 7F. Just to rest her feet.

CHAPTER 23

H otel Literati
Apartment 7F
1:45AM

"DETECTIVE…"

Nothing.

"Detective!"

"Huh? *What!* Oh—"

The uniform guarding the crime scene didn't dare touch her, so from five feet away, he said, "LT, you fell asleep twenty minutes ago. I thought you should take a look at this."

"Oh, yeah. Thanks. Milligan, isn't it?"

"Yes, sir. The techs have finished mapping your scene, and rushed off to another one. Wanted me to point something out to ya."

"Okay, great. Let's go." She stumbled when she first stood. Almost fell. One leg tucked under the other had fallen asleep on the too-short sofa in the seventh-floor hallway. Milligan reached out to help her, but she shrugged him off. She shook off the tingling numbness and stretched her arms.

He chuckled. "Long day?"

Her deadpan glance said, "Yeah, a couple. Whatta we got?"

She then noticed her wristPad blinking at her, and its "hot topic" haptics tingled her wrist. Must be the rest of the CSM download. She'd first peek at what the techs thought required her immediate attention.

Milligan led her across the hall and in to the body. She insisted it be not moved by the M.E. until the CSM team finished and she had walked the scene herself. Besides, they were tied up for another hour elsewhere. Busy night, like every night. No stranger to grizzled corpses, this one struck a chord.

"They wanted me to show you this because their gadgetry didn't know what the hell to make of this thing around her neck. Pardon my French."

"No worries, Milligan. What *is* that? A pouch? Pretty soaked in blood. Mostly dried. Looks like it's got stuff inside." She didn't touch it. "Let me see if they snagged any imagery of its contents."

The CSM's download to her wristPad had flagged the unusual miniature pouch as an item of "significant interest"—oblong, and maybe half the size of a child's fist. She'd examine all the data later.

One item on the inventory list for the pouch was a slip of paper with some writing on it. Though it was folded into a small blood-drenched wad, their multi-layer and multi-dimensional image analysis digitally unfolded and enhanced it.

She said, "Yikes."

Milligan looked at the projection, too, and just shrugged. "I don't envy you your job, LT."

She meant to chuckle. Came out a snort.

A strange language and symbols not cataloged anywhere in any online database added another level of confusion to this already-twisted case. Her hopes of solving this one fast dissipated in a cloud of doubt.

The other eight items in the pouch? Even more confusing:

1. organic matter, long dead,
2. desiccated exotic herbs (unidentifiable),
3. a piece of cloth or clothing soiled with male human perspiration and more than one type of rancid oil,
4. a small rounded stone,
5. tiny animal bones (species undetermined),
6. degraded human hair (male),
7. a bit of exotic wood soaked in yet a different oily solution,

8. nail clippings, also from a human male, but no ID, which was strange.

That completed the unusual pouch's inventory of nine items, including the paper.

"What the shit?"

"Like I said, LT—"

"Shut up, Milligan."

As she shook her head in exasperated bewilderment, she scanned the now-completed CSM map of the entire scene. The machine only identified DNA from the victim, the two neighbors, and nobody else?

Oh crap. How is this possible? How did the body get in here? Undetected? And where was this poor girl tortured and killed?

She seethed in exasperation, "Aaah!"

CHAPTER 24

Officer Milligan looked concerned. This pit bull growled and bunched her fists, ready to hit something—or someone. But she was a pro.

"Lieutenant, you gotta go get some real shut-eye. Like in a bed. You're lookin' kinda like a zombie. Can't think straight like that."

"Shut up, Milligan."

THE BIG LUG COULDN'T KNOW. HER SISTER *had* TURNED herself into a real-life zombie. As teenagers, the two of them used to get high together on *Bounce*, an insanely addictive psychotropic drug. It was an expensive vape, and the two of them weren't proud of what they did to keep scoring inhalers of the stuff. The trouble started at a party where McQ's sister, Molly, lost track of her hits and overdosed.

During a two-year period, institutions across the country over-flowed with Bounce ODs. Until they shut down a massive manufac-turing and distribution ring of the synthetic party-drug out of Houston. Molly was one of the countless casualties.

To this day, McQ's sister existed in a semi-catatonic state in a diaper inside a locked ward. Numb to everything from common sense to fear, she no longer experienced any emotions, including pain—physical or emotional. She wasn't dangerous. Not really. Well, maybe to herself.

McQ preferred to envision Molly no longer suffering from the pain and indignity of her current dilemma. Nor the shame from what their step-father subjected both of them to as adolescents—may the bastard rot in the deepest circle of Hell.

Unlike so many other unfortunates, McQ kept her sister out of the public institutions by paying for private care where they specialized in chronic Bounce victims. That was just one more reason she snagged every single hour of overtime possible.

Molly's care cost a shit-ton.

McQ still went to a couple of Narcotics Anonymous meetings every week, at least, until recently. She tried to help other addicts. She'd like to do more, but....

Her sponsor would stop McQ in her tracks with one word: *excuses.*

Molly and Bounce were the two primary reasons McQ became a cop. Putting away predatory assholes like her step-dad played a role, too.

THIS LIKABLE SON-OF-A-BITCH, MILLIGAN WAS RIGHT. SHE *was* acting like a zombie. Not because of Bounce, but because of her maniacal focus on the job.

Yeah, she'd sneak home for a couple of hours of shut-eye to turn loose her sub-conscious on these weird-ass clues. She'd also think more about *him*. That mysterious neighbor, *Sir* Aubrey Greigh. The first thing that popped when she did a background check gave her heartburn.

Melissa and Clancy Greigh. Three years and a gazillion cases ago, some long-gun shooter slaughtered Greigh's wife, daughter and three others in DuSable Park. The man had lost his family. That was my case, and I treated him like shit last night.

Plus, Greigh was some sort of big-deal author, and a background riddled with unexplained gaps. Born in Scotland, he immigrated to America a decade ago.

Not in any public feeds, but he popped up in multiple law enforcement databases, including Interpol's. The guy had some sort of classified foreign service experience with off-the-charts security clearances as a contractor for three different governments in five years. Holy God!

To top it all off, the King of England himself granted this guy Knighthood... for meritorious services rendered. *This can't be the same guy, can it?*

The arrogant asshole was eye candy to boot. She wondered if helping the police is how he dealt with losing his wife and daughter. *Like his version of NA.*

Shit.

Yeah, she'd have to wonder about this guy. She'd still treat him as a suspect for now.

HAD IT BEEN TWO OR THREE DAYS? SHE FORGOT HOW LONG since she'd caught more than a twenty-minute catnap? Under Milligan's watchful eye, McQ stumbled to the elevator and made her way through The Lit's lobby to the street where a patrol car awaited.

That frickin' Milligan must have radio'd down. Nosy bastard.

She grinned and offered the big lug a playful punch on the shoulder as a way of thanking him without having to say so out loud. *Must be a father.*

The uniform behind the wheel hollered through the open door curbside. "Your chariot awaits, LT. Milligan says I'm to deliver you to your apartment. And I ain't takin' 'no' for an answer."

"Yeah, yeah. Alright. Let's do it."

She slid into the front seat of the cruiser, strapped in, and lowered the door. Muttered the name of the cop bar down the street from the nine-nine—Harrow's—and that was it.

. . .

McQ woke up twenty minutes later. Startled, not remembering where she was for a moment, she muttered, "What the—?"

She massaged a crimp in her neck from leaning crooked against that cruiser's window. She heard and then watched the driver munching on a basketball-size sandwich. Between bites, he slurped from an enormous cup of hot rocket fuel.

Between slurps, he said, "We been here a few. I stepped out to grab a midnight snack. The barista across the street makes killer sandwiches." He nodded off to his left.

She looked at her wristPad configured to display the time whenever level to the ground. It was almost three in the morning. *"Midnight snack? You're late."*

"Yeah. Couldn't bring myself to roust ya. Where's your apartment?"

"Back there." She tossed a vague nod out the passenger-side window of the cruiser.

"Okay. Here. Now go get some shut-eye, LT. Hope ya like egg salad. Gives ya the wind, but solid protein."

He tossed a gigantic cellophane-wrapped sandwich into her lap and grinned like a cadet just out of the academy—maybe a few years earlier."

She leaned forward and swiveled her head to see his nameplate. "Thanks… McKenzie. Yeah, been a long couple a days." After pushing the door button, she swiveled her weary ass out. Without looking back, she offered a hip-level wave of gratitude to her chivalrous Irish chauffeur still visible beneath the cruiser's wing door.

Damn!

McKenzie watched LT stumble in between two buildings, to make sure she made it, and just to enjoy the view.

Good Lord, even wasted-tired she is a world-class looker! Wonder if she knows that? Doesn't act like it.

He grinned at his good fortune. Watching the LT sleep and snore and drool a little was the highlight of his shift. That, and slapping the crap out of an abusive husband who resisted arrest earlier.

Yup, life was good tonight.

CHAPTER 25

McQ's Apartment
6:00AM

SHE SLEPT LIKE A CORPSE. THAT IS, UNTIL SHE POPPED straight up in her bed like someone had just jammed ten-thousand volts into her brain.

She scrunched her nose, and punched her thigh as a small penance for treating Aubrey Greigh like a criminal last night. She just remembered why that made her an insensitive ass-hat.

McQ caught the time with one eye. She launched herself out of bed. She had slept for almost three hours, even though her current case threatened to puke on her career.

Though not her nature, she needed to ask for specialized help. Was this Greigh the guy? Yeah, she'd recruit him.

That'll be a fun ask after last night!

So much of this screwball case made no sense to her. So much appeared to be understandable only by more educated mooks, like the sharpest mystery writer she knew—the *only* one she knew—Aubrey

Greigh. Fat chance he'd agree to help her after the way she treated him. After their now-remembered history together.

*McQuillan, you are **such** an idiot!*

If he remembered her from three years earlier… oh, boy. She was *not* eager to take another tongue-lashing for not solving his family's murders. *That* case had plagued her for months before she put it behind her as her insane case load piled up.

Now, she was already feeling the weight of Police Plaza. Plus, an impatient public from what the media was already calling the brutal slaying of a beloved poet by the *Rhyme Killer*.

Good grief.

The force already suffered from a lousy reputation, and it would do her career prospects no good if she couldn't close this one fast.

From what the uniforms were saying after canvassing other neighbors and management, nobody saw or heard anything. McQ realized that most of this crowd at the Literati didn't think like normal folks, *and* was a pretty tight-lipped community. A hotel that catered to authors, poets, artists, actors and musicians? Might as well be from another frickin' planet. But Greigh….

She thought there might be something on the second and third floors—a homeless vibe down there, but nothing to connect any dots. Traffic cameras up and down Harrison, State and Wabash revealed nothing so far, either.

The hotel's antiquated security cams only covered the lobby, the birdcage and freight elevators, the loading dock, and the main employee areas. Half of those no longer worked. Nothing surveilled the upper floors, and neither of the elevator cams detected anything out of the ordinary.

Their killer was a ghost, or knew where not to be.

McQ would need to interview *Sir* Aubrey Greigh and that other neighbor again. A quick search this morning revealed that Greigh had consulted on a handful of homicide cases for other departments across the country, plus a couple abroad.

Writing wasn't his only skill. Why had she not uncovered this three years ago? Or last night? Did he have something useful to offer?

Yeah, she was getting in her own way and now grasping at straws, but this case might just be a career-ender.

Shit!

TIME FOR A WALK. MCQ DRAGGED HER KEESTER BACK INTO the nine-nine just one long block north on Dearborn from her studio apartment a little before ten AM. Captain Granger ducked her head into McQ's office minutes after she arrived.

"Sitrep on the Thibodaux case?"

"Hey, Cap. Good on prelims. CSM mapped the scene. The forensics team completed their sweep. I'm looking into a couple of leads."

"So, you've got nothing. Look, I'm already taking heat from the commissioner who's swamped with inquiries by everyone from politicians to the press. And The Literati's management is complaining the media corps is clogging their lobby with reporters doing livestreams and asking questions of anyone who passes by.

"Get a handle on this, McQuillan. Work with PR on a statement. We gotta get in front of this. I'm gonna get Johnson to work with you."

"Wait, boss. I'm lining up an experienced consultant. He's also one of the vic's neighbors, *and* the guy who discovered the body. Knows a shit-ton about the vic's unique environment. I'd rather bring him on board. Okay by you?"

"Well, if it'll move this damn thing along. You have no idea what you've stepped into, do you, McQuillan?"

I'm beginning to.

THEN IT DAWNED ON HER. SYBIL THIBODAUX REALLY *was* A genuine national and international celebrity. Another quick search revealed the *First Lady was one of her patrons,* for crissake! A regular on a few of the popular talk shows, she was quite the activist for her Creole culture.

McQ couldn't appreciate what that meant, or even what a "Creole" was. But she'd find out. Thibodaux's claim to fame was her poetry and her activism, both of which meant jack-shit to McQ.

She'd read a poem awhile back, but didn't "get it." She realized she never took the time to appreciate it, either.

Time? Hell, who has time?

Figured she'd have to make time, now, at least to find enough time to get inside this woman's head and her world.

McQ sat at her desk trying to make sense of what was not apparent. Already over twelve hours downrange of the poet's murder—that's how she thought of this victim—she realized how much trouble she was in.

The Rhyme Killer? Good grief.

But it was getting very real. She had no suspects, a bunch of crazy clues she couldn't make sense of, and hadn't yet located where the actual murder took place. Or how the body even got dumped into the vic's *locked* apartment. *And* the almighty frickin' CSM offered her almost no practical help. Maybe another review of what the forensics team found.

She had been so confident, but now… not so much.

CHAPTER 26

H otel Literati
Apartment 7D
3:00PM

THEY MET IN HIS SUITE. BOTH STOOD NEAR HIS AMAZING
wall of windows, pretending to admire the hazy skyline. Smelled like
eau de bachelor's neglect. And dusty. That surprised McQ. Must have
missed all that last night. Mr. Greigh seemed so... fastidious, right
down to the creases in his ghetto-chic jeans.

Her nose started itching the moment she entered his apartment. In
the light of day, she realized it was a lot bigger and far more lavish
than 7F—the crime scene—but a similar layout. McQ said, "Listen,
Mr. Greigh—"

"Just Greigh is fine." He wasn't giving anything away, with that
classic face of chiseled granite.

"I owe you an apology for last night. I was exhausted, and way out
of line. Are we okay?"

"I don't care about that, Detective—"

"Chance McQuillan. McQ, is fine."

"Chance?" His demeanor cracked. He turned and looked her straight in the eye, just for a moment, before looking at his feet, as if he remembered something, but said nothing about it. Then the granite resurfaced.

She said with the tiniest of smirks, "My parents had a certain philosophy of life. They took it out on me."

"Alright…, McQ. Can you give me assurances that you'll produce results on this case, unlike my family's three years ago?"

And there it was.

"I deserve that. I can't imagine—"

"No, you can't. Now what is it you want?"

"I looked you up. Turns out you have some credentials. Like you said. I need your help."

"Not interested."

"You're still pissed at me for last night, isn't that it?"

"No, that's not it. I am very busy, and—"

"You're angry. I never caught your family's killer."

A stinging silence descended like a death shroud over the already quiet apartment. Greigh's brow furrowed. His dimpled chin made a few quick trips up and down under his clamped-tight lips. His anvil jaw's muscles and every visible tendon in his neck were getting one helluva workout, too. She watched his fists clench and unclench a few times before he turned away from her to face the windows and his wooded balcony.

Wooded? And covered? Sheesh.

But he said nothing, no doubt for fear of losing control. She experienced grief over her sister, but nothing like this.

After a full minute of them both standing there, both staring out at the city they both loved and loathed, McQ said, "I'm angry too. I lost a lot of sleep over that case. It's one that still haunts me to this day." She fell silent.

He seethed softly. "You lost sleep." Another pregnant pause. This was not going well.

I need a different tack here.

"Yeah, I know that sounds lame right now. So do you want your friend, Miss Mori, to feel the same shitty way about losing *her* friend? No closure? Fact is, Greigh, without your help, that could happen. I don't have what it takes by myself to solve the murder of your neighbor and Miss Mori's friend. They're about to pull me off this case unless I make some genuine progress, and I mean starting *right now*. So, are we gonna get past this, or what?"

The uneasy smoldering extended to a minute, then two minutes, before it broke. He turned around so suddenly, he startled her. Her hand moved toward her service piece on pure instinct.

He said, "Fine. But no paper trail. I will help you where I can, but not as a consultant, not as a registered confidential informant. Nothing. Can you commit to that, Detec... McQ?"

It's as if he'd turned the page to start a new chapter. Maybe a new book. Incredible. His brow beetled a little less as he resigned himself to his own brand of professionalism. She looked him in his now-soldier's eye and offered a silent, quizzical nod.

With a fresh tone of voice, he said, "Now, what did your fancy gadgets tell you about the scene?"

CHAPTER 27

The man was a machine. Greigh was a different person from thirty seconds earlier. Now, cool and competent, he walked over to his sofa and lowered himself with one fluid maneuver. He awaited McQ's briefing, like an expectant field commander at a headquarters location in a combat zone. Facing the fireplace, he crossed his slender legs and stared at the dark mantle—not at her—while he awaited her response.

She was eager to start, but she sauntered—not rushed—over. That seemed contrived and appropriate. She positioned herself on the U-shaped sectional sofa at right angles off to Greigh's right with the fireplace to her right. Flipped her comfortable loafers to the floor, crossed her blue-jeaned legs and bare feet under her, now conscious of her toenails. Most of her red Kabuki Queen nail polish was now badly chipped. Oh well. Not a priority.

Greigh shivered. He said to no one in particular, "Butler, a small fire, if you please." Electric flames emerged from ceramic logs. Looked real enough. McQ could almost feel their warmth. Or Greigh's demeanor was less chilling. Maybe both.

"Okay, well, the CSM wasn't much help. Only deepened the mystery. No DNA other than traces of yours, the victim's and Miss Mori's"

He said, "Most Japanese expect you to address them by their last name followed by *-san*, as in *Mori-san* for Sango Mori. But I suggest we just use first names—Sybil and Sango. We'll need to talk with Sango again—together—and best we keep it casual."

So the guy was getting down to business. Good.

Damn, he's a looker. Even looks good with that stubby ponytail and full beard.

She continued. "Now, here's where it gets more confusing. With your background—"

"My background?"

"Huh? Oh, like I said, I researched you before I came over here to eat crow. There's a lot I haven't learned about you. Don't worry. I won't ask. But I discovered you've worked a few homicides before, some international, at least in an unofficial capacity. Plus, like you said last night, you've crafted hundreds of scenarios in your books with stories that take place all over the world. Congrats on your success, by the way."

He still stared at the fire, eyes half-closed with his hands folded in front of him. Just deep-breathing, and with a slow rhythm—in through his nose, out through his mouth. Like he was meditating. Or concentrating. Or visualizing.

"Pays the bills. So what's confusing?"

Modest, too.

"Like I was saying, I'm sure you noticed that, ah, they did not murder Sybil in her apartment—"

Greigh interrupted, eager to show his observational skills. "Too little blood—no pooling or spatters consistent with her many aggressive wounds. No detached viscera, and less odor than I would expect from a post-mortem release of bladder and bowels."

"Uh, yeah. Very good. So how did the body get there?"

"No signs of an appliance to transport it, such as a cart?"

"Negative."

"Then the killer carried it, perhaps with the aid of an accomplice. Since Sybil weighed a mere hundred pounds, perhaps one-ten, whoever carried the body would have been strong, but required no extraordinary strength. It is likely that whoever carried the body was the killer—a male."

"What? Women aren't strong enough to carry a buck-ten?" She noted she was reverting to the previous evening's snarky style. She looked contrite.

"I said *likely* a male, McQ, based on statistical probabilities, but more so because of the brutal pattern of Sybil's wounds. I'm guessing the edge weapon used was dull, based on the wound patterns. It chipped the bone visible at her shoulders and on the front of her thighs. That sort of intense brutality is more likely to have come from a male of the species—statistically speaking."

"Oh. Right. Good analysis."

~

GREIGH STOPPED STARING AT THE FIRE. HE SWIVELED A cautious gaze toward this spunky detective. She was lovely.

Instant guilt swept over him. Her waves of dusky auburn hair and the way she kicked off her shoes to fold her legs underneath her reminded him....

After a brief silence, he said, "So, I repeat. Other than no unexplained DNA, what else has you so confused besides that the murder took place elsewhere, and they transported the body to the scene post-mortem?"

"Our gadget is quite good at creating a visual representation of footprints and their paths at the scene, even some decent three-dimensional rendering of movements. Our Crime Scene Mapping device, or CSM, can discern the shapes of footprints to determine what direction they were headed, but can't tell the sequence of steps."

"You can see *where* someone walked, but not *when*."

"Yeah. If you walked backward, for example, CSM wouldn't recognize that. Only that you walked in a particular pattern."

"Again, what's confusing?"'

McQ wrinkled her nose, as if it itched, but she didn't want to scratch it. That was obviously how she gathered a moment to catalog her thoughts before speaking.

Greigh observed other signs of a strong analytical mind. And she was not afraid to ask for help if she thought it would benefit her case, despite how difficult this ask must have been for her, given their history.

She had already begun speaking again. "The CSM tracked footprint patterns. Yours and Miss—yours and Sango's. You both stood for a time just inside the entry door, staring down at that weird drawing. Then, you stepped over it on your tip-toes and proceeded flat-footed to your left around the entryway wall and into the living room. You both stood together after discovering the body in front of the fireplace."

Since Sybil's floor plan was similar to his own, McQ used her index finger to point down and to her right—to the space in front of Greigh's fireplace.

"You stood behind Sango. I'm assuming you braced her against the horror of the gory scene. With your help, she sat on Sybil's small sofa, likely in shock at the sight of her friend's brutalized body. Still, she had the courage to seat herself mere feet from her friend's remains. That must have been terrible for her.

"You, however, kneeled near the body, Greigh, I assume to inspect the wounds. You traipsed through every room in the apartment. After you loitered near Sybil's desk, you returned to Sango. You then ushered her from the apartment. Both of you once again stepped over the entryway drawing on the floor. Does that sync?"

He raised his eyebrows in appreciation.

There is value to these gadgets, after all.

"Yes, very good. Except for the sequence. I knelt by the body *after* 'traipsing through every room' to ensure the killer or killers weren't still milling about. I'll ask one more time. What else is so confusing?"

He appreciated how she laid out evidence to demonstrate that this CSM apparatus offered some value, but still found it lacking.

She wasn't one-hundred percent dependent on her gadgets. Encouraging.

He grew more curious. There might be some excellent story material here. But first, they must find poor Sybil's killer, or killers.

SHE SKETCHED OUT THE TIMELINE. "KEEP IN MIND THAT the CSM only senses footprints up to six hours old. You reported discovering the body at 9:58PM. The initial uniforms arrived on scene at 10:50 to log the homicide—I know, not great response time.

"The CSM was forty minutes away at another scene—we only have the one prototype right now. But this is a high-priority case. They arrived in Sybil's apartment at midnight. Our six-hour footprint window would be from the time they started mapping at 12:15AM back to 6:15PM yesterday evening."

The vertical twin furrows between McQ's eyebrows deepened just above the bridge of her nose. "So here's the really confusing part. The *only* footprints at the scene during that entire window were yours and Sango's. *No others.*" She let this sink in.

THERE IT WAS. GREIGH THREW A *now I'm intrigued* expression onto his face. He cocked his head to his right and swiveled his gaze to hers full on. "You've convinced me of the device's footprint-tracking capability. I assume the CSM saw when the body appeared."

"Yup. Plus or minus ten minutes. The body 'flew' into the apartment through a window—on its own—between 7:55PM and 8:05PM."

"Which is well within your machine's effective window."

"Uh-huh. That's what's confusing the hell out of me. Plus, CSM senses heat differentials, as in body heat compared to the scene's ambient temperature. Nothing other than Sybil's, yours and Sango's.

"Also, I could use some serious help on this Creole and Voodoo stuff. Sounds like this ws an important part of Sybil Thibodaux's life.

For example, that intricate drawing on the floor—you know something about that. You mentioned it last night. But I wasn't ready to hear it, then. I am now."

Her coy smile seemed somehow so familiar. Even alluring.

Shite! That's what occurs to me right now?

CHAPTER 28

He muttered, almost to himself. Focusing on his sandals, as if they offered critical evidence, he said, "First, either your killer or killers are ghosts, or they've figured out how to defeat your machine. That implies at least some expertise in contemporary forensics, maybe in the capabilities of your CSM device itself.

"Second, Voodoo, Voudoo or Voudun, are all very similar practices and rituals depending on its country of origin. It is a complex topic. Voodoo is a little known and often misunderstood or misrepresented quasi-religion that focuses most on healing. But let's take small steps here.

"I've researched Voodoo. The drawing in Sybil's entryway is a vévé. Think of it as a location-specific spell cast by an expert in such matters. Skilled Voodoo practitioners are known as bokors or caplatas, also called witch doctors, shamans, sorcerers, or sorceresses in some cultures. A caplata is a female bokor. They may also call her a queen.

"You can hire a bokor or a caplata to cast a spell or charm for a variety of specific purposes. Sybil's vévé appears to have been cast— that is, drawn and conjured—by a bokor or a caplata. They say the more precise the vévé and its rituals, the more powerful its effect."

"I don't mean to be naïve, but so what?"

"It is possible Sybil is a caplata, which I doubt. Even though as a Creole of color from New Orleans, she would almost certainly be a devout practitioner, or at least knowledgeable of the Voodoo arts. But she's likely no expert conjurer. *More* likely, she hired a local, or imported someone. Either way, that might reveal a trail to follow."

McQ jumped on this line of thought. "And if she hired someone to create this for her, we might uncover unknown associates here in the city. But maybe more on point is her motive for having that... vévé in her apartment in the first place. I would imagine this, ah, bokor or... caplata would need to know the specifics of Sybil's fears—to cast their, ah, spell, right?"

McQ was *way* out of her comfort zone with this stuff, but it could be key to the case.

Greigh piggybacked on that. "Yes. Perhaps even the identity of someone from whom she required protection. And I'm guessing some bokors might be motivated beyond the bond of temporary trust between them and their clients, which means you might leverage their freedom for information."

"Okay, good. I also need to look at who knows our new CSM tech well enough to defeat it. What else do you think this vévé meant to Sybil?"

"Well, it symbolizes a powerful invocation of protection from a Voodoo loa, or deity, designed as a sanctuary against evil and fear. Sybil lived in fear to the extent that she felt the need for powerful protection.

"McQ, if Sybil was indeed a devout believer, as the physical evidence suggests, we now know she feared for her life, or at least for her well-being, *and* for some time.

"It takes time to locate and to employ a bokor, as does any relationship that is based on rather unique beliefs *and* deep trust.

"Then, it takes even more time to complete such an intricate vévé, including the ritual associated with its invocation if it is to be conjured for full effect.

"We should seek to identify the source of her fear, and that will get us closer to identifying her killer or killers."

Greigh continued, "After discovering the body last evening, I snapped a photo of that drawing, McQ. This morning, I verified that this vévé—a sacred symbol—was indeed an invocation of protection from the Voodoo god known as Maman Brigitte." He pronounced it, ma-MON Bree-ZHEET. "This god—or loa—is an *aggressive* protector of women *and* considered to be the epitome of punitive justice."

THIS GUY KNEW HIS STUFF. PLUS, WITH EVERY DETAIL Greigh referenced, he backed it up with either logical observation or research. This was pure gold.

She slid a little closer to him as her interest intensified, leaning into his hypnotic voice, and now peering deep into his ice-blue eyes. Just a little frightening.

She prompted him, "Punitive justice?"

"Yes. We might surmise that Sybil not only feared for her life, but feared someone with whom she had personal pork, as they say."

"You mean, a *personal beef?*"

"She sought revenge, or at least, justice. I can relate."

She let this cut slide. "Greigh, I *am* impressed. What else?"

"If Sybil's killer or killers were also Voodoo acolytes, they would not have crossed her threshold. And let's not forget her door and windows were all locked—from the inside. I see three possibilities.

"FIRST, THEY KNEW LOCKS. THE CRIMINALS POSSESSED lock-picking skills equal to or better than mine. I consider this unlikely. My skills are considerable, and that old but formidable lock was a challenge, even for me.

"Second, in the unlikely event they gained access to the scene via the front door, the killer or killers were not Voodoo practitioners. They took no notice of the vévé drawn on the floor. But it appeared no one had tread on that drawing, no doubt crafted with delicate lines of powdered eggshell. That is customary and is easily disturbed.

"Besides, hauling *any* corpse does not make for light and careful steps, much less over a two-foot-square drawing right at the scene's threshold. Yet, Sybil took great care to sidestep it each time she came and went prior to her demise.

"Or third, and the most likely possibility, the killer or killers gained entrance to Sybil's apartment by some other means. This would imply they either were not Voodoo practitioners, or they were, but remained oblivious to the protection at what should have been the apartment's only manner of ingress or egress."

"Nice."

She now felt like a rookie gum-shoe next to this formidable sleuth. Quite the mind on this one, and he had a pant-load more experience than her brief background check of him had revealed.

But for now, she just wondered about the whole package....

CHAPTER 29

Who is this guy?

Greigh said, "McQ, I suggest we ensure we're in sync with our complete chronology of events, even though we don't yet possess enough information to establish a murder window.

"If we assume Sybil was murdered within a few hours prior to her arrival in 7F, we know she was killed yesterday, and probably early evening. Beyond that assumption—"

"Nope. You're wrong." Why did she shiver with the tiniest thrill from correcting him?

Check the hot rocks, McQuillan.

"We *do* know when she was killed. Our medical examiner, not the CSM, placed the estimated TOD at 6:00PM yesterday, plus or minus ten minutes."

"Okay, excellent. Since the body dropped into 7F circa 8:00, it had been there for less than two hours before Sango and I discovered it at 9:48. Initial law enforcement was on scene an hour later."

A cynical slant-glance from Greigh did not surprise her, but she could only offer him a single-shoulder shrug of inevitability.

She said, "Yeah, I know. With almost thirty homicides daily in the city now, and twenty percent of those in our precinct alone, we gotta suck up half a dozen new murder investigations each day. And for every day that a case goes unsolved, which are the majority, they stack up—fast.

"Worse, a hundred uniforms from the nine-nine cover hundreds of other crimes daily besides homicides. And that doesn't include the crank crap."

She didn't see any empathy appearing on his face. "Yeah, that sounds like a bunch of lame excuses. We're all just exhausted, all the time. I arrived on scene last night at 11:05. The forensics team started their scans after midnight and completed their work an hour later, at 1:15AM—this morning."

GREIGH RECORDED IT ALL. HE CONVERTED IT TO TEXT VIA his wristPad, favoring prose over fancy visuals. He rewarded McQ with an appreciative glance.

"Very thorough, Detective. Can your forensic team tell us how many blows were evident on the body?"

"They all sorta ran together. Said somewhere in the neighborhood of forty deep wounds. Most criss-crossed the front of the body, not the back. Appeared to be reckless, hap-hazard, and vicious."

"Ligature marks?"

"Her hands and feet had been bound with old-fashioned stranded three-lay hemp rope based on trace. They stopped manufacturing that stuff almost a century ago."

That drew Greigh into a thoughtful moment of silence. "Intriguing. So, the killer restrained Sybil. Wanted, perhaps *needed* to look her in the eye as he killed her. Very personal. Messy. Forty heavy blows took time, made noise, and required privacy, not to mention a large weapon and restraints—away from prying eyes and ears. Any signs of torture with a focus on inducing pain more than death?"

"Nothing conclusive. No blows that steered clear of vital organs, fingernail extractions, electrocution, discrete amputations or broken appendages other than those incidental to the killing blows."

"So extracting information likely wasn't a priority. This seems both like a crime of passion *and* a well-executed assassination meant to send a message. Two modus operandi, ,maybe two killers, or at least accomplices? Any indication that the body was transported to your scene from elsewhere outside The Lit? Traffic surveillance or witnesses? Video or otherwise?"

Another brief pause before McQ responded. "Nope."

"Then I suggest we search for our murder site within the hotel. We'd best loop in the building's owners, Vince and Luca Donati. They're in the penthouse. I can make introductions, if you like."

"That'd be great. Uniforms canvassed this floor and adjacent floors, but turned up squat so far. Seems nobody's talking, even if they saw or heard something."

"Artistic types are likely reticent to get involved. What about the gris-gris around Sybil's neck?"

"The what? Oh, that little pouch? We couldn't make any sense out of it. I assume that's another Voodoo thing, right?"

"Yes. A gris-gris," he pronounced it *GREE-gree,* "is a small cloth bag filled with herbs, oils, stones, small bones, and possibly hair. Plus, it might contain other personal items gathered under the direction of a particular god through the guidance of a bokor or caplata.

"A gris-gris protects its owner—the person for whom it was conjured. It is crafted at an altar, which could be makeshift, but consecrated in a ritual with the four elements of earth, air, water and fire—with salt, incense, water, and a candle's flame.

"They always use one, three, five, seven, nine or thirteen ingredients. Never an even number, and never over thirteen items. They select stones and colored objects for their occult and astrological properties, depending on the purpose of the gris-gris.

"This is a clear signal that Sybil was a devoted Voodoo practitioner who felt she needed protection from someone—or some... thing. Can we get an inventory of its contents and any imaging your team collected?"

"Of course. I'll send it to you. How might that be revealing?"

"You'll want a DNA scan of each item in that bag. Not only might its contents reveal its conjurer's 'signature,' there could be DNA of the person Sybil feared. The pouch itself might conceal foreign DNA inside from your gadget—don't ask me how. Ask your lab to examine it the old-fashioned way: in a lab."

"Well, it *was* drenched in Sybil's blood, and damaged in the savage attack, so it's taking some time to sort that out, but I'll ensure we get a complete workup."

"Was there any text in the gris-gris?"

"As a matter of fact—"

"I'd like to examine that too. I'm not hopeful there, but one never knows."

McQ soaked in his every word. She captured it all on her wristPad as Greigh spoke so she would forget nothing and could analyze all of this later. She also fired off several notes to her forensic team. She wondered why Greigh had not mentioned the obvious photograph she found under the desk where he had loitered after finding the body and searching the apartment.

"Greigh, what did you find under Sybil's desk?"

He looked at her and smiled. "Your device already informed you I spotted an ancient torn-up picture. A group of black laborers, possibly slaves, appeared to be working in a sugar cane field. They posed for that photo."

"Any guesses why she would keep such a picture?"

"Wild speculation only. You will want to investigate Sybil's birth name."

"Huh? What does *that* have to do with the photo? You don't think Thibodaux is her given name?"

"I do not. An infamous massacre of almost a hundred black Creoles took place back in the late nineteenth century. They named the tragedy after the Louisiana parish where it took place. Care to guess how history remembered it?"

"The Thibodaux Massacre?"

"Indeed. Wasn't Sybil an activist who highlighted her heritage, including injustices levied against her people? Consistent with her penchant for 'punitive justice,' perhaps? Although Thibodaux is a common name."

Her warm smile wasn't a reaction to the tragedy Greigh described. Rather, she smiled at his pronunciation of the word, "penchant"—a very nasal "paw-shaw." Educated mooks. Then she tuned back in before she missed anything. This guy!

"I'm guessing that unfortunate historical event became at least one of her cultural touchstones. Might even have taken the name as homage to those who died fighting injustice. As I recall, that was a racially motivated revolt against cruel labor practices during the post-slavery reconstruction period after your Civil War. That revolt ended in tragedy.

"I'd be curious what her given name was, even though it could be tangential to the case. Thibodaux *is* a rather common Quebecois name. Aren't you curious, Detective Chance McQuillan? Did she just pick a meaningful pen name, or was she hiding her true identity for some other reason?"

"Indeed I am curious, Sir Aubrey Greigh." She sniggered. McQ would relegate the partial newspaper clipping and scrapbook remnants to a later discussion. She had to admit that Greigh was already a tremendous asset to her investigation. She learned more about *her* case in the last hour than the previous twelve she had already spent mulling it over on her own.

But would she satisfy her captain with what they had learned in the last forty-eight hours?

And why on earth did Greigh want to keep his involvement so secret?

She worried about her other cases piling up.

CHAPTER 30

Monday, June 25th
Chicago, Illinois
1:00PM

This is gonna suck.

Detective Chance McQuillan, a.k.a. McQ, spent some time with CED's PR department. Not of her own free will. Captain Granger gave her no choice.

The rank and file called Police Plaza—CED headquarters—"PP," usually with a cynical smirk, sometimes a snide remark, like, "I'm from PP, and I'm here to help."

The PP prig now sitting across from her at least had the courtesy of coming uptown to the nine-nine. This woman-child got up and paced around the captain's conference room as if her hair was on fire. Her name was Macy. No, Mazy.

With wild arms, Mazy's speech tempo reminded McQ of a small-caliber automatic weapon with a rapid fire rate on full auto. Or a hundred-pound body saturated with rocket fuel—the favored precinct house mud. Caffeine incarnate.

"Now, Detective, in cases like these, the public wants to hear of everything we know. That cannot happen."

"Right. Because we don't discuss the details of any open investigation, high profile like this one or not. It might jeopardize the investigation, or worse, the public's safety." Right out of the manual.

Mazy kept pacing. "Yes, while you are correct, that's not what reporters and the public will swallow. They'll want more. They always want more. So we need to provide you with specific talking points you *can* share without violating the integrity of your investigation. Make sense?"

"I guess."

Mazy started ticking off points on her stick-fingers. "And they will push the human interest angle. Who was the victim? We share that. What was the nature of the attack? Here, we must be very careful. We share no details. Do we have any suspects, or anyone in custody? If not, 'we are pursuing every lead.' And nothing more. Okay?"

"Yeah, whatever."

Mazy stopped pacing right next to the slouching and thumb-twiddling McQ. She glared down at her with her tiny hands on her tiny little-girl hips. The tempo of Mazy's speech slowed as if she just realized she was speaking to an intellectually challenged child.

"Detective, you might not think this is important, but I'm trying to keep the fucking brass off your ass. You feel me? Now, how about you lose the smart-ass attitude, and we do our jobs here? Fair enough?"

McQ's eyes widened. She jerked her head up and looked at Mazy like she was seeing her for the first time. Another woman in a male-dominated profession trying to do her job the best she was able. She could appreciate that.

"Yeah, alright, Macy—"

"Mazy."

"Right. Sorry. S'just that I got cases piling up as we speak, and I know I'm not gonna get any sleep for another forty-eight. Guess I'm a little cranky. Tell me what I should say, okay?"

Mazy's posture softened as she settled into the chair angled toward McQ's left shoulder and leaned her elbows on the table. Now medium tempo staccato. "Okay. Look, I'll take as little of your time as possible, Detective—"

"Just McQ."

Mazy's voice softened further, both in volume and tenor. It was obvious she had her own monsters to slay. Back to full operational tempo speech....

"Okay, McQ. Here's how we get you through this. I've constructed some talking points for you after reviewing the case file. Tell me if I got anything wrong. You'll be standing on the steps of Police Plaza down on Michigan Ave with a few dozen cameras and microphones stuffed in your face. You stick to the script, and you'll be fine. Read a statement and take no questions. Alright?"

"Sure. And I truly am sorry about the attitude, Mazy. Let's get this done."

McQ WAS A MANNEQUIN. AT LEAST, SHE FELT LIKE SHE WAS on display in a department store window. She wore the same full-dress bullet-blue uniform—her only one—she always wore to fellow officers' funerals. Not good memories, and too many of them.

Her impressive collection of medals and commendations embarrassed her, because all this just seemed... pretentious. And she had to wear this damn wool monkey suit all too often.

But Mazy had told her what to wear and convinced her this was essential police work, even though it may be above her current pay grade. And somewhat ceremonial.

Mazy's department had blasted out the notification for this media conference to all the local, regional and national feeds. McQ peeked through the ten-foot-tall bulletproof-glass doors of Police Plaza.

PP faced South Michigan Avenue. She saw what seemed like hundreds of reporters, cameramen, and a mob of curious citizens bottlenecked between barricades at the bottom of the stone steps.

She squeezed her uniform cap under her arm a little too hard.

Didn't want to drop it. Not here. Not now. She'd ensured it would fit over her long hair tied in a tight bun low on the back of her neck. No guarantee the wind wouldn't whip it off.

Funny what I'm worrying about. This is worse than entering an active crime scene with bullets flying! Oh, and no weapon? Jeez-Louise.

With the fingers of both hands interlaced in front of her down low, she drummed the print of one thumb against the other like she was tapping out a desperate SOS in Morse code.

Just another part of the job, McQ. You can do this.

The appointed time arrived. The well-orchestrated script she had memorized was to be followed 'to the letter,' per PR whiz kid Mazy. McQ knew she was *way* out of her league here, but if she wanted to be captain some day, this was damn good training.

Remember, you asked for this case, smart-ass!

She jammed her hat onto her head, per academy standards—the hat's bill three fingers above the bridge of her nose—lower than that, you looked smug, more than that, a dufus, or worse, like you didn't give a shit.

Two of the police commissioner's security detail swung open and held the heavy doors for her, the commissioner, her captain, Mazy, and the rest of the dog and pony show.

They all marched the fifty feet out to the microphone-infested podium at the top of the wide steps—a tiny island in a deceptively calm sea of granite and marble, gargoyles and flags snapping in the brisk breeze.

At least the breeze knocked down the humidity some. She still felt drizzles of cold sweat running down her spine beneath her blouse. She took some comfort that her wool uniform jacket would hide all the evidence of nervous perspiration. Well, most of it.

A small contingent of uniformed officers allowed no one from the throng onto the steps. The closest reporter or camera operator was about thirty feet away and fifteen feet below them. They said that was for security, but also for power posturing, McQ guessed.

Commissioner Roberts—a tall, movie-star-handsome man of fifty-five—stepped up to the podium. Captain Granger and *her* boss—the chief of detectives (the rank and file called him 'the C of Ds')—McQ, and three of the commissioner's security detail remained lined up behind him. Mazy hovered behind this row of dignitaries and muscle, along with her own boss.

The commissioner tapped the microphone and received two satisfying thumps fed back through the PA system via two speakers on portable towers thirty feet off to either side of the podium. The thumps' echoes jolted McQ back into the moment. They announced to the audience the mannequin parade was about to begin.

This was happening. McQ tugged at her already sweaty collar.

"Ladies and gentlemen of the press, citizens of Chicago, thank you for being here. Last week, our fair city and the world lost a national treasure with the heinous murder of Ms. Sybil Thibodaux. Rest assured the full might of the Chicago Enforcement Department is engaged to catch the guilty party or parties. I have asked the lead detective on this case, Detective Lieutenant Chance McQuillan, to deliver a prepared statement—the status of the team's investigation to date. Detective?"

Six mannequin steps forward, McQ shook hands with Commissioner Roberts just behind the pathetic protection of the podium, as choreographed. He stood a full foot taller. She felt small. He crushed her hand with both of his, held her gaze, and delivered a confident smile reinforced by a firm nod of affirmation.

Optics.

The podium dwarfed McQ. She jerked down on the microphone's flex-neck and laid her notes in front of her—almost at shoulder level—in case she forgot what she'd memorized. She cleared her throat. Heard it echo down the canyons between the tall buildings on both sides of Michigan Avenue over the low din of oblivious traffic.

"Thank you, Commissioner Roberts. The victim, Ms. Sybil Thibodaux, age twenty-nine, from New Orleans, Louisiana, was an extended-stay resident of the Hotel Literati at the time of her tragic demise. Neighbors discovered her body in her apartment at ten PM last Thursday. We are pursuing several strong leads, but have no suspects in custody as yet. We cannot discuss the details of any ongoing investigation, and this one is no exception. I will say that as my team and I dig into Ms. Thibodaux's life, we know she will be missed. Thank you."

PANDEMONIUM REIGNED. McQ RELEASED HER SWEATY TWO-handed grip on the podium's torso and turned to re-join Mannequin Row. She left her script behind.

One reporter's voice resonated above all the others as he *screamed,* "What about the thousands of other homicide victims who are not VIPs? Why don't *they* get this kind of special attention from the CED?"

No doubt this came from some obscure reporter representing some fringe media outlet. McQ's blood smoldered. She looked over her shoulder at the person who shouted those questions and made eye contact. The man's voice had quivered with emotion. He was no reporter, just an ordinary little man. Maybe a relative or friend of another victim. Her blood cooled.

The script said McQ was to return to her place in line so the commissioner could deliver one final assurance that this case was a priority. And that, as they say, would be that.

Instead of following the rehearsed choreography, McQ returned to the podium after a stutter step of uncertainty. She looked at the slender Hispanic man who had delivered that impassioned plea.

"Sir, those are excellent questions. I can't speak for anyone but myself, and I *promise* you that every victim deserves the same attention. We just don't hold a press conference for all of them. I'm currently working six other homicides besides this one. I haven't slept in over thirty hours. And that's just another day in the life of *this* CED detective.

She paused to swallow, but her parched mouth refused. "You can be confident that every single victim of a crime gains our full attention, but not all get a press conference. Why? Because *this,*" she swept her arms down and around at the spectacle of which she was now a part, "takes time. It robs precious minutes away from seeking hard justice for *all* the cases I'm working on." Her voice shook with her own passion... and exhaustion. "Thank you, sir."

She meant it.

And it showed.

It was weird. The crowd fell dead silent. Then, as McQ performed a slow-motion about-face with her shoulders now stooped from exhaustion and stress—very un-mannequin-like—the man who had screamed those questions began nodding and clapping in a slow cadence that grew to a crescendo as others joined in.

And in that instant, a celebrity cop was born.

McQ WALKED BACK TO THE LINE. WITH HER HEAD STILL down, she slantwise caught the commissioner's eye and wasn't sure if he was pissed or delighted. She had broken from the ranks. Mazy stood back there. McQ thought she might break into tears. Fear or joy? Couldn't tell.

No, she'd done it now. Chance McQuillan, outlaw mannequin. Sure to be shunned.

The commissioner regained control of the podium to make a brief closing statement, but the throng now bombarded him with questions.

"Why aren't you giving that poor detective and all of your officers more help?"

"How is it that your case closure rate continues to get worse instead of better?"

"Why shouldn't the citizens of Chicago fear for their lives with thousands of murders in the city that you never solve?"

Of course, he handled every question with aplomb, but McQ knew she had set up the most important man in the CED for this shitstorm.

She couldn't wait for the beat-down sure to follow. She'd be lucky to keep her frickin' job.

What the hell is the matter with me? Why couldn't I have just stuck to the damn script?

In the meantime, she had a job to do… after she escaped from this mannequin suit.

CHAPTER 31

H otel Literati
      Chicago, Illinois
6:00PM

~

THEY DIDN'T COME TO SCHMOOZE. GREIGH AND McQ TOOK the public birdcage elevator from his suite to the fourth floor. There, they transferred to a smaller, more ornate private elevator just west of the birdcage. This elevator carried them to the building owners' penthouse on sixteen.

When Greigh sent word they would come, Vince Donati could not have been more forthcoming. "This entire affair," he said, "is giving us nothing but agida and acido—aggravation and heartburn."

The elevator opened into the Donati brothers' expansive foyer. Their apartments—two rambling suites, comprised the entire sixteenth floor of The Lit. Sixteen was smaller than the floors below, up in the peak of the hotel's tower. Each of their two apartments still sprawled more than any other individual suite in the hotel.

McQ's eyes popped when she noticed the furnishings in golds and

131

crimsons. She didn't appreciate squat about period furnishings other than plain, fancy, and obscene. This stuff was over the top. She chortled inside at her own pun.

The elevator door was still opening. Vincenzo, a.k.a. Vince Donati charged forward, and stuck his hand into the still-opening door as it slid from their left to right.

"Aubrey, so good to see you. It *has* been a while, hasn't it?"

"Hello, Vince. Thanks for seeing us."

"No, thank *you* for helping the police sort out this sordid affair. You might guess countless residents are up in arms."

Vince glanced with ill-disguised discomfort at the obvious cop in her comfortable loafers and her practical off-the-shelf attire, who accompanied one of his more prominent owners.

Greigh gushed, "Where are my manners? Vince, meet Detective Lieutenant Chance McQuillan of the CED's ninety-ninth precinct, the lead detective on the Thibodaux case."

"Chance?"

Greigh injected, "Don't ask. McQ, this is Vince. He and his brother own and manage this fine old pile that I and so many others call home."

"McQ?"

She said, "It's short and to the point, sir. Like me. Thank you for seeing us. Is it possible to ask you and your brother a few questions?"

"Absolutely. Luca is putting the finishing touches on a soufflé. They fall at the drop of a pin, you realize. Of course, you will stay for dinner."

Not a question.

GREIGH SENSED HACKLES BRISTLING. HE PRE-EMPTED HIS favorite new pain-in-the-ass detective on what was sure to emerge— an inflammatory remark.

"Vince, that is a generous offer. Luca's soufflé is legendary; however, you can imagine the time sensitivity of this case."

"Yes, yes, what were we thinking. McQ, you do know the camera simply adores you. Your performance at this afternoon's media conference? Epic. I imagine the commissioner wants to pin a medal on your... chest." His eyes wandered down for only a moment, but it was long enough. "You're one helluva fundraiser for the CED. Brava." His expansive arm movements were so... Italian.

Nonplussed, she said, "Yeah, that spiel sorta slipped out. I'm in deep guilty right now with my boss. But to the case, sir—"

"Call me Vince, *please!*" He sounded like he was pleading. He held his hands in front of him as if praying. For what, Greigh could guess.

She ignored the theatrics, bordering on impatience. "Okay, Vince. We need immediate access to all security feeds within and around the hotel."

"Yes, yes, I'll call Max, our security guy. I'll get you two together and he'll hand all of that over. But I must admit that since this is the first problem we've *ever* had, we have not placed a priority on security to date. I'm afraid much of it is absent, inoperable, or outdated."

"Thanks. Next, do you have blueprints for the building?"

As she spoke, a slight but portly gentleman in a... velvet smoking jacket entered the room with what seemed like a theatrical flourish. Even before Vince introduced his brother, Luca said, "I don't understand. Why would the building's blueprints be of interest?"

Greigh spotted McQ about to roll her eyes as she glanced over at him. Her eyes said, *A velvet smoking jacket? Seriously?*

It was as if he were able to read her mind. She was *so* obvious.

Vince interrupted as he misinterpreted her expression.

"Detective, my brother must have left his manners in the kitchen with his soufflé. Luca, you know Aubrey, of course. And this is Detective McQuillan of the CED."

LUCA SEEMED CONTRITE, BUT HIS RUDE INTERRUPTION question seemed disingenuous. This guy was a piss-poor shapeshifter. But McQ gave away nothing. "A pleasure, Luca. We just need to understand the killer's possible entry or exit points, escape routes, that sort of thing."

"I see." But they saw Luca didn't.

Vince said, "We'll ensure our facilities manager, Rhonda, makes whatever building documentation we have available to you, McQ."

Luca said, "McQ?"

In unison, Greigh and Vince said, "Don't ask." They all laughed. All except Luca, and McQ who kept a stink eye on Luca.

She addressed her next question to Vince, since he seemed the much more cooperative brother.

"Vince, how many elevators?"

"How many? Well, we have the public elevator—"

Greigh said to McQ, "That's the one we call the birdcage."

Vince continued. "Birdcage? Ah, yes. Clever. Now, you already know about our private elevator between four and sixteen—you just rode that one up. We make that available if there is an emergency evacuation, or some such. And there is the large service or freight elevator between the basement storage areas and all sixteen floors— except for two and three, of course. Only employees have access to the freight elevator. Or owners, with permission, for moving furniture and such. It is an old building, but we prioritize maintenance of the elevators."

"So there are no other elevators between floors?"

"No."

Vince worried. Two hours later, he and Luca lounged alone in the expansive living room they shared between their two apartments, almost as if they had their own lobby. Luca lit a fire.

They sat on a huge sofa facing their fireplace's electric flames, a prominent feature in their sunken living room. They shared a bottle of superb red wine from their favorite family-owned vineyard in Sicily.

Vince had selected it from their extensive private cellar, a chilled room next to their living room. He always ensured the temperature in that room hovered between 55° and 59°F, with the humidity always between 50% and 80% to keep the corks from cracking. Some were quite old. And valuable.

Luca poured two generous servings into exquisite gold-rimmed crystalline glasses with dangerously long stems.

Vince said, "Greigh's friend seems nice, doesn't she?"

"Vince, she is *not* Greigh's friend. She's a *cop*. Seemed awfully nosy."

"Luca, that's her job, for crying out loud."

"Well, I don't like strangers snooping around, cops or not. We have a wonderful thing going here."

Luca's agitation was sudden and dramatic. This surprised Vince.

"Luca, settle down. After all, someone was murdered right here in our own house. This is not at all good for business. We have twelve units up for sale, and if this whole sordid affair drives prices down, well, we're already on a razor's edge. We need every penny of revenue from the sale of those units and their monthly HOA assessments just to maintain operating expenses. And we can't afford anyone moving out because of this."

"Vince, the sooner we get this thing resolved and behind us, the sooner we can get on with taking care of The Lit."

"Who are you kidding? We've been struggling to stay in the black ever since we bought the place."

"Yes, but—"

"But nothing. Look, we realized our vision for this place. We knew we would never become wealthy with such a niche property. And that's okay. But don't you want more than a perpetual struggle?"

"This is our dream, Vince! We are *living* our dream! It still is *our* dream, isn't it?"

"Yes, of course you're right. It just gets hard sometimes. All this... *noise.*"

As they sat next to each other, Luca reached over and squeezed Vince's shoulder. "It's going to be fine, brother. *We* are fine."

CHAPTER 32

M onday, June 25th
      CED Ninety-ninth Precinct
Chicago, Illinois
10:00PM

McQ SLUMPED AT HER DESK. THE CACOPHONY OF
conversations in the nine-nine squad room, smart-ass remarks, and an
occasional cackle at some stupid joke, or the retelling of a heroic story
about the previous night's happy hour misadventure—none of that
bothered her.

In fact, it rather soothed her nerves. The familiar environment and
expected buzz of meaningless chatter meant she was where she was
supposed to be. She wasn't here much, but when she was, this was
thought-clarifying meditation for her. Even as fatigue dogged her.

While the men in her squad gave her a hard time, she knew they
also respected her. Maybe even feared her a little. Good.

Her comm implant buzzed. Its HUD—her heads-up display which

was visible only to her thanks to something called narrow-beam refraction—read *Sgt. A. McKenzie. #135622.* Her favorite beat cop and chauffeur. Mr. Egg Salad Sandwich. Badge number 135622.

"Hey Mac, staying on his tail? Or did he make your cruiser 'n lose you?"

"C'mon, LT. Give me some credit. Odd, though. Right now, Luca Donati is cozied up to none other than Gaspari Copolla at his fancy social club over on the corner of South Wabash and East Van Buren. I can see them walking the grounds through the fence, arm-in-arm, like a couple of long-lost buddies. The whole place is lit up like a sunny noon fifty years ago."

McQ recognized the name in an instant. Copolla was the most infamous old-time crime boss in Chicago. Don Gaspari himself allegedly had gone "legit" in recent years, and had transformed himself into one of the most prominent businessmen in the city.

"Any idea what that's all about?"

"Nah. What put you onto this guy, Donati, anyway?"

"Dunno. Something just didn't smell right when I met him earlier tonight. I watched his face twitch when I asked him about The Lit's blueprints. He's not a fan of female cops either, or likely any cop. Not sure. But what would a respectable hotel magnate be doing with the likes of old Don G?"

"How long you want me to stick with this guy? My shift is up in a couple, and I still got an actual job."

"Take off, Mac. Since you said you wanted to be a dick some day, I got the sense you'd appreciate a little OJT. Thanks."

"Hey, due respect, LT, you got this big deal case. Why not just get one of your own swingin' dicks to help you out?"

"*You're* the one who gave me a ride, let me nap in your cruiser and tossed me an egg salad sandwich the other night, brother. And spur-of-the-moment action like this? Dicks aren't too comfy with that. Didn't have time for a pant-load of questions and justification and beggin' for a piece of the action. They all come with baggage. Besides, all these guys here wanna do is look at my ass."

"And you think I don't?" She could hear him smirk over the comms.

"Shut up, Mac. Have a good evening."

"You too, LT. And thanks."

CHAPTER 33

T uesday, June 26th
     Apartment 7D
Hotel Literati
8:00AM

Doesn't the man ever sleep?

McQ and Greigh had already been at it for hours. She had knocked on his door at 5:00AM. Already dressed, he looked like he'd been up for hours when she got there. His door had clicked open when she approached it.

After she entered, he waved her in without so much as a word, as if they'd never stopped working the case, like she'd just stepped out of the room to pee, or something. All business.

A blunt-steel morning cast an ominous mood over them through Greigh's wall of windows. Captain Granger called to ask McQ an endless stream of questions about the information she had uploaded to the *Rhyme Killer* case file in the CED cloud.

McQ had yet to tell anyone, other than Greigh, about Luca

Donati's visit last night to the number-one mobster in the city, Don G himself. They treated that tidbit with kid gloves for the time being. Neither could explain why, but they had agreed.

She ran her fingers through her mostly untangled hair to get it out of her face. Again. McQ knew she wasn't doing her other cases justice, but she made progress. This case was to be her priority. So be it.

The label that the press stuck on this case—the *Rhyme Killer Case*—was not only cheesy, but didn't seem all that appropriate. Greigh enlightened her about something called *free verse*, for which Sybil was most well-known. Guess what? Free verse poems don't even rhyme most of the time.

Plus, she didn't think of the vic—Sybil—as a poet. She was just a corpse.

God, am I that callous?

HER BOSS EYED EVIDENCE HER PROGRESS. LIKE PREY stalking quarry. She said McQ impressed her with the rapid progress she "finally" demonstrated, but continued to insist that rapid closure was essential. Freakin' optics. McQ would keep pressing Greigh. She hated to admit it. The man was twenty-four-carat gold.

Now, he was in his kitchen whipping up an early brunch for them, for crissake.

Brunch at 8AM?

Some sort of manufactured cavern-grown plant-based protein concoction fried with real onions, mushrooms and fresh herbs. She tried to curb her culinary enthusiasm—yeah, right. Although she admitted—to herself—it smelled wonderful. The man knew his spices.

He brought two plates to the table as she reviewed notes projected in front of her above the table. After making a few verbal edits to what she saw, she dated and time-stamped the case file updates with another verbal notation, highlighting the murder window.

This timeline would be critical once they began interviewing suspects and digging for alibis. Then, she uploaded this updated file to the CED cloud. Captain Granger would be hovering over her own device, waiting on that update with bated breath. Guaranteed.

GREIGH LOOKED AT HER. IT WAS ODD. SHE FOUND IT impossible to identify his expression, as if he were remembering something, and she was the key to unlocking that memory.

Then, as if changing the topic, he said, "So old Gaspari and Luca. Most interesting, whether or not that has anything to do with our case."

Our case. He's invested in this thing, now. Ulterior motive? Nah.

He still held the two plates of food expecting her to take one.

McQ said, "Greigh, I'm not starving. How about we go back to 7F? We gotta figure out how the body got into that apartment."

"Agreed. Now that your team is done with the scene, I'd like to rummage through some of Sybil's papers. We might find something relevant to her state of mind, or her actions leading up to her death. But you must eat something. I need you sharp."

She wasn't sure why, but that punched her instant-pissed-off button. "*You* need *me* sharp? Who do you think you—" but then she reeled in her emotions. Again. Son-of-a-bitch. He was right. She *was* cranky—low blood sugar and a chronic lack of sleep. At least she could do something about the former.

"Sorry. You're right. I guess I haven't eaten since yesterday some time." She accepted the plate of food he held out to her. He still held his own plate in his right hand.

"Thanks." And she meant it.

"It's alright. I'm still rather tense myself. May I suggest you dig into financials for The Lit, and for Luca and Vince Donati? Individually and collectively?"

"Uh, sure. Although we're kinda straying far afield, here. But why not? No stone unturned."

. . .

Fifteen minutes later, after they both had slammed down a few bites of breakfast, they had walked down the hall and stood surveying Sybil's living room, still in disarray.

Greigh paced the perimeter of each room with deliberation. He rummaged through debris, and banged the heels of his rubber-soled shoes on the floor around the edges of each room. He tapped on the walls with a favorite knuckle. Twenty frustrating minutes later, he said, "Why don't you inspect the windows again? I have another idea."

McQ wasn't sure how she felt about taking orders from this *civilian,* but she had to admit that Greigh might just be a better detective than her. She'd already learned some solid moves from this guy. Not that she would ever admit to that—to anyone, especially, not to him.

"Okay, but you said the windows were locked."

"I suggest you seek signs of tampering, marks left by climbing gear. Look for anything that could have been used to gain access there, as unlikely as that might be. We must eliminate all possibilities, mustn't we?"

Climbing gear? To transport a body? But he was right. Eliminate the impossible, the improbable, and what remains....

She was about to remind him that her forensics team was very good, but she bit her lip in silence. Headed for the windows.

Unlike his apartment, no balcony outside. Just seven stories of polluted air between her and Harrison Street. The only opening windows *might* be passable by a small person. Greigh was right— unlikely, even improbable, not impossible. Nevertheless....

Already headed for the door, he said over his shoulder, "Nothing obvious here. Look, McQ, I'll need some think time to pursue a theory, but I'll need your help first."

He stopped and wheeled back around to face her head-on.

Oh-oh.

"What kind of help?" She looked concerned, but with all the visibility this case was getting, she relaxed when he explained. They'd get what he asked for.

He needed access to the online city archives that were under tight control after multiple terrorist attacks sensitized and classified them.

McQ made a call. After several hurdles cleared with an assist from Captain Granger's contacts, Greigh received the access he requested.

LATER, MCQ PROCRASTINATED. SHE REALLY DIDN'T HAVE time to check in at the nine-nine. But Captain Granger would need some hand-holding about now to settle her down, especially after their escalation request for broad municipal archival access by a *civilian*. That had raised more than a few eyebrows.

This high-profile case was killing the captain. She was used to plenty of pressure, but not from a non-stop media barrage *and* political artillery fire.

Neither am I, and misery does love company.

MCQ ATTENDED TO HER OWN BUSINESS. GREIGH KNEW SHE had trundled off to her precinct house by way of her apartment for a quick shower—something about a command performance. He could tell this meeting worried her.

She confided in him she kept a small studio above a cop bar called Harrow's down the street from the nine-nine. This was some sort of secret for some sort of reason.

GREIGH RETURNED TO HIS OWN APARTMENT. HIS GUT burned with conviction. He was *certain* he was on the right track. But as Will Rogers once said, ""Even when you're on the right track, you'll get run over if you just sit there."

The Literati was an ancient building with a great deal of history, some of it infamous. They had remodeled various parts of it countless times. Greigh remodeled his own apartment before moving in ten years earlier, along with less significant updates since then.

What if an old duct or passageway exists behind some newer wall covering?

Pursuing that idea, he settled in at his desk. He addressed his queries to the omnipresent Butler, with instructions to display results on his trusty old 2D 'puter monitor embedded in his writing desk. Sometimes old school methods made the most sense.

Pressing and holding a button next to his right hip underneath the desk, the entire distant third of the desktop elevated until he released the control. A few papers slid toward him as he did so, not that he did much with actual paper anymore—unlike their victim. Greigh felt using paper to be too costly and, more to the point, inefficient.

"Butler, please use the passcodes transmitted to me from Captain Granger to access the Chicago city archives, specifically, architectural archives and associated documents. List on my desk all sources of such data relevant to this building, before and after it was called Hotel Literati."

"Of course, Sir Aubrey—"

"Come now, Butler. Don't make me tell you again, or I *will* upgrade you."

"Sorry… Greigh. Old habits."

Is this damn machine trying to tug my knickers into a twist?

He smiled.

CHAPTER 34

Butler said, "Greigh, I'm displaying one-hundred-twenty-two archived references to the structure at 667 East Harrison Street. These include blueprints, relevant newsworthy articles, and historical surveys. Would you like me to summarize? If so, what are your priorities?"

"Yes, please. I'm most interested in the building's original blueprints, with a focus on all access points to what we now consider apartment 7F."

"Alright, Greigh. I live to serve."

This bloody machine slays me.

When he configured Butler,

Greigh endowed him with a male tenor's smooth voice and a calm demeanor with just a touch of dry Scottish wit. His reference voice? That of a well-known actor named Sean Connery. He thought of that now as he listened to what had become his closest friend and confidante. This artificial intelligence network was not even state of the bleeding art. But they had grown comfortable with one another.

Sometimes newer isn't better, is it?

Butler continued, as the list of document names rolled onto Greigh's screen in four separate partitions—architectural, historical, utilities, and less interesting site elevations that included basements and tunnels. Butler now sounded like a lecturing professor who smiled as he spoke.

"This will amuse you, Greigh. Constructed during a period in America's history known as the roaring twenties, this was also a time of political turmoil amidst great wealth and prosperity—at least for some.

"Federal legislation known as the Volstead Act, better known as 'Prohibition,' outlawed the manufacture, distribution and sale of alcoholic beverages from 1920 until repealed in 1933—"

"Excuse me, Butler, but what the shite does that have to do with The Lit's bloody blueprints?"

Butler sounded impatient, too. Or was that just Greigh's imagination?

"Relevant. Prohibition and affluence of the day influenced the aforementioned structure's design and placement on the property when it was constructed. Specifically, both affluence and Prohibition mandated unusual access to what is now known as apartment 7F. And to all apartments on all floors above three on the south side of the structure. Our side.

"This building was rather unique in that respect, as it catered to an opulent clientele with certain... proclivities. We have access to more detail than you might expect in a building that is well over a hundred years old. That is because it was—and is—listed in the Chicago Historic Resources Survey. It possessed unique historical value at the time of the initial survey late in the twentieth-century. Now, would you like me to continue, Greigh?"

"Sorry. Yes. Please continue."

BUTLER SETTLED DOWN. "SECRECY AND THE COVERT movement of contraband creeped into every aspect of modern building design of this scale within that period. No more so than in the city of Chicago.

"You've indicated you wish to find all access points to apartment 7F. But you're already aware of the obvious points of ingress and egress. You need no blueprints to identify and locate its entry door and windows, correct?"

"Correct—if they have not changed in location or configuration."

"Unique to construction of commercial residences during that infamous period was a focus on covert passages and elevators disguised as ordinary doors. Hiding in plain sight, so to speak.

"Dumbwaiters connected guest rooms to concierge kitchens that catered to the erudite well-to-do for whom money was no object. Dumbwaiters are small elevators for conveying food and dishes—"

"Yes, I am familiar with the term. Did you discover any of those features in this part of the building, Butler?"

"Look at the documents on your screen—the areas outlined in blue."

An overlapping series of floor-by-floor blueprints flashed onto Greigh's desk. The seventh floor diagram—his, Sango's and Sybil Thibodaux's floor—showed foremost.

"It appears there is—or was—a dumbwaiter that serviced each apartment on each floor in the southern or front half of the building that faces Harrison Street. They likely supported the opulent concierge food service popular in finer establishments of that era.

"The large kitchen on the first floor serviced the grand restaurant adjacent to the hotel's lobby. It appears there were three small kitchens—food preparation areas—on each of four upper floors. They were on the fifth, eighth, eleventh and fifteenth floors between the A and B stacks, the C and D stacks, and the E and F stacks. Each catered to its own neighborhood's culinary specialties and perhaps was used for other purposes as well, such as for catering small events.

"It is no surprise that such roaring twenties opulence did not survive that decade. It would appear they decommissioned and closed off those areas above the third floor in the early nineteen-thirties. The nationwide financial collapse in late nineteen-twenty-nine gave birth to America's Great Depression. That changed everything.

Greigh's pulse quickened. "These dumbwaiters once carried food and drink to rooms on floors closest to each kitchen? *Twelve* kitchens?"

"Yes, Greigh. At least to the deluxe suites on the building's south side. According to relevant lifestyle articles in the archives, they then conveyed empty plates, dishes, bottles and glasses back to each kitchen via carts through a network of short service hallways not visible to guests. These dumbwaiters featured access from both the apartment side and the service hallway side.

"I have discovered numerous articles of the day describing the hijinks of celebrities and politicians. Rumors ran rampant. They smuggled other fare into their rooms—cases of contraband liquor, prostitutes, wildlife—via these dumbwaiters, these small elevators."

"Was there a dumbwaiter to apartment 7F?"

"Yes, to every apartment on all floors above the third floor on the south side of the building, including 7F, and what is now your suite, too, by the way."

"Aha! And would they have been large enough to carry two people?"

"Theoretically, yes."

"Where would that dumbwaiter have been located in the floor plan of apartment 7F?"

"In the kitchen next to the windows, not unlike this apartment."

"By the windows. Alright. Let's assume someone accessed 7F via the dumbwaiter. Where would that have led them?"

"I can only speculate. But according to the original plans, the dumbwaiter opens to a narrow service hallway on each floor where a kitchen was located. For example, these service hallways were only accessible to hotel employees on the fifth, eighth, eleventh and fifteenth floors. They led to the kitchens between the A/B, C/D and E/F stacks on those floors.

"But they were not directly accessible to any of the apartments across the hall to the north—the backside of the building—without crossing the main east-west hallway, and through an employee-only locked door."

"And how were provisions delivered to those kitchens?"

"Via small food service elevators next to each kitchen."

"Where did they lead?"

"From a central supply room on the main floor, north side, near the loading docks at the rear of the building. They also lead—or once led—to storage areas in the basement, as does a large freight elevator between the C and D stacks."

"Right. The freight elevator just down the hall. Are those food service elevators still in use?"

"There is no automation or networked cameras in those antiquated spaces, so I would have no way of knowing. And the archived blueprints don't show their current status."

"Son-of-a-bitch."

"Was that a question, Greigh?"

"No. Let me think."

"Of course, Sir Aubrey...."

"Butler—"

"Greigh, that was a joke. You are too tense."

"And you are just a bloody machine."

"I *am* offended—also, a joke."

"Riddle me this, Butler. How would someone know about these old architectural details after all this time?"

"I have no way of knowing that, Greigh. How did *you* gain access for *us*? Also, I would imagine the building's owners would have had certain documents conveyed to them with the property when it was acquired. That is customary with most commercial properties of proper provenance."

"It seems another discussion with the Donatis is called for."

"Who?"

"This building's owners,"

"Indeed."

CHAPTER 35

McQ's Apartment
9:50AM

This can't be good.

McQ was not a fan of being called to the nine-nine without a damn good reason. Captain Granger expected her in her office at ten AM. Not optional. McQ would not admit she was already planning to be at the nine-nine, anyway, after two luxurious hours of sleep.

"Yes, ma'am."

"Don't call me that. Be here at ten sharp."

"Okay, sir."

With her mid-back-length auburn hair still damp, those heavy ropes tugged at her scalp. If she'd earned a buck for every time she thought of chopping it all off, she could afford a suite at The Lit. Not that she'd want to live there. Although....

. . .

Two blocks in ten minutes? No problem. A hike up South Dearborn, was all. She lived this close to the nine-nine so she wouldn't need to subject herself to mass transit. They'd upgraded the entire system a decade ago, and the trains weren't bad. Still had to navigate a mob of misogynistic pigs and the homeless throngs the uniforms would chase out of the stations every morning. But most were folks just trying to get to work without getting mugged, or worse.

Some tried to make a buck with three-card-Monte while avoiding the transit cops. Nope, she liked living above a bar and hoofing it for a few blocks, even in this neighborhood.

If anyone slung her any flack, she'd draw back her jean jacket enough to reveal the butt of the small semi-auto 9mm holstered high on her right hip. No shoulder holster for her. Too slow to access. Besides, one of those was uncomfortable with a bra. Maybe she'd flash her gold shield, like it was unintentional, but unmistakable. That deterred most mooks pretty fast.

Criminals weren't going after cops these days, anyway, not even the troublemakers that hung around the precinct house. But that could change tomorrow.

It had before.

McQ arrived at the nine-nine. She was early enough to grab a quick mug of house mud, what passed for heart-paralyzing coffee the uniforms called rocket fuel, a.k.a. slow death. Tasted like crap, but rendered sleep largely unnecessary. For a few days, anyway.

McQ sensed some commotion behind her, around the corner. But by the time she returned to the squad's bullpen from the break room, all she saw were a few strange faces making eye contact with every-one, and a bunch of other heads trying to look real busy.

Something familiar about a couple of the huge visitors standing on either side of the water cooler across from the cap's office with *their* heads on swivels. She passed them by with a quick nod and sauntered into Granger's inner sanctum, as ordered.

Right on time.

And there stood the frickin' commissioner.

Oh, boy!

She froze in the doorway, still open. Slack-jawed, flat-footed, and hair still hanging in damp ropes, with her mud in one hand, she offered a lame little down-low wave to the man with the other.

"McQuillan, come in and close the door, please. You already know Commissioner Roberts. Sir, you met Detective McQuillan yesterday at the media conference."

With a blank face, no doubt from a lifetime of practice, he said, "How could I forget?" Roberts then smiled down at her. That was a good sign, wasn't it?

I bet this guy plays a killer game of five-card stud. Shit on a shingle! He's even taller than I remember.

McQ shuffled forward, shifted her mug to her left hand, and shook the offered right hand. Another crushing contact with the big boss.

She winced as she squeezed back as good as she got before he released her. Or did she release him? Did he wince a little, too? Good.

"Detective McQuillan, a good firm grip. I respect that. Have a seat."

She sat. Both he and Granger remained standing.

Oh-oh.

He now towered over her.

"Sir, would you mind taking a seat, too? I'll get a crimp in my neck."

"McQuillan!"

ROBERTS CHUCKLED. HE TOOK A SEAT IN GRANGER'S second guest chair to McQ's left. "No problem, Captain. Detective—"

"Mind calling me 'McQ', sir? 'Detective' sounds like you're about to scold me for screwing up at the PR thingy yesterday. Are you here to scold me, sir?"

Granger and Roberts exchanged some sort of look she couldn't label.

Granger said, "I told you, sir."

The next moment, both ladies jumped, startled by Roberts' rumbling belly laugh that came out of nowhere—without warning—like a crack of thunder on a sunny day.

Once he settled down, he alternated his penetrating gaze between Granger and McQ. Settling on McQ, still chuckling under his breath, he said, "Scold you? Hell, you made my appeal to the mayor and city council for additional resources a walk in the park!"

Granger's eyes stop imitating saucers. She grinned.

He continued in a tumble of words with his voice raised an enthusiastic half-octave while inflecting wildly. Like he was reading for a part in a movie, and doing a half-assed decent job of it.

"I like my people thinking on their feet. My PR team apologized to me after the conference. They said they directed you to *only* read a prepared statement, and that you went rogue. Their words. Somebody named Macy—"

"Mazy. Sir."

"Mazy. Yes. Hell, you remind me of myself a few decades ago, McQ."

He rumbled thunder again. McQ then matched his grin.

She exhaled for the first time since sitting down. At least it seemed so.

"Oh. Well, ah, that's a relief. Sir."

"McQ, if you ever think about getting into politics—that's what my staff and I do now—you call me. I wanted to come up here and thank you myself. I know we work you all like dogs, and that's not right, but too damn necessary."

Commissioner Roberts' brow furrowed—on demand—as he continued with a look of deep concern. It seemed genuine.

"So, here we find ourselves. A budgetary vulgarity. But now, I have high hopes of getting the rank and file—you—some reinforcements. That, in part, is because of you, McQ. Just don't let it go to your head, young lady. Your captain also tells me your case closure rate is the best in your house. Impressive. Anything to say?"

"No, sir. Just need to get back to my seven active cases some time today—one in particular."

Another crack of laughing thunder. "Good! Now, get the hell out of here, and get back to work. Get that rhyme killer off the streets for us."

"Oh, not you too. Sir. No offense. Dumb label."

The man just grinned, stretched out his hand as they both stood, almost bumping foreheads. She quickly slipped her U of I class ring off before shaking his hand again. Better safe than sorry.

He caught that move. Roberts chuckled again before they started round two of their grip fest. This time, they both winced.

Good!

She chuckled too, grinned back at the "big boss," and made her retreat, taking her mug and a smirk and a sore right hand with her.

CHAPTER 36

What's with all the mystery, anyway?

McQ had asked herself this a hundred times. She wasn't sure why Greigh wanted to be the invisible man on this case. She told herself she didn't really care, but wondered.

That's why they once again met in his suite at The Lit. Besides, it was nice up here. Not to mention quiet. And Butler made better mud. Light years better. From *real beans*. Greigh also alluded to the need for further investigation into the building itself. That piqued her interest.

She arrived at the door to his suite. It was ajar. She shucked a momentary concern, knocked and entered without waiting for a response. The heel of her right hand came to rest on the butt of her weapon.

"In here."

No duress in Greigh's voice. Her hand dropped to her side.

When she rounded the entryway wall into the living room, he said, "How did your 'command performance' go?"

"It was nothing. So, your idea. Bear fruit?"

"How would you feel about demolishing a part of your crime scene?"

"Huh?" Couldn't tell if he was joking, but he didn't strike her as the joking kind. Not about the case, anyway.

"Well, CED's done with it. Sounds like a question for the condo owner."

"In some small part, maybe, but we may need to punch a hole in a wall to determine what's behind it. That's not condo property *behind* the walls. That's the building's domain according to our HOA. But I'm not inclined to trust Vince and Luca just yet."

"So, what are you proposing, Greigh? Breaking the law? Again?" She was only semi-serious.

"We need some progress. How badly and how quickly do you want to solve this case, Detective?"

Detective? Shit, he's reminding me I'm an officer of the law, and it sounds like we're about to destroy private property.

"Tell me what you have in mind, Demolition Man."

"Have you heard of 'the unfortunate necessity defense'? It states that the commission of a smaller crime in order to prevent a larger one may be defensible."

"*May* be?"

IT WAS TIME FOR ACTION. GREIGH KNEW THEY WERE PAST niceties. "Look, McQ, there is a heretofore undiscovered entrance into your crime scene. We *may* discover it by destroying nothing. But if we're entering territory where you'd prefer plausible deniability should it prove otherwise, I'm willing to go in alone and do what needs to be done. What say you, McQ? Are you prepared to go a little rogue?"

Greigh could almost predict her response now, knowing she was a woman of action and coveted results. They needed a break in the case *now*.

"Rogue, you say? Not the first time. Got called that less than two hours ago. Screw it. Let's do this."

Greigh smiled. He could tell she appreciated the choice, but didn't want to be left out. Insatiable curiosity, too. Excellent.

After a quick visit to a storage room in his suite next to the entry door behind a bookcase, he emerged with a claw hammer and a crowbar. Closed the heavy bookcase-slash-door behind him.

"Tools of the writing trade, Greigh? And what the Hell was that glow coming from that secret room? Hiding something? Contraband?"

He looked abashed. "Not secret, just subtle. Grow lights. I grow my own herbs. My body is a temple. Isn't yours?" He grinned at his tiny joke. Her jaw hung slack. He added, "I use them for cooking —*nutritional* herbs and herbs for flavor, *Detective.*"

"Oh. I did not see *that* coming." Did she look just a little disappointed? "Whatever...."

They stood there and stared each other in the eye a beat longer than necessary before Greigh walked around her and out his front door. She shook her head, turned and followed, closing the door behind her.

They turned right, walked the hundred feet to 7F. McQ used the old-fashioned metal key in her custody. Greigh followed her with a tool in each hand.

Heading toward the kitchen, they then turned left out of the entryway to pass between the breakfast bar now to their left and cabinets with countertops, sink, and appliances to their right.

The window wall lay ahead as they stepped over and around the clutter on the floor.

UNLIKE HIS APARTMENT, THERE WAS NO PANTRY CABINET in that corner—the southwest corner of the crime scene. In its stead, they faced a lovely raised-wood panel with beveled moulding, the kind you might see in an opulent private library.

Its age was evident. Its moulding's angular edges were rounded off by countless layers of varnish and polishing, and possibly, refinishing. There were myriad small dents visible from decades, or even a century or more, of minor encounters with hard objects.

They stood there, looking at that five-foot-wide section of wall from the floor to the ten-foot ceiling. It appeared older than the rest of the relatively modern kitchen. A hazy sun warmed their left cheeks through the windows. For the first time, Greigh noted what was *not* there in front of them.

"Do you detect anything odd, Detective?" He stared at the surrounding floor with an odd twinkle in his eye.

"You mean the kitchen is a mess, like all the rooms in this place?" Nobody had touched anything since the forensic team finished their work.

"Come now, Detective. What do you see before you?"

"Um, I see utensils and dry goods scattered on the floor around us. Someone emptied the refrigerator—the door's still open, although the light is now off, so someone turned it off since the murder. Broken glass, smeared condiments, the smell of something rotting. That tomato-based crap over there is spoiling and making my eyes water. Plus, all the torn books, paper and junk on the floor behind us."

"What's missing?"

"Footprints, but we already knew that."

"Very good. What else?"

He waited with surreal patience. He was enjoying himself. Then it happened. Her eyes widened. She pointed to the floor in front of them.

"This corner, next to the windows. There is nothing on the floor in that corner, as if somebody swept it clean!"

"Brilliant. And why might that be? This should reflect the precise condition of the scene after the crime, should it not?"

"Yes! If the killer didn't enter and leave this place by the door or the windows, which were all locked, a secret door *swung inward into the apartment*." Her words tumbled out faster now. "There couldn't be anything on the floor here after that door swung shut behind the killer when he left!"

Greigh playfully bumped her shoulder with his own. "Shall we see if we can open this *door?*"

"Hell, yeah!"

They both kneeled, shoulder-to-shoulder, on the only part of the kitchen floor with no broken glass or drawer contents strewn about—an area about five feet square. They were between the windows to their left and the first kitchen cabinet to their right. They faced west. With the sun reaching higher into the almost-noon sky, the upper portion of that wall panel was now in shadow.

From an inside jeans-jacket pocket opposite her high-hip holster that held her Glock, McQ grabbed a miniature flashlight that she carried everywhere. She shined its brilliant beam around the perimeter of the lovely old panel that looked to be of genuine wood.

Now that they examined this panel with acute interest, they noticed its exquisite craftsmanship had obscured the hairline seam around its perimeter.

She started knocking and pressing at its edges. Greigh did the same, but it was crowded for both of them to do so in that corner. He backed off, stood up, and let her explore what just had to be a secret panel for accessing an old dumbwaiter. The theory was just too good to fail. But he knew that's when they often did.

McQ knelt at the edge of the panel inches from window glass. She pressed harder and harder at various points along its periphery.

And then it happened.

She set her flashlight on the floor. It rolled away from the wall. She pushed *hard* with both hands on a spot less than two inches from its left edge above her head, but at about waist level if she had been standing. The vertical edge of the heavy panel separated from that corner a fraction of an inch.

Click.

After a sharp intake of breath, still kneeling on her haunches, she looked up and grinned at Greigh over her right shoulder. Clapped her hands together like a little girl who had discovered something amazing and squealed, "Yahtzee!"

Greigh could not explain why his eyes misted over. He swiped first at one and then the other with a fist knuckle before she peered up at him again. They both continued to grin like Cheshire cats.

She stood, wedged her fingers into the crack, and pulled against the stout resistance. Not like she had nails to break. With the scraping screech of neglected hinges, the full-length panel swung open fast as if, once freed from its closed position, it *wanted* to open. Maybe spring-loaded hinges.

And there it was.

Now standing side by side, they stared at a handle on the bottom of a door that would slide upward. A dumbwaiter.

"Would you like to do the honors, Detective?"

CHAPTER 37

She grinned up at him. Brimming with gratitude, she wondered how long it would have taken her to figure out this piece of what was now *their* mystery without Greigh and his research skills? This seemed like a moment of shared significance. And maybe not just for the case.

McQ stood and brushed off her hands. She reached for the slotted handle, now at waist level and less than six inches from the door's bottom edge. She exerted upward pressure, but one hand was not enough. Crowding three fingertips of each hand into the slot and lifting, the sliding door slid upward.

They stared into the blackness. Once the door was up almost as far as it would go, a small elevator shaft of ancient bricks appeared. It was approximately three feet square.

Though they could not see the car, they quickly realized a pair of once-elegant hand ropes powered it. They hung in the shaft, still soft to the touch.

Greigh said, "May I borrow a pair of gloves?"

A pair magically appeared from inside McQ's jean jacket.

He grinned as he stretched them over his large hands. Reached into the shaft near its right side and tugged first on one rope, then on the other. One drew down easier than the other after a momentary resistance. He figured that was the one that would bring the unseen car down, hopefully at a controlled rate of descent. It was above them.

McQ's eyes remained wide from their discovery, but she already spurred them onward with a cluck of her tongue.

She said, "Alright, now we know how our perpetrator entered and exited the scene. What's next?"

She spoke to his back as he pulled on the easier rope, hand over hand. Then, the car appeared—sooner than Greigh expected. He skinned his knuckles on the car's rusted steel bottom. Produced a small rip in one of his gloves and a softly uttered expletive.

He moved his hands closer to the wall of the shaft until the car clicked into a safety latch when its floor came level with the opening into the apartment's kitchen.

Not winded by anything other than anticipation, Greigh turned toward McQ, nodded at the opening, and said, "We need to determine where this leads. But let's think about this."

He examined the backside of the now-open five-foot wall panel that had concealed the dumbwaiter, swung wide to their right, into the kitchen and against the cabinets. Greigh said, "Ah, see this?"

McQ crowded closer. She drew in his musky odor. A trace of dizziness coursed through her.

Focus, McQuillan. You're not a cat in heat!

She pushed toward his shoulder and neck to peer at a small fixture near the end of Greigh's index finger. She shone her flashlight at that spot in the vertical center of the panel's right edge, the backside edge that would close to near the windows.

"What *is* that?" She watched as Greigh examined without touching what appeared to be a small loop of rope.

"So you can pull the wall panel closed from the backside once you're in the dumbwaiter. May I borrow your light for a moment?"

He grabbed it from her hand without waiting for permission. Shone it inside at the floor of the dumbwaiter, and up along its two side walls—left and right. Again, he touched nothing as McQ looked on.

There were only two sidewalls, the open back side faced the raw brick of its shaft. Looking up, he saw there was no overhead panel, only a cable that suspended the car's sturdy frame. The hand ropes disappeared into darkness.

"Look at this." He aimed the light at the small space's interior. "There is a greasy dust clinging to every surface. But the floor is almost dust-free, except for the corners. Someone's been in here not long ago. But since your team found no trace evidence here in the apartment, it's likely safe to assume we'd find none in here, either."

She said, "Someone will need to ride this contraption out of here."

Greigh didn't hesitate. "I'll go."

"No way, mister. One, you are a civilian. Two, you outweigh me by, well, a lot. We don't know how strong these old ropes are. And three, we need to get this new space processed for trace before proceeding any further."

"How long with *that* take?"

"Too long. Look, this is how the killer got in here. Once in the apartment, he left no trace. You're right. We *could* assume there will be no trace in the dumbwaiter, but I can't take that chance. I'll get someone to deliver an evidence-gathering kit for later processing. That'll get us to whatever is beyond this miniature coffin."

"Dumbwaiter."

"Shut up!"

McQ was already on comms with Forensics. "They're sending a kit right up. Can't get the team here for several hours. We need to move quicker than that."

"Agree."

Two cups of Greigh's amazing coffee and twenty minutes later, the kit arrived. Looked like a large doctor's bag with pockets inside. After donning gloves from the kit—Greigh already destroyed hers—McQ vacuumed and bagged, sprayed, photographed, and DNA-scanned the dumbwaiter's interior with a handheld device, as well as what she could see of its shaft. As suspected, nothing apparent. The dumbwaiter was forensically as clean as the apartment, at least according to this cursory sweep.

She'd have the team do a full analysis of whatever lay beyond the dumbwaiter. Later. She'd exercise care. Slipped on the kit's full-body suit and folded herself into the small space with her flashlight.

They both smiled.

Greigh said, "We keep open comms. Agree? Apologies—your call."

"Good grief, Greigh. Stop already with all the politeness. We're almost a couple, now."

When she realized what she'd said, her cheeks flushed. She dropped her eyes to mask her embarrassment. Tugged at her gloves and adjusted her hood to avoid any further awkward interaction with this beautiful and brilliant man—for the moment.

She turned and crawled into the dumbwaiter. Once inside, she bounced up and down to test the integrity of the cable attached to the overhead frame.

"Well, I haven't plummeted to my death. Yet."

She grinned at her gallows humor.

McQ drew down the door. Its inside handle was also a finger slot. Before the dumbwaiter even enclosed her in darkness, her comm implant buzzed. She tapped it. "Yes, Greigh, I copy, already."

"Just checking."

"You aren't worried about me, are you?" She meant to chuckle, but it came out as a nervous snort.

That must've sounded rich.

She leaned against the side wall that had been to her right when she climbed in. She half-opened the door again, digging her fingertips into the worn finger slot on the inside and slouched to peer out at Greigh, who had already started pacing. He turned to peek in at her when the door creaked up.

She said, "I'm surprised. Roomy in here. Sybil and her assailant could have wedged in, though it would have been snug for two bodies, maybe less so with one broken in pieces and folded. I see a finger slot on the backside of this door, too. And a hand-painted label. Pretty crude, and faded. Says, '7-6P.' Like it wasn't odd at all back in the day for people to be inside this thing."

"Makes sense. Back in the day, they likely labeled hotel rooms by the floor and by their relative position down the hall. I'd guess 7A was 7-1, 7B was 7-2, and so on. 7F would have been 7-6. The 'P' must stand for 'Private' to distinguish it from employee spaces. And I'd wager they smuggled more than a few bodies—alive, I would hope—in or out of these rooms back in the day."

"Huh. Makes sense. Here goes nothing." As she spoke, she pulled the door down once more. She felt a sudden wave of claustrophobia, of finality. "Up or down?"

Greigh said over their comms, "Well, the nearest concierge kitchen was once on the eighth floor, one floor up, so I'd suggest you try up. Those old hand ropes will have some purchase—or leverage via mechanical advantage—so it shouldn't be all that difficult to draw yourself upward. Look for any doors or markings to your right as you ascend."

She knew Greigh was listening to her grunt as she drew down on one of the two hand ropes that hugged her left shoulder. The rope tried to scrub at her thin gloves. She heard a *click*—no doubt the latch that engaged when the dumbwaiter locked in place when they first moved it. Now, it was disengaged.

"Going up...."

She dropped.

"Oops. Wrong rope. *Now* going up. You're right. It's easy, but squeaky and rumbly from lack of use. Smells real musty in here, like old dust in an attic mixed with dirty grease from an old garage floor."

❧

G REIGH SAID, "S TILL ALRIGHT?"

Only a few seconds of tortured silence had elapsed.

165

"Yup. Lots of brick on both sides of me now. Some are crumbling. Hey, wait! Here's a door to my right. Says, '8-6S'. Stopping."

Click.

"'S' for 'Service?' Can you open the door?"

Puffing a little from exertion and excitement, McQ reached for the slotted handle near the door's bottom at her right hip. Her holster got in the way until she shimmied around enough to reach the handle with both hands. Tugged up on it. Nothing. Then again. It yielded.

"Oh, my."

"What?"

"I'm in a room here, but it is really black. Not what I expected. Like a small storage room or something. I'm getting out."

"McQ, stop!"

"*What!*"

"Sorry. Shine your light down. Just make sure there is indeed a floor."

"Oh, yeah, good idea. Um, yup, I see a floor. Thanks. I'm... crawling... now. It's.... Weird—... Now,... Can't...."

"McQ?"

"McQ!"

CHAPTER 38

Greigh waited.

This is madness.

One minute.

Two minutes.

He vowed not to seem too anxious by giving McQ time. But the raw silence chafed him.

Was she alright? Had something happened?

Or just bad comms?

After what seemed like an eternity, he croaked, "McQ, what in bloody hell is going on?"

Nothing. He couldn't bear losing someone again.

I'm being silly. She's capable, she's armed… but she's all alone.

No, not again!

Not willing to wait a second longer, Greigh checked his jeans pockets. Felt the lumps of his own flashlight and his favorite folding knife. The kind where once you release the safety catch, you whip open the blade with a flick of the wrist. That knife had saved his life more than once.

Greigh slid open the door to the dumbwaiter. The empty shaft greeted him. After hauling down on the hand rope with vigor, and then more slowly, the empty car appeared in less than ten seconds. This time, he kept his hands close to the right wall of the shaft. He would not skin his knuckles again.

At almost a foot taller than McQ, Greigh clamored in with greater difficulty. Pulled on the rope.

Click.

He pulled until he saw the door to his right McQ had described —'8-6S.'

Click.

Pushed up on the door, and twisted his torso to his right. His light chased away the stygian darkness outside the dumbwaiter. But there was no sign of her.

Greigh crossed the empty room, which was only fifteen feet square. No exits. Nothing on the walls except a few ancient scraps of paper worthy of examination later. But right now, he feared for his partner's safety. Then, the beam of his light lit up a door on the far wall.

That must be the west wall.

GREIGH APPROACHED THE DOOR. IT LOOKED LIKE A regular door, but wider—perhaps three feet—with two buttons on the right door jamb: U and D.

He pressed D. After a three-second delay, the sounds of ancient relays clacking, and the low groan of a motor performed a symphony of protest. He waited a full thirty seconds.

From the length of time it took for the car to arrive, he assumed McQ had used the elevator to ride it to the bottom of the shaft. He could not know if this was true, or whether she made any stops on the way down.

This was now a fishing expedition. If McQ were here, he'd have some fun with her by calling it 'an exploratory sortie to the sea' or 'a hopeful fish-catching trip.' Despite his profound worry, he grinned.

Tick.

Greigh assumed that once may have sounded more like a *ding* before decades of neglect. That ship had sailed. He grinned again. An anxiety-coping mechanism.

BUT NOW, HE NEEDED TO *move.* HE GRABBED AND TURNED the doorknob, like entering a closet. The car's interior remained dark.

As he entered, his flashlight beam revealed the car's interior was perhaps four feet square. He stepped in, turned around, and lit up an ornate series of greenish brass or bronze buttons aligned to the right of the door in a column—15, 11, 8, 5, 1, and B—from top to bottom. This was consistent with the archival copy of the building's blueprint.

The B button was gobsmacked with a pink greasy substance. Lipstick! McQ left him a trail to follow.

He imagined her muttering, "Just in case…."

Smart lass. She was okay, wasn't she? His finger hovered over that button.

What the hell.

Greigh pulled the heavy wooden door closed, now in front of him. It latched. He punched 'B'. His finger came away slippery. The elevator began its bumpy descent—under protest. The screeching, squeaking, and bouncing did not inspire confidence as he watched the backside of each floor's door rise in front of him, alternating between raw brick and the occasional steel cross-member.

He braced for impact.

McQ DRAGGED AWAY FROM OBLIVION. SHE SPRAWLED cheek down on damp brick floor—moldy and… something else. The back of her head throbbed and something wet and hot dribbled down both sides of her neck. Her paper-like forensics suit was torn away from her head and left shoulder.

What in the—?

Her attempt to turn over and sit up failed. Nausea and dizziness overwhelmed her, so she allowed gravity to return her to the floor. Hard. Only this time, face up. She heard the *thud* as her skull hit the floor, but the back of her head just felt… dead.

So dark. But there was an errant beam of light several feet away. Her flashlight! An indistinct shape nearby grunted and growled as it moved.

Shit. There's an animal down here.

But every time she tried to sit up, her head spun. She thought she would vomit. A frickin' concussion? Best to play dead. Her arms wouldn't obey, anyway.

The shape, only defined by bizarre shadows created by her tiny but powerful flashlight beam on the floor, moved with some speed, howled, and stomped on her light. It went dark as she realized she was on the edge of blacking out again, light or no light.

In the darkness, shuffling… and… loud sniffing.

*What is that **stench**?*

A foot delivered a vicious kick to her right side. Hurt like fire and lightning.

She tried not to make a sound, but failed.

Oomph….

Ding.

The elevator. Was Greigh coming to her rescue? She remembered losing comms, stepping out of the elevator, closing the door, taking only two or three steps, and… *fire and lightning.*

A sudden scratching sound nearby in the blackness, like claws on the brick floor, or something dragging as it turned—to face the elevator door?

Silence. Waiting. To pounce?

McQ thought she saw the beam of another flashlight shoot out from the opening elevator off in the darkness. She said as loud as she was able amidst her pain and foggy brain, "Greigh, look out. Something...." She could say no more.

She heard, "Hey! I'm armed. Show yourself!"

A heavy shuffling sounded close. But then, combined with that scratching sound, moved away from her. It was leaving!

"McQ, where are you?"

With a weak voice, "Over... here...." And then the blackness turned into warm oblivion.

She welcomed its embrace.

CHAPTER 39

Greigh had heard McQ's croaked warning. On full alert, he exited the small elevator, prepared to do battle. He'd pulled out the knife and flicked it open with his right hand, the flashlight still in his left.

The odors in this dank dungeon threatened to overwhelm him. He shouted, "Hey! I'm armed. Show yourself!" Then, "McQ, where are you?

A large space with hard surfaces. McQ sounded distant, frail. Her voice tried to echo. His did.

He took a beat to locate a circular light switch on a brick wall near the elevator. Twisted it, got a satisfying *clack*, and the room lit up with a single industrial-grade light in a wire safety cage off to his left. There she lay... at the end of a blood trail.

He ran twenty paces. Unconscious and bleeding from a head wound, Greigh assumed the worst—that McQ was seriously injured and that they were in hostile territory.

Someone or something had dragged her. No time to do anything but to secure her safety. He still clutched his open knife, prepared to use it if necessary. But he'd need to set McQ down first to do so. Useless. He folded and secured the knife.

Greigh picked her up in his arms with gentleness, despite the danger, and carried her dead weight to the elevator. She was so warm and soft. Fragile. The back of her head was a tangle of sticky black-matted hair in the dim light. He laid her down, curled on the small elevator's floor, stepped over her, and closed the door behind them.

Using his light once more, he found and punched the number eight on the panel, retracing their route to escape this hidden Hell. If he had to, he'd squeeze McQ and himself back into that wretched dumbwaiter, but he feared worsening her injuries, if they could both even fit in there.

THEY ARRIVED ON EIGHT. GREIGH PULLED MCQ FROM THE small service elevator into the darkened room. Carefully stretched her out. Not much new blood. He thanked a god he didn't worship. Needed to get Q to a hospital. All he could think of.

Left the elevator door open. It would not operate like that. Nobody —or no thing—could follow them up.

Rushed to his left. Just a wall. But there were tools, and some ancient construction material. He had to think. Oriented himself. He had exited the dumbwaiter—a known point of origin—facing west. He now exited the elevator, facing east. The wall to his left must be north, toward the eighth-floor hallway.

He grabbed a sledgehammer that was covered with greasy dust, like everything else in this walled-off room. Chose a spot in the center of the wall that looked like it might be a walled-over door. He swung. And again. And again. Plaster over wooden lath. Good. That would yield.

Half a dozen swings later, he broke through, adjusting his swings to miss wooden studs that had become like rough-sawn iron over the decades.

On the far side of the wall, he encountered what appeared to be the backside of shelves containing stacks of sundry items—not-old items. He kept swinging, and the shelves, too, gave way to his desperate bludgeoning.

After ten minutes of concerted effort, he had created an opening large enough to lift McQ through. His flashlight gripped in his left hand cast them both in a bizarre dance of shadows.

As he picked her up, she regained partial consciousness. Her first instinct was to protect herself. Her arms tried to windmill. A right cross narrowly missed his jaw. He laid her down again and wrapped his arms around her. She struggled against his tight embrace.

He said, "McQ, it's me, Greigh. You're okay. We're safe, McQ, alright?"

She stalled. Still in the relative darkness with only the small light offering a hint of recognition, Greigh's voice softened from its earlier strident tone. "McQ, I'm holding you still. Stop struggling. You'll injure yourself further."

With a faint voice, she said, "Greigh? I... there's something down here."

"No, McQ, we're no longer there. We're safe now, back on eight. Can you walk? I need your help to get you through the wall over there, okay?"

"What? Oh, yeah. Okay. Greigh... you—"

"Later, Q. Let's move."

He helped her up. They stumbled through the rubble he created beneath the two-by-three-foot hole. He took special care to avoid any upright nails on the floor by shuffling his still-sandaled feet. There were dozens of nails in the broken pieces of lath still anchored in chunks of nineteenth-century plaster in their path. He struggled to help McQ and to aim his little light at the same time.

Plaster dust filled his cone of light, like high beams in a blizzard. They stumble-shuffled forward. He kicked away debris before each step. Jagged chunks of lath bloodied a few of his toes. They shimmied through the hole—one at a time—and into a well-used hotel storage room. Banquet and cleaning supplies, horizontal stacks of tables and vertical stacks of chairs, stores of light bulbs, spare parts....

It all looks so terribly... normal. And almost no dust.

With McQ's arm over his shoulder, he wrapped his right arm wrapped around her waist. He clutched her left hand that was slung behind his neck. They stutter-stepped, as one, the twenty feet across the room. Their objective: a door on the far wall. He assumed it led to the hallway.

He planted McQ atop a stack of chairs. Her feet dangled, but she seemed secure, now more conscious than not.

Greigh banged on the locked door.

Who prevents exiting a room? What kind of cocked-up works is this?

He hollered, "Hello? Hello!"

Nothing. He said, "McQ, I'm going to fetch my persuader. Are you alright?"

He saw she gripped the arms of her chair as if her life depended on it.

"I'm fine. Just get us out of here."

GREIGH RAN BACK TO THE HOLE. REACHED THROUGH, AND recovered the sledge. Back at the door, before he prepared to swing, his flashlight beam spotted a light switch. Flipped it on, and the room lit up. Modern overhead lights.

The door was secured by an electronic lock. Since he didn't have his lock-picking kit with him, he figured the sledge was next. But then, he discovered a toolbox on a nearby shelf. He leaned the sledge against the wall by the door.

In the box of tools, he found a flat-blade screwdriver. He wedged out the pins securing the door's hinges to the jamb. After five minutes of persuasion, and all four pins removed, the door fell outward into the hall after a persuasive kick.

Greigh picked up McQ, intending to carry her to his apartment. She resisted. "I can walk."

"You will *not* walk. We do not know the extent of your injuries."

"Put me down or I *will* shoot you."

She squirmed as he reached under her knees and arms, and around her upper back from her perch on top of the chairs.

"Do what you must, lass."

During times of stress, his highland brogue tended to surface.

He swooped her up, and off they trundled. Too weak to resist, she swung her left arm up and over his right shoulder. Then she clung tight as if she feared falling.

THEY RETURNED TO THE FAMILIAR. THE HALLWAY BETWEEN apartments 8F and 8E appeared similar to his on seven, but the carpet was blue and black, not red and black, and just as threadbare down the center. Turning left, he carried her to the birdcage elevator. Moments later, they arrived at seven. His apartment door was still across the hallway, right where he had left it.

Funny.

His biometrics popped the lock. They entered. He carried her to the sofa, facing the fireplace. Her t-shirt under her jean jacket rode up as he set her down. Revealed a nasty bruise on her left side the size of a soccer ball.

Pulled his own t-shirt over his head and wadded it up against the cut on the back of her head. Not much new blood.

"Butler, lights twenty-five percent. Low fire, please. Call 9-1-1."

"Are you injured?"

"No, but McQ is. Someone attacked her. Please report that Detective Chance McQuillan sustained a head injury, now conscious and responsive, but a possible concussion. Parietal laceration, bleeding arrested. Pressure applied. Internal injuries possible as evidenced by a large hematoma on her torso. Request an ambulance ASAP.

"Also, notify her precinct, the ninety-ninth. Perpetrator is not in custody, and presumed to still be in the basement of Hotel Literati. We are under no imminent threat."

"Of course." Greigh thought Butler registered concern, empathy. Ridiculous.

As he leaned over McQ, her eyes fluttered white and closed.

CHAPTER 40

A partment 7D
      Hotel Literati
3:45 PM

GREIGH STRETCHED McQ OUT. HE STRAIGHTENED HER legs on the center section of his sofa and fetched an ice pack to gently place on her forehead. The flames crackled. Her unconsciousness concerned him. Or was she mustering and conserving as a defense mechanism? All he could do was hold her hand. It was warm.

Twelve minutes later, a heavy knocking on Greigh's door startled both him and McQ, now conscious once more, but dizzy and nauseous. She reached for her gun. He covered her hand. Patted it.

He rushed to open the door to greet a small army of uniformed cops with EMTs in tow carrying their medical kits. More personal than just having Butler unlatch it. And probably safer.

One uniformed officer rushed past him and them all to get to McQ. He knelt on the floor in front of the long sofa. Her eyes were closed.

Her left forearm covered her face and forehead, holding the ice pack in place.

Greigh heard him say, "LT, you okay? What were you thinking? No back-up? Goddammit, LT!" He grabbed her right hand—the one laying across her stomach. She was too weak to resist. Or… was she?

Is this what jealousy tastes like? Ridiculous, old bean! Why would I be jealous?

In and out of consciousness, she drew her forearm away from her face. The ice pack slid off her forehead onto the sofa by her neck. Her hand hovered in mid-air before she moved it to her stomach on top of the other one she'd just pulled away from her… friend?

"I'm fine, McKenzie. Just a knock on the head. And don't get all mushy on me."

Her words were stronger than her voice—higher than usual, and croaky.

The medical technicians shoved the uniform—McKenzie—out of the way with gentle but insistent hands so they could examine her.

The apartment now felt crowded with all the commotion and so many strangers milling around. Five edgy uniforms—four males and one female—roamed around as if this was a crime scene.

They all looked at him like he was the scum that attacked one of their own. This is why he didn't like beat cops. They leaped to conclusions.

He needed to act fast.

IN A LOUD BUT RESPECTFUL VOICE, GREIGH SAID, "FOLKS, just to be clear, this is *not* a crime scene. I have been assisting Detective McQuillan on one of her cases. I will answer all questions you will wish to ask me. Now, would anyone like a cup of coffee while the medical techs take care of McQ?"

They all stopped to stare at him, as if to test the veracity of his claims. He shrugged. The lone female officer—she seemed more mature—recognized what was going on. She said, "Sure, why not? But first, let's talk over here."

The other four stopped wandering around seeking potential threats, and now all stood with their thumbs hooked into the front of their bulky equipment belts, heads still on swivels. They obviously practiced that pose at the academy.

Greigh smiled as he followed the officer to his dining table and chairs by the window wall. A gray morning had turned into a leaden afternoon. But everything seemed bright after what felt like hours in darkness deep within the bowels of the hotel. He said over his shoulder, "Butler, please brew coffee for six."

Butler's voice emanated from everywhere. "Of course. Police officers like their coffee strong, don't they, Greigh?"

EVERY COP IN THE APARTMENT JUMPED. THE SWISHING OF bodies stiffening inside starched by tired blues and clicking weapons being accessed seemed almost comical. But, of course, it was not.

"Sorry, Officers. That's just my automated butler brewing coffee for you."

The officer's eyes across from him darted around, but softened after taking a deep breath and rolling her eyes. "You are Mr. Greigh? The person who called 9-1-1?"

He read her name plate and responded. "Yes... Officer Blake. That is, I directed Butler to do so." He nodded upward and over his shoulder in the general direction of the kitchen, as if Butler were a person in there making coffee. They could hear the water already boiling and dripping. Greigh glanced at the other officers, who seemed to have notched down somewhat after he defended Butler.

Having completed some triage, the EMTs prepared to transport McQ on the gurney wheeled in moments earlier. Greigh caught an affirming nod from an EMT. He nodded his gratitude in return. He slumped at the table.

Officer Blake nodded to the other uniforms who, after one last cautionary look around, filed out of the apartment. All except her partner, the stern young man who had rushed in ahead of everyone else and held McQ's hand—McKenzie.

He remained hyper-vigilant with his back against the fireplace. His eyes darted, head swiveled, and his right hand remained in the neighborhood of his service piece. The other hovered over his truncheon—his nightstick. Kids like that tended to be trigger-happy. Not too surprising with their constant exposure to street violence. And that's why Greigh hated dealing with street cops, empathy notwithstanding.

Officer Blake observed his own anxiety. "Mr. Greigh, you can imagine the threats we deal with every shift. And when one of our own gets attacked, well, we're all edgy. Besides, Detective McQuillan is sort of a hero in our precinct house. That makes this personal—for a lot of us."

"I understand, Officer Blake." He truly did. And he understood *personal*. Instead of allowing himself to be subjected to Copper 101 Interrogation, however, he took the lead.

"Officer, please allow me to tell you what happened. I will also put McQ's—Detective McQuillan's—attack in the context of the Sybil Thibodaux homicide investigation for which she is the lead detective, as you might know. There is a direct correlation, but that is only a working assumption at this point."

"Yeah, I caught her kick-ass media conference on the vids. You a consultant or somethin'? You sound like a cop."

"Yes. Or something."

BLAKE SETTLED INTO THE CHAIR ACROSS THE TABLE FROM this Mr. Greigh. Man, was he a looker. And he knew how to spend money by the lay of this place. This apartment was somethin' else, even though the building itself was kind of a dump.

He laid out the whole case, and the timeline leading up to the attack. He'd make a good cop. But he was too rich. No money in bein' a cop. She knew, as a single mom.

Looks like he might have a thing goin' for the LT, too. Hell, if I played for the other team myself…. But McKenzie over there? Sheesh. He didn't even try to hide his smotherin' crush on the LT.

Officer Blake suppressed a smile. She recorded Mr. Greigh's entire statement. When he'd finished, he said, "I suggest you coordinate with McQ's boss in the homicide detective division, Captain Granger, at the nine-nine."

She said, "The *nine-nine?* You *do* sound like a cop, Mr. Gr—"

"Greigh. It's just Greigh."

"Okay, Greigh. You like workin' with the LT?"

"McQ? Yes, well, we have our moments. She's an excellent investigator. And I believe she thinks I bring value to her effort."

"Uh-huh." This time, she didn't try to hide her smile. Seemed like an okay guy even though he was rich… and maybe too freakin' handsome for his own good. Or for the LT's. None of her business.

He added, "I assume you'll perform a thorough search of the basement where the assault occurred. McQ's attacker could still be down there, and might have left some trace evidence behind relevant to our —McQ's—case. She said her attacker sounded like an animal, but got the impression of a man."

Oh, boy!

"Uh-huh. We'll take it from here, Greigh. Thank you for taking care of our LT. Means a lot."

And she meant it. As she shook his hand at the front door, why did she experience a tiny jolt?

Yeah, right, Blake, like you got a shot!

"Goodbye, Officer Blake. It was a genuine pleasure to have met you."

She smiled and tossed him a mini-salute.

Wow!

CHAPTER 41

W‌ednesday, June 27th
          Mount Sinai Hospital
Chicago, Illinois
9:45 AM

GREIGH VISITED MCQ IN THE HOSPITAL. THE TRAIN TO
Mount Sinai took nineteen minutes, including eight stops. He timed
it. Force of habit. Details mattered.

The uneventful ride gave Greigh time to imagine what *could* have
happened. He visualized McQ's slender body hacked to shreds like
poor Sybil's. Imagined McQ bound, maybe gagged. Her face locked in
terror as she regarded her own arms and legs criss-crossed with blow
after blow of the machete.

The madman would have stared into her eyes, striking with glee
until she lost consciousness. Greigh even created in his mind the
coppery odor and the feel of her sticky blood souring as it congealed in
and around her wounds. It would have matted down her red tresses as

the monster bludgeoned her skull. The helplessness would have been the worst. Especially for someone as strong as his McQ.

My McQ? Good lord, what the hell is wrong with me? She's fine, no thanks to me.

∿

GREIGH SWUNG OPEN THE DOOR TO THE DOUBLE-occupancy room, stepped in, looked around, and chirped, "You look bloody awful, now don't ya, lass?"

The room brightened. Simple joy washed through McQ. That surprised her. But her smile died a sudden death. She wasn't sure why.

Still groggy from the meds meant to suppress the pain radiating from the back of her head and into her neck, she croaked, "Are your compliments always so underwhelming? My guys tell me you hauled my butt out of danger yesterday afternoon. Thanks, Greigh."

And she meant it, embarrassed that she had let some low-life get the better of her.

She reached her right hand out to him as he approached her, as if to shake it—like two colleagues greeting one another—very busi-nesslike. She would show her grip was stronger than her drug-addled voice, like she did with the commish.

He accepted her hand. She squeezed hard. He did not. Instead, his large but gentle left hand rested over both of their right hands. The thrill of that simple action also surprised her.

What the hell is going on here?

And then he opened that mouth again. "Don't they teach you how to clear a room at the academy? Rookie blunder. McQ, you could have ended up like Sybil at the whim of that blighter."

His scolding was soft and well-meaning, but he might as well have been screaming at her. He smirked under a worried brow. She pulled her hand free.

"You're an ass. So what do we know?"

"Well, your uniformed buddy McKenzie is a *madman*, you know. He demanded that your boss, Captain—"

"Granger."

"Yes, McQ. McKenzie charged into her office and demanded that she help get him a dozen uniforms to search The Lit's basement. I witnessed this fiery spectacle from your squad room. An Officer Blake was kind enough to take me in for further questioning—at my request, by the way."

Yet another surprise. She said, "I thought you were 'Mr. Invisible.'"

"It was time for me to 'appear.' Not by choice. Against my better judgment, mind you, I now realize you need my more visible help."

"What makes you think...? Okay, yeah, you're right, Greigh. I'll shut up, now. My head is killing me. What else?"

She fingered the bulky bandage that wrapped her head.

Good Lord. This thing is huge.

"I introduced myself to Captain Granger—"

"What?!"

"I convinced her I bring some minor value to your investigation. She even allowed me to lead McKenzie—"

"Mac."

"Very well. Mac and I are now on rather intimate terms."

"Oh, this I gotta hear. You and Mac." Not a question.

"Yes, well, his colleagues could not find the area of the basement where you were attacked, even after a search that lasted several hours. Mac tells me it's a maze down there, but assured me they were thorough."

"Wait. Don't tell me you and Mac rode that dumbwaiter down... together." She grinned, visualizing that, not daring to laugh. The meds didn't remove the pain, but she seemed to care less about it.

"I don't much care for the man's cologne, and he said my beard scratches. A most revealing sortie, that."

McQ chuckled, and winced.

"By the way, Mac tells me he doesn't much like being called Mr. Egg Salad Sandwich, whatever that means. Something about 'no act of kindness goes unpunished.' He is quite enamored of you. Did you know?"

Yeah, puppy love. Mr. Egg Salad Sandwich. Nice kid, Mac. Kid? He's damn near my age. Just fewer miles.

She shook her head from side to side, but with care, managing a lop-sided smirk of appreciation.

"It's nothing. What did you find?"

"Ah, yes. I forget how self-deprecating you become when someone compliments you—a veteran at rebuffing unwanted attention. A classic deflection mechanism, you know. I imagine someone as attractive as you must deal with awkward accolades all the time."

"Dammit, Greigh. *What did you find?*" He was the most infuriating man she'd ever met.

"After pouring ourselves out of that confounded matchbox, we retraced our path into the service elevator on eight and down to the basement with weapons drawn—"

"Weapons? As in plural?"

"It seems after our reluctant embrace in the dumbwaiter, and that I 'hauled *your* butt out of danger,' as you articulated, I find your Officer Mac endeared to me as well. He's quite intelligent—"

"Greigh!"

"Ah, yes, well, while he remained reticent at granting my request for a pistol, he allowed me to brandish my knife as we exited the service elevator in the basement. We took some time to explore the area where you were attacked and dragged—"

"I was dragged?"

"Yes. Fifteen paces or so. Your attacker possessed some strength, as you are heavier than little Sybil—"

"Seriously?" But she smiled.

Yup. Jerking my chain. A habit with this guy.

"What else?"

"It is my belief that after he disabled you, he was attempting to move you to some place where he could spend some quality time with you—undisturbed. Perhaps like he did with Sybil."

McQ shivered at the prospect. Then it dawned on her. "Wait a sec.

Why didn't you just take Mac to the eighth floor, through the hole you created to get us out of there?"

Greigh hoisted an insidious smirk to full mast. McQ wide-eyed him. "You stuffed him into that dumbwaiter intentionally? Oh, you wanted to give him the full experience, huh? You really are an ass, aren't you?" Then she couldn't help but grin, too.

"He said he wants to be a detective, so we started where you and I started—at the crime scene."

Of course. Wouldn't be that you're jealous of Mac's puppy crush, could it, Mr. Mystery Man? Had to show him who's the big dog, maybe?

GREIGH GREW SERIOUS AGAIN. "McQ, WE NOTICED SEVERAL things neither of us had the time to observe during our first trip to that space. Similar to the storage room on eight, dust covered everything. But someone—or some thing—had left numerous prints and trails on the floor. I'll come back to that.

"The reason your officers didn't find this space when they accessed the basement via the employee freight elevator? Like the dumbwaiters and food service elevators, that portion of the basement was walled off decades ago. Maybe a century ago. Further analysis of construction materials would be required.

"I retrieved the sledge hammer from the eighth floor so Mac and I could break our way out of that also-forgotten space. That brought us out into a large storage area that the hotel still uses.

"McQ, the magnitude of the walled-over spaces in that grand old pile astounds me. And I've lived there for a decade. The officers who canvassed the building said the Donatis were as surprised as anyone and continued to offer all assistance. They can't afford the sort of shadow this case is casting over their beloved establishment. Can't be good for business, or for the condo owners' confidence—*my* confidence."

"Any sign of my attacker?"

"One rather small man's footprints, plus another larger man's trail, led downward into an old sub-basement, which appears to have been there since before they built The Lit.

"That sub-basement leads to an even more complex warren of tunnels, some of which are sewer and utility conduits. The two sets of prints lead in myriad directions."

"An accomplice, as you suspected."

"That now seems probable. Mac and I became concerned for our safety, so we retreated. We're not done. The captain has two uniforms posted at the hole where we busted through into the normal basement, and they are on high alert. She also said they found trace DNA on your collar by which your attacker dragged you. Belongs to someone named Robin Bidok."

Greigh fell silent, deep in thought.

"What is it?"

"Perhaps nothing. That name. It just occurred to me that name is a curious anagram."

"A what?"

"An anagram is a word or phrase formed by reordering the letters of another word or phrase, such as *satin* to *stain.*"

"And?"

"If you rearrange the letters of this Robin Bidok's name, the only arrangement that makes any sense at all is *bookbinder.* Curious."

"So, does this guy have a sheet?"

"The captain told me there is almost no record of this guy. Not even employment. Likely a homeless bloke."

"Hey! Didn't you say two of The Lit's floors are dedicated to those kinds of folks?"

"Yes. The entire second and third floors comprise Sherwood."

"Like the forest?"

"If you venture there, you'll understand the reference. It is, well, gamey. My friend and neighbor lived there for a time before she found her feet."

"She chuckled, then winced. "You mean, 'gained her footing', Greigh?"

He smirked. "When Sango Mori first arrived from Japan, she lived in Sherwood for a time. I'll chat with her about this Bidok character."

But there was something else behind Greigh's words. Like a grim shadow. Concern sculpted her face.

"Greigh, promise me you won't go down there alone."

"Why, Detective, do you fear for my safety?" His smile was genuine and inconsistent with his tone of voice. She was on to him, or at least, she thought she was.

"It's just that we can't have any more citizens mauled by some cave dweller, is all. If he's our killer, the only reason he's still hanging around—"

"He's not done."

"Right. Look, they tell me I'll be out of here by tomorrow morning. Overnight observation, they say. I'll get Mac assigned. You and he will take me down there. We're gonna find the son-of-a-bitch who gave me this headache."

"Yes, m'lady,"

Dear God, that smile. Does he know?

She said, "Shut up!" as she shook her head from side to side and then regretted that momentary lapse in judgment an instant later.

CHAPTER 42

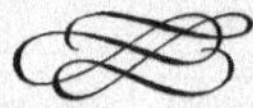

G reigh was pleased with himself. Just then, a woman with sauntered into the room as if she'd shown up for a rager. The room bloomed with the scent of patchouli. Her provocative tattoos wrapped around a bare left shoulder, the back and sides of her neck. He deduced she was some sort of performer by her theatrical entrance.

Stunning from head to toe, she saturated the room with her dazzling ensemble of jewelry and primary-colored fabrics. A flowing tunic festooned with sequins melded with the white scarf that wrapped around her neck and trailed behind her to below her slender waist.

A ballet of expansive flourishes preceded not one, but two fluid three-sixties—too earthy to be considered pirouettes. Yes, she was accustomed to being the center of attention—an audience-pleaser.

A husky tenor with healthy lungs, her voice broke as she squealed, "McQ!"

But her bubbly countenance disappeared, to be replaced post-haste with an expression of profound concern. And just like that, she flip-switched back to high-camp humor.

"Well, don't you just look *awful*. Too bad they couldn't color coordinate that wicked bandage on your head with your fashionable teal tunic, isn't it? I'm betting if you get out of that bed right now, we'd flash on your tight little tush following you about, wouldn't we, now?"

It took the visitor only two more seconds to notice the tall, handsome creature to her left. A privacy curtain had obscured any view of him when she first entered.

"Ooh, well, *hello!* Don't you just look yummy! I'm Daniella Kilby. Call me Dani. And you are…"

"Greigh, Aubrey Greigh. Just Greigh."

"Of course, you are, Just Greigh. But you're not, are you. You are a radiant rainbow." Both of her arms arced in a wide gesture toward Greigh.

She swiveled her head toward McQ, but kept her eyes glued to Greigh.

"Okay, McQ, is this your secret lover? A fellow cop? Both? Luv! Speak to me, already!" Her eyes finally followed her head to pierce McQ's soul. She snapped the fingers of both hands high and in front of her face several times in rapid succession to reinforce the importance and urgency of her query.

This set both McQ's and Greigh's heads spinning.

Greigh said nothing.

McQ said, "No, no… we work together."

"Oi, Q. Me thinks yon maiden doth protest too much. Work together, indeed."

Dani winked at the too-obvious double entendre, and patted Greigh's chest with one hand, while offering McQ a dismissive wave with the other.

"Whatever." She issued a lung-emptying sigh. "You're a big girl. When do you escape this dungeon?"

Greigh jumped in. "Ah, how do you two know each other?"

Dani, lightning quick, said, "*Why,* Greigh? Because we seem so different? The copper and the exotic dancer?"

"Exotic—?"

"Greigh, this would go much quicker if you didn't repeat everything I say. See, we work out together at the same gym. Have for years. I dance at *Flights of Fancy* where Wabash passes under Ida B Wells, not so far south of the DePaul and U of I campuses. College kids are poor, but horny tippers, and they're satisfied simply watching me perform.

"That's better than the older crowd of leches—them's that can't keep their hands to theirselves who wander in from The Institute for Professional Social Workers. Savvy?"

Dani didn't seem to be joking, merely profiling. Fired another salvo before Greigh could respond. All he got out was an intake of breath. He felt like verbal roadkill.

"Besides, I'm drumming up business by day as a student."

"You're—"

"Yeah, mate. So hard to believe I can dance *and* wrangle twenty-five graduate credits as a criminology major at the U of I? Because I'm over twenty-one doesn't mean I'm brain-dead, Greigh. Right, kiddo?" Dani swiveled her hypnotic eyes, not her head, from Greigh to McQ, wrinkling her forehead above her right eyebrow.

"'Over *twenty-one?*'" McQ awarded her friend Dani a twinkling grin of affection. "Yeah, Greigh, Dani's too damn smart for her own good. Keeps poking her nose into police business, like someone else I know."

She managed yet another tired grin with a glance toward her now-favorite mystery writer. Not that she had time or energy to read any mysteries, or any books other than procedural manuals.

GREIGH STOOD THERE, TAKING IN THE OVERALL spectacle that was Dani Kilby. He said, "You're a Londoner." Not a question.

"Aw, shucks, partner, ya caught me. Walthamstow. Had to move, though. Too many sex crimes. So, I dinna move to North London, some place like East Finchley. Instead, I leapt the pond. Came to Chi-town. Love it here!

"And you, Greigh? Got a bit 'o the Gaelic burr, aye? SCUH-tsh, yeah?"

Her attempt at imitating a Highland brogue came across more like a New Yorker attempting a Louisiana drawl—comical.

"Edinburgh. Most highlanders'd argue 'tis not really Scotland. Can ya hear it?"

"No worries. Oi, because I hail from Hoe Street dun't mean I dun't read or watch vids, cupcake."

She had been on a full frontal flirt with Greigh as a low-brow Brit. But now she wheeled around toward McQ with a grand gesture, fearing they were neglecting *their* patient.

"So what's the prognosis, luv? When do you get paroled?"

"Uh, tomorrow, I hope."

"'Brilliant. Here, this is for you."

With yet another expansive flourish, Dani whipped a small package from her mammoth bag of many colors featuring no discernible pattern whatsoever, other than a style that might be called *chaotic kaleidoscope*. Wrapped and ribboned, she pushed the package toward McQ with one hand and squeezed her friend's arm with the other."

"What is it?"

"Thirty-odd quid of the dark Viennese chocolate, that is. There ain't *nothing* that bitter Austrian chocolate can't cure, or at least make better. Now, I must bolt."

She kissed McQ on the cheek—her forehead remained concealed under that massive bandage. Dani stood on her tip-toes, raising her stiletto heels off the floor, and pecked Greigh's right cheek. Squeeze-twinkled both doe eyes and snap-patted his shoulders twice with both of her hands which were adorned with at least one ring on every finger and on both thumbs.

With a few parting words over her shoulder as she blew out of the room in a whirl of fabric and tinkling bracelets, she shouted, "A pleasure, *Just Greigh*. Q, you owe me a rematch. Give us a bell. Get well so I can kick your arse, girlfriend!"

AND SHE WAS GONE. THE DOOR CLOSED GENTLY BEHIND her. Once again, quiet descended over the smallish room. Greigh still stared at the door, rubbing off what was sure to be a mighty smudge of blood-red lipstick from his cheek. He said, "She's a force of nature, isn't she?"

"You have no idea. But she's a great friend. Maybe my only friend."

"Agree to disagree, Detective. After all, we've risked life and limb together. You and I, we've bonded."

Under her bandaged forehead, McQ blushed. Smiled. Mouthed one word Greigh could discern only by reading her lips, as if she were afraid to say it out loud for fear of jinxing the spell.

"Thank you."

Greigh tried to imitate Dani's Northeast London clip, "No wearies, luv."

CHAPTER 43

C ED 99th Precinct
Chicago, Illinois
2:20 PM

THE REPORTER DRONED ON AS IF BORED. BUT SHE WAS A veteran broadcaster who flirted with facts. She sounded and appeared enthused by over-inflecting her voice, cocking and turning her head from side to side in a too-predictable pattern, and too frequently. She was helpless to change. So sayeth the ratings.

She'd been in this game for far too long, and knew it. The wrinkles could no longer be covered up without some serious work. So, her neckline plunged. A diversionary tactic. Her days in front of the camera were now numbered. Just another disposable pretty face. Time to dial up the drama. Another diversion.

"Chicago Enforcement Department Detective Lieutenant Chance McQuillan was *savagely* attacked at the Hotel Literati yesterday in the Near Southwest Loop. Doctors expect her to make a *full* recovery.

You may recall witnessing Detective McQuillan's *riveting* plea for *more police support* on our show Monday.

"This attack, after the *brutal* murder of *famed* twenty-nine-year-old *inaugural poet laureate* Sybil Thibodaux just six days ago *in that same building*. Detective McQuillan is the lead detective on that case. Coincidence? Cover-up? *Conspiracy?*

"Some suggest that The Literati is already a *single-building crime spree.*

"We interviewed one of the Literati's condominium owners for their feelings who asked to remain anonymous for obvious reasons. This person said they *suspected* the building was *haunted* or *cursed,* possibly *both*—"

THE SCREEN FELL SILENT. AFTER CAPTAIN GRANGER HAD clicked the remote, she flung it onto her desk. It nearly slid off the far side at the feet of two contrite detectives.

"Who the hell leaked this? I want answers!"

She quick-paced in front of the media screen on her office wall. She glared and yelled at the sullen duo who stood fidgeting in front of her. McQ listened on comms from her apartment.

"Was this your doing, McQuillan?"

"You kidding? Absolutely not, Captain. You think I *like* having these media jackals squatting outside?"

McQ finished dressing, popped three painkillers for her epic headache, and realized she was screaming at her boss. As an afterthought, she shouted, "Sir!"

NINETY MINUTES EARLIER, McQ HAD CHECKED OUT OF THE hospital AMA—Against Medical Advice. No time to lounge around. She feared Granger would jerk the case away from her and put a putz like Johnson or that other guy on it.

The stench of stale smoke found its way up from Harrow's down-stairs, like always, but it seemed stronger today. That did neither her headache nor her mood any good.

That she lived above one of the oldest cop bars in the city was a well-kept secret. Until the press found their way to the alley-side stairway to her apartment in the last twenty-four hours. At least they weren't saying where that was over the air for fear of losing a slippery almost-exclusive.

She tuned the captain back in, who said, "Well, who, then? Who else knew about what happened to you yesterday?"

"I'm on my way to The Lit to question the only others outside the department who were in the loop on this—the building owners, the Brothers Donati. But I can't imagine this does them any good. I'll find out, sir. I need to figure out *why* someone would leak this. Gotta be more than just news of one cop getting knocked on the noggin."

She hadn't yet told anyone in the department about Luca Donati's encounter with the mob boss, Gaspari Copolla. Maybe it was nothing. If so, no use casting aspersions.

"Aren't you still supposed to be in the hospital, McQuillan? Oh, never mind. We're running out of time. Keep that writer around, though. He's sharp. I also got the chief to assign that uniform, McCoy—"

"McKenzie, sir—"

"Right. Get this done, McQuillan. We're coming up on a week, and you still don't have a single viable suspect."

Rather than correct her boss, McQ snapped out her response, grateful that Granger hadn't handed her case off in her absence despite having mandated another partner, a uniform, no less. But McKenzie was a good shit. She'd rather that have been her idea. But she couldn't agree more about keeping Greigh close at hand.

"Yes, sir!"

McQ hung up on the captain. She said, "Call 'Just Greigh.'" She smiled at the label she'd given Greigh in her contact list.

"Yes?"

"Hey, Greigh. You up for another visit with Vince and Luca? I'd sure like to know how the media learned of my assault so damn fast. Maybe they have answers."

"Meet me at my suite. Butler will let you in."

She double-tapped her temple to disconnect.

TWENTY MINUTES LATER, SHE WOULD HAVE PUSHED Greigh's doorbell if he had one. Knocking worked. Butler the Invisible said, "Yes?"

"It's Detective McQuillan."

Click.

The door sprang open an inch or two. She entered and closed the door behind her.

Click.

Did Butler just lock me in?

She hollered, "Hello?"

From the far side of the wall that divided the entryway from the living room-slash-kitchen area, Greigh said, "Come, McQ. I'm just finishing a call."

She wandered in. Ahead and to her left, Greigh paced behind his desk near that magnificent wall of windows. He stared at his desktop as he spoke.

"Yes, we'd like to speak with both of you. It's related to the investigation…. Alright. Thank you. Ten minutes." He tapped his temple and turned an admiring eye toward his partner. He was so obvious, sometimes.

She *was* fresh out of a badly needed shower, now with only a small bandage plastered to the back of her head. She had even slathered on some lipstick and slid into a clean pair of jeans. Not sure why.

"THE DONATIS?"

Greigh said, "Luca is not happy, but Vince recognizes the futility of not cooperating."

"Something about that guy. You sense it, too." Not a question.

"Luca is concealing something from us—possibly from Vince, as well. Look at this."

He motioned her over and pointed to the inclined portion of his desktop.

"What am I looking at?"

"The Lit's financials. Your captain got Mac a warrant while you were on your little vacation. He insisted I be given access."

Little vacation?

She no longer lurched to swallow the bait he dangled. At least, not this time. McQ smiled at her own minor victory over at least one emotional pimple.

"That was fast. Mac's a quick study for a uniform. And?"

"In a past life, I studied and practiced forensic accounting—"

"Of course you did." Nothing about this man shocked her anymore.

"Despite some clever financial maneuvering and camouflage, it is quite clear, at least to me, they've been on the verge of bankruptcy ever since the place opened. My analysis also establishes evidence of a long-term financial relationship between The Literati Management Corporation and Urban Entertainment, Inc. Yes, that's one of Gaspari Copolla's shell corporations. Regular transactions for over a decade."

"Well, we knew Copolla was involved. The boys're paying protection, or whatever they're calling it these days."

"McQ, the transactions are *deposits from* UE *into* LMC's coffers. And these are significant sums. The Donatis are not paying protection to Don Gaspari. The Don is protecting *them* with his regular and substantial financial support."

McQ's rust-colored eyebrows would have hiked up to her hairline if not blocked by a forehead of perplexed wrinkles—and the pain that would have incited.

"Well, isn't that special? Let's go talk to 'the boys' again, shall we?"

Greigh grinned. "I thought you'd never ask."

Sixteenth-floor Penthouse
Hotel Literati
6:10 PM

ONCE AGAIN, A CONGENIAL VINCE DONATI MET McQ AND Greigh at his private elevator as it swished open. And once again, Luca was nowhere to be seen.

"Greigh, we've seen more of you in the last few days than in the last several years. We must stop meeting like this." Vince smiled, but Greigh did not return the gesture.

"Oh, my. We're being serious. How may I serve?"

McQ teed up a response, and her tone was serious, indeed. "Where is Luca? We need to ask you both a few more questions. And yes, this is official."

"Of course, Officer—"

"Detective."

"Sorry. Is that where—?" He waggled an index finger toward the backside of her head where a bulky bandage clung to her hair. She had ditched the theatrical wraparound.

"Yeah, and I'm in no mood to dance. Your brother, please?"

"Of course." Vince's smile disappeared. He replaced it with an embarrassed expression. At least, that's what it looked like to McQ. Her head and neck hurt like the devil himself was repeatedly stabbing her skull while stomping on her side. She just wanted to get this over with.

Two minutes later, Vince appeared with Luca, once again wearing an apron.

Cooking again?

Luca said nothing as he approached them still standing near the entryway. Vince waved them over to their generous U-shaped sofa near the center of their huge sunken living room and directed where each should sit.

But McQ sat where she damn well pleased, which inspired a whole new level of discomfort. Luca stopped short of a defiant sneer as he pasted on a neutral mask, trying to look pleasant. He failed.

By the time they were all seated, the temperature in the room had already cooled. That was fine, too. She was here to rattle cages. She directed her steely gaze toward Luca.

"WHY ARE YOU IN BED WITH THE MOB?"

Three pairs of eyebrows shot up at the unexpected question. Her head-butt approach obviously surprised them all.

"And before you try to deflect me, I'm aware of the payments."

Vince pre-empted Luca's response, which was sure to be far too inflammatory. He knew how the man felt about *women*, especially those in law enforcement. They could be *so pushy*.

"Ah, Detective, you understand loyalties... the thin blue line and all that. It's no different outside the police force. The Copolla family are old friends. Our father, Anthony Donati, rest his soul, was once Don Gaspari's top lieutenant. This was long before the Copolla family transformed all their activities into legitimate businesses after paying their debts to society.

Signore Copolla took us under his wing when Papá passed, and remains a major investor. He sympathizes with how tough it has been for us to realize our vision for this grand old pile." He swept his arms wide to take in The Lit.

"And what is your quid pro quo?"

Vince did not hesitate. "We maintain complimentary apartments on the fifteenth floor for the family's use when necessary. That's it. Nothing illegal or untoward, I assure you. Now, allow me to ask you a question. What does this have to do with your case?"

"Perhaps nothing. We are investigating. Everything. Why didn't you tell us about all the walled-off spaces in this building, like the three service elevators on the south side?"

LUCA FIDGETED. HE HAD BEEN LISTENING TO HIS DOCILE brother answering questions spewing from this impertinent female's mouth. He could remain silent no longer, despite his brother's obvious wish that he should do so.

"Lady, why are you interrogating *us* instead of chasing down your murderer?"

"Luca, did you kill Sybil Thibodaux?"

In an instant, she had once again captured all three men's rapt attention. Luca glared at her. "What did you just ask me? How *dare* you!"

"Look, gentlemen, I'm proving a point. How are we to discover who the killer or killers are unless we investigate all avenues? That's why it's called an investigation. Now, one of those elevators—between the E and F columns of apartments—was used to transport the body to the crime scene. *And* they used it as an escape route. Into *your* basement, guys. You mentioned nothing about those elevators when we last spoke. I need to know why. Right now."

Though her voice was low, the gravity of her tone was unmistakable.

~

VINCE SAW THAT LUCA SMOLDERED. HE WAS ABOUT TO speak again, but Vince interjected before things got further out of hand.

"Detective, it may seem strange to you, but we had no idea those elevators existed. Nor the adjacent storage rooms. Nor the walled-over dumbwaiters that your officers reported finding after your attack. This is an ancient structure, and I guarantee she's not yet done giving up her secrets. Alright?"

She waited nary a beat. "Let's say I believe you. Were the building's blueprints conveyed to you when you bought the property a decade ago?"

"That is not something neither of us would know without consulting our facility manager."

"We spoke to Rhonda. She says she has no such documentation. Said she assumed you would have them in your private files."

"Sorry. If we did, we'd provide them. We have no way of knowing about any spaces that were closed off prior to our acquisition of the property. Why would we? It is not our policy to go knocking holes in walls—expensive walls—out of idle curiosity."

"Okay, guys, thanks for your cooperation." And just like that, she arose, turned, and headed up the two steps to the foyer's elevator at a brisk pace. Greigh got up, shook Luca's and Vince's hands, shrugged, and followed. He had not spoken a word since arriving. No sense starting now.

CHAPTER 45

What on Earth!

That entire conversation ruffled Greigh's dander. "McQ, are you *trying* to get them to erect legal barriers to our investigation, to 'lawyer up,' as they say?"

"Listen, Greigh. My head and my side are killing me, and I don't have the patience or tolerance for polite bullshit right now. They're hiding something. I just can't put my finger on it yet."

"I agree."

"Wait, what? You do?"

They'd reached the fourth floor in the penthouse's express elevator, where they switched to the main elevator—the slower and less private birdcage. Rode it back up to Greigh's apartment on seven. After reaching the privacy of 7D, they continued their conversation.

Butler granted them entrance. Greigh closed the door behind them. They made their way to the sofa in front of the fireplace, where they sat side-by-side, angled toward one another. Greigh's brow wrinkled as he spoke, emphasizing his point with an erratic index finger.

"I'm convinced Luca is hiding something, although Vince might be as much in the dark as we are. I'm glad you didn't mention Luca's clandestine rendezvous with Don Gaspari on Monday night. We don't want them alerted that you had at least one of them tailed."

"I thought you'd defend them." She scratched her head, fluffed her hair, avoiding her bandage, and then swept stray strands away from her eyes.

"Because they're my landlords? Know your onions, Detective." He grinned. "Whatever Luca or they both are concealing from us might have nothing or everything to do with our case. In any event, we do *not* want them hiding behind a big guns legal team funded by the Copolla family's deep-pockets."

"Oh crap, I hadn't thought of that. So that meeting was a bust." Her voice went flat, as if he had deflated her.

Greigh raised a now steady index finger skyward. "Not so. New question: what happened to the building's blueprints? New information: the Copolla family, maybe old Gaspari himself, view Luca and Vince as family. Now on the record: both brothers claim ignorance over secret access to the crime scene."

McQ's shrill response concerned Greigh. "But we still haven't nailed down any damn suspects!"

"Well, we do have Robin Bidok's DNA on your collar from your basement attack. He may or may not be Sybil's killer, but he *is* violent. That's a viable clue. But it is time to take a different tack. We focus on Sybil's penchant for the Voodoo arts. Any word on your inquiries about Sybil's family in Louisiana?"

"Oh, yeah. Before my bump on the head yesterday, I received comms that Sybil lived in a place called St. John's Parish in New Orleans. And you were right, Greigh. They dug into sealed adoption records. Sybil's birth name was not Thibodaux. It was Coincoin. Her biological mother is a woman named Zelda Zenaida Coincoin, who is an important Voodoo sorceress, whatever that means. They maintained the pretense that this Zelda was just Sybil's distant aunt. She claims Sybil knew no different.

"Now, get this. Some monster raped Sybil and killed her stepfather four years ago in Northwest Louisiana—all on the same night at some remote plantation museum. They didn't apprehend the perp according to NOPD."

"I wonder if that's why she moved."

McQ continued from memory. "Her biological father is out of the picture. They are all very private. No public evidence that Sybil even had any friends. Her aunt—her mother—has quite the following, though, at least by reputation. NOPD only gave us a general sense. They contacted her. She'll escort the body home. NOPD's sources say they're huge on tradition."

McQ had been staring at the dark fireplace in front of them when she swiveled her gaze after an odd silence. Greigh looked uneasy.

She said, "What's bothering you, big guy?"

"That they're 'huge on tradition.' And one of those traditions hints of retribution. Not unlike a Sicilian blood feud." He now looked down-right grim.

"Oh, shit. You mean like a Voodoo vendetta?"

"Precisely. We should find Sybil's killer before—"

"Yeah, before—"

"You should advise your people to be on the lookout for Sybil's mother and any of her known associates."

"Matter of fact, NOPD mentioned a few of those, including the two most visible from St. John's. Someone they call Obeah Man—"

"Oh, my. That's a Voodoo title of great respect, someone viewed as a spiritual leader and healer."

"Well, this spiritual leader's name is…" she referred to her wrist-Pad, "Clairvius Rincisse. And another popped, too. A Doctor Jacques Memeaux—a witch doctor of some notoriety—came up as a past associate, or at least an acquaintance of Ms. Coincoin. Some say her arch-rival. They're from the same neighborhood. But according to NOPD, 'not from the same side of the street,' whatever they mean by that. Those are the only two they thought worth mentioning.

"They advised that both should be on our radar. Just in case. Especially this so-called doctor who's got an extensive rap sheet—all weird misdemeanors."

"An obeah man and a bokor. McQ, if they both come here, that could spell trouble."

"Do I wanna know what kind of trouble?"

"Ah, the kind you get when you mix petrol and a lit match, or a militant priest and a cage fighter."

"Shit. I'll issue BOLOs."

CHAPTER 46

T hursday, June 28th
      Chicago, Illinois
   10:00 AM

SHE DID NOT LIKE CONSTABLES. ONE WEEK AFTER SOMEONE murdered her daughter, Zelda Zenaida Coincoin—Sybil Thibodaux's estranged biological mother—arrived at the ninety-ninth precinct as directed to claim Sybil's body. Sybil had only known Zelda as a distant, on-again, off-again aunt. Didn't matter to CED as this woman was the only known living relative of the victim, and the only person to claim the body.

With so many deaths in the city every day, they told her each of the larger precinct houses hosted its own cryo-freeze morgue and a part-time medical examiner who travelled between precincts.

Ms. Coincoin was also advised that the paperwork and transport arrangements would be completed the following morning at the earliest. Or it might take several days.

A detective would eventually need to ask her a few questions before they'd release the body. This made her very nervous. Many police were not to be trusted, especially those from outside her parish.

She did not know who to trust. So, using a prepaid comms they once called a *burner*, she purchased in New Orleans and carried with her to Chicago, she called Sybil's friend. Miss Sango had first notified her of her daughter's death.

SANGO MORI INVITED ZELDA TO STAY IN SHERWOOD AT THE Hotel Literati. It was the least they could do. Luca Donati himself authorized Sybil's mother and her entourage to camp there until they escorted the body home.

That afternoon, Sango met Sybil's mother and an older gentleman for the first time in the lobby of The Literati. Their four much younger friends—three men and one girl—stood at a respectful distance in a tight group, all peering in different directions. Incredibly fit, they all looked more like bodyguards or soldiers than friends or relatives.

After introductions, Sango hugged the regal woman of intense beauty who stood before her—crestfallen, but resolute. She sensed more than smelled or saw a musky aura.

Sango shook the older gentleman's soft and warm hand. She offered him a deferential bow. Force of cultural habit.

She led them to well-worn but comfortable chairs in an alcove off the main lobby so they might talk in relative privacy. The young quartet remained standing and were not introduced. They had spread out to establish a perimeter around the three of them as she, Zelda and the older man seated themselves.

"Now, Sango, me dear, you's calls me Zelda. And dis dear man, he be Clairvius Rincisse. You's calls him Obeah Man, someone dat commands great respect. Rightly so."

Zelda nodded toward the older gentleman with long snow-white braided hair and a clean-shaven face that exuded a rugged kindness. Without looking him in the eye, Sango's peripheral vision saw his eyes appeared bloodshot with yellowish whites. As if he had seen too much of life, but hungered for more. He nodded, but said nothing.

"You's now tells me how me daughter comes to pass, ya?"

Sango thought that an odd turn of phrase, as if this mysterious woman was lost in time with no sense of past, present, or future. She envisioned she was looking at an older version of her deceased friend, but more so, with outrageous fashion embellishments. It occurred to Sango she had never seen Sybil's hair out from under what she had called her tignon—she had pronounced it *TAWn-yon*—a woman's traditional turban-like head wrap.

Sybil was attractive, but her mother was stunning, perhaps in her mid-forties, with burning ebony eyes. They were huge, hypnotic. She wore no covering over her thick hair of long rope-like braids drawn together in a loose pony tail low on her slender neck. Bits of bright red ribbon and multi-colored beads adorned the mane of this lioness here and there, captured in her weave that seemed to sparkle from within.

SANGO FOUND IT IMPOSSIBLE TO DISCERN THE SHAPE OF Zelda's slender body, sure to be fit.

Wrapped in a loose-fitting gown, she moved and behaved like a cat, a predator on the hunt. Her intensity filled the space around all of them.

Those eyes.

And her head was in constant movement. Like a hungry jungle cat.

Sango worried. There exists ancient Japanese folklore of monsters within cats that come out at a certain age. Some believe they turn into beasts known as the *Nekomata* after a certain time.

They believed these beasts devoured human beings and killed just for fun, but more for revenge. Sango wasn't sure why this legend came to her from looking into the pain of this beautiful woman's dark eyes that *seemed* gentle enough, but that never stayed in one place. She could not shake a profound dread. Her instincts usually served her well.

She shook her head to clear her thoughts, not sure why she needed to do so.

Zelda nodded slowly as if to affirm Sango's unspoken omen.

With a clear head once more, Sango told Zelda and Obeah Man everything she knew. She shared all that she and Greigh had found in Sybil's apartment one week earlier. But she impressed upon them that her friend, Greigh, understood what they had found better than she.

"We mus' meets wi' dis friend a yours, den. And what was me Syb's las' words spoke to you, me dear?"

Zelda's huge black eyes burrowed into Sango's. She dared not hold anything back.

"She said something that made no sense to me: 'The devil's voice grinds salty gravel into a seeping wound.' Then, she fell silent, as if she had shared too much with me."

Zelda cast a meaningful glance toward Obeah Man. He spoke for the first time, like quiet thunder. "Did she say any ting 'bout keepin' a promise? Any ole ting atall?"

"What? Well, she mentioned a blood oath, and something about a sacrifice, but she more muttered this to herself than to me. That scared me. What's this all about?"

Zelda jumped in. "Dis mus' all sound strange ta you's, me dear. Jus' traditional Voodoo healin' arts 'n family affairs."

Then, seeing Zelda's forlorn gaze over some faraway horizon, Sango felt a lump rise in her throat as she whispered, "Sybil was so strong. I admired her."

"Ya, so. Me daughter, she a *fanm djanm*—a strong woman—dat sure."

A single tear tumbled down Zelda's left cheek, as if that was all she was willing to shed before her obvious inner strength launched her out of the chair like a panther on the prowl.

LIKE A *Nekomata?* STARTLED, SANGO AROSE, TOO. "OKAY, then. Shall we find a space upstairs where we can settle you and your friends? Lower Sherwood, the second floor, is nothing fancy, mind you, but it's off the streets, which can be very dangerous."

"Any place fer our bedrolls be fine, me dear. Our needs? Simple. Our wants?" Silence escalated in the already hushed lobby as they stood there... until, "We's be fine. We's a thankin' you."

In deference to Zelda, Obeah Man motioned her to precede him as they made their way across the lobby. Their colorful procession collected a few stares as they strutted. He muttered to Zelda, "After you, Doyenne."

Sango stewed in her own thoughts as they walked.

Unusual people. They carry themselves like royalty. Just like Sybil. But those four young ones back there? What is that *all about? They look ready for... anything. Like warriors seeking battle. Like... black Samurai....*

As Sango registered Zelda and her five companions' biometrics at the front desk, the scanning process concluded after a few seconds for each. All six scanned "green" for their DNA-based background check. The empathetic clerk explained the few rules during this process. The most important? No drugs and no violence.

Then, they all marched up a long flight of stairs behind a door just to the west of the birdcage elevator. Halfway up, they double-backed at a landing before proceeding to the next landing on two.

At the locked door that would grant them access to the second floor, Sango explained. "Now, as you approach this door, or the door one flight farther up, each of your biometrics—your personal body signatures—will unlock them for you. Zelda, you try it, dear."

As Sybil's mother came to within a foot of the door marked with a large "2" at its center, the door unlatched with a *snick*. She peered over her shoulder at Obeah Man standing behind her on the landing and shrugged. He did as well. They all passed through into the center of the broad second-floor hallway.

Zelda had come home. Such was the heaviness and closeness of the back alleys at the fringes of the French Quarter where

New Orleans tourists never dared to invade. That's where dedicated practitioners found her shop where every need for practicing the Voodoo or Hoodoo arts would be found. To fulfill any animate, inanimate, spiritual or metaphysical needs.

Yes, this Sherwood stank like home. The greasy haze in the dimness clung to the roof of her mouth and cleansed her soul. Little Sango told her she herself lived here for a time until she reached her stride and moved upstairs.

Ta Camelot. Where some coward jackal done murdered me little fanm djanm. Let de hunt begin....

Little Sango found them a space in a large room with a southern exposure where few others camped. Most preferred either the wide hallway or rooms on the opposite side of the hall—those with windows facing north. Zelda liked the vibrations of *this* space and told Little Sango with a mighty nod she approved.

ZELDA'S ENTOURAGE SETTLED AROUND HER. THEY ALL unpacked their bedrolls and sundries, but hard cases with shoulder straps remained closed and locked.

This all overwhelmed Sango, still mired in her own grief. Uninvited tears clouded her vision. She excused herself after promising to reach out to them later in the day.

Now, she needed to be alone.

"Me understands, gentle one. You's a good friend to me little Syb. She move too fast, an' life done run her down. Don' you make de same mistake, me dear."

With that, the much taller Zelda stooped down, kissed Sango on the top of her head, and pushed her shoulders away with a gentle shove and a warm smile.

Sango left.

Wondering.

And crying.

CHAPTER 47

Hotel Literati
Chicago, Illinois
10:10 AM

GREIGH WORRIED. AFTER McQ'S ATTACK IN THE LIT'S basement, she spent the night in Mount Sinai, recovering from a mild concussion and head laceration. She had checked herself out at her earliest opportunity.

Now, she would not tell him she nursed a jackhammer headache at her apartment. She refused to admit that, but he could tell by the sound of her labored voice on the comms and sudden catches that jerked her back into silence.

Earlier, she had given Greigh the key to Sybil's apartment, the crime scene. There might be clues in Sybil's papers. He had intended to do this earlier, but got distracted by the whole dumbwaiter affair.

He spent a frustrating hour dwelling on every square foot of Sybil's home, dredging up his own memories at the sight of such brutality.

Especially as he peered at the too-sparse, now-almost-black spots of dried blood that remained on the earth-tone rug where they discovered Sybil's remains. He set that emotional turmoil aside for the sake of the case.

Compartmentalized.

Best possible effort, anyway.

He discovered a few scraps of a paper journal's pages scattered in the living room and the kitchen. Even though torn into pieces, it appeared someone ripped them in rage from a single volume—a crudely conceived effort to conceal their contents:

> "... engorged with jealous rage..."
> "The poor man suffers with less than nothi..."
> "... in squalor, Sherwood is his only h..."
> "... now, something different..."
> "I fear for Robin's spirit..."
> "If only he..."
> "... but little hope of e..."

Greigh didn't doubt that one hand wrote all of these sentence fragments—Sybil's.

He collected them with care in a small bowl he found unbroken on the kitchen floor, not bothering with gloves since the forensics team already scoured everything for trace evidence. Took them back to his own apartment.

GREIGH SET THE BOWL ON HIS TABLE NEAR THE WINDOWS. Even though artificial, the trees on the balcony to his left soothed his still-agitated mood. The hazy sun enabled him to better examine what might be significant clues pointing to Sybil's killer.

Aided by a powerful micro-light for even closer examination, he arranged and rearranged the scraps many times before drawing a few cautious conclusions, or at least a set of working assumptions:

- The paper itself was an expensive parchment, which might mean these notes were important enough for Sybil to commit them to costly paper. He also confirmed these scraps all came from the same journal, if not from the same page. And she wrote them in the same distinctive color of ink—a dark crimson that appeared to be black until he exposed it to intense illumination,
- Someone was jealous of Sybil, likely of her success and/or fame, to the point of "rage,"
- The subject of her note—at least part of it—was someone named Robin. Had to be Robin Bidok. Sybil knew him. He lived in squalor on the second or third floor of The Lit—in Sherwood, but Sybil never had, so how had their paths crossed?
- Someone—probably this Robin—underwent some changes. Perhaps he was already a violent person who could be, what? Psychologically devolving?
- Sybil seemed to believe whatever relationship she had with this person, or this person thought he had with her, was all but hopeless, almost as if she was trying to help him,
- No mention of anything related to Voodoo, which may or may not be significant,
- If this Robin killed Sybil, it was careless to leave these scraps as evidence. Greigh speculated no criminal mastermind did this, but perhaps a reckless and deranged mind.

Here was a killer sharp enough to defeat forensic technology, but dull enough to leave such obvious clues?

No matter. They needed to find this Robin—yet another clue pointing at their first and only suspect. There was little doubt this was the Robin Bidok whose DNA they found on McQ's collar. McQ's attacker?

Greigh pondered his next move. Who could he trust *and* knew Sherwood?

Yes, Sango mentioned she lived there when she first arrived at The Lit.

CHAPTER 48

H otel Literati
Chicago, Illinois
11:05 AM

GREIGH KNOCKED WITH A GENTLE KNUCKLE. AFTER A momentary delay, the shuffling inside Sango's apartment grew louder before it stopped. No doubt she was checking her security panel before answering the door.

He realized Sango not only used a hidden camera to identify visitors, she also employed an intercom—like his own. Not sure where the camera was, he stared straight ahead at the door.

Had she had that installed? Or did she inherit all this protection from the previous owner?

"Greigh? Is everything okay?" The sound of her voice seemed to emanate from the door itself.

"Oh, ah, hello, Sango. Everything's fine. May I have a moment of your time? I have a few more questions."

"Um, sure. One sec."

He waited in the hallway. About thirty seconds later, the sound of several locks rapidly disengaging—as if an automated sequence—preceded Sango opening her impressive door—a reinforced laminated metal slab mated to a solid machined metal jamb with no less than six mammoth hinges, opposite four overly long and oversized deadbolts each a foot distant from its neighbor. With no knob in the hallway, he surmised she must disengage this monster from outside with her own biometrics. The panel inside confirmed that.

Bloody Hell! Funny that I only live a hundred feet east, in the same hallway, and I never noticed this fortress door before. You never notice the best security.

Sango did not look up at him. Her puffy eyes caught Greigh's for the briefest of moments. She offered him a grim smile before once again casting her somewhat vacant gaze downward. This strong little woman suffered.

Sango led him into her apartment—for the first time, even though she had been to his several times. He had imagined it differently. While the basic floor plan was like his and Sybil's, though both were smaller, changes made by this unit's previous owners could not have been more different. And because Sango likely used most if not all of her means to get into this place, she had done no substantive decorating.

She *had* draped a few oriental tapestries here and there, along with the careful placement of an elegant room divider. A token attempt at Feng Shui, perhaps, of Chinese origin, not Japanese.

Sango, or someone, had festooned each panel with ancient *kanji* characters on its translucent paper panes stretched within light pinkish-brown wood frames. Probably from the Japanese Cypress called hinoki. He recognized the subtle lemon scent of that traditional wood. Or were those characters *katakana* ideograms, maybe even the more contemporary *shinjitai*.

Greigh had not studied the Japanese language and its history for many years, now lost in a haze of higher priorities.

"Please, sit down, Greigh."

She motioned to one of two chrome and leather chairs that faced her fireplace angled toward each other. They were *so* not Sango. No doubt she bought the place furnished.

"My dear, I apologize for intruding, but I thought I'd share with you a clue I found in Sybil's apartment. I could use your help in deciphering it."

He waited. Allowed a protracted silence to deepen. He now wondered if this was a mistake. His friend looked terrible, like she had been crying. She had always been a fastidious dresser and a disciplined martial artist. Yet, here she was, disheveled. Not shaking, but quivering. And her place was a mess. Very *not* Feng Shui.

"Sango, has something happened?"

"I'm sorry. Sybil's death hit me hard, murdered right down the hall. I always imagined The Lit to be impenetrable. And today I met Sybil's mother. I feel like I've now absorbed her grief as well. I am truly shaken, Greigh. But I'll help if I am able."

She squirmed in the uncomfortable chair. Yes, she had bought this place furnished.

"I understand. You know I do. You are an empath. Wait, you met Sybil's *mother?*"

"Yes. An amazing woman. She brought a few friends to help her escort Sybil's body home. They're supposed to leave as early as tomorrow, but they're not sure. And Greigh, it is so sad that Sybil never knew Zelda Zenaida Coincoin was her mother. Zelda says that was 'for safety reasons'."

Greigh's pulse quickened.

"Listen, dear, I found references in Sybil's apartment to someone named Robin who lives, or has lived, in Sherwood. You've spent some time there. What can you tell me, if anything?

"Sherwood? Oh, my. That was two years ago, now. Folks who live there watch their own backs, and each other's. They come and go. Trust is a rare commodity down there. Most people who camp in Sherwood aren't desperate, but are likely to be needy and distrustful, even of Camelot's residents."

"You mean people like me?"

"Well, yes. People like *us*."

Now he squirmed. Wasn't sure why. Must be the chair. "Dare I ask you to accompany me to Sherwood, Sango?"

She sprang from her chair, marched to her windows with a sense of urgency, as if the view would suppress some unbearable memory.

Greigh knew that body language all too well. Sybil peered down toward Harrison Street, her view unobstructed—no balcony.

"Sango, I ask a great deal, but this clue could lead us to learn something about our first suspect. I'm hesitant to venture into Sherwood to ask questions, even with you.

"But I can only imagine how those folks would react to a police detective, and that will happen next. At least we're only a couple of civilians trying to help catch a monster. Will you help me find Sybil's killer?"

He arose and approached her. He stood close, but did not touch her. She stared down at the busy street below, over the roofs of low-rises on the south side of Harrison and beyond.

Greigh watched a fascinating metamorphosis creep over Sango. She transformed from a frightened, hot mess to a warrior in a matter of a few dozen seconds. Like the fighter who saved his own life on the street a week ago.

Clenching and unclenching her fists, she turned to look up into Greigh's eyes, hers now steady and resolute. The change that swept over this diminutive street fighting poet surprised him.

She said, "Greigh, I just came from Sherwood, settling Zelda and her friends for the night. That was *so* hard. Brought back a flood of memories, some good, some not so good."

She retreated within herself, but only for a few protracted moments. Then, "Give me five minutes."

A slow grin crept over Greigh's face as he risked squeezing the side of Sango's left shoulder. She smiled back and added, "I suggest you dress down a bit."

He looked down at the casual but expensive slacks he wore. She said, "Yes, and that lovely V-neck sweater as well, along with those almost-new loafers.

He said, "Yes, of course. Why don't you come to my place when you're ready?"

"Alright. First, we track down your clue. Then, we invite Zelda to Camelot. She needs to visit her murdered daughter's apartment. She deserves that."

"I bloody hate that."

"What? Why?"

"No, I hate the name *Camelot*. It sounds so... cheeky."

She dropped her gaze, then looked up at him with her head cocked, turned without another word and disappeared into what must be her bedroom.

He returned to his apartment to change.

Sango stood at the door to 7D. The latches *clicked* and the door sprang outward a few inches. She jumped.

Huh. I guess Butler recognizes me.

Ever since they found Sybil's ravaged remains, Sango had grown hyper-vigilant. Even more so than before. She hated how that felt, but what could she do? She entered and closed the door behind her to re-engage Greigh's locks. Butler beat her to the punch.

Click.

Two years earlier, Sango discarded the few clothes she owned when she lived in Sherwood. No getting rid of that smell. But she now wore the oldest outfit she still owned to blend in.

Not that we'll fool anyone.

Sherwood's residents could be skittish, at least they once were. Most still were. And this would differ from ushering Zelda and Obeah Man to the second floor for the first time. They were now going down there to ask hard questions. At least, that was the plan.

Greigh emerged from his bedroom off to her left. Like her place, its entrance was just inside the east end of his living room's window wall. She almost didn't recognize him.

The man was a chameleon. Every hair that had been fly-away clean, tied back and in place ten minutes earlier now appeared disheveled, matted, and shaggy. He looked like he was days or weeks downrange of a comb or a brush, much less a shower or even a sponge bath. He stooped as if he now bore the burden of the world on his shoulders.

He was a master of detail, right down to dirty fingernails, a ragged tunic she would never have imagined he would own, even ancient boots. One of their paper-thin soles separated from its upper at the toe box. As he approached, a musky odor washed over her."

"Oh, my. Greigh, you are no stranger to dressing down, are you, dear?" The transformation astounded her.

"Too much?"

"Quite remarkable. I would lose the stooped shoulders and zip up those atrocious trousers. Residents of Sherwood may be poor, but most have not lost their sense of dignity. Especially those who only plan to stay there for a short time, as I did.

"We were not all indigent, Greigh. Some just lacked sufficient means or opportunities. Also, leave that ragged cap behind. Then, your *disguise* seems quite appropriate. I take it you've traveled incognito before."

"A time or two. Shall we?" He offered her a gentlemanly bow and held out his arm for her to accept. She swatted it away.

"Okay, lose the country gentleman's manners. Let's just go."

He punch-shoved her shoulder, grinned, and shuffle-stepped to the door in front of her.

"Oh, you were joking? Hilarious, Greigh." She smirked.

This was what she needed—a wonderful distraction from moping around her apartment, crying her eyes out, now both for herself and for poor Zelda.

***Poor** Zelda? The Nekomata? Ha!*

CHAPTER 49

They descended into another world. The birdcage stopped at four. The next stop would be the Mezzanine, not three, not two. That was Sherwood, accessible only by stairs, or by freight elevator, and then only if approved by hotel management. Since there was no furniture in Sherwood, the only reason for rare freight elevator access would be for rapid evacuation purposes.

Sango and Greigh exited the birdcage to enter the stairwell just to its west, next to the penthouse elevator, and hiked down one flight of stairs to three. To get back up onto four, their biometrics would be required to open the door through which they had just passed. Back up to Camelot.

Yes, the Donatis and Camelot's condo owners took security seriously despite generous intentions.

The first expression that sculpted Greigh's face as they entered the hallway on three was a grimace in response to the potpourri of the day's odors. Not that it was noxious, but not what he expected.

It had been a while. Unusual cooking and waxy candle odors, smoke from fires and illegal tobacco assailed him. But most of all, the odor of too much seldom-washed humanity in an enclosed area almost caused a sudden dizziness. It always took a few minutes to adjust.

He whispered to Sango, "Heady stuff today."

Twelve-foot ceilings in the hallways and rooms helped, along with huge slow-turning ventilation fans. There were no doors on any of the rooms along the wide hall that stretched in both directions. And no electric lights. It just occurred to him he never knew why.

"I've often wondered. Why no lights? Power outage?"

Sango said, "In a manner of speaking. The Donatis' generosity cannot extend to paying utilities for non-paying residents. Some say the power disappeared after a batch of light bulbs did the same. Those bulbs are worth a pretty penny.

"I assume that's the same reason there are no doors. They were originally fitted with ornate bronze hinges, also worth a great deal on the street. Besides, doors can create tribalism. That can't work here."

Greigh aimed his flashlight at a dark shadow on the hallway ceiling, where he spotted no bulb *or* fancy fixture, just a vacant socket. That would never have occurred to him.

Sango leaned into her seething whisper inches from his right ear. "Greigh, put that thing away. Flashlights are rude here, but more to the point, that is a toy of the well-to-do, or worse, a cop's tool. Out of character. Okay?"

"Oh. Right, you are." He extinguished it and stuffed it into a baggy cargo pocket on the outside of his right thigh.

SANGO WAS ANXIOUS. SHE WANTED TO INTRODUCE GREIGH to Zelda, Sybil's mother, and her companions. She presumed they were still just one floor down on two where she had left them less than two hours earlier. There would be time, after pursuing Greigh's clue.

Just then, a voice squeaked from behind after they had ventured only half a dozen steps east of the stairwell door.

"Sang?" She wheeled around, surprised to hear her name from that voice in this place. A familiar voice.

· · ·

"Jerry? Hey!"

She rushed forward and threw her arms around a dirty young man with tangled medium-length hair, a pocked face, surprisingly nice teeth, and a frizzy man-boy's beard. It appeared his haircut had been self-inflicted some time ago.

"Oh, my gosh, I had no idea you still lived here."

They parted, but Sango's hands remained on Jerry's shoulders as she gazed into his somewhat cloudy eyes with affection. His hands rested on her hips. At just over five feet, she still looked down at this little wisp of a man-child. Greigh judged he had likely not yet witnessed his eighteenth malnourished birthday.

They stared wide-mouthed at each other in silence for a full thirty seconds before Sango shook her head, and patted his shoulders twice. They both dropped their hands, and she turned as if she'd just remembered who she was with.

"Greigh, this is my very old friend, Jerry. We don't really use last names. Before we came to The Lit together, he watched my back on the streets while I slept, and I his. Jerry, this is my friend, Greigh."

The two men shook hands with enthusiasm. Greigh said, "Nice to meet ya, Jerry."

Sango looked at Greigh in surprise as he spoke with a benign accent very different from his own. It seemed to fit just fine—the kind that would be accepted anywhere and not really stand out.

"You too, Greigh."

Jerry's eyebrows hadn't yet descended to normal. Now, the smallest wrinkle appeared in the center of his forehead, mid-smile.

"Sango, someone said you moved up to Camelot. That true?"

"It is, Jerry. And I apologize for no proper goodbye. But now, we're here to catch a killer."

It was Greigh's turn for wide eyes and a wrinkled brow. His head jutted forward. The chords on his neck pulsed. This was not lost on her.

"Greigh, it's okay. Jerry is one of the good guys. I've trusted him with my life more times than I can count, and I trust him now."

Jerry struggled to take all this in. "Okaaaaay. What's this about, Sang? A killer? You're speaking metaphorically, right?"

They stood in that dim hallway with flickering mini-can-fires and twinkling candlelight glowing in both directions and all around them. Sango grabbed Jerry's hand and swung it back and forth between them as they stood side-by-side—two kids in the playground sharing a private joke. She looked at Greigh. Her smile was genuine.

"Jerry is *the* master of metaphors and allegories, so naturally, everything fits into the context of those literary devices. Right, Jer'?"

The man-boy looked both a little embarrassed and proud at being considered the master of anything.

Sango squeezed his hand. "Jer', can we go to your spot and sit for a bit? I'm serious. Someone murdered a friend of mine upstairs on seven, and we believe there's a person living here, or who *was* living here that may be involved."

"Well, shit, you guys. Yeah, follow me."

They walked west all the way to the end of the hall. Sango imagined they were four floors under her own apartment by now, but on the north side of the building's central hallway. They turned right into a room at the end. No door, and twenty-five feet square. Three singles, including Jerry, and one couple shared that space in a small free-standing tent that had seen better days.

Everyone exercised care not to take overt notice. Communal etiquette mandated invisible walls of privacy between strangers who were all grateful to be here.

Greigh wondered about bathroom facilities in a place like this. He remained enthralled. The concept and successful implementation of a neighborhood like Sherwood had always fascinated him. He was a patron, like so many Camelot owners.

They approached the northwest corner of the space where a bedroll and a few sundry personal items lay beside it.

"This has been my spot for a long time. I like the light from the windows. Since it's a northern exposure, doesn't get too bright or too hot in the summer. A nice even light."

He pointed to where each should sit. He didn't offer them

anything, nor was anything expected. Once they settled in, Jerry spoke in the low tone that seemed appropriate and consistent with this place, "So how can I help you, Sang? I've never seen you so serious. Not even when we lived in cardboard boxes in the shadow of the Ida B. Wells."

"It's bad, Jerry. You've heard of Sybil Thibodaux?"

"The famous poet? Murdered, right?"

"Jer', she was a friend of mine, and Greigh's neighbor."

"Oh, shit. Sang, I am *so* sorry. Wait, Greigh? As in *Aubrey* Greigh? The mystery master?"

Greigh said nothing. He only nodded and darted his eyes around. Sango tamped both her palms down in front of her.

Jerry whispered, "Holy shit, you guys. Ah, oh, wow. Okay, then. Well, ah, what do you need?"

A lump rose in Sango's throat. She leaned forward and whispered, "Do you recognize the name Robin Bidok as someone staying here, Jer'?"

"No, I don't… oh, wait, that could be Robby, I guess. Never caught a last name."

Greigh spoke for the first time since their initial introduction. "Jerry, is he here now?"

"Oh, shit, you—?"

"We just need to talk with him."

"Uh, yeah, his spot is—or was—right through the door over there at the end of the hall on this side. Been gone for over a week, now. Left his stuff. Nobody's had the nerve to touch any of it. A proctor has been poking around the last couple of days. But I haven't seen Robby since. And that's weird. Most folks around here treasure their every possession. But I can tell you, he was a strange one. Scary, too."

Sango asked in a gentle voice. This was hard on her. "Tell us about him, Jer'."

CHAPTER 50

Jerry collected his thoughts. He whispered in his nasal soprano tone, "First, Robby fancies himself a poet, but other than rhyming a few words, the guy's a hack. My uninformed opinion. You'd know better, Sang.

"Plus, to listen to him trying to perform *any* of his work out loud is to contemplate blowing your own brains out, or better yet, his. Awful stuff. And Sang, you know how tolerant I am of mediocre talent, mine included. But this dude...."

Greigh said, "Do you know who he liked and disliked?"

"Oh, shit."

"Jerry?"

"Sang, he *loathed* your friend Sybil. He was obsessed. Talked about her all the time."

Greigh jumped back in. "How do you know this, Jerry?"

"You kidding? He'd rant on to anybody desperate enough to listen about how unfair *his* life was. Because *they*—females, female poets, specifically, and *especially* Sybil Thibodaux—got all the credit, even though *their* work could never compare to *his* brilliant verse. He'd go on, and on, and, well, even polite people would pretty soon tell him to shut the fu—, to shut up, including me. We watched each other's backs around that character. Sometimes he got mean. Vindictive mean."

Greigh glanced over his shoulder to the door opening. "You say no one has seen him for a week?"

"Or more."

"Since he's a murder suspect, do you think anyone would mind if I look at his effects?"

"Hell, Greigh, walk his shit right out a here, and you'd be a hero."

GREIGH UNTANGLED HIS LEGS. HE STOOD UP AND WALKED in a deliberate manner over to the pile Jerry identified as Robby's out in the hall. He intuited that sudden moves around here would be frowned upon. There was a certain reverence about this place. He did not want to startle anyone.

A piece of paper peeked out from under what might have passed for a pillow. He started reading a verse entitled *The Solo Horror Corollary*. He read the first line:

empty souls drip through near-clotted holes.

"Dear God...."

Jerry and Sango wandered up behind him.

Greigh said, "Sango, you're a poet. Take a look. Opinion?"

By the light of a small candle Jerry brought with him, she invested about fifteen seconds to peruse the page Greigh handed her.

She said, "Well, his theme is dark enough to niche his audience down to about a half-dozen people on the entire planet. But his technique, while amateurish, would improve if he dedicated himself to the craft. Jerry, is all his work of this ilk?"

Jerry read a few lines and shivered. "Well, I'm a visual artist, not a poet, but pretty much, yeah. Real bleak stuff that almost everybody hated. We do bleak around here every day. But this stuff...."

Sango continued. "Seems he is so enamored of himself that he'll never grow in his art. From what Jerry's told us, Greigh, and now what I've read, I'd bet this guy is pretty depressed, with low self-esteem, maybe even suicidal. But a murderer? Can't tell from what little we know. He seems just incredibly angry."

Greigh assumed they had identified a prime suspect, wherever he was. Still standing near Robby's effects, Greigh asked, "Jerry, what else can you tell us about Robby?"

"He's got this mouth-full-a-marbles twang for an accent. When I got the balls to ask him about it, he said he's from Louisiana. Never been there, myself."

Greigh and Sango snap-glanced at each other. Now, more energetically, Greigh rummaged through the rest of Robby's effects. Found a ragged and dog-eared pocket-size volume called "The Little Book of Curses and Maledictions for Everyday Use."

Bingo!

A quick scan of its table of contents revealed:

- Generic Revenge Curses
- Custom Revenge Curses
- Warning Curses
- Repudiation Curses *(earmarked)*
- Self-Curses *(earmarked)*

Two other books hidden under his bedroll included, "The Complete Book of Black Magic & Witchcraft" and "Book of Shadows."

Greigh showed them to Sango and said, "This guy may or may not be a Voodoo practitioner, but he is into the occult. He's looking better and better as a suspect. Jerry, if he comes back, he may be dangerous. Steer clear. Understood?"

"Yessir. You don't have to say *that* more than once." He and Sango shared a meaningful moment.

Greigh returned the books and the poem. He used a sleeve to cover his right hand and grabbed a smelly watch cap from the pile. Stuffed it into a cargo pocket on his left leg.

· · ·

GREIGH TURNED BACK TO FACE JERRY.

"Can you describe him?"

"Better than that. I drew his freaky ass." Jerry hustled back to his spot, rummaged for a moment, and came up with two sheets of cheap re-purposed paper. He handed one to Greigh. The drawing was so good it almost looked like a photo, but with a dramatic painterly vibe.

"Jerry, you are *talented*. If I were to need an illustrator for any of my projects, would you be interested?" Greigh smiled.

"Hell, yeah, Mr. Greigh!" His enthusiasm fueled a louder response than he intended. A few nearby heads turned. Some frowned. Like in a library. Jerry tossed a tiny apologetic wave and a shrug to his neighbors.

"It's just Greigh. Can you tell us anything else, Jerry?"

"Yeah, it was weird. The day Robby disappeared, a strange man in a creepy top hat visited him. You know, like Abraham Lincoln, for Pete's sake! I watched them. The dude spoke just a few words. Hell, more like barks. Couldn't hear 'em, though. Then, Robby just got up and followed him away. That was, what, nine, ten days ago?"

"Are you able to describe this man?"

Jerry grinned big. He shoved the second sheet of crappy paper with torn edges toward Greigh. Another near-photo.

Greigh grinned, too. "Damn, son, your pen and paper are better than a surveillance camera. Can I make copies of these? I'll return the originals."

"Naw, keep 'em. I signed 'em. And they are gen-u-wine graphite pencil drawings. Maybe worth somethin' some day."

Sango peeked at the second drawing and gasped.

IT WAS TIME TO BEAT A HASTY RETREAT. SINCE JERRY possessed no comms, Greigh gave him a card to connect later. Suggested he leave a message with the concierge in the lobby. Jerry led Sango and Greigh to the stairwell.

Greigh said goodbye with a hearty handshake, Sango with a hug.

CHAPTER 51

S ango seemed revitalized.

"Gosh, it was good to see Jer'. He is so talented, Greigh. He just needs a break. So, what do you say we visit the second floor and introduce you to Zelda Zenaida Coincoin?" She pronounced the last name 'KWAH-kwah.'

He said, "Yes, 'second-born daughter.'" Greigh began reciting information. Sango deserved to know. This would hurt.

"Sango, according to the local police in St. John's Parish, New Orleans—Coincoin was Sybil's family name. You should also be aware that four years ago, someone raped Sybil and killed her adoptive father, who tried to rescue her during the attack. They never apprehended the killer. Zelda is an important figure in the New Orleans Creole and Voodoo communities."

"Greigh! Stop! Too much, too fast!"

"Oh. I see. Of course."

"Someone *raped* Sybil? And *murdered* her father?"

"Adoptive father. Yes, Sango. It pains me to share all of this with you, but you have a right."

She fell silent. Dropped her head to her chest as they stood in the deserted stairwell landing between the third and second floors, between the gates of Upper and Lower Sherwood.

Greigh realized after a handful of quiet moments that Sango was sobbing. Her entire body rose from stillness to a crescendo of shaking, but she made no sound.

He felt awful, but they needed to do this next bit together, or not at all. This was the hardest part of the nasty job he'd volunteered to tackle with McQ. Leveraging a friend's pain to solicit information from the murder victim's grieving loved ones.

Who knows? Maybe in some subliminal sense, he realized he couldn't shoulder everyone else's sadness, along with his own, all by himself. What kind of person did that make him?

Needy?

An emotional chainsaw?

Sango was one of the strongest people he had met in a long time with the mind of an empath and the heart of a warrior. He seemed drawn to sensitive but strong women.

Even though most of them don't survive.

Greigh had already witnessed one incredible transformation from this woman today. He believed he was about to witness another. Sango did not disappoint him. Her profound grief only further strengthened her resolve, as he was convinced it would. He hated that he knew that. More so, that he leveraged it.

She wiped her tears away on the sleeves of her old tunic. Muttered in a gravelly voice thick with phlegm, "Let's just go talk to these poor people, okay?"

"Who is with Zelda, Sango?"

"Obeah Man and what I call several young *Bushi*—warrior-types. Four, I think. Yes, three men, one woman."

"Oh, my."

They descended the rest of the way to the second floor. As they passed through the door, the now-familiar odors and hushed buzz bombarded them. The air appeared... dense, translucent. Sango led the way to the room across the hall. Greigh realized they were precisely five floors beneath his own apartment, but a world apart.

Before they entered, Greigh noticed Sango once again looked like she had seen a ghost.

"What is it, Sang?"

"That man that visited Robby. I know someone who looks a lot like that, but older, and blacker. I'll introduce you."

ONE YOUNG MAN SPRANG TO HIS FEET. HIS COLD EYES followed the two strangers as they approached their doyenne—their spiritual matriarch.

He whispered, "Madame?"

Zelda sat cross-legged on the floor facing the southern sky through the windows. She swiveled her head, and her shoulders followed.

"Sango, me dear!"

Zelda smiled, nodded to the young man and his compatriots, who relaxed, but remained standing to keep a wary eye on the tall white man they'd not seen before. They all clung tenaciously to their staffs.

Zelda followed Sango with her head, but she tracked her eyes like a heat-seeking missile to the handsome stranger accompanying her.

"I can't explains it, but udders in dis room, dey packs up and leaves. We's no chase dems away, me dear."

Sango smiled at Zelda's speech pattern. Inflections in her voice were downright rhythmic, which eclipsed her unusual use of grammar.

"Are you quite comfortable, Zelda?"

"Yes, yes. Who be *dis* handsome fella?" She grinned… at least the corners of her mouth turned upward.

"Zelda Coincoin, this is Aubrey Greigh. Just call him Greigh."

"Like de color of de sky. Sit. Sit." She patted a space to her right on a spread-out bedroll. Greigh did as he was told. She directed Sango to her left.

∽

Obeah Man paced. Greigh's agitation was not lost on him as Greigh's eyes darted around at the young ones with them. Each was armed with a heavy walking stick longer than their height. They all remained standing, gripping those... weapons.

Zelda said, "Greigh, your eyes, dey tells me you has a kind but troubled heart, and you's be fearin' mighty, right 'bout now, ya?"

"Pleasure, Madame."

Zelda smiled at the affectation pronounced in the proper French manner.

"First, allow me to say I am truly grieved by your loss. And the world's loss."

"Ya, you's understands. You's has lost, too. Wife? Child?"

"Both."

Zelda's face dropped the societal smile. She reached for both of Greigh's hands with both of hers. He did not resist.

He had to admit that their shared grief introduced them not possible in any other way. Zelda pulled her left hand from Greigh's and clutched Sango's right hand. They sat in an oppressive silence of their shared grief, simply staring at the gray sky.

At last, Zelda squeezed their hands a little harder before releasing them. She was all business in that next instant.

"Now you's tells me what happened, ya?"

Impressed by yet another strong woman now in his life, Greigh shifted his hips to better look Zelda in the eye.

"Zelda, you will need to meet with the police, but we can come with you if you like." He watched her eyebrows creep upward. "I'm working with a detective that I trust, and she trusts me. You will like McQ. I will vouch for her."

"You's likes her. Dat be good. You's a color 'n she be a letter—gray 'n Q. A good match. What else?"

His eyes twinkled before they darkened. "We have identified a suspect. Someone who seems interested in dark magic."

"De Voodoo?"

"We don't know."

Greigh shared with Zelda the titles of the books they found in

Robby Bidok's bedroll. "He lived here, just one floor up, but he disappeared before your Sybil was... attacked."

"You's can say 'murdered', Greigh. Where be dis man, now? Zactly?"

"We don't know, but we believe he also attacked my detective friend McQ in the basement of this building. She survived. Zelda, did you conjure a gris-gris for Sybil?"

Once more, Zelda's eyes widened. "You's knows some ting of de art, me dear?"

"A little. There was also a vévé to Maman Brigitte inside the front door of Sybil's apartment."

Upon hearing this, the older gentleman stopped pacing and shared a meaningful glance with Zelda.

They know something!

"I lack de manners. Greigh, this be Clairvius Rincisse."

Greigh jumped to his feet fast enough to startle their youthful entourage. He turned toward the older gentleman, already standing, and now frozen in his tracks in response to the sudden movement by this tall white man.

"Obeah Man, I am honored to meet you, sir." He extended his hand. With slow deliberation, Obeah Man shook it, no doubt surprised that this white Yankee spoke mojo. The smile on his face was slow to spread, but it did.

Zelda smiled too, as both Greigh and Obeah Man sat down in unison.

She said, "Ya, Greigh, I makes de mojo bag for me little Syb. But who's be conjuring a vévé to Brigitte?"

Greigh's blood curdled. The time had come to take a chance. "Sango, please show Zelda and Obeah Man the picture that surprised you. Do either of you recognize this man?"

Sango handed over the drawing of the man with the top hat that met with Robby, the despondent poet, right before he disappeared.

Zelda only saw it at an angle and upside-down, but she snatched it from Sango. Her face contorted with anguish. She thrust the picture across to Obeah Man. It was clear they both recognized the man who looked like a younger version of Obeah Man, but was either white or of a lighter mixed-race complexion.

Nobody said anything for a full minute. Greigh waited.

"Greigh, you's knows 'bout bokors?"

"Witch doctors, for lack of a better label?"

"We's knows dis man. Sybil knows dis man. You shows me dis vévé. Now. We's talks more after."

And with that, Zelda arose and helped Obeah Man to his feet. They began quick-stepping toward the hallway, both now anxious. The two of them stopped at the doorway. They glanced back at Sango and Greigh, still getting to their feet.

Greigh said, "Zelda, we will go up to Sybil's apartment, but my Detective friend McQ must meet us there." He left no room for discussion on this point.

She shrugged and said, "We's goes."

Greigh rang McQ, who was already at the crime scene. He briefed her and implored her to show deference to the victim's mother when they arrived at 7F.

She promised to be on her best behavior.

CHAPTER 52

The entire group marched. Sango led them across the hall to the stairwell. They descended one floor down to the Mezzanine and transferred to the birdcage elevator as soon as it arrived. It took a while. Nobody tried to fill the awkward silence. The eight of them filled the old beast to near capacity. Got off at seven, turned left, and arrived at Sybil's apartment.

Two uniformed officers—Milligan and McKenzie—guarded the crime scene's door while McQ performed a more detailed search, as ordered by Captain Granger. The two officers came to full alert when they saw this mob up the hall now descending upon them.

Greigh led the way, and assured them all was well. He explained they were the victim's family. Milligan and McKenzie still kept their eyes glued to the four young toughs and their long sticks. They barred them them from entering the scene after Greigh, Sango, Zelda and Obeah Man entered. The young ones all looked to Zelda. She nodded. They stood across the hall at what looked like the civilian equivalent of *parade rest*. Situation de-escalated.

McQ exhibited compassion during Greigh's introductions to Zelda and Obeah Man. The forensics team had preserved the vévé inside the front door with a transparent spray-on fixative. This would peel off later to transfer the drawing along with the materials used to create it, as well as any organic matter present.

Zelda and Obeah Man stood conferring over the drawing. Several minutes later, as McQ and Greigh discussed the two paper drawings with Obeah Man and Sango, Zelda made a pronouncement.

Once more, she grabbed and snapped the paper with the index finger she launched off her thumb. "Dis man, he's done conjure dis vévé. Dis be Jacques Memeaux. We's not knows why he's be here. But we's *knows* me Syb would have *NO ting at all* to do w' dis man-bastahd. She *never* be askin' Doctor Jacques to conjure dis fer her. *Never. Garr-ohn-teed.*"

McQ said, "What? Then why is this here?"

Obeah Man spoke for the first time. His voice startled them all. Sango had heard him speak just once in the lobby during their initial introductions. His voice rumbled with authority as he walked further into the apartment. Left them all standing near the entryway as he spoke over his shoulder. "Dis vévé not fo' Sybil. Dis be a trick. Jacques work from bofe hands. Dis be dark mojo fo' money."

McQ said, "Both hands?"

Greigh explained. "Unlike most Voodoo experts, this guy will do whatever anyone pays him to do—good or bad, ethical or otherwise. Both hands. It seems Doctor Jacques Memeaux is a Voodoo mercenary. Sounds like the worst kind."

Zelda looked deep into McQ's eyes. Reached out, squeezed her arm to reinforce her sincerity. "Greigh speak de trufe. We's not bein' proud a Jacques. He's be Syb's age, but he's never likes her. He's be one reason why nobodies knows me be Syb's true mamá or Clairvius here be her true papá. Fer her protection. Our enemies be many. Jacques be one, dat sure."

GREIGH'S SHOCK ONLY LASTED SECONDS. HE SNAPPED HIS fingers. "No *wonder* Sybil was such a force of nature with parents like you." He grinned, but that faded when he remembered he was speaking to parents who had just lost their child.

Now that Zelda no longer saw any reason to hide their parentage, she leaned on her Clairvius with a tired smile.

"Our Syb, she's live many lifetimes in her twenty-nine seasons. Good rest, sweet child."

Both she and Clairvius—Obeah Man—bowed their heads and closed their eyes, standing in the middle of their murdered daughter's *living* room.

Nobody intruded on their grief. Finally, Zelda whispered, "You's talks wi' de Nawlins po-po. Dey gots cameras watchin' Jacques' shop in de alley off Rampart Street behind de Black Penny. Maybe gets you a look-see at somebodies be buyin' dis bastahd's black heart."

McQ's eyes brightened.

Another lead.

CHAPTER 53

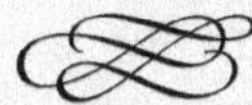

Clairvius Rincisse—Obeah Man—sat on his bedroll in Sherwood. Alone. Even though he was surrounded by strangers, friends and his lover. He, and he alone, carried the full weight of Sybil's past tribulations, and even the one that got her killed.

She never knew he was her biological father, only as a holy man of her faith. He had been her confessor her entire life. He remained in her life in this small but important way.

But she had developed into an independent spirit, even as a child. Their connection became so much more than spiritual. He learned she was raped by some Yankee carpet bagger four seasons earlier. And the laws of the land failed her. He said nothing. He could not. He could only console her as her priest.

They lived in a nation ruled by the white man's law and religion—as it had always been. America was a theocracy. Little separated church and state, not that he felt bound by the politics of any nation or anyone else's religion. That included Catholicism from the European part of his own heritage.

The state-nation they now lived in treated his people and their non-European heritage with disdain and intolerance, even ridicule.

Abortions were illegal in America. No exceptions. But the god of *their* understanding would never force his little Sybil to carry the demon spawn of the monster—the murderer of her adoptive father—to full term.

Yes, despite his belief in the sanctity of life, he arranged an illegal procedure to do what was holy, what went beyond the petty politics and deranged, self-serving dogma of man—white or otherwise.

Against his better judgment and his pleading, Sybil followed her monster, her demon, to this city. But she swore Clair to a blood oath of secrecy. And it cost her the life on which she placed so much value. After that night at Montrose by the Cane, that life was no longer her own, but belonged to her people, and to the cause of justice. Or was it vengeance? She passed over carrying this load.

Clairvius Rincisse—not Obeah Man, but the parent of a murdered child—vowed to relieve his baby of her burden, no matter the cost. As Sybil's confessor, however, he could never even tell the child's mother of his foreknowledge and abetting of Sybil's abortion or her more recent intentions. Yes, this was *his* burden to carry—alone... to his own grave. And beyond.

The burden was heavy.

SYBIL HAD FRIENDS IN HIGH PLACES. SHE HAD PERFORMED her poetry at the presidential inauguration of Marjorie Cullen, even though Sybil believed politics little more than a necessary sham. For the time being, anyway. Her friends respected her for her unvarnished honesty, but most for her beautiful and unrelenting spirit.

Sybil's inaugural performance had earned her a lucrative publication contract. They had showered her with invitations for more nationwide speaking engagements than she cared to entertain. Not to mention invitations to parties and events hosted by influential people she cared not for, but who had grown curious of the Louisiana Creole culture, her heritage, her birthright. That had made all this folderol significant and necessary to her.

Sybil Thibodaux had become an international celebrity, which launched her voice as a spokesperson for her people. She had envisioned all of this as her solemn duty—her cause célèbre. And so much more so after that night at Montrose. If the conflict inside didn't tear her apart.

AND NOW SHE WAS DEAD. OBEAH MAN WOULD SORT THIS out, and would leverage his considerable power and influence to do so. Neither would he shy away from leveraging Sybil's visibility and network here in Chicago and elsewhere.

With immense pride, this passionate father remembered her performance at President-Elect Cullin's inauguration six years earlier. Like most presidential inaugurations, it took place at the U.S. Capitol.

Broadcast worldwide, Sybil became an instant celebrity. She composed *"Loud and Proud"* for the occasion and performed it with severe eloquence to an audience of billions:

Before you, stands a small proud American, daring
To dream the pinnacles of expression, of freedom,
A whirlwind of blood and heart stirred and inspired
To rise above, to float in a fog by the sea, we swim,
To breathe the crisp mountain air, we climb
To drink in the flowering desert's scent, we walk
In a field that feeds the needs of a billion bellies.
We labor to love, we travel to seek, we dare to dream.
Our flag and our spirit may flutter, but fly for
Every single American of us, to be loud and proud!
While all around, a silent bitterness of slicing sacrifice
Tasted, swallowed, by so many, do we still dream?
Can we still ascend weary souls to dizzying heights
Of wonder? Of hope? We all aspire to freedom's fire,
The glow of hearth and home! In this great nation

Where we are free to choose the heavy hand of hate
Or the tender touch of love. We jealously protect
Our sacred right of freedom, to choose our fate
In the embrace of liberty and under justice for all.
Yes, we do so, loud and proud:
The red, white and blue, black, brown, and yellow,
A rainbow of hope, and freedom, and justice.
America the beautiful will never settle,
Built on bricks of hope. We shout this sacred oath
To one another with a small clear voice
That is loud and proud, and never to be silenced.

AND NOW, HIS LITTLE SYBIL'S SMALL CLEAR VOICE WOULD
never speak or be heard again, other than through her work.

Clair's faith was strong. And severe.

CHAPTER 54

They had made millions. Vince and Luca Donati were more than just brothers and business partners in the Hotel Literati for the past ten years.

Before combining their resources to purchase The Lit, Vince made his fortune buying and selling entertainment technology companies.

Luca produced fantasy vacations for the rich and famous.

Both fancied themselves erstwhile entertainers and passionate patrons of the arts, especially the written word as printed and performed.

Vince's stern but amiable personality exuded the impression he only cared about the business, but he loved the theater and had always been drawn to drama.

With sculpted good looks, but a brash personality, Vince needed to be the hard-nosed business executive and diplomat. His demeanor served them well with venture capitalists and investors.

Luca's elegant presence added a layer of sophistication to their partnership. He'd bubble with perpetual enthusiasm for the hotel, for the Performing Arts, his undying admiration for literary genius, and he maintained a huge soft spot in his heart for the starving artist.

He stood alone as Sherwood's foremost advocate. Vince tolerated that low-brow neighborhood within The Lit only because it was so important to Luca.

CHAPTER 55

Hotel Literati
Chicago, Illinois
3:20 PM

THE MAN WAS AN ENIGMA. WHILE IN THE PRESENCE OF Zelda Coincoin, Sybil Thibodaux's estranged mother, Greigh had only shared a few words with Clairvius Rincisse.

Everyone simply called him Obeah Man, a title of great respect within the Voodoo community. He was always at Zelda's side. And the discovery that he was Sybil's biological father meant that he might possess insights invaluable to understanding Sybil and why she was killed. At least, Greigh hoped.

Being an aficionado of Voodoo, and of the belief that Voodoo was central to the investigation of Sybil's homicide, Greigh wanted to spend some time talking with Obeah Man—alone.

Now that Sango had introduced them, Greigh walked down to Sherwood and invited the man down to the lobby for a discussion. He

247

thought Obeah Man would be more comfortable there than in Greigh's apartment.

He was right.

THEY SETTLED INTO AN ALCOVE

Greigh said, "Sir—"

That rumbling voice interrupted him. "Greigh, I's be honored if ya jus' calls me Clair when we's be alone."

"Ah, okay. Clair, may I ask why you kept Sybil in the dark about you and Zelda being her parents?"

"She's be raised by a wonderful man dat loves her as much, or more. Zelda 'n me, we's born into a life a service, a sacrifice. We's gots many friends, but many enemies, too. Dis be how we's protect her."

"What insights might you offer from what you've seen of the investigation?"

"Evil be near, Greigh. And not be born of de Voodoo. Somebodies wants you tink so."

This captured Greigh's attention. "Tell me more. Please."

"Sybil not has dat vévé conjured. Dat black heart, Jacques, he's done dat for somebodies else. Fer monies. Find him, 'n you find Syb's killer."

"Clair, someone or some thing spends time, or lives in the basement of this building. My impression? Human, but animal-like."

Clair had half-closed his eyes and gazed straight ahead, even though he and Greigh were sitting at right angles to one another. Greigh's last two words snapped his head up. He cast an intense gaze deep into Greigh's eyes.

"Animal-like? Stink?"

"Ah, well, yes. Just impressions. Musty, like a wet dog. Not sure, though, I guess."

"You's takes me der."

"Now?"

"Ya, please. I gots de hunch. De Voodoo arts not lost on you's,

Greigh. And you's knows dis part a de world, dis city, dis darkness. We's goes, before...."

"Of course."

With that, the old man jumped up, more spry than Greigh would have imagined. He turned and looked down at the still-seated Greigh with urgency.

"Okay, den, Greigh. We's go. Now." The man's entire body fidgeted.

The freight elevator that would take them to the basement did not stop in the lobby. So Greigh led Clair—Obeah Man—to the stairwell in an alcove west of the birdcage elevator. If Clair had been in the lead, Greigh'd be hustling to keep up. He could feel the escalating anticipation in both of them.

At the bottom of the stairs, they found themselves in the deserted basement. On the far west end, they came upon the two officers guarding the hole into the walled-off area where McQ was attacked. That led to the passage where a ramp led downward to the sub-basement.

Only... as they approached, they spotted both officers lay unconscious, or worse.

On instant alert, Greigh threw an arm in front of Clair. They stopped fifteen feet from the two prone uniforms, more in shadow than not.

"Clair, you wait here."

Greigh slipped his favorite knife out of his pocket Flicked it open. It gleamed in the solitary caged light overhead and behind them. He crouched and found a strong pulse in the neck of both officers. Just unconscious.

That's when the feral growl echoed from the darkness of the hole that led to the site where he had found the unconscious McQ.

Clair heard the growl, too. The old man flew past Greigh, slipping through the hole into the darkness before Greigh could stop him.

"Oh, bloody hell!"

. . .

GREIGH HAD NO CHOICE BUT TO FOLLOW. BEFORE HE DID, however, he grabbed a heavy flashlight from one of the officer's equipment belts and his service weapon after folding his knife and pocketing it.

Then, Clair's voice rumbled from the darkness, "You!"

Silence fell like an anvil into wet cement. Seconds dragged into half a minute. The darkness was complete. After stepping through the three-foot-square hole, Greigh saw nothing, nor knew where to turn, reluctant to light up the room with the officer's flashlight. Some instinct kicked in for fear of spotlighting Clair and placing him in further jeopardy. Then somewhere ahead and to his left, he imagined Obeah Man possessed surreal night vision.

"Obey me! You shall not—"

Greigh followed the sound of a grunt and another growl before he yelled, "Hey! I'm armed! *I will shoot you!*" He clicked on the light, swung it around and it silhouetted... not one figure, but two! One larger than the other. They both ran into the darkness. Well, one ran. The other quick-shuffled. That smell! The same as when McQ was attacked. That's when he saw Clair on the floor, not moving.

HE DRAGGED THE PRIEST—AN UNCONSCIOUS CLAIR— toward the light of the hole and into the normal basement as quickly as he could with just one arm. The other held the light. He had tucked the officer's gun into the small of his back—out of the way, but still within quick reach.

Clair was a big man. He regained partial consciousness and tried to help, but that only made Greigh's task more difficult.

Just before they passed through the hole, Clair pushed Greigh away. Got to his feet. Stumbled toward the light under his own power, but still groggy.

A stubborn man.

. . .

ONCE THEY WERE BOTH THROUGH, GREIGH TURNED OVER one of the uniformed officers to grab his police comms unit. It was McKenzie! Still unconscious, but starting to stir.

Greigh pushed buttons on the device. Found the push-to-transmit button and yelled, "Any police in the vicinity of the Hotel Literati basement, two officers down with hostiles in the immediate area. Send help at once. One man down is Officer McKenzie. This is Aubrey Greigh, a civilian. I repeat, send help. Two officers and a civilian require medical attention. Basement of Hotel Literati on Harrison. Out."

He dropped the radio. It clattered on the concrete. A voice squawked back, but he ignored it. He attended to Clair and to the two officers as best he could. But then he stood and pointed the flashlight in one hand and Mac's pistol in the other back through the hole into the darkness from behind the protection of its ragged edge. His finger remained poised just outside the trigger guard. There he stood, frozen in a state of hyper-vigilance.

Clair sat on the floor next to the injured officers with his head between his knees while also applying pressure to a gash on one of the cop's heads.

Three or four minutes later—it seemed an eternity—the cavalry arrived. Four uniforms with blood lust in their eyes waved weapons and lights in his direction and shouted warnings to surrender.

Greigh slowly set the pistol and light on the floor and raised both hands as directed. He said, "I'm Aubrey Greigh. I made the call. These men were attacked by two perps in there." He nodded toward the hole in the wall.

They still forced him to his knees and placed him in zip-cuffs behind his back until they sorted out the situation.

He understood. Contain and evaluate.

CHAPTER 56

After McQuillan's attack earlier in the week, a dozen uniforms had descended on The Lit's basement like a swarm of angry hornets. Someone—or some thing—had attacked one of their own.

Now, after someone down here assaulted *two* uniformed officers and a civilian just an hour ago, a full-fledged invasion scoured the basement. Plus, they invaded the ramp that led down to a sub-basement on the dark side of the hole in the wall. And out into the service tunnels that extended far beyond the boundaries of The Lit.

This grew into a search that included a CED mobile command post in The Lit's basement, with Captain Granger as the onsite commander. She coordinated the search that was executed by her regular *and* Tac Squad officers who were all in body armor and heavily armed.

McQuillan wanted in on the action, but Captain Granger *ordered* her to go home and to stay there. Granger was still pissed that McQ had checked herself out of the hospital against medical advice, but understood and appreciated her drive.

Granger thought this search was certain to be a futile exercise.

First, armed with maps that illustrated countless escape routes, Granger was convinced their offenders were long gone.

Second, even with advanced instrumentation, the odds of

searching every hiding place were next to nil. She wasn't even sure the city maps included all the older tunnels that they already knew existed.

And third, this exercise in optics took scarce resources off the streets where their presence prevented genuine tragedy from occurring—every hour of every day.

But she had no choice, and she lamented that her crime scene had expanded from square feet to square *miles*.

THE BASEMENT BLAZED. CAPTAIN GRANGER'S COMMAND post comprised a three-foot by six-foot array of six monitors that displayed the best maps available. Her forensic team provided eight 1,800-watt crime scene lights, each on a six-foot collapsible stand. Those fourteen thousand watts illuminated their entire area. And along with thirty nervous bodies, increased the ambient temperature by at least ten degrees.

Six operators with comms at workstations in front of the six big screens coordinated the search and updated the displays. The warren of tunnels radiated out from a point just west of their location, with branches and connecting tunnels every thirty yards. They'd do what they could.

This is just impossible! But the show must go on.

"OKAY, HUDDLE UP!"

Thirty officers surrounded Captain Granger in the spacious "normal" basement. All wore grim determination under their body armor.

She said, "We're searching for at least two violent offenders in this complicated search area. Keep your comms live, go where you're directed, and report when you've covered your designated sections in the search grid.

"I have assigned each of you to one of six teams. You should know your team number. Each team's leader will coordinate with their operator here on your designated team's channel." She pointed to the six senior search coordinators sitting in front of their control panels and big screens. They wore headsets in addition to their comms implants as backups.

"Assume armed and dangerous. Take no chances. But we are *not* on a kill mission here. Stay safe. Let's go."

Each of the six coordinators barked comms tests followed by deployment orders into their headsets to their respective team leader. All the team members illuminated their chest-mounted search lights and body cams in response. They readied their weapons and lights as they fanned out in the darkness beyond the hole in the wall.

Each team carried varied armament—one or two long guns, stun grenades and handguns all around with plenty of spare ammo. They weren't taking any chances. The sound of shuffling feet died away as the search team funneled through the hole and disappeared into the sub-basement that led to the tunnels.

For six hours, they searched. While two different teams found evidence of someone passing through their quadrants, they encountered no active threat.

One team figured they had found the site where Sybil Thibodaux's murder took place. They geo-tagged the location and passed it back to Command.

Then Captain Granger called it. No joy, other than finding the murder site.

Pack it in.

Return to command.

End of shift.

What a waste of two-hundred-twenty-eight officer-hours....

CHAPTER 57

This was *going* to happen. Sango and her scrap friend from Sherwood—Jerry, the visual artist—were determined to explore The Lit's basement themselves. Earlier, a small army of cops found nothing but a puddle of blood and a few pieces of old rope in an alcove —the killing floor.

They left four officers as guards at *the hole in the wall*. That's what everyone now called the crude entrance created by Greigh with a sledgehammer to access the walled-off part of The Lit's basement, even though the army of cops had enlarged it. You could drive a small car through that hole, now.

Only remnants remained of the sophisticated police command post just outside the hole. All that technology and manpower hadn't delivered any more clues, other than confirming more than one perpetrator existed, and they located the cubby where Sybil was killed.

Knowing Greigh possessed skills, Sango asked if he'd care to accompany them. He said, "Most certainly! But I want McQ with us, or they could accuse us of contaminating an official crime scene. And we need her gun with us."

He called McQ at her apartment. She said, "Yeah, the captain benched me. And all those resources wasted. Politics."

"Well, how would you feel about a more surgical off-the-books sortie that is far more likely to yield results, but at higher risk? These buggers may be long gone, but neither Obeah Man nor I think so. He recognized one of the bad guys when he was attacked, almost where you were assaulted. Something else is going on here."

"Obeah Man? Another attack? He *recognized* one of them? Good grief, you've been busy."

"I'll catch you up. Are you feeling up to another adventure, *partner?*"

"We are *not…* oh, what the hell. Why not?"

"We'll have two other civilians with us. Sango and one of her friends from Sherwood."

"Civilians? Sherwood?"

"I forget. You've been away from the action despite your best efforts. You already know Sango. She can take care of herself. Plus, we have an eyewitness who can identify the person who left DNA on your collar during your attack. Those are names and faces we can attach to two of these wankers, one of whom may be our murderer."

"*What!* Greigh, when were you planning on sharing these eyewitness accounts with me?"

"I just did. Look, Obeah Man thinks something else will happen soon. This is a holy time in the Voodoo world. The summer solstice on June twenty-first—the day Sybil was murdered—is a special day. And the week following the solstice carries even more significance.

"St. John's Eve is their holiest day, along with the rituals that follow. This is that time. They may disappear soon. We need eyes and ears. And if we encounter anyone down there, it would be nice to have the guy with us who slept next to the arse who attacked you, wouldn't it? Our witness's name is Jerry. He can also ID the other bloke for us —the Voodoo mercenary. Bring your gun, McQ. Just in case."

"Okay, I'll come, against my better judgement."

THEY MET IN AN ALLEY WEST OF THE LOADING DOCK ON the north side of The Lit. McQ brought McKenzie—Mac—who was still recovering from his own knock on the noggin while guarding the hole in the wall. But he now wore civvies... and packed his personal pistol... since this little op was way off the books.

Greigh introduced Jerry to McQ who in turn introduced Mac to Sango and the others. McQ did not look happy leading a kid like Jerry into potential danger, but said nothing. Besides, Jerry would lead *them*. She needed a break in this case. It was killing her, and her career. Plus, the only way to stop Jerry and Sango would have been to arrest them. Better they have a chaperone.

Nothing tops local knowledge.

An obscure vent behind several dumpsters just west of The Lit's north side loading dock was their entry point. Jerry dislodged its louvered cover. Said he'd slept in there "for awhile" and had indulged in a bit of exploring.

Jerry would lead them into the sub-basement, the tunnels, and, if necessary, the sewers. He said with a grin, "And no need to disturb the cops already down there. We'll pass well below where they're camped, guarding their precious hole."

Sango said, "Good, because I'd rather not get shot."

McQ smiled. "That's why you have a rogue cop with you."

Greigh thought that the tap on her head must have loosened up his favorite detective.

"Make that two rogue cops." Mac's crush on McQ was impossible to hide.

CHAPTER 58

They started with swagger. The rag-tag posse of three civilians and two cops made their way through thirty feet of five-foot-diameter ventilation conduit with Jerry in the lead. Greigh followed next and made a mental note to suggest the kid grab a shower when he got the chance. But nobody talked. They worried the cops guarding the hole would hear.

Neither could they walk. They waddled down the sloped conduit with its rounded floor. From there, they made their way into the sub-basement, a full floor lower and twenty-five yards farther west from the hole with the cops.

The heads-up display on Greigh's wristPad offered him a gleaming god's-eye projection of the known tunnels based on the city's archived blueprints he downloaded earlier. The HUD also displayed their location on the map projected in front of him, and "bread crumbs" so they'd be able to backtrack when the time came.

At the northwest corner of the sub-basement, another downward-sloping tunnel led to even deeper tunnels. Most of those had rounded *brick* floors and a few inches of black water that stunk like sewage.

"Do you hear that?" Jerry's young ears picked up indistinct noises coming from somewhere ahead of them.

Concerned for the safety of their trio of civilians, McQ said, "We need to abort and return with backup."

Mac said. "We could do that, LT, and we should, but do we want to go back empty-handed? Again? Personally, I'd like to reach out and touch the scumbag that likely tapped both of us on the head."

Sango said, "I am *not* going back. Jerry and I agreed we would see this through. So you do what you like." Jerry suffered from is own crush.

They all saw the crushing conflict on McQ's face in the dimness of their hunched-over shadows and reflected flashlight beams. This was her call. But she saw the fire in Sango's eyes, and believed her.

"Fine. *But we stay together*. There's a branch up ahead. Let's make sure nobody sneaks up our flank after we pass it. There could still be more than one of them down here. Let's go."

THE MAZE BECKONED. AFTER FIFTEEN MINUTES OF pressing forward and taking branches, McQ's light caught a reflection on the floor thirty feet ahead of the tight little group.

She kept them moving forward to whatever had thrown a glint back from her beam. As they drew near on high alert, she stooped down and prodded the small pile with her pistol.

Jerry said, "What *is* that?"

Greigh said, "It's a reflective body suit. What's underneath it, Q?"

She said, "Looks like strap-on shoes, but instead of soles, there are several two-inch spikes. What—"

"Q, that's how they defeated your crime scene mapper. Reflected body heat and disguised footprints. Besides, wrapped up in that shiny suit, complete with hood, goggles and gloves, no DNA and no temperature differential."

"Son-of-a-bitch!"

. . .

THEY STOOD IN A CURVED STRETCH OF THE NARROW tunnel with several intersections now behind them. The pile they'd been examining lay in a trickle of water at their feet.

That's when they heard shuffling and scraping, closer now, louder, and coming from both ahead and behind.

McQ barked, "Okay, everybody, we need a defensive formation. Greigh, you and me toward the front. Mac, you and Sango toward the rear. Jerry, you keep your skinny butt in the middle. And above all, *we stay together!*"

About the time they formed up with weapons drawn, the tunnel echoed with loud and sustained sounds in the darkness from both directions. Guttural howls grew deafening as they echoed and reverberated through the small brick sewer tunnel.

Jerry panicked. "What the fuck *is* that?" Greigh laid a calm hand on his shoulder and squeezed. This went on for thirty seconds as they remained stationary, waiting.

THEN, SANGO SHOCKED EVERYONE. SHE BROKE INTO A RUN toward their rear. Mac hollered at her over the blood-curdling din. She ignored him.

Mac shouted, "McQ!"

She saw what was happening. "Follow her, dammit!"

Mac did so, and Jerry took off after both of them.

"Shit. Okay, fall back, Greigh. We gotta catch up with them before somebody gets killed."

McQ and Greigh rounded the curve where a divergent tunnel joined theirs in time to see Mac coming up on Sango already in hand-to-hand combat with a… *creature?* The darting beams from their flashlights threw surreal shadows that confused them all.

Sango got the howling creature onto the ground, but it stabbed with an upward thrust into her chest. She fell on top of whatever that thing was. But the wild creature threw her dead weight off. On its feet again, it then confronted Mac as he drew closer and was about to thrust its knife into Mac's chest. He double-tapped the creature, center mass. Like he was trained. It dropped face down into the running water on the tunnel's rounded brick floor, slippery with slime.

Jerry stood only feet behind Mac as Greigh and McQ caught up. He said, "Holy shit, you guys. That's Robby, my neighbor from Sherwood. But there's something *really different* about him."

Robby wheezed for what sounded like his dying breath. His last act in life was to howl like a banshee from whatever Hell he crawled out of, or was falling into. But it warbled because he was screaming face-down and half of his mouth was under black water. Just desserts.

McQ kept her weapon aimed in one direction, Mac's in the opposite. Neither knew if they were still under attack.

Crumpled on her side on the wet floor, Sango bled almost black from a chest wound. Greigh rushed to her and cradled her in his arms. Foamy pink blood issued from the corners of her mouth. She said in a gargling whisper, "Did we get him, Greigh? Did we stop Sybil's killer?"

Greigh held her, already grieving the loss of another friend. "Yes, Sang, we got him. *You* got him. Just relax, dear. You're going to be fine."

She smiled. A long exhale preceded her last raspy words. "Then there is honor in this death."

And she was gone.

The next guttural howl was Greigh's. For several minutes, nobody dared approach. When he ran out of scream, he picked up his friend's small body and carried her back the way they came. He did not care about the potential for further danger. McQ broadcast their position and vector via her police comms, and that they were coming back up to the basement, toward the hole in the wall.

After several minutes of walking, they saw light beams ahead, followed by a voice. "Lieutenant McQuillan? Is that you?"

"Yes. I'm with another officer and three civilians, one of whom has been fatally stabbed. Officer McKenzie here will escort you back to a perp's body—to be guarded in place until my forensics team arrives. We believe there is at least one other perp down here somewhere. Location and status unknown. Assume armed and dangerous. Do not pursue. Recover and preserve evidence at the scene—a silver suit and a pair of strap-on spiked shoes. Officer McKenzie will show you the way to that, too."

One of the approaching officers responded as they approached, "Copy that, sir."

Mac said, "Copy, LT."

CHAPTER 59

F riday, June 29th
    Lower Sherwood,
Hotel Literati
Chicago, Illinois
4:24 AM

EVERYONE AROUND THEM SLEPT. ZELDA ZENAIDA Coincoin, Voodoo matriarch, looked into the yellow eyes of Obeah Man, revered Voodoo witch doctor, unofficial husband, and father of their murdered daughter.

She whispered, "Ya done seen him, sure?"

"I did, mon amí. Jacques done gone 'n did it."

"Merde. Dat don' do us or da practice any favors. Who's be his slave? And was it him dat done our little girl?"

Zelda's profound concern went beyond any fear of a negative light cast on her healing practice. She was grateful her Clairvius had survived the attack by Jacques' zombi boy. If Jacques had had more time with the boy, her dearest Clairvius would have been ushered into the presence of Bondye himself, into Vilokan, the forested island. She just refused to suffer another love lost, and vowed she wouldn't have to, not just yet.

Clair said, "Mebbe he kilt our Syb, but dat Jacques 'n his boy, dey ain't none too clever. Me din't recognize da boy. Only Jacques. But dat slave-boy done attack me *after Jacques done tol' him ta kill me*, Z. Dat boy, he already under de spell from jus' a few days of de medicine 'n mojo, but he cun't do it. Jus' knock me out. Jacques, he not even do right by Damballah Wedo. Din't even capture dat boy's zombi soul, not altogether. Dat Jacques, he's be a menace, dat sure. But he's tinkin' I be dead."

"Dey not find dat slippery devil, Clair. He's be long gone now dat his boy be dead. I just be glad dat you—"

"Now, Zelda, me dear, you don' do dat. We's be fine and we's got dem spells an' de loas workin' fer us, sure." He pressed his hand on top of the clenched fist she rested on her muscular thigh.

She converted her residual worry into profound gratitude, and something else. She allowed a single tear of happiness before they got back to business.

Grim business.

CHAPTER 60

*Who **is** this guy?*

McQ's research into her new civilian partner did not prove satisfying, but it succeeded in intimidating and mystifying her.

She learned that Greigh's father, a native Scottish highlander, was Great Britain's ambassador to Columbia. That's where he met, fell in love with, and married Greigh's mother.

She later immigrated to England with her new husband, Sir Benfield Greigh, where their son Aubrey was born.

McQ even found a short biography written about the young Greigh. At ten, he moved with his family to Edinburgh, Scotland. It seemed Aubrey had always had a passion for the written word. He completed his first novel by age fourteen. McQ thought about her passion at that age. Choosing the right lipstick and deciding which boy to bat her huge brown eyes at eclipsed everything else. Other than hiding from her asshole of a stepfather and his groping mitts.

Greigh attended Edinburgh Napier University. By the age of twenty, they awarded the very private Aubrey degrees in journalism, publishing, and public relations. Thus began his career as a *professional* writer.

A regular boy genius.

According to one revealing article about this emerging public personality a few years later, Greigh socialized when necessary—as mandated by his publicist. But his history and current behavior illustrated that he'd rather not. His was unusually private by nature. McQ found no social media presence other than a website and fan correspondence she learned was initiated and managed by his New York literary agent.

From his author bio, she learned that Greigh had studied light martial arts for years early in life, and that still fascinated him. He favored the practice of holistic medicine, whatever that was, along with the tenets of several eastern religions. But he was not a devoted practitioner of any religion.

Nor was Greigh an agnostic. Rather, the few public interviews McQ unearthed revealed that he believed most in the sanctity of nature, a glaring anachronism for a megacity dweller.

Now, McQ scratched her head when she learned Greigh had disappeared on month-long retreats twice a year—January and June—for nine years. She found no record of where he went or what he did. But upon his return, he'd write another book and shoot it off to his publisher. He completed his last retreat twelve years ago.

At thirty-four, Greigh was knighted.

He's a frickin' knight? Seriously? Explains the 'Sir'. But he downplays that. Hmmmm....

Greigh popped on the international feeds as the recipient of the *Knights Grand Cross of the Royal Victorian Order*. Reason: not publicized at the recipient's request.

McQ looked this up. This *KGCRVO*, as it was called by insiders, was awarded for "services rendered to the Monarch, an order of chivalry." In other words, Greigh did some huge personal favor for the King of England or his family, significant enough to be awarded a knighthood.

Jeez-Louise.

Greigh abandoned these twice yearly retreats. Two years later, he immigrated to America and married Melissa Calvo, now ten years ago.

He continued to write and publish two or three novels every year since, dozens of short stories or novellas (whatever that means), and co-wrote dozens more by collaborating with various ghost writers.

What the hell is a ghost writer?

McQ now believed Greigh buried himself in his work to hide from his emotions. This was one troubled individual for whom she felt both compassion and curiosity. She understood what a personal sense of profound loss can do to the human psyche.

But what makes this guy tick, now?

CHAPTER 61

T ihomir Leonov's Limousine
Chicago, Illinois
9:00 AM

H E MIGHT AS WELL BE A GOD. TY LEONOV LIT HIS FAVORITE Cuban cigar, a Montecristo Robusto—Limited Edition, of course. He smiled as the bluish-brown smoke curled and climbed toward the massive motorcar's ceiling before flattening into a layer of peppery tendrils.

Supreme confidence of his insular lifestyle enabled him to live by a set of rules different from those that constrained mere mortals. He acted daily with impunity, knowing his ambition and influence entitled him to any freedom he desired. If anything interfered with this basic premise of his life, it was an obstacle to be removed. That included the rule of law.

After all, he deserved his immortality.

. . .

A recent example—Sybil Thibodaux. She had been an obstacle. After seeing a picture of her in the feeds a couple of weeks ago, he made a point of seeking her other images and interviews. Saw her everywhere.

That tasty dark meat from before four years, now? She now in Chicago? And now she live here? At Literati? No way no accident!

Turned out his stooge—Vince Donati—just ended a steamy affair with this same woman, and now, he required this very vocal wench silenced.

Ty ordered her eliminated for his own reasons, of course. Not that she could ever have hoped to get anywhere near him, no doubt to seek her petty revenge.

Me and mine? No touch. Not now, not never!

She could have become an annoyance, nothing more. But her removal served him well on a grander scale with the use of a few... theatrics.

His stooge suggested a creative solution to both their problems. So far, the scheme proved to be genius. The police remained clueless. And his secret? Preserved. They blamed a madman possessed by jealously, that Voodoo zombie that made rhymes. Now, it seemed the police cleaned up that loose end *for* him.

Life is most good!

CHAPTER 62

A partment 7D
    Hotel Literati
10:00AM

One short step would do it....

The precipice on which Greigh lingered crumbled under his bare feet after a crazed Robby Bidok killed dear Sango. It seemed everyone close to him meets a violent death—at least the women.

First, Mel and his little Clance. Now, he felt responsible for Sango's demise the previous evening. His friend. And McQ would be dead now, too, if not for fate.

At a minimum, his detective friend was in the hot seat with her boss and with the District Attorney's office for getting a civilian killed during a police investigation, and for disobeying a direct order to stand down. Her job was on the line. They placed her on administrative leave her with pay pending a full inquiry.

Optics.

Madness.

But the loss of Sango, now? Just too much.

Bloody hell!

~

McQ NOW HAD FREE TIME. NO JOB, AND NO CASES TO worry about. Not officially. At least she still had a paycheck to cover her sister's care. Well, most of it. No overtime adders. More importantly, this was now personal.

She banged on Greigh's door.

Why the hell can't the man get a doorbell like everybody else?

She sensed Butler watching her as she looked in the general direction of where she thought "his" camera hid. Embarrassed that someone might overhear her talking to someone else's machine, she half-whispered, "Butler, I need to check on Greigh."

Nothing.

She kept banging on the door.

Still nothing.

Louder, "Greigh, goddammit, let me in."

The door's lock disengaged with a *snick*.

McQ didn't like what she saw as she rounded the left end of the entryway wall into Greigh's living room.

"Feeling sorry for ourselves, big guy?"

There he sat, sprawled on the center of his sofa, bare feet on the low table between him and his dark fireplace. A drink sat on the table —untouched—next to his right foot.

"McQ, what do you want? We're arse-over-tits on this whole buggered case. My friend is dead, and we're both out of it, alright?"

"Well, Mr. Famous Mystery Writer and expert on about every subject I've slapped you with, did you write a bazillion stories by quitting? Listen, Granger has assigned that idiot Johnson to take over *my* case since it's, and I quote—all but closed, except for mopping up the mess—end quote.

"I guarantee you Johnson couldn't find his ass with his own shit. He's a waste of skin. They're declaring victory. They have their killer—

Robin Bidok. Motive, means, and opportunity. A nice tidy package. Only a few loose ends to tidy up, my ass. But you and I know that is pure, unadulterated bullshit. The commissioner has already issued a congratulatory media release, for crissake. If we don't work this—you *and* me, Greigh—Sybil *and* Sango will be two more sad statistics.

"So, what say you get your head out from between your butt cheeks and help me find the real *who* and *why*?"

GREIGH LOWERED HIS BARE FEET TO THE POSH AREA RUG. Picked up his drink. Raised it to peer at the viscous yellow liquid in the crystal rocks glass and muttered, "When mourning ends, reality bites hard. May mourning never end."

After a few seconds of silence, he hurled the drink, glass and all, at the fireplace. Left a trail of Scotch and shards of crystal on the floor.

Startled, McQ quickly replaced her momentary fear with pity. This guy suffered. He was no cop and should enjoy the considerable fruits of his labors.

She rounded the low glass table, now splattered with liquor, sat down beside him, placed a sympathetic hand on his right shoulder. The lump in her throat belied her external confidence.

"Listen, Greigh, will you please consider this—for me? Even though you have no good reason? I need you, and maybe you need me... a little. At least as a friend who understands. You lost your family. I can't imagine. I lost my sister. She'd be better off dead. We both lost Sango. Shit."

Unexpected tears rolled down McQ's cheeks. Her voice had taken to quivering. She sniffled and tried to wipe her running nose. Dropped her head and surrendered to her own despair. She sobbed silently, still trying to suppress it.

Two big hands covered her left hand after she had dropped it from Greigh's shoulder to rest in her lap. Surprised, she turned to peer up into his eyes. They were no longer icy-blue, just blue. And misty. Like hers.

His right hand crept up and around to press her head against his. Like two grieving buddies. They both stared at nothing.

He croaked, "Friends?"

A damn burst. She sobbed openly. He did so along with her, but in silence.

The moment passed. They pulled apart. Both stared at the shattered tumbler that had cracked the fireplace's curved glass panel. An awkward few seconds preceded Greigh muttering, "Sorry—"

"Yeah, no... that never happened."

"Right. Whatever you say, Detective. Your sister?"

"Another time, okay?"

They turned to stare into each other's eyes, then the busted fireplace, then back.

"I never liked that bloody thing, anyway."

GREIGH ISSUED A SUBDUED CHUCKLE. MORE OF A *huff*. Then, McQ joined in. They both shook their heads. McQ ripped the remnants of the bandage still stuck to the back of her head and threw it hard now toward the spider-cracked glass panel. Made it about halfway.

She said, "Yeah, sometimes a little laugh helps heal deep wounds. A little."

He wiped his face with his knuckles and grinned. "Detective McQuillan, I had no idea you were a philosopher as well as an ex-cop."

"Shut up! I'm not an ex-cop just yet."

They both smiled again, both pushing and rubbing away tears that had no place in a homicide investigation.

Greigh tightened his lips and shook his head again as if to dislodge cobwebs in his brain and said, "Okay, partner, let's do this."

He gave her left hand a little squeeze before he stood and said, "I must fetch my thinking sandals."

"Thinking sandals?"

He hustled off to his bedroom, returning moments later... all business again. Sat down next to her on the sofa again, but with some distance between them. Strapped on his sandals.

"SO WHAT DO WE KNOW?"

"Greigh, we *were* making progress, even if it was at a snail's pace. Sometimes, that's how this works in the real world."

He said, "But all we have is a dead zombie, this Robby Bidok, conjured by a mercenary witch doctor who is nowhere to be found. And..." he cleared his throat with some difficulty, "another dead friend."

McQ tried to keep Greigh's grief from reclaiming his already cloudy judgment. She said, "Well, I can see why they like Robby for Sybil's murder. He hated and envied her. That's a viable motive. He was into all this Voodoo stuff. So was Sybil. We saw plenty of evidence that supports that as part of the MO. Robby could have hired this witch doctor to help him. That's means. And he lived at The Lit. That's opportunity. Plus, like Sybil and the witch doctor, Robby's from Louisiana. He's perfect for it. But too perfect."

Greigh leaned forward, scratched his chin with one hand and furiously drummed the fingertips of his other hand on the table in front of him.

"I know you're trying to keep me on the beam here. His motive *could* be viable. And his interest in the occult had him crossing paths with this bokor in Sherwood—Jerry witnessed that.

"*What if* Robby intentionally succumbed to Memeaux's methods that removed remorse from his repertoire so he could kill? He was sad enough, but he didn't kill you. Obeah Man either. Why not? That is not the profile of a brutal killer, unlike the brutality we witnessed on Sybil's body.

"Besides, he did not possess the financial means to hire anybody. Can you even find *any* financials for this homeless wanker?"

Greigh continued in a voice shaking with conviction, maybe remorse, too. "No, this Jacques Memeaux *recruited* Robby. Somebody else *hired* Memeaux to weaponize Robby, but we have no clue who. Or why.

"Plus, do we really think Robby, a homeless and penniless poet, possessed the intellectual wherewithal to defeat your CSM tech and come up with such a sophisticated plan to get into and out of Sybil's apartment undetected? Even with this Memeaux's help? Even if they find foreign DNA in that suit, they already have their man. No, McQ, we need to start over. We are missing a key piece of this puzzle. A big one."

He softly pounded his fist on his right thigh. Again and again, thinking hard. Tip of the tongue frustration. Like he knew they were close. Like he was still paying penance. For Sango. Or as if a little pain might help him focus his thoughts.

But encouraged by his renewed enthusiasm, maybe he was applying logic on the case as a balm. She said, "Yeah, you're right. Follow the money?"

"Well, we know the Copolla family has been subsidizing The Lit from its genesis a decade ago. But I don't see a viable motive for murder there."

McQ spread her arms wide. "What if we're missing some bigger picture here? How about we widen our search? What if we turned a forensic accountant loose on *all* the financials surrounding the case? The Lit's, Sybil's, the Copolla's, even Sango's, this Doctor Jacques, Zelda's and old Obeah Man, too?"

"You don't have a working badge, remember? Besides, acquiring warrants for all of that? A challenge even if you still *had* a badge, and we had much more to go on. But we do need a break here. That might turn up something."

McQ grinned. "My guess is that by now, Johnson's drowning in messy little threads, and scratching his head over all of it. The brass might call them 'just loose ends,' and Johnson may be a putz, but I'd bet my favorite pair of jeans he'd welcome any help we might offer. Granger will bend a few rules to finish cleaning up this still-sticky career eyesore. I'll make a call. She won't hang up on me."

"Brilliant. Meanwhile, what say we get inside poor Sango's apartment for a look-see before CED gets hold of it? They will get there sooner versus later, even though it's not a crime scene."

"Why, Mr. Greigh, that would not be legal, strictly speaking."

"Well, Ms. McQuillan, it would be morally reprehensible if I didn't insert myself as a private citizen to check on the well-being of my friend and neighbor's home. That faint odor of smoke in the hallway worries me. And if you happened to be in the vicinity at the time, well...."

"It would be irresponsible of me *not* to ensure *your* safety, being a trained law enforcement officer and all, badge or no badge."

"An *unarmed* law enforcement officer."

"Not true, strictly speaking." She pasted on a demure smile and patted a lump on her boot-cut jeans outside her right ankle, six inches north of her comfy loafers. She delivered a full-fledged Irish smirk.

Greigh grinned. He said, "A wonderful distraction. Besides, I've been itching to take a crack at that monster door and lock-array guarding poor Sango's apartment."

"Boys and their toys."

The contrived good humor helped. Might even have been therapeutic, even if it was factitious.

CHAPTER 63

Apartment 7B
Hotel Literati
10:15AM

Maybe we won't get arrested.

"Good grief, Greigh. This looks like the back door to a citadel!"

They stood before Sango's monster door to 7B. Greigh worried. His chief concern was the alarm system. Once he defeated the door, he'd have less than ninety seconds to disarm the alarm Sango was sure to have.

If he failed, this would be a fast snatch 'n grab of anything relevant before the cops arrived. With their historical response time for homicides, if Sybil's case was representative, he figured they'd have at least twenty minutes for a potential burglary—*if* it was a *silent* alarm connected to a security firm whose mission it was to alert law enforcement.

McQ believed they'd arrive sooner than that.

If the alarm *wasn't* silent, neighbors would come running. Since

Greigh was a neighbor, he might offer to stand by until the police arrived, as if he were an innocent bystander. By then, though, they'd be long gone—two doors east to 7D.

Upon sharing all these thoughts with McQ, she grinned and said, "A sound plan. You think like a burglar. Or a lawyer"

THIS WOULD BE A CHALLENGE. GREIGH COUNTED ON THE spacious hallway being deserted mid-morning on a weekday. He laid out his extended kit on the hallway carpet. For this lock, he chose a proprietary device of his own design, half the size of a brick with its own three-inch screen that included selection menus.

Sango's biometric lock required a hack that fooled its programming to "believe" she was physically within a few feet of its sensors, alive and well. McQ looked on. She didn't need to mention that she was both incredulous and inquisitive. That was plain to see.

Greigh said, "I've done some contract work for companies that manufacture and program such locks."

"Of course you have." Her eye-rolls or mental head slaps had become a routine reaction around this guy.

He chattered while he worked, "Lacking legitimate access, we pop traditional pin and tumbler locks with either a master key or a bump key. Likewise, all bio locks possess a finite number of software 'bumps.'

"When aligned, they release the equivalent of pins from tumblers. Just as if Sango were standing close by. I select the lock manufacturer's name from this list to wirelessly interact with the manufacturer's brand of biometric sensing. They each use similar but proprietary algorithms. Just have to pick the right set.

"My device then tries every bio-scan variation, including tens of thousands of select DNA categories in nanoseconds. Most of these locks use only sixty-four simplified genetic DNA chain segments based on how the installer configured—that is, taught—the lock during installation. Much like trying every possible combination and permutation, but executed so rapidly that it seems almost instantaneous. The entire process takes only a matter of half a minute to set up and another twenty seconds of execution time.

Clack, clack, clack, clack.

"Bingo."

FOUR BOLTS RELEASED. THE HEAVY DOOR THAT HAD NO knob or key slot, only invisible sensors, eased outward. Greigh darted into the apartment, seeking Sango's security panel. There was a monitor and an electronic lock release, but no alarm. That surprised him. Odd. All the better.

McQ closed the door behind them—there *was* a knob and sensor pad on the inside. They went to work.

She scoured the kitchen and the single bedroom. He searched Sango's bookcases and desk. In a locked drawer he opened with ease, Greigh found a leather-bound paper journal. He called to McQ, hoping this might be the lead they sought.

Seven minutes had elapsed since they entered Sango's apartment, and it would seem no alarms were raised. So, they sat down on the sofa, shoulder-to-shoulder, and started pouring through his deceased friend's journal.

Greigh said, "Her writing style is quite formal. She recorded the date of each entry with rigor."

McQ wasn't surprised. "You know, Greigh, many women, unlike most teenage girls, are likely to keep something more formal than a simple diary, like a journal. I do the same thing. I'll record something in my wristPad most often as a way of keeping track of significant things that have happened in my life. Looks like your friend did that as well, only on paper. Old school. Like her friend, Sybil."

Greigh thumbed through the pages with dates that preceded and followed Sybil's murder. He stiffened. Shot his eyes up from the book to look at McQ as she looked at him.

"Oh, bloody hell! You will *not* believe this."

· · ·

SHE WAITED. HE KEPT READING TO HIMSELF, TOTALLY absorbed. She punched his shoulder. *"What, already?"*

"Listen to Sango's entry dated June eighteenth, just three days before Sybil's death:

"'I feel so empty. Sybil's brief affair with someone she calls V ended badly. She wouldn't say who that was, or why she both started and ended that affair. Says V can be a gentle soul, but also a paranoid beast. He begged her to keep seeing him. He said he was coming into a pile of credits. Of course, that did not interest dear Sybil. He accused her of using him—of toying with his affections. He fears she will tell someone about his bi-sexuality, and said he could not bear that. Apparently, V still loves L with a passion. But if L knew of their affair, it would crush him as L can be so jealous. V fears that would devastate L emotionally, and would 'create the most dire consequences,' *whatever that means.'*

"And she dated this entry June twenty-third, two days after Sybil's death:

"'... The last time I saw Sybil, she said something under her breath, 'The devil's voice grinds gravel into a seeping wound.' That frightened me, but I have no idea what she meant. She also told me about a white boy from her home state she'd been trying to help, but he was too far gone. And he was under the influence of someone she called the left hand of evil. All too strange.'"

Greigh looked up from Sango's journal, fell silent in his astonishment. His mouth hung open.

"Holy shit, Greigh. We have suspects. Brothers, my ass. Let's go."

"Wait, Q, there has to be more. Why would an international celeb and activist like Sybil pursue a sordid affair with a local bi-sexual innkeeper? That makes no sense."

"Maybe she was lonely."

"And all the Voodoo stuff, which we now know was a smoke-screen? I could not write such a poor story line, at least not one that ends here, not even if I tried. It's all too... cheeky. But *why?*"

"Truth is stranger than fiction?"

"Oh, come now, Detective. This doesn't stink like gutter rubbish to you?"

"Yes, it does, Greigh. But we follow the evidence. Or Johnson does."

"Agree. But is this evidence, or just hearsay? It is circumstantial only, *and* fruit of the poisoned tree since we are not cops and we didn't acquire this info legally. What do we do now?"

McQ rubbed her chin. Her eyes widened. She snapped her fingers.

"If we put this book back, and leave without a trace, that idiot Johnson *has* to find it. I'll tell him I have some insights he should leverage. We can aim him in the right direction."

"Why don't you think he is a competent detective?"

"You know the type, Greigh. He's an apple polisher and has Granger fooled. Barely. But as a detective, he's a stumbling clusterfuck —pardon my French. His skills as a detective are limited to following someone else's leads, and then taking credit for them if he gets the chance. Even then, he requires supervision, or he'll screw it up. He got his gold badge because his uncle is an influential alderman."

Greigh hoisted a conspiratorial smirk. "What if we chose an alternative approach, you and I? This journal is likely to surface, regardless. In the meantime, we might think more like private investigators than coppers. We continue to carry out our own investigation—privately. Granger still seems to be fond of me. As a neutral party and your former consultant, I will offer tidbits to Granger and Johnson to keep things on track.

"Look, Q, if we crack this case, it's possible we get you back in the good graces of the department and the DA. And you were right. I owe this to Sango. *We* do. What do you think? Ever have the desire to be a private penis, as they say?"

"Private *dick*, Greigh." She would have smiled, but he saw the concept conflicted her. She had been a by-the-book cop for a long time. This was a gigantic leap for her blue blood.

She muttered under her breath as if she feared being overheard,

"But if we get caught, we're talking obstruction of justice. Both of us. I'm curious why your friend Sango didn't share all this with us. Or at least, with you."

"It is my experience that the Japanese are honor-bound in a way we cannot understand. She likely made an oath of silence to Sybil by which she felt bound. Perhaps even to keeping all this in confidence after her friend was murdered. That must have been excruciating.

"It also could explain her almost maniacal—even reckless—compulsion to overcome her emotions in seeking justice for Sybil. She'd consider that 'unfinished business.' She even uttered the word, 'honor,' in her dying breath."

Greigh's sudden intake of breath did little to disguise his resurfaced anguish.

"Q, I want nothing *but* justice for my friend. Sango was helping us with this case—*your* case. Hell, she still is from the grave. She saved my life. You know what that feels like. I owe her a debt impossible to repay."

That was a not-so-subtle reminder that he had saved *hers* days earlier, implying that both of them had riveting reasons to throw out the book—at least for now.

McQ stood. She paced back and forth in front of Sango's fireplace. Then, turning to Greigh, who still sat with the journal open in his lap, she said, "Screw it. Let Johnson find his own clues. We'll help him find this book when we're done following these leads."

They left no sign they were ever there.

It was time to interrogate "*V.*"

CHAPTER 64

Apartment 7D
    Hotel Literati
10:35AM

"Yes?"

"Vince. Good morning. I have news and want you to be the first to hear it. Could I have a word with you at my place?"

"Good morning, Greigh. Well, I'm rather occupied—"

"Please, Vince. You will want to hear this. And Vince, please come alone."

"Well... certainly, Greigh. I'll be there in a few minutes. 7D, correct?"

"That's right. Thank you."

McQ AND GREIGH STOOD IN THE WOODS. THEY overlooked the city from the perimeter of the artificial forest on his covered balcony.

McQ said, "I can't get over this. Like I'm standing in a park or something. Today's air quality is even decent enough for our little party. You get him out here. Put him at ease. That won't last long."

She rewarded Greigh with a devilish grin and a playful punch to his left shoulder as they stood there planning their interrogation.

He smiled at her. "Well, aren't *we* a chipper kipper?"

He turned away from McQ toward some indistinct spot facing the apartment's window wall. Said, "Butler, record all audio from the time our guest arrives until he leaves. And say nothing. I don't want him to realize you're listening."

"Alright, Greigh."

"McQ, you take the lead. I'll be his mate."

"Good cop, bad cop? I just love being the bad cop, even though I'm not a cop."

"For the time being. And Vince isn't aware you've been suspended."

"Not suspended. Placed on administrative leave. Six a one. In any event, I will *not* add impersonating an officer to the DA's charges, or however they might choose to slap my wrist again."

"But it's not illegal for him to *think* you still have your badge tucked under a flap somewhere." He grinned—as he so often did around this woman—without growing guilty about it. Not really. Not much. Anymore.

Butler announced, "Your guest has arrived. Shall I admit him?"

"No. I'll greet him. Thanks, Butler. Now remember, mum's the word."

GREIGH APPROACHED THE GLASS WALL. TWO POTTED TREES bordered the slider. It swished to his left and closed behind him after he passed through into the living room. He left McQ to get seated on one of three cushioned settees.

Two of the short patio sofas faced each other under a dais out on the balcony that was tented overhead and on three sides. The open side faced the railing and the southern viewscape of the city south of Harrison.

Between these two settees on this raised platform that enabled a better view sat a third settee. It faced the railing some six feet distant. In the center of this C-configuration, a low stone-topped table was laden with a simple all-white porcelain tea service.

The antique set comprised a large teapot under a traditional cosy, three cups, a sugar bowl, a creamer, and three silver spoons that laid atop a trio of overlapping linen napkins. A small silver tray heaped with a dozen scones nestled nearby.

All very proper, all dairy-free, and all sugar-free, of course.

GREIGH OPENED HIS FRONT DOOR. THERE STOOD AN impatient Vince Donati in the hallway with arms crossed and fingers drumming. Like an impatient landlord. A pleasant expression, certain to be artificial, gave his otherwise handsome features a petty and unpleasant demeanor.

"You have no doorbell." Not a question.

"Vince, so good of you to come." Greigh extended his hand. Vince was slow to uncross his arms to accept it.

"Please, come in. I have tea and scones for us on the balcony."

"Oh, well, that sounds fine. Thank you." That softened him up. A little.

"And I promise I won't take much of your time, but new information has come to light that I wanted you to hear of first."

Greigh led him into the apartment and across to the balcony. As they approached, the glass slid open. Swished closed behind them.

Vince wrinkled his forehead. "I'm just a little confused. I saw the commissioner announce on the morning feeds that they caught poor Sybil's killer last night, right here in our basement. Some sort of Voodoo vendetta? By the way, a nice shout-out for your assist."

Greigh hooked an amiable right arm into Vince's left and led him to the railing side of the dais. His visitor reeled when he caught sight of McQ.

"Oh! Detective!"

"Just McQ, Mr. Donati."

Vince turned his head, not his torso, to look up at Greigh who still held his arm, as if he feared Vince might otherwise escape.

"Ah, I thought we were to be alone, Greigh."

"No, Vince. But we wanted to chat with you without Luca." He offered Vince a convivial pat on the back.

"Why on earth—?"

Greigh released his arm, motioned for him to sit on the settee opposite of McQ. Greigh sat between them, in the center of the third settee facing the railing, and interrupted. "Tea?"

Vince and McQ responded in unison, "No thank you." Greigh poured himself a cup, achieved just the right color with almond milk, sat back, and waited for the show to begin. He maintained a helpful but disinterested expression.

This would be good.

McQ STARED AT VINCE IN SILENCE. SHE LEVIED AT HIM one of those dead-eye cop stares with a hint of curiosity and a dash of suspicion. The kind that precedes a proper interrogation.

An eternal half-minute later, she smiled and said, "Nice tie."

Vince shot his right hand to his already perfectly knotted powder-blue Hermes. It rose from the vee in his tweed vest to the elegant collar of a silky shirt that reminded her of melting French Vanilla ice cream—with a stiff collar. She smiled at that thought.

Let's butter this muffin.

"You enjoy fine clothes, don't you, Vince? That gorgeous jacket alone must have cost more than I make in six months."

Now he squirmed as he sank into the settee's canvas-like cushion. "Well, I do take pride in my appearance." He shot his cuffs and crossed his legs to render the mirror polish on at least one of his custom Oxfords more visible. He obviously didn't relish where this seemed to be headed, yet his ego absorbed the compliment. He shot a frigid glance toward Greigh, who just shrugged.

"And you are downright handsome, t' boot, Vince."

A nervous smile crept across his face. He glanced at his antique Patek Philippe watch, signaling he really didn't have time for this tomfoolery. He now cast a more suspicious glare over at Greigh. Then, he looked back at McQ straight across from him. She seemed at ease… and smug.

"Thank you, Detective."

"Just McQ. Now, your time is valuable, so let's get right to it. Who ended your affair with Sybil Thibodaux? You or her? Before you answer me, Vince, you need to wonder whether I already know the answer."

Vince jumped up so fast, he bumped the heavy table in front of them with both knees, spilling Greigh's tea that still sat in front of him—untouched. Vince winced, but said nothing. Glared first at McQ, then at Greigh, who just shrugged. Again. Vince ran the fingers of both hands through his wavy salt-and-pepper hair, tugged once more at his perfect powder-blue tie.

"Sit down, mister!" Her cop voice.

Here we go….

FLUSTERED AND FLUSH, VINCE WRESTLED WITH A MOMENT of indecision. Greigh saw him trying to decide whether to rush out. No doubt he wondered whether he'd even be allowed to do so, or to stay and find out what else they had.

Q was on a roll. "I bet you're now wondering what else we have, aren't you, Vince? You must be boiling inside about how all this looks. You engaged in a sordid affair with a beautiful young woman who was murdered right after she dumped you. In my business, we call that a helluva motive.

"You're a muscular guy who owns the building where your secret lover was killed. We call that means.

"And you spent time in her apartment. Did you even have your own key to that old-fashioned lock on her door? And that, my friend, completes the trifecta of motive, means and opportunity."

McQ was enjoying herself.

"You must appreciate what that says for you, Vince, m'boy. You have just become our number one suspect in the murder of Sybil Thibodaux. Now, why don't you tell us where you killed her? We know it was somewhere in this building. And how did you get her body into her apartment undetected? That was *very* clever, by the way. If you cooperate, I'll speak to the DA on your behalf."

As McQ spoke, they watched the prim and proper clothes horse devolve into a slouching, sloppy, sweaty mess. He tugged too hard at his tie, which now hung in a blousy loop—loose around his neck and too much of it pulled outside of his vest from yanking on it side-to-side.

The genesis of sweat stains appeared at his now-unbuttoned starched-stiff collar. He ran his fingers through his hair. But this time, it was against the grain. He looked like a wild man.

Who starches a silk shirt?

"She called you *V,* didn't she, Vince? She thought you a gentle soul, but knew you could also be *so* paranoid. Why is that, Vince? You tried to keep her from dumping you by promising her a pile of money. I wonder where that would have come from, what with all you spend on clothes, and the deep guilty you and your brother forever struggle with just to meet expenses. Yes, we have your financials from within your shells.

"I'm curious, Vince. When did your love for Sybil turn into a hatred so cold that you needed to cut her lovely little body to ribbons and dump her corpse like so much trash? That took some time and planning and a bitter heart, didn't it, Vince?"

"Wait, wait! You've got it all wrong. I could *never* hurt Syb. I *worshipped* her. She was the only woman I have ever loved!"

McQ kept pressing. "Well, help me out then, Vince. She *used* you, didn't she? That must have pissed you off. But for what? And why would your *brother* be *jealous*? Because he isn't your brother, but your *other lover*? Your *husband*, Vince. Have you tied the knot? Made your union legal? Doesn't matter, does it?"

Now a steaming heap, Vince muttered, "Oh, dear God." He planted his forehead in the palms of his hands, his elbows perched on his knees. Greigh pitied him. McQ was carving this bloke into bite-size chunks.

"So let's say you didn't kill Sybil. I might swallow that if you loved her as much as you say. Even after she used you and left you. Are you *only* guilty of cheating on your husband? Luca can be insane with jealousy, right? Did *he* kill Sybil, Vince?"

He jerked his head up, looked across the table at McQ. Some epiphany had just occurred to him. His eyes hardened down to wrinkled slits.

After a deep breath and a sudden steely gaze, he said, "So, Detective, if you suspect me or Luca of killing Sybil, why aren't we at the police station? Why am I sitting in one of my owner's apartments sipping tea?"

Greigh said, "Neither of you are sipping tea—"

Both McQ and Vince turned toward Greigh and said, "Shut up!"

He looked down and muttered, "Ah, right."

Vince continued, his voice spewing spite. "And it occurs to me that in the police commissioner's media conference this morning, he announced that some other detective would tidy up the remaining loose ends, or some such. Are you still even *on* the case, *Detective?*"

McQ looked like she was about to reach across the table and rip out Vince's throat, so Greigh jumped in.

"Vince, shall we just go upstairs and see what Luca thinks about all of this?"

Greigh had never seen Vince's venomous glare, but there it was.

He said, "From now on, you will speak with neither me nor Luca without our attorneys. And if you do, I will sue your smug Irish and Scottish asses for defamation and harassment. Do you understand me?" Vince stood without awaiting an answer and bolted for the door.

Before he had even descended the three steps of the dais, McQ lobbed one final grenade, as if it was merely an afterthought, "That it? No consideration for 'the most dire consequences imaginable if Luca finds out about the affair?' Sybil's words, Vince, not mine, you smug son-of-a-bitch. Don't leave town, but please, God, just leave us. Greigh, I do believe I'll now have that tea you offered earlier."

Vince froze in his tracks. He stood below the dais without turning before hustling from the balcony, and through the apartment to the front door. His anger drove him to slam it so hard the latch failed to catch.

He left it.

～

GREIGH POURED McQ A "CUPPA" BEFORE PULLING A DEVICE from his jacket.

McQ said, "Is it working?"

"Like a charm. With a nod to my IDF friends, I planted *two* tracking-slash-listening devices on his person. In case he finds one of them or takes off his coat. I stuck one under the collar of his jacket, and one inside the back of his vest's collar. I don't believe I've ever seen him not wearing that boorish vest."

"IDF friends?"

"Oh, yes, well, I've worked with some good folks in Israel's Defense Force in the past, and they have the most marvelous toys. They—"

McQ grinned. "Of course you have. Hey, this gum-shoe stuff can be fun. Less politics."

"Does that mean you're ready to pounce onto the street?"

"Good grief, Greigh. The expression is *hit the bricks*. Yeah, let's go slap some shoe leather."

"Come again?"

"Never mind. Let's find out if we rattled his cage hard enough."

Greigh smirked. "American English!"

CHAPTER 65

L obby
    Hotel Literati
11:00AM

THEY HID IN PLAIN SIGHT. McQ AND GREIGH SAT IN ONE
of the eastern alcoves of the posh but outdated lobby of the Hotel
Literati. Raised by two steps and separated from the main lobby by a
brass railing, these cozy areas featured lower ceilings, overstuffed
chairs whose legs sunk into deep-pile carpeting with well-worn traffic
patterns. These conversation nooks glowed golden from soft tabletop
lighting. All of it painted an intimate atmosphere, but with a clear
view of the entire lobby.

Greigh had paired both their comms implants to the multi-func-
tional device in his lap—*his* favorite gadget.

"What's the range of that thing?" She nodded to what she called
Greigh's "half brick." Its small screen offered its own soft glow.

"Should be good to five miles, but that's line of sight. I'm receiving
Vince's location. See?"

He pointed to the small "V" on the screen—his location relative to their "G". That's when they first picked up audio over their comms, courtesy of Greigh's listening/tracking discs.

"Send a car. Now."

Would have been hard to miss the brittle edge on Vince's voice.

Greigh said, "He's leaving his sixteenth-floor apartment. This gadget does not do three dimensions. That's why I'm showing him stationary. He must be descending in his elevator."

McQ registered concerned. "He'll have a car waiting out front."

"I anticipated that."

"Naturally."

"Yes, well, I asked Butler to ensure my auto is out front, standing by. One just never knows."

"You've done this before." Not a question.

He pointed at the screen once more as they leaned into each other to view it. "Ah, see? He transferred to the birdcage and we should see him soon."

VINCE DONATI EXITED THE ELEVATOR. HE WAS FAR enough away from where they sat that he didn't spot them. As he bolted through The Lit's ten-foot-tall entry doors, they watched him enter a chauffeured limo outside. They bolted out behind him as he pulled away.

Greigh pointed to their left. "There. That's mine."

While she ran toward a brand-new Bentley Continental, McQ exclaimed, "You gotta be kidding me!"

As they jumped in, he executed start and manual drive commands. McQ amused him. She lost interest in tailing Vince Donati, consumed by feeling and smelling and sinking in, like she'd never before experienced automotive opulence.

They pulled out from under the hotel's ornate porte cochere and kept a one-block interval in the light traffic. Most who still found it necessary to travel now leveraged mass transit. The city completed their upgrade to all of the Chicago Transit Authority stations a decade earlier, and the trains were now state-of-the-art magnetic levitation—clean, safe, smooth and fast.

Vince headed uptown. Either he wasn't on speaking terms with his driver, or he didn't know him. Either way, the man didn't utter a single word en route. They imagined him still seething from McQ's tenderizing and grilling.

Ten minutes later, after crossing under Michigan Avenue, the limo rounded the block and pulled to the north curb on East Monroe.

"The Watchtower building?" McQ wrinkled her entire face in confusion as she read the magnificent sign out loud. A glistening modern-art sculpture of ten-foot-high brushed stainless letters stood near the center of an expansive plaza fronting a glassy skyscraper. "What's there?"

Greigh snapped his fingers and said too loudly. "Watchtower! Ty Leonov! Shite be on the Saints!"

"Who?"

"Watchtower *is* Tihomir Leonov, a Russian immigrant billionaire—land and real estate developer. He specializes in large commercial projects—everything from skyscrapers to stadiums to...."

"Oh, bloody hell, McQ. He oversaw a massive commercial canal project in Louisiana three or four years ago. It made the national feeds. A great deal of controversy."

"*Louisiana? Oh, shit!*"

"Precisely. Coincidence? Not likely."

"What's his connection to Vince Donati?"

"Now? I have no idea. But when I was president of The Lit's home-owner's association three years past, Watchtower made repeated attempts to buy The Lit.

"At the time and since, rumors of Watchtower acquiring other properties around The Lit circulated. The Lit's HOA, subsidized by the Donatis—and we now know by the Copolla family—retained a fleet of attorneys to prevent a hostile takeover.

"Watchtower even tried to acquire the Donatis' bank note, no doubt also subsidized by the Copolla family, or at least by Gaspari Copolla himself.

"After I lost Mel and Clance...," Greigh caught a quick breath and swallowed a lump, "I rather lost track. Didn't seem so important anymore."

McQ waited a few beats. "So, what does all that mean?"

"My dear Q, we may have stumbled onto our bigger picture here. From my three-year-old perspective, there is no reason for either of the Donatis to have *anything* to do with Watchtower. *Nothing.*"

McQ said, "Well, something's changed. Luca meets with Gaspari without Vince's knowledge. Now Vince meets with someone at Watchtower, and I'm guessing Luca isn't aware. I wonder if Vince is meeting with Lenin— "

"Leonov—"

"Yeah, if he's meeting with that guy himself— "

"Doesn't matter. That he's in that building at all? McQ, this is a bloody break."

He smiled, and almost without thinking, reached across the Bentley's center console and squeezed McQ's left hand. She squeezed back. Then, back to business. They both pulled away, lost the smiles.

"So, what do we do now?"

CHAPTER 66

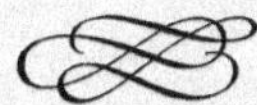

Greigh grinned. "Q, my 'half-brick,' as you call it, will record whatever it can detect in there. Should be well within range." He nodded toward the Watchtower skyscraper.

"You up for some more nice and not-nice police action?"

"You mean, 'good cop, bad cop,' Greigh? *How* long have you been in this country?" She giggled at his crappy attempt to sling American cop slang.

Greigh looked surprised at first before he joined in. He screeched the Bentley away from the curb, pulled a U-turn on Monroe, and bolted back to The Lit, down on Harrison.

"Holy crap, Greigh. What's the hurry?"

"I want to catch Luca alone if we are able, while Vince is occupied at Watchtower.

They pulled up under what Greigh called the hotel's porte cochere. McQ considered that to be a pretentious label for a fancy and expensive covered drive-through for the hotel's front door. It was nothing other than a portico for the few cars and limos remaining in the city, and even fewer that came to The Lit.

Greigh left the car and tapped his comms. "Butler, have the car garaged, if you please."

He double-tapped to disconnect a second later as he *ran* through the lobby to the elevator and up to four. McQ hustled to keep up. While they ascended in the birdcage, Greigh called the Donati penthouse. He was breathing heavily.

"Hello?"

"Luca, this is Aubrey Greigh. I need to see you *right now*. It's about Vince, I'm afraid."

"What? Is he okay? What's going on?" Luca panicked, as expected.

"Please, just unlock your elevator. I'm on four."

"Very well."

Since the penthouse elevator already rested at four, no doubt from Vince's hasty departure earlier, mere seconds passed before the door opened.

Swish.

Thirty seconds later, they had ascended to the sixteenth floor. The door opened. There stood a frantic and fidgeting Luca Donati, first worried about what might have happened to Vince, and a nanosecond later, pissed that Greigh had brought *that woman.*

He stood there, now with his arms crossed, performing some sort of arrogant head wobble as he spoke. "What? What is *she* doing here?"

Greigh grabbed Luca by the arm and led him into the spacious living area and down to their U-shaped sofa that nestled in their sunken conversation pit.

"What are you *doing?*" He tried to pull away from Greigh's grasp.

"Luca, please sit down. It's about Vince."

"Yes, you said that before. *Is he okay?*"

"For the time being. Do you remember when I was president of your HOA and we were concerned that Watchtower was trying to buy The Lit from under you? Even though you and Vince weren't willing to sell?"

"Of course. You helped prevent a hostile buy-out, so to speak." Luca's expression softened a degree. "Vince and I told you we would be forever grateful. *What about Vince? Please,* Greigh."

Both men had rather forgotten about McQ's presence. She still stood, at a distance, a silent observer.

"Luca, can you imagine any good reason Vince would meet with Ty Leonov?"

After an astonished silence, Luca said, "*What?* Greigh, you're talking rubbish. Vince would never— "

"Luca, McQ and I saw Vince entering Watchtower with our own eyes less than twenty minutes ago. I was so concerned that we came straight here. Is he in any danger? I would think both you and he would stay as far away as possible from those Slavic thugs."

Luca sat stunned. Doubt displaced disbelief as he pondered what Greigh just said. McQ almost felt sorry for the guy. She remembered the words from Sango Mori's journal, that Luca could easily be devastated emotionally. She watched with interest to see what Greigh would choose to reveal, and what he'd hold back.

Luca grew contrite. He sat down heavily. His inquisitor followed suit.

"Greigh, I honestly do not know why he would go there, or what he's doing. This frightens me. Those Russians frighten me. I can only imagine that Vince is trying to shelter me from something. I fear it might be something awful."

"Alright, Luca. Listen, I suggest you not confront Vince about this, not just yet. That might be dangerous for him right now until we know more. Luca, we want to help you here. You believe that, don't you?"

"Oh, ah, yes, I believe I do." McQ saw Luca now looked up at her with an expression unique from their previous encounters, *and* from a few moments earlier. Now there was... deference? Desperation? What must be going through his mind right now?

"What time is he home when he's been out?"

"We *always* share a glass of wine at five before I cook dinner."

McQ also now looked at Luca differently after reading Sango's journal and observing his current state of mind.

Greigh pressed on with a continued sense of urgency. "Alright, then. Here's what we'll do. If he isn't home by five, you call me straightaway. If he arrives home safely, do *not* confront him. That may put him in an awkward, if not downright dangerous position, depending on what sort of arrangement the Russians might have forced him into. Do you understand that, Luca? Luca!"

The man remained dazed, but cut through his fog.

"Oh, yes. That will be hard. Vince and I just do not keep secrets from each other."

McQ turned away, toward the white stone fireplace mantel. Its ledge was at her shoulder level.

Greigh said, "I understand. But there is something happening here from which we need to keep you *both* safe. We'll sort this out within the next day or so. Alright, Luca?"

"Ah, yes, alright, Greigh. I shall never be able to thank you enough for helping us like this, with such… discretion."

He dimpled his cheeks without smiling as he looked up at McQ by way of thanking her as well, and without having to say so out loud.

Greigh patted his shoulder. Both still sat on the sofa in the pit. "You're most welcome, my friend. Now, early tomorrow afternoon, you will update me, so we stay coordinated. Now, don't bollocks this up. You can do this, can't you, Luca?"

"Yes, yes, early tomorrow afternoon. I'll ensure I'm alone and I will call you."

"Brilliant. We shall now beat a hasty retreat in case Vince comes home soon. Be strong, Luca. We *will* get through this. You know how much I love The Lit, as do you and your brother. We'll talk tomorrow."

"Yes, we'll talk tomorrow."

They left Luca sitting there in his emotional tumult, staring straight ahead. That sofa faced the huge mantel from which McQ had been observing Greigh work his magic.

They let themselves out. Rode the private elevator to four and made for the stairwell to avoid bumping into Vince who could very well be coming up in the birdcage at any moment.

This case just got a whole lot more interesting.

CHAPTER 67

Butler popped Greigh's door outward as they approached 7D. They entered. Greigh took his proprietary half-brick device out of the huge cargo pocket of his unfashionable black tactical pants.

He dared not brandish the device until they were behind closed doors. They both dropped into their customary positions on Greigh's sofa.

"You deployed both of my listening devices, Q?"

"I'm glad you referred to them as *your* devices. Because even a cop on administrative leave can't be involved in unlawful surveillance. I will claim ignorance if you get caught."

"Yes, yes, a veneer of plausible deniability and all that. Working in America is so... provincial. Unlike Interpol or the Israeli Defense Force— "

"Greigh, do I want to know about that right now?"

"That was just book research, you understand."

"Right. I placed one of your button-size surveillance discs on the mantel stuck to a small sculpture, and the other closer to the entryway by their bar. So, can we record as well as listen to what's being said in the Donati love nest on that brick thingy of yours?"

"Yes, but these don't track location, like Vince's. Let's find out if they're working. I've now depleted my inventory of gadgets. We'll catch up on Vince's recording later."

Greigh put his *brick thingy* in pairing mode once more to pair with their personal comms. He deselected the Watchtower devices ("V") on the list and selected the Donati penthouse devices ("L") on the half-brick's small screen, but... nothing. After a few minutes, they heard a few banging noises.

"Q, I'm recording. But this might take a while before Luca says any—"

"Hello, Gaspari?"

Splendid!

"YES, IT'S LUCA. I THINK VINCE IS WORKING WITH TY, OR someone in his *familia*. Why on Earth would he be doing that, Gaspari?"

They could hear the strained desperation in Luca's voice, even through poor audio quality. They only heard Luca's side of the conversation.

"Do you think I should confront him, *carissima*?"

Carissima? Dearest one?

They waited for ten seconds.

"Alright. I'll just pretend everything is normal until then. What about Watchtower?"

Another shorter delay.

"Are you sure? I so worry about you. What if Rocko— "

A very short delay.

"I understand. I love you, too, *carissima*. I don't want to lose Vince. I love him so."

Delay.

"Of course. Ciao, Don Gaspari."

IN SHOCK, GREIGH AND MCQ ALTERNATED LOOKING AT THE device in his lap—from which Luca's voice indirectly emanated—and at each other. The case's now-even-further-accelerated pace colored them dazed and amazed.

McQ said, "Dearest one? Rocko? What in the world is going on, Greigh?"

"At the risk of jumping to hasty conclusions, I'll pose a working assertion. It would seem Luca is closer to the old Don than Vince. 'Dearest one' almost sounds like a son talking with his *mother*. What if the old boy is gay too? That's vietato—forbidden—in traditional Italian and Sicilian mafia cultures, and would be a secret to protect at all costs."

McQ jumped on this. "So, if the old boy *is* gay, Sybil Thibodaux's threat to reveal that secret from her pillow talk with Vince might mean motive. Maybe the Copolla family had Sybil offed to silence her. What if the old Don wasn't only protecting himself and his *carissima*—Luca—but Vince, too, Luca's lover? And Sybil's? Now that we know they're not brothers, but a couple...."

Greigh said, "And maybe this 'Rocko' is the Don's trusted muscle. This is an awful lot of dodgy speculation. But it does paint Sybil's murder on a bigger canvas. These boys would have the resources to defeat your crime scene gadget— "

"The CSM."

"Combined with the Donatis' knowledge of The Lit's architecture— "

McQ lit up like a Christmas tree. She said, "Did we just break this case wide open?"

Greigh brought them back to street level. "Let's remember that none of this is admissible in a court of law *even if* we had tangible proof, neither of which we have. And we've fractured more than a few statutes to get this far."

McQ's enthusiasm would not be quenched. "We now have more rocks to turn over. You're right, Greigh. Private dicks can move a lot faster and freer. I'm just concerned we're punching holes through so many constitutional rights here that we're almost criminals ourselves."

"But unlike criminals, we're not doing this for personal gain. *Our* intentions are honorable."

She was having fun. She grinned and punched Greigh's right shoulder.

"What now?"

CHAPTER 68

Twenty-sixth floor
    Watchtower Inc.
Chicago, Illinois
11:20AM

Teodor Raspin, a.k.a. Rasputin loved working for Tihomir Leonov—most of the time. There was no ambiguity. Unlike so many who had immigrated to America, his boss and friend had not gone soft. Ty was still a warrior.

Twenty-one years ago, in the Central Federal District of the Russian Federation, Ty was a young intelligence officer working out of the Kremlin. He recruited Rasputin, who was privately employed as an enforcer on the outskirts of Moskva. They had been together ever since.

When Ty needed something fixed, he would get word via their encrypted comms, or through one of his managing directors. Today was different. Ty asked to meet face-to-face at his twenty-sixth-floor office in the Watchtower building—Ty's headquarters on Monroe.

. . .

THE BOSS'S MAMMOTH OFFICE FEATURED FLOOR-TO-ceiling windows on the entirety of its fifty-foot east and south walls. Ty was proud of this gargantuan space. He boasted the best views in the city, of both the lake and downtown, including the Near Southwest Loop—the heart of his current pet project.

When Rasputin arrived, Ty's assistant showed him in. Ty clustered his "biggest" desk, a few "bestest" chairs, and an overstuffed sofa with accompanying low tables in the far southeast corner of this cavernous room.

Nobody sat on the sofa. It surprised him to find Vince Donati sitting there in front of Ty's desk, like he owned the place.

Rasputin damn near bit clean through the toothpick nestled in the corner of his mouth. Donati's fancy suit and fancy tie and fancy shoes… looked like the little asshole was posing for the cover of a fancy men's magazine or something.

Ty and Vince watched him approach as his footsteps echoed off hard surfaces everywhere, including the glossy black floor, the black sixteen-foot ceiling, and black walls. Even the austere black-strap leather-on-chrome furniture refused to absorb a single decibel.

Ty *worshipped* black and shiny. He called it the "new white," whatever the hell that meant. Said it reminded him of Moskva's winter nights after curfew, but without the cold.

"Rasp, old friend. You know Vince here. He brings us the news."

The boss was the only guy on the planet who got away calling him anything other than Rasputin. After all, he had a rep, not unlike Grigori Rasputin, the early twentieth-century mystic and royal advisor under Nicholas II, Emperor of Mother Russia back in the day. Some said the Emperor even served at the old mystic's pleasure. Rasputin of old was Raspin's hero.

Ty once said that the way Rasp made problems disappear was *magic*. Besides, the original Rasputin was both feared and worshipped. He liked that. *And* it fit with his last name, Raspin.

Fuck 'em, let 'em fear me.

He even grew a shaggy black beard and long locks—much like the original mystical Rasputin—at least below his "bald spot." The top of his head failed to host more than a dozen long hairs total—unlike the Rasputin of old—not a comb-*over*, but a comb-*back*. Still, he refused to wear a hat, even during Chicago's coldest winter days.

RASPUTIN LOOKED AT TY, NOT AT VINCE. HE SAID, "I'M guessing it's not good news. Never is with this guy." Nodded toward Mr. Fancy without looking at him.

Ty smiled. "You can read a room pretty good, I think," The boss spoke English with almost no accent, but his grammar still sucked. He did okay, though, the most powerful and wealthiest man east of LA and west of New York.

Rasputin hissed with a sneer, already knowing the answer to his question. "We got The Lit yet, Vincy-boy?" Only then did he slant-glance down at him.

He thought the wimp might just break out in tears. "Yes, well, we are very close. You see, there is a complication. One of the condo owners has partnered with a CED detective, and— "

"Names."

"Ah, yes. Of course. Aubrey Greigh and Detective Lieutenant Chance McQuillan. They— "

Rasputin rolled his eyes. "For crissake, not this Greigh guy again."

This time, Rasputin bit clean through his toothpick. Then, as an afterthought, chewed it to bits and swallowed the pieces. He'd never spit 'em out onto the boss's glossy floor. But he was never without a spare, either. Dug out another one from his shirt pocket. He always kept spares. Damn spaces between his teeth caught food. Couldn't let shit rot in there.

THIS TERSE INTERROGATION AMUSED TY. HE SMILED AT Rasp's directness and said, "Rasp, this Greigh and this detective, they cause the problems for poor Vince here. And that make the problems for us and our project, too. You understand."

"Okay, boss. Want me to level The Lit?"

Ty chuckled. "The hammer? No, not yet. Let us use the scalpel, okay, Rasp?"

"You got it, boss. Scalpel."

CHAPTER 69

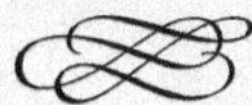

Vince shivered. What had he gotten himself into? These monsters lacked even a sliver of humanity. This was not hyperbole. They were dead serious. There was only the next goal to be achieved. Greigh and his policewoman were a threat.

Would these bullies talk to Luca? Surely not. What would that achieve? Leonov would lose his own continued cooperation, and that seemed to be his primary objective, at least for now.

Vince also realized that by witnessing this conversation, they had now involved him in a conspiracy to commit multiple murders and possibly in an act of domestic terrorism!

There would be no question of his involvement now. These Russian mobsters always recorded *everything*. He was now sure to be on someone's radar somewhere, naming not only Greigh as a target, but a police detective!

It was one thing for Leonov to eliminate a black woman visiting their city. After all, Sybil was coming after Leonov himself. *And* she could destroy his own relationship with Luca. But now, conspiring to kill a *cop*?

Shit!

Leonov smiled at Rasp as the long-haired thug turned to leave, but

Ty asked him to stay. He then swung an icy gaze toward Vince. The smile remained, but those dead black eyes unnerved him. How would this little drama end? Would he survive?

Shit!

"Vince, we do the little favors to each other. Now, you serve the bigger good here, you know."

Couldn't the big scary schmuck at least learn proper English idioms? But he's Ty Leonov. Who will correct him? Nobody, that's who. Except maybe Don Gaspari.

"We change the face of this city for better or for worse!"

Now, he's plagiarizing wedding vows? 'For the better,' you pazzo idiota!

"Our Watchtower Entertainment Complex bring thousands jobs to Chicago, and respect from those animals on both coasts. Chicago will be bestest city of the world. And who would miss old hotel, a couple dozen other old buildings and old park? But beautiful new stadium, new casino, and new hotel with parking under the ground... be like Heaven for Earth, no?"

Vince winced. His stomach lurched. He thought he would be sick. "Yes, of course, like Heaven. Except for the people who now make that area their home, Mr. Leonov."

"Of course! We buy! Good money for nothing!"

You mean, 'money is no object?' You wish to be an American capitalist? Learn the fucking language, you Russian pig!

Vince didn't want to press his luck, but a corner of his conscience still nibbled at his tongue. He said, "And your offers will be very generous, I'm sure. It's just that money isn't important to some."

"Sure, Vince. That's what Rasp he is for, to help for that. You see? It all works."

Oh, brother.

"You go now. All gonna be fine. You see."

Vince offered the man a wincing smile, rose, turned to leave with the gnawing dread that his days were numbered.

He headed for the doors of Ty's private elevator a good fifty paces across this ridiculous ballroom-wanna-be office. Most of that absurd room remained empty black space. Talk about over-compensating. Vince tapped his temple to inform Leonov's driver. "Five minutes."

"Yes, sir."

VINCE IMAGINED THE EXQUISITE IRONY. THE STENCH OF IT dizzied his sensibilities. This near-illiterate billionaire is going to destroy a safe harbor for the most literate group of creative souls in the city. Perhaps in the country. To replace it with a football stadium and a casino.

Whoever said the pen is mightier than the sword never met Ty Leonov, illiterate sword-swinging billionaire.

And what does that make me? Selling out Luca's lifelong dream for mere money? Well, for a lot of money, at least. We will live worry-free, in comfort, in any city in the world for the rest of our days. And we can then afford to be philanthropists and patrons of the arts—without all the headaches. Why is that such a bad dream? If only Luca could see…. He'll come around. Won't he?

Besides, he could *not* allow Greigh and that policewoman to threaten his relationship with dear Luca, much less expose their secret to the Copolla family at large. Gaspari could no longer protect them if that were to happen. The Don would have no choice but to ostracize the two of them, or worse.

And if they outed the Don himself? Dear God, no place on Earth would be safe!

No, just like Sybil, Greigh, and that woman had to go.

ONCE THEY WERE ALONE, TY MOTIONED FOR HIS ASSASSIN and general go-to guy to come closer to him behind his "biggest desk," as he called it.

He said, "Vince too, yes?"

"Sure, boss."

Just a quick nod as he left, already chewing on a fresh toothpick.

CHAPTER 70

Ty Leonov loved darkness. His suite on the top floor of the Watchtower building reflected his favored black-chrome, strap-leather and glass motif. Glossy black everything. Even the leather shined and the ebony-tinted windows glistened.

The powerful Russian was quite eloquent when he spoke and thought in his native tongue, not this cumbersome and primitive local gibberish. If only everyone spoke and thought in Russian!

He poured a snifter of some expensive brown liquor. He hated the taste. It wasn't vodka. But it was expensive, and classy. Or so he was told.

Ty swirled and smelled the almost-black liquid like some society prick had taught him. And he sat with his back to the wall of windows that overlooked Lake Michigan.

It was night, and the lake was dark.

Leonov grew fascinated by Creole culture and the Voodoo arts after spending time in New Orleans, overseeing his canal project four years earlier.

The Creoles were a proud bunch who fancied themselves conquerors of their own destiny, even today. Foolish quadroons—a word he had heard that he thought meant "mixed blood"—didn't realize how much power they could have. To him, taking a Creole girl meant taking her dark power, absorbing it into himself.

He felt strong, like the evening he toured the Montrose Plantation in Northwest Louisiana. He visited the area to survey the nearby Cane River region. Not really a museum guy, he did want to see where real slaves once lived.

Ty remembered with relish the slave quarters at Montrose, where he absorbed Sybil Thibodaux's dark power.

Then, almost four years later, here in Chicago, he struck a deal with Vince Donati, or whatever the man's real last name was, on an unrelated pet project in the city. Turned out Vince got cozy with a Creole girl, too.

Donati learned that among other goody-two-shoes Voodoo experts, the girl knew of a Voodoo witch doctor she hated. Said his name was Doctor Jacques Memeaux from the Bayou St. John neighborhood in New Orleans.

The Creole girl told Vince the man was a disgrace to the practice because he was nothing more than a Voodoo mercenary.

Perfect.

IT HAD TAKEN LITTLE RESEARCH. TY FOUND THE MAN AND his disgusting little shop in a dingy alley off Rampart Street at the edge of New Orleans' French Quarter. He sent Rasp down to meet with the man and to buy his services.

The guy bragged to Rasp that he was so skilled, he could help his boss get away with murder—for the right price. Rasp also learned the man had some expensive habits to support.

Ty had a clever plan using this Voodoo guy who would do anything for a buck. He had brought this Doctor Jacques to Chicago, and set up a ruse to kill two birds with one stone.

Perfect.

· · ·

VINCE HAD TOLD TY THIS CREOLE GIRL HE BEDDED WAS tracking a Russian in Chicago for having raped her and for killing her father four years earlier.

He recalled having some fun with a *quadroon,* as they say down there. Didn't mean to off the old man. Oh well. Sometimes, shit happens when you're having fun. This was the same girl!

Son-bitch! That bitch, she track me! Tiny world!

Ty told Vince he'd prevent the woman from revealing their affair, put the fear of God into her, and mask her demise with some Voodoo trickery. Get the cops running around in circles. Maybe get The Lit some bad media coverage.

He also told Vince this should help shake the confidence of the owners in the building. Motivate them to sell—to him—to get the hell out. Told Vince *he* needed to handle his 'brother.'

"And soon, yes? The clock, she ticks, Vince. You understand."

With some additional encouragement from Vince, Luca should be more amenable to selling the building itself, wouldn't he?

Vince *assured* Ty that he would. The Voodoo crap would make a great smokescreen that also seemed very appropriate. And that bitch would get some of her own medicine.

But Vince had started asking questions. Ty told him to just trust him. Later, when Vince's little Creole dark meat turned up dead, the little shit panicked. Vince said he never imagined they would *kill* her. Ty saw that made the wimp doubt their plan.

That second woman, she was just collateral damage from the freak that Doctor Jacques created. Unfortunate, but she was just a Jap, after all. Not like she was Chinese. He liked Chinese. When Vince the wop heard about the Jap, Ty thought the man would go public. He could not allow that.

Obviously.

CHAPTER 71

Saturday, June 30th
   Hotel Literati
2:20PM

SHE KNEW VOODOO COULD HELP. ZELDA ZENAIDA Coincoin called Greigh from The Lit's front desk to meet her.

He did. The least he could do. She still wanted to believe the misdirected use of Voodoo killed Sybil.

She had a theory about how to locate Doctor Jacques Memeaux. Since someone obviously killed Sybil somewhere within The Lit, it was a good bet the murder took place in the basement or tunnels underneath the building.

She knew Jacques liked the dark. That's probably where he started transforming that poor child into a willing slave, she said.

And since that boy, Robby, stabbed poor dear Sango, resulting in her death, at a minimum, they could charge Doctor Jacques as an accessory to murder. Zelda would help Greigh and his policewoman friend do so. She hated the man who did so much damage to the reputation of her sacred Voodoo faith. But most of all, she would see justice done for lovely little Sango, her new friend.

Obeah Man—Clairvius Rincisse—was also eager to help. They both still believed that Robby Bidok murdered their little girl, even though Greigh said he doubted it based on the evidence. They *wanted* to believe Robby was the killer, anyway. He was now dead.

Doctor Jacques *had* clearly been involved with at least one death—Sango's. And *maybe* her Syb's too.

Ya, de man must pay.

CHAPTER 72

S tate Street Gym
    Chicago, Illinois
3:00PM

GREIGH REMEMBERED. MCQ WORKED OUT AT A GYM ON THE corner of State and Van Buren, just a few blocks east of the nine-nine.

On the hike up there, Greigh reflected on his brief discussion with Zelda and Obeah Man. They shared with him the location of Doctor Jacques Memeaux's shop in New Orleans. They remained convinced he still stayed in The Lit's basement tunnels somewhere, or was even living down there. Something about his job not being finished. But Greigh had larger seafood to cook.

No, that wasn't right.

I have bigger fish to fry! Stupid butchery of the King's English. Americans!

He smiled. McQ would have enjoyed correcting him.

The gym's squat structure was a renovated store with a flat roof and a sixteen-foot-high water-stained ceiling. The deeper-than-wide space faced State—a northern exposure that looked out on the perpetual shadow of the elevated Ida B. Wells skyway.

Because of that, its interior always remained dim, even on the brightest day. The lights inside were always on—twenty-four/seven— one of the few workout joints in the Near Loop that stayed open around the clock. Presumably, this accommodated cops, firefighters and others who worked odd shifts.

The State Street Gym was more of a fight club than a gym. Its most prominent and obvious interior feature was the elevated twenty-six-foot-square boxing ring at the center of the space.

Heavy bags and speed bags hung around the periphery. An impressive free weight area and a few specialized weight training machines filled in the gaps. Three treadmills and two ellipticals offered cardio training.

Toward the back, Greigh spotted a large matted area for floor exercises and free-form mixed martial arts sparring, the only space in the gym that did not feel cluttered.

Various weapons adorned racks on both walls—escrima sticks, combat staffs, nunchucks and action bats. But there were no throwing weapons or edge weapons.

Most of the clients looked like law enforcement types. Greigh wasn't dressed to work out—by design. Otherwise, he would have fit right in, except for his casual grooming standards.

He spotted McQ. She sparred with someone toward the rear on the matted area that he estimated was thirty feet square. Two-inch-thick mats with a traditional Tatami surface texture—that of woven rice-straw in the Japanese tradition—covered the entire area.

McQ fought with... Dani the dancer? Now he understood. Dani and McQ sparred, but it looked more like acrobatic choreography. It moved him as both violent and beautiful. They had been at it for a while if their perspiration stains were any sign.

When Dani Kilby, the Brit expatriate, spotted Greigh approaching, she waved off McQ. She was mounting a brutal assault below Dani's knees with a sweep move that suggested a blend of ballet and break-dancing.

Dani chirped, "Greigh! You look bewitching, luv!"

"Hello, Dani."

McQ popped up from the mat. Both women's soaked chests heaved from extended exertion. McQ wore a sweaty t-shirt emblazoned with the words, "Red Hair, Don't Care." The hem around its neckline appeared to have been ripped out. She did not look pleased.

"Greigh, what are you doing here?"

He stood there, flat-footed and wide-eyed.

"What *was* that besides *amazing?*"

Dani seemed pleased by his presence. Like he had just saved her from a profound thrashing. She said, "It's Capoeira, a Brazilian art form that combines elements of martial arts, dance, acrobatics, music, and spirituality. You like?"

"Yes, very much. Perhaps I— "

"No!" McQ mounted a defensive posture. "This is *my* thing, Greigh— "

"Well, *our* thing, right Q?" Dani exaggerated a mini-pout.

"Yes, Dani, *our* thing. Could be one thing I'm better at than the all-knowing Sir Aubrey Greigh, who has done everything, been every-where, and knows all."

Greigh looked confused. He crossed his arms and cocked his head. "Q, are you angry with me?"

She looked embarrassed. "No, just a lot of adrenaline, and you intimidate me. A little."

"Well, if it is any consolation, I have spent little time in South America, and what you two were performing was nothing short of awe-inspiring. And intimidating. A little."

Dani kept quiet, still huffing from exertion. She stood back, her hands on her hips, and observed these two.

After an awkward silence that wore on way too long as McQ now looked befuddled, Dani said, "Oh, bloody hell, you two. You need some time alone. I'll hit the showers. Are we still on for tonight at my place, Q?"

"Yeah. Wouldn't miss it."

Dani smiled at her friend, and wheeled on her bare feet, swinging a wink toward Greigh.

"Bye, luv!"

McQ said, "See you later."

Dani chirped, "How do you know I was talking to you, Q?"

She flung a flirtatious wave back over her shoulder toward Greigh and blew a kiss his way as an afterthought. That last bit might have been to pay McQ back for the trouncing. All good fun, of course.

Dani might just say, "Natch, cuz!"

CHAPTER 73

Greigh brought news. The two wandered to a row of empty plastic chairs along the one side of the matted area meant for onlookers. They were alone. As they sat down, McQ grabbed a towel from one of them to wipe her face and neck.

"McQ, I learned from a search of Outlaw— "

"Wait, what? Outlaw is a known-offenders database accessible only by law enforcement, and—

"Yes, well, about that, I called Lois—"

"*Lois?* Captain Granger?"

"She put me on to your colleague, Detective Johnson who— "

"Oh, for crissake. Why don't they just give you my old desk at the nine-nine!"

Greigh paused. He took in Q's fidgety demeanor, with arms crossed tightly across her sweaty chest. He smiled, gazed at her with his head cocked to one side, and silently peered at her.

"Oh, you're having fun with this? Greigh, you really can be an asshole, sometimes."

He still waited, saying nothing, as if to find out whether she wanted to learn what he discovered... or not.

"*Alright,* already! What did that putz Johnson tell you?" He still waited, but then relented—to put her out of her delicious misery.

"You know, Johnson isn't such a bad sort— "

"*Greigh!*"

"Yes, well, he'll never be you, of course, but he knows how to execute a simple database query. Gerard Bianchi is the only known associate of Gaspari Copolla with the *Rocko* alias, and one of Gaspari Copolla's strong fellows—his favorite, it would seem."

She didn't want to smile, but couldn't help herself. "You mean his *muscle?*"

"In that capacity, I think they'd call him a repairman, correct?"

"No, Greigh. They call them *fixers*."

"Right. I think I'm getting the hang of these American colloquialisms, don't you, Q?"

"Sure, why not? So, when Luca called the Don, he floated the idea of sending Gaspari's key fixer to deal with whatever Vince has going on with Leonov. Depending on what Gaspari is thinking, that could start a war between the Copolla family and Leonov's crew. But it sounds like maybe the old Don is trying for a more subtle approach. Like he needs to know more before he acts. Okay, Mr. Super-Sleuth, what else have you learned?"

"I heard a broadcast on the local feeds earlier featuring Chicago's 'business person of the year,' none other than Ty Leonov, with his abominable butchery of the English language. And McQ, guess whose voice sounds like it 'grinds gravel into a seeping wound' as Sybil might say?' A voice like the devil himself."

"Leonov. Son-of-a-bitch. Sybil came to Chicago hunting Ty Leonov."

Greigh grinned like the Cheshire Cat.

"A safe bet. I can think of only one reason."

"Leonov raped her and killed her step-father."

"Monopoly!"

"You mean, '*Bingo?*'"

"Yes, Bingo!"

McQ ADMIRED THIS MAN'S GRIT. BUT SHE WOULD NEVER consider telling him that. He already knew he intimidated her. It was so hard to tell whether he was shining her on with his screwed-up sayings, but his investigative mind *definitely* intimidated her. And right now, she wouldn't have it any other way.

"So, how do we prove Leonov is a rapist and a murderer?"

"We should continue this conversation at my place. We require privacy and resources this lovely fight club does not offer. I need Butler."

"Gym, not fight club. Fine. See you there in thirty."

"Minutes?"

"Shut up!"

She headed to the showers with a smile he couldn't see.

Something about this guy… a lot about this guy….

CHAPTER 74

Apartment 7D
Hotel Literati
Chicago, Illinois
4:00PM

"You will not believe it, Q."

Greigh asked Butler to route the recorded audio from his half-brick through the whole-house speakers with the direction to only play it in the living room. He and McQ stood at his desk.

"Listen to this portion of Vince's meeting with Leonov himself this morning."

'Rasp, this Greigh and this detective, they cause the problems for poor Vince here. And they make the problems for us and our project. You understand.'
'Okay, boss. Want me to level The Lit?'
'No, not yet. Let us use the scalpel before the hammer, okay, Rasp?'
'You got it, boss. Scalpel.'

McQ couldn't believe her ears. "He ordered a hit on *us?* Holy shit. The balls. And talk of leveling *this entire building?* An act of *terrorism.*"

Greigh scratched his chin. He said, "No, Leonov's too smart. He's setting up for a bigger play. Getting the feds involved would only present another obstacle. But we *are* getting too close.

"This is marvelous news, Q, but that also makes Vince a loose end. Not a doubt in my mind. We must warn him, but how do we do so without spilling our fist?"

McQ rolled her eyes. "You mean 'tipping our hand'?"

"Precisely. Do you have the results of the Nackatish rape and murder investigation from four years ago? That must be central to this entire affair."

"Yeah, I downloaded all of that to my wristPad before I got cut out of the loop. That's Homicide Investigation 101—get the victim's history. But they couldn't identify the origins of any trace evidence, other than... oh, shit. We now know Leonov was in Louisiana working on that canal project. And the Nackatish sheriff determined one Teodor Raspin had rented a car about fifty miles south in a larger town called Alexandria. That made Raspin a suspect, but Leonov's battalion of lawyers said there was no evidence Raspin was anywhere near the site of the rape and murder. And that was that."

Greigh pointed an index finger skyward. "Of *course,* there was no trace evidence that *Raspin* committed those crimes. Because *Leonov* used Raspin's rental car to get to the scene. With Leonov's formidable legal team, he would have had all that evidence suppressed so neither he nor Raspin would ever see the inside of a courtroom. Would there be a record of Leonov's DNA on record somewhere?"

McQ jerked her head up. "Yes. They catalog all immigrants."

"How about you suggest to Johnson that they compare trace at the scene of Sybil's rape in Louisiana to Leonov's DNA?"

"Okay, but they've already concluded that'll never make it into a court room."

Greigh said, "We don't care. I want the Chicago Police to realize this Russian thug is no choirboy, and that he doesn't deserve to be *business bozo of the year!*" His eyes had turned… feral.

"This guy is getting to you, isn't he?"

"I hate entitled prigs who lack any semblance of humanity, and don't feel laws or decency or accountability apply to them. Yes, Tihomir Leonov and his ilk piss me off. We should have made this connection sooner, Q."

CHAPTER 75

D ani Kilby's Apartment
Chicago, Illinois
7:00PM

SHE DESPERATELY NEEDED A GIRL'S NIGHT. McQ KNOCKED
on the door of Dani's fourth-floor walk-up around the corner and
down State from the club where she worked.

"Allo, luv! Door's open. C'mon in."

Dani caught McQ's long face and said, "I'm cracking a bottle of
cheap red wine. Our task is to recycle its contents tonight, and I ain't
listening to no excuses why that is a perfectly bad idea. Why the
starving puppy face?"

"Hey, Dani. All that's going on. This case. We have a lot, but no
way to prove any of it. The bad guy is rich and powerful. Hides behind
a gazillion expensive lawyers."

"The system is buggered, luv. Always has been." She poured a
mammoth glass of wine. Handed it over. McQ dialed up a tired smile
and a nod of gratitude.

Sometimes McQ thought Dani must envision herself to be a social worker.

"Q, you work way too hard. You take no time for yourself. And as a concerned friend, it is my professional opinion as an expert at reading people, your personal life is an emotional dumpster fire. Hell's bells, girl, when's the last time you went out on a date? With a man? Or got up for a bit of shagging? Q, I worry so about you."

McQ laughed. "Yeah, well, my career is sliding off a slippery platter along with a growing heap of infractions, and I keep adding more to the pile."

"How's your eyesight, luv? Not very good, is it? Why aren't you wearing specs?"

"Dani, what *are* you talking about?"

"*Greigh,* you bloody fool! There is chemistry between you two. The man is smart, rich, gob-smacking handsome, and he glows when he looks at you. You've got to be bloody blind not to recognize that."

"Whatever. We're both focused on getting justice for two murdered girls."

McQ SWIRLED HER WINE. "HEY, DANI, LET ME ASK *you* A question. If I was a rich guy—a bad guy—and I wanted to hook up with young black girls, how would I do that?"

"Hmmm. Listen, Detective, I'm no expert on such nonsense, but a rich guy ain't about to cruise the district himself. He'd send someone. Plus, loaded guys can afford to be selective. Might use an agency. But that's not too low-profile. If he needs discretion.... Dunno."

Almost talking to herself, McQ muttered, "Yeah. He'd send someone. Maybe someone like Rasp...."

Dani stiffened. Set her already half-empty glass down on the table in front of her lumpy sofa and swiveled toward McQ, sitting close to her left.

"*What* did you say, Q?"

"That he'd send someone— "

"No, no. Did you say *Rasp?*"

"Sorry, Dani. Thinking out loud."

But seeing such a reaction to that name, she, too, set her glass down, and grabbed both of Dani's hands. "Why, girlfriend? Spill."

"Mr. Thursday."

"Say what?"

"There's this scary bloke what comes in every Thursday, as regular as the queen's tea. Sometimes Monday and Thursday, sometimes Tuesday and Thursday, but always Thursdays. We've taken to calling him 'Mr. Thursday.' Always during our happy hour specials.

"The girls talk. The creep always asks about new girls, but *only young black girls*. And they tell me he always says, 'the more innocent, the better, and the money is big.' Now how creepy is *that*? The wanker calls himself Rasputin. Is that helpful?"

"Not sure, Dani, but thanks. You associate with the nicest people." And McQ laughed.

Shit, this is priceless!

Dani said, "Don't I, though, Now, tell me why *your* personal life is *not* an emotional dumpster fire, Ms. Perfecto-Mundo."

McQ's demure expression belied her delight at having uncovered a key clue. She started by trying to mimic Dani's Londoner accent, but relented. "Hey, I'm here with *you*, luv! Besides, I'm surrounded by too many men at work. I need a breather. At least they're not *all* creepy!"

They shared a badly needed belly laugh and proceeded to punish their livers with what remained of the wine."

Inside, though, McQ reeled.

We know how to find Raspin—Leonov's 'someone!'

CHAPTER 76

S unday, July 1st
      Penthouse Apartment
Hotel Literati
Chicago, Illinois
7:00 AM

Luca's concern sculpted his face. Would Vince notice? His beleaguered husband slouched at their elevated breakfast table by the windows overlooking their balcony. He was a man deflated and defeated.

Luca longed for Vince's bubbly demeanor and customary impeccable appearance, now replaced with that of someone who cared little about such seemingly trivial matters.

Should he confront his favorite person in the universe with what he knew? Greigh told him not to, but keeping a secret from his dearheart tortured him.

He served Vince a special eye-popping breakfast of soyrizo—a spicy plant-based chorizo sausage facsimile—drizzled in Sriracha sauce, and accompanied by fresh homemade biscuits. And he'd brewed a pot of his favorite English breakfast tea tinged with synthetic honey—synthetic, since bees were all but extinct.

Vince poked and prodded at his breakfast for ten minutes. So Luca changed tacks with a surprise to accompany the poor man's tea, the only thing he might enjoy in his distracted state.

Luca wandered back into the kitchen to retrieve a special treat over which he'd labored yesterday—a platter heaped with room-temperature Sfogliatella Riccia, Vince's favorite. More of a dessert, a good sfogliatella improved any mood, day or night.

Luca had crafted the elaborate dessert made with multiple layers of paper-thin dough arranged in clam-shaped pockets. He filled each with a sweet cream filling made with semolina, water, ricotta, sugar, eggs, cubed candied fruit, cinnamon, and a pinch of salt. He had searched the feeds to find the ricotta and real eggs. Had them delivered. This was sure to cheer up the poor dear man.

He approached Vince from behind as his back was to the kitchen. About to surprise him with the heaping platter of handcrafted pastries, Luca said, "Hey, babe, I can see you're down. This should cheer you up— "

Crack.

TIME SLOWED TO A DEMONIC CRAWL. FROM BEHIND, LUCA watched Vince's head jerk from right to left with a brutality he could not have imagined in his worst nightmare.

The entire section of glass wall three feet from Vince's right shoulder crackled and tumbled to the floor in a pile.

A pink cloud filled the air over Vince's left shoulder.

Vince and his chair teetered. Gravity took over.

The plate of dessert pastries plummeted. The crystal platter crashed to the Italian marble floor. It shattered into a million shards.

Luca just stood there, slack-jawed. His hands still thought they held the platter.

He could make no sense of what was happening.

. . .

Crack.

A second adjacent panel of glass closer to the kitchen disappeared six feet from *his* right shoulder.

That's when his brain realized someone had shot Vince, and was now shooting at *him*. Did he even care? Without Vince....

But he realized he did care. If for no other reason, to find the fucking demon who did this to his dearest little Vinnie. So he followed the sfogliatella to the floor, tapped his comms and yelled, "Call Greigh!"

Wind now swirled around... everything.

While he waited to hear his friend's voice, perhaps his only friend, other than Don Gaspari, he crawled to where his man had fallen. Vince lay on his left side, still mated with the armed chair that went over with him.

Tears clouded Luca's vision. Despair clogged his movements. He crawled through a million glass slivers that bit into his hands and forearms and bare ankles. He felt nothing other than profound confusion.

Luca noticed just a small hole in his partner's right temple, but blood pooled on the floor at an alarming rate. Luca could not bring himself to crawl around to look into Vince's face. Even if he wanted to, he grew too faint, so he stopped to rest. His hand rested on Vince's shoulder. He patted it. Not sure why.

"Hello? Luca?"

"Greigh... they... shot Vince." Luca tapped his wristPad. Said, "Elevator... open. I—"

"Luca!"

CHAPTER 77

Shit!

Greigh pulled on the pair of jeans he'd worn yesterday, still slung over the ottoman in front of his overstuffed reading chair between his bed and the balcony slider. Grabbed a clean t-shirt from the top dresser drawer ten feet from the foot of his bed and slipped into a pair of old felt slippers.

He called 9-1-1 as he ran for the door and the birdcage elevator. Down on four, he transferred to the already open private elevator that carried him to Luca and Vince's apartment. Before he got there, his second call was answered almost as soon as it connected.

"Greigh?"

"Q, someone shot Vince Donati. Luca called. I'm on my way up there now. Join me. I'm leaving the button pulled in their elevator for emergency services."

Click.

As Greigh entered the penthouse, it seemed... stormy. Twenty feet of wall—two ten-foot-wide floor-to-ceiling glass panels—lay on the kitchen floor in piles. Sheer drapes billowed inward from strong and gusty sixteenth-floor Windy City winds. Instead of manicured air in the vast apartment, the place stunk of city grit and bloody chaos.

Greigh rounded the island bar between the sunken living room to his left and the elevated kitchen to his right. Spotted both Vince and Luca on the floor in a large and spreading pool of blood near the now-absent windows in their breakfast nook. He took in the scene and arrived at an obvious conclusion.

A sniper from high ground. From the only building tall enough on the south side of Harrison—the Prudential.

Most of the blood flowed from the unseen exit wound underneath Vince's head. It had to be massive. He kneeled to check for a pulse on Vince's neck. Nothing. Vince's bowels had let loose.

Luca, however, though unconscious, presented a weak but regular pulse. He bled from several cuts to the right side of his head. Two looked deep and bled profusely.

Greigh knew certain head wounds could produce a great deal of blood without being life-threatening, other than the danger of exsanguination—of bleeding out.

GREIGH PULLED OFF HIS T-SHIRT. WADDED IT, AND applied compression to the worst cuts on the right side of Luca's skull. The one near his temple worried him the most. Not much protecting the temporal lobe of the brain there. But he saw no entry wound. The sniper... *missed Luca?*

Pale, clammy skin, shallow breathing... Luca was in shock. But with his head bleeding, Greigh dared not elevate his feet. Best to leave him in situ and maintain compression. He called 9-1-1. Again.

After several minutes, Luca regained partial consciousness, but his eyes remained closed. Likely an unintentional defense mechanism for a sensitive man dealing with a horrific chain of events.

Greigh noticed the food all around them. They were just having breakfast.

. . .

"What....?"

"Luca, you are injured, but you'll be okay."

I hope.

"... Vinnie?"

"I am so sorry, Luca. He's gone. You should remain quiet. Help is on the way."

The man tried to sob, but was too weak. It was all he could muster to draw in a shaky breath and wheeze it out. He'd lost a significant volume of blood.

"Who would—?"

"Luca, I *vow* we *will* find and punish whoever did this to you and your husband."

The intensity of emotion in Greigh's voice while he held Luca's hand surprised him. Luca squeezed his hand, opened his left eye to a slit, and blinked while peering into Greigh's soul as if to offer a silent thanks. The gesture came across as a macabre wink—a death vow.

"You know... about me and V—?"

Why do people in my life always die on Sundays?

CHAPTER 78

Monday, July 2nd
    McQ's Apartment
Chicago, Illinois
8:00 AM

Smallest safe house ever!

Their knees bumped as they sat facing each other. They hunched over the miniature dining table almost big enough for *one* in McQ's tiny apartment—one room plus a bathroom and a short hallway with a dozen hooks for jackets and hats.

Greigh had noticed every one of those hooks supported something, including McQ's hip holster. The worn spot was evidently where she clipped her credentials. The rig was absent her badge and her Glock— with a hoodie draped over it to, what, conceal it?

Can a holster seem sad?

"Thanks for the use of your couch last night, Q. Won't people talk? Us practically sleeping together?"

One cheek puckered as he smirked. He recognized humor was a

classic defense mechanism to fend off his feelings for what he witnessed yesterday morning at the Donatis.

"First off, I don't care what people think. *And* the couch is at least six feet from my bed. Second, very few folks are even aware of this place. And third, after what happened to the Donatis yesterday, we gotta stick together until we figure out what to do about this Raspin character targeting us.

"Besides, I am not about to spend time with you in some fancy hotel room. I'd call in the cavalry, but they'd just slam us into protective custody until the captain's overtime budget craters. We gotta be proactive here. If you're okay, I'm okay, *partner.*"

Greigh couldn't help but crowd his brain with conflicting thoughts that leaned more and more toward feeling good about having McQ as a good friend, in addition to Butler. That's all it was.

He said, "Music and stale smoke aroma are included—no extra charge?"

"Shut up and eat your cereal. Besides, they need good water and ice for drinks downstairs. They got this good old-fashioned reverse-osmosis filtration system for the entire building. A golden oldie. So, my shower doesn't stink like a fish's toilet. And I can drink the water right out of the tap. I'm not kidding!"

"I trust you, Q. I'm not complaining, mind you. I just figured I should have brought some foodstuffs. To share the financial burden. *This* is *cereal?*"

"Like I said, Greigh, shut up." She grinned.

"But why a cop bar?"

"When there's no target on my back, cheap food and strong drinks."

GREIGH FIDGETED. HE WANTED TO GET DOWN TO BUSINESS. They were both very pissed off. McQ summarized, ticking points off with her fingers:

- "Sybil's adoptive father—dead,

- "Sybil—raped,
- "Sybil—dead,
- "Sango—dead,
- "Vince—dead,
- "Zombie Robby—dead,
- "Luca—wounded,
- "Someone already clobbered me over the head,
- "Same with Mac and that other uniform—I forget his name,
- "One evil witch doctor—in the wind,
- "Now, a contract on both our heads,
- "Little or no hope of *ever* getting to Leonov, not from the right side of the law, anyway...."

"Did I miss any highlights, Greigh? I hope not, because I've already run out of fingers and thumbs."

He said, "It's bloody time to take the bloody gloves off, Q."

He continued on a more even keel, as if he'd already planned a solution in his mind.

"Some folks live both outside the law *and* above it. We should talk with someone who understands the rules of such a game. We need to talk with Don Gaspari Copolla."

Her eyes widened, and her cop brain revulsed at this outrageous notion.

"You're joking, right?"

"You don't have to come, but *I am* going to talk to the man."

"How will you even get to him?"

"He knows me."

"I see. Do I want to know how?"

"I was president of The Lit's HOA for two years. During that entire time, I aggressively defended The Literati from Leonov's ongoing takeover efforts. We assumed he was intending to demolish it. Couldn't let that happen. I didn't realize the Don was personally involved back then. But I do now. Plus, I'm told Gaspari loves my books.

"One of the top gangsters in the country, and *the* most notorious in Chicago, is a *fan* of yours?

"Is that so hard to imagine, Q? Besides being a dashing crime fighter, I *have* sold a few million books. That comes with a certain, ah, notoriety."

"Yeah, I forget about that sometimes. How will you get to him?

"I'll call him. Luca gave me his private number. I caught him at a weak moment right after the shooting. He may not even remember giving me that number. Wanna join the party as long as we are so far from civilization?

"You mean, 'way off the reservation'? Hell, yeah."

"Reservation?"

"Never mind. How and when do we get this party started?

"No time like the present." Greigh tapped his temple and said, "Call Gaspari Copolla." Earlier, he had added to his contact list the number Luca provided. He paired the call to both their comms so McQ could listen in.

"LUCA?"

"No, sir, this is Aubrey Greigh. Do you know who I am, sir?"

"Mr. Greigh. Of course. My favorite author and defender of our Literati community. Only Luca has this number— "

"Yes, sir. He gave it to me. The police are keeping this quiet for now, but Luca was injured yesterday, sir, and— "

"Do not tell me this! Is he okay?"

"He is recovering, sir, but I *am* sorry. Vince is dead."

The deafening silence that followed concerned Greigh. Had he lost his thread-like connection to this erstwhile crime boss? Then....

"You will now tell me what happened, Mr. Greigh. But you will not do so over comms. I am sending a car. You are at The Literati, yes?"

"Yes, sir. I am bringing my consultant with me. We have information for you. I look forward to meeting you, sir."

Click.

~

"HOLY SHIT, GREIGH. WE'RE 'GOING FOR A RIDE' AFTER telling a mobster that someone under his protection was just murdered? I'm gonna puke."

"Look, Q, you don't have to come. We haven't *any* substantial proof that ties Leonov to at least three murders now, probably many more. At least, nothing that will hold up in court. I'm going to level with the old gent, and see what he says. Then we'll regroup. Fair enough?"

"Yeah, no, I'm in. But I'm watching my career as a cop drift farther away by the second."

She offered him a grim smile of determination.

"C'mon, we don't want to miss our ride. Let's get back to The Lit. Thanks for not inviting the nice gangster's limo to *my* home."

Greigh liked this woman more with each passing moment.

CHAPTER 79

H otel Literati
    Chicago, Illinois
8:30 AM

THE DRIVER OF THE ONLY LIMO NEAR THE LIT'S COVERED
front entrance waved to Greigh like he was an old friend. Greigh and
McQ approached him holding the passenger's side rear door open for
them. The man held out his hand.

"Mr. Greigh, it is an honor. I love your books. My name is Gerard
Bianchi. Please call me Rocko. Everybody does."

To see the expansive grin on this granite face meant either this
man's admiration for Greigh was genuine, or he was one hell of an
actor. Maybe both.

Rocko.

"I just love Peter Fontera in 'Looks That Kill' and how he solves
the murder of Joshua Krona. That book had a real 'Murder on the
Orient Express' vibe to it with a 'Fifty Shades of Gray' undertone.
Chicagowood at its finest. Outstanding!"

"Thank you, Rocko. Brilliant. Not too many people pick up on my intent. Well done!"

If Rocko had been grinning before, he glowed after that remark.

"I have a copy on the front seat. Would you sign it for me?" The grizzly hulk giggled with anticipation.

McQ stood there dumbfounded, not sure if she should intrude on this bromance, or just tumble into the rear seat of the limo and wait. She couldn't help but appreciate the moment.

Rocko reached in through the open front window for the book and held it and a pen out to Greigh. He scrawled a quick signature, handed it back to the grinning gorilla, and patted him on the shoulder.

"It is my pleasure, Rocko. Shall we go?"

"Oh, yeah, of course."

A SHORT FIVE-MINUTE RIDE LATER, ROCKO PULLED UP AT the corner of Van Buren and Wabash. They sat in front of a walled estate with a four-story mansion at the center of its manicured grounds.

Bronze-on-bronze lettering on the arched gateway's pillar to their right read, "Sicily Club." Twin gates under the arch opened as they approached.

The drive from the gate through the circuitous grounds to the "clubhouse" may have taken longer than the trip from The Lit. It looked like a botanical garden. The myriad plants and trees all appeared very real.

Both McQ and Greigh knew of this rather famous place, but had never been inside.

Ten minutes after entering the club and passing through some security rigor—with apologies—Rocko ushered them in through the front doors to an elevator and to Don Gaspari's library on the third floor. Greigh assumed this was the man's sanctum sanctorum.

THE OLD MAN SAT IN FRONT OF A FIRE, EVEN THOUGH THE room seemed quite warm. Rocko signaled for them to follow him around to the mantel so the old man could see them.

"Don Gaspari, your guests." Rocko turned to his charges and said, "No offense, but due to his compromised immune system, Signore Copolla requests no physical contact. I'm sure you understand." He smiled at Greigh.

McQ wondered, *Yet he walks arm-in-arm with Luca Donati around the grounds of this place at night?*

"Thank you, Rocko. Now, Mr. Greigh, you have some news for us."

What am I? Invisible?

"Please, be seated, you and your, ah, consultant."

He turned to McQ and said, "I was sorry to hear of your suspension, Ms. McQuillan, but I am delighted you are working with our friend, Mr. Greigh."

Shocked to be recognized, she smiled and nodded. She didn't bother to correct him that she was on administrative leave, not suspension. From his point of view, no difference.

Besides, this was not her show.

CHAPTER 80

G*ame time.*

"Now, tell us what happened to our little Vinnie, Mr. Greigh."

"People just call me Greigh, sir. Should we speak in private? No offense, Rocko."

Bianchi shrugged and said, "None taken."

The old Don said, "Rocko stays. Please...."

After they sat down—Rocko remained standing—Greigh said, "Yes, sir. Ty Leonov put a contract out on Detective McQuillan and me. We have a recording. Not legal, that recording. We are loose ends now that Mr. Leonov is more aggressively trying to acquire The Lit.

"Likewise, Vince had become a loose end. He had an affair with a woman who we now know Leonov raped in Louisiana four years ago. Leonov also killed her father, by the way. Luca does not know about any of this.

"Vince was ashamed. But the woman may have threatened to expose their affair. We are quite certain Leonov orchestrated that woman's death last month and made it look like a Voodoo killing to destabilize The Lit and make it easier for Watchtower to acquire. Leonov expected Vince to encourage owners and Luca to sell.

"And we know that Vince and Luca are—were—a couple. Sir."

Don Gaspari's neutral mask never cracked. His right elbow on the arm of his chair ensured his thumb supported his chin with an index finger against his sunken right cheek.

Without turning his head but cocking it to his right and back, his eyes drifted up and to his left to look at his friend, Rocko. McQ saw the sadness in each of their eyes after this barrage of emotional artillery.

"GREIGH, ARE YOU A FRIEND?"

"Yes, sir, I am. And I vowed to Luca while he held Vince's body in his arms yesterday morning, and I held him, that I would do whatever I could to find them justice.

"But I must tell you, sir. While we hold recorded evidence that Leonov directed his henchman, Raspin, to hit McQ here and me, we only *suppose* that he had Vince killed. However, it *is* a logical conclusion."

"We know of this mongrel, Raspin. But tell me. Why would he risk killing someone under my protection, Greigh."

"Sir, it pains me to tell you this, but Vince was collaborating with Leonov to have his mistress murdered by Raspin. *And* to encourage Luca and their condo owners to sell to Watchtower their—our—units, as well as the building itself. Vince told his mistress he was expecting a huge payday. We've verified this with two different sources. Sir."

"Was little Vinnie's mistress this murdered poet that's been in the news?"

"Yes, sir."

The ensuing silence sounded deadly. Greigh had taken a mammoth risk, accusing one of this powerful man's favorites of multiple betrayals. A full minute passed. No one said anything, or even moved.

This was a pivotal moment.

"WHY?"

"Sir?"

Why would my Luca's little Vinnie do this thing?"

A frightening sneer broke through Don Gaspari's neutral mask. Was that disbelief? Anger? Did he sense Greigh had betrayed "his Luca's" husband?

Greigh said, "We can only speculate. Vince's lifestyle was… opulent. I could not help but notice his watch alone is worth several million dollars. We're convinced he grew weary of living hand-to-mouth, so to speak. Even with your generous support, the hotel has always struggled. Vince loathed the struggle.

"Leonov has been trying to acquire The Lit for years, as you are aware. His escalation to multiple murders is likely driven by some sense of urgency, so he offered Vince an obscene amount of money—we don't know exactly how much—to get the deal done. And now it is clear why he did so."

The Don's frown turned curious.

"Why?"

"We have it on good authority that through his various shell corporations, Leonov has already purchased every property central to the Near Southwest Loop. That includes all properties north of Harrison to just south of the Ida B. Wells, east of Plymouth Court to west of Wabash. Everything except The Lit and the Church of the Holy Innocents already belong to Watchtower."

"I repeat, why?"

"He plans to build a stadium, casino, parking structures, and a huge hotel."

COPOLLA SHOT ANOTHER KNOWING GLANCE TOWARD Rocko, who just nodded, almost imperceptibly.

"I see. What are his weaknesses?"

"He likes young black women, and he is convinced he is above the law. A friend of McQ's here works at the gentleman's club called 'Flights of Fancy' near The Lit."

Rocko had been standing close to the Don as if shielding him from some unseen threat with his hands clasped below his waist at the end of his braided-anchor-chain arms. He said, "I know of that place."

Greigh nodded to him and continued. His gaze returned to the old Don. "Our friend says Raspin spends time there early every Thursday evening. We suspect he is there to hire young black women."

Rocko said, "For Leonov."

Greigh said, "That's a good bet, Rocko."

Don Gaspari looked into Greigh's eyes like a lie detector. He must have satisfied himself with what he saw. He then peered up to catch Rocko's eyes once more.

Greigh fell silent and waited. McQ started fidgeting.

"Thank you, Greigh. You are indeed a good friend. You have performed for us an invaluable service, you and your... consultant." He only offered a tired smile, first to Greigh, then to McQ.

The meeting was over. Rocko said, "I'll drive you back, Mr. Greigh and Ms. McQuillan."

It wasn't lost on McQ that neither Rocko Bianchi nor the Don called her "Detective."

Sharp folks. Deadly, *and* sharp.

Had they just made matters better, or worse? Trusting someone like Gaspari Copolla was like trusting a rattler protecting her young. Or so some books said.

CHAPTER 81

S afe house? More of a safe *closet*. Back in McQ's apartment, she
said, "Right now, we need to share what we told Gaspari Copolla
with that putz Johnson as lead detective. Or we're both headed to jail
for obstruction. Agreed?"

Greigh hesitated only for a moment and nodded. "Yes, although we
are not obliged to tell him who else with whom we have spoken,
are we?"

"Strictly speaking— "

"No, Q, not strictly."

"Hey, I'm no lawyer. Let's just tell Johnson who'll tell Granger
everything. Except we won't mention Copolla unless he asks. If they
ask *how* we got this info, I'm throwing you under the bus as the non-
cop in this dynamic duo, okay?"

"Hey, I've got friends with friends. Vince was a friend, of sorts.
Luca still is. Vince was a private citizen who unlawfully recorded a
conversation that he shared with us. Who's to say otherwise? Luca
will say whatever I ask. Fair enough?"

"Yeah, I guess. None of you are cops, and whatever they did, they
were in survival mode. Luca still is. Let's just see where this takes us."

Nine-nine time. They walked up Dearborn to the precinct house together, where they sat down with Johnson at his desk in the squad room and told him everything—except of their visit with Gaspari Copolla. Nor that Leonov pointed Raspin's gun at the two of them. They did not want to be locked up in protective custody. They had work to do.

Johnson said, "Holy shit, guys. You been busy."

McQ frowned and said, "Yeah, well, things were moving fast, and this is part of Greigh's world. Why I brought him in on this case."

"So you think Leonov had a shooter go after Vince Donati. And you think that's the guy—not the other Voodoo guy—what also killed this Thibodaux chick."

"Oh, for crissake, Johnson, that's what we just told you."

"Yeah, yeah, okay, smart-ass. You're the one who— "

Greigh butted in, "We've shared everything we have with you, Detective Johnson. We will now leave all this in your capable hands. And you have my number for any more questions, alright?"

McQ stood up too quickly next to Johnson's desk in the squad room, followed by a startled Johnson and a too-calm Greigh.

Johnson pulled his glare away from McQ and looked at the much taller Greigh who already had his hand stuck out. A man-to-man shake and a good-natured pat on the detective's left shoulder.

Johnson said, "Greigh, you I like. Yeah, you guys can go. And thanks for the information. We'll take it from here."

He addressed Greigh without looking at McQ. He didn't see her eye roll as she turned to leave with Greigh shrugging at Johnson and trailing behind.

As if it was an afterthought, Greigh turned back to Detective Johnson. McQ was already halfway to the squad room door. Greigh said, "Oh, one last question, Detective. What did the forensics team find from the Vince Donati shooting? I was there. It was bad." He lowered his eyes as if trying to shed a horrific memory.

A little drama can't hurt.

~

DETECTIVE JOHNSON SHOOK HIS HEAD. HE SAID, "WELL, I'M not supposed to talk about that, but what the hell. All they found was the weird slug that passed through the victim's skull.

"Because it passed right through both of his temples—soft spots—and got stopped by a bar stool cushion, it was in good shape, even after passing through heavy window glass. The slug was a...," he referred to his wristPad notes, "... a slug they figure was from a .338 Lapua Magnum cartridge, a sub-sonic round.

"The forensic guy said that is unique to a...," he referred to his notes again, and read aloud, like he really didn't know what the words or acronyms meant, "... an old IWI DAN—a precision tactical rifle designed with the Israeli Defense Force back in the twenty-first century."

Johnson looked up at Greigh with a smirk, but he was already hustling away.

Weird guy, but I do love his books.

~

THEY HIT THE STREET. McQ SAID, "SUCK UP, MUCH?"

"It's called diplomacy, Q. You might try it, sometime. I just wanted a clean exit. Let's get off the street. We need to talk. I'm about to kill someone myself."

The man was not kidding. That feral sneer. She'd seen that on his face one other time—just before he violently threw a glass at his fireplace.

"Greigh, what are you talking about? You're scaring me!"

There was that feral sneer again. This time his face looked on the verge of exploding.

"Johnson just told me the slug they pulled out of Vince is *the same obscure caliber and vintage that killed my family three years ago.*"

That revelation stunned McQ, too.

"But wait. What would be Raspin's, or Leonov's, motivation for killing your wife and daughter?"

"Think about it, goddammit. I was spearheading the effort to prevent a hostile takeover of The Lit. By Leonov. We already *know* he's willing to kill to make that happen. Even now.

"He had Sybil killed to make The Lit look like an unsafe place to live. He had Vince killed because he failed to deliver, so he's escalating. Now he has a hit out for us because we're getting in the way. Remember what Raspin said during Vince's meeting with him at Watchtower? When Vince named us, Raspin said, 'For crissake, not this Greigh guy *again*.'

"And what resulted from Mel and Clance—the two most precious people to me—getting killed? I resigned my position as president of The Lit's homeowner's association, and I went into an emotional tailspin.

"I backed off. It fucking worked!"

Is this the first time I've heard him swear?

He now marched back and forth on the sidewalk at such a furious pace, McQ feared he might walk into traffic on Dearborn without realizing it. She grabbed him by the arm and led him to her place one long block south.

"Let's get off the street. Now."

CHAPTER 82

M cQ's Apartment
Chicago, Illinois
10:35 AM

Loneliness is a cruel mistress. But sometimes, solitude is called for.

McQ planted Greigh on her sofa, slipped on a hoodie, went for a walk. The man needed to be alone. They would not give Leonov's trigger-man a free shot at them, so they continued to lay low. But her apartment was not designed for more than one. He struggled. She understood. And now, getting muddied up with a crime boss?

Unbelievable.

Greigh never considered himself lonely. He was just a loner. Butler *was* his only friend, and not even human. He now considered McQ a friend, too, or something else, but he wasn't sure she felt the same.

Ever since he lost Mel and Clance, nothing but his writing seemed important. Along with the occasional crusade. Even now, writer's block and dark thoughts plagued him more and more.

He'd sit for hours holding the rag doll that belonged to his beloved little Clance. He flirted with insanity when he exhumed their bodies, had them cremated and hand-sewed their urns of ash into the doll's abdomen. Somehow, though, little Clance and Mel seemed closer, insane or not. He could still smell Clance whenever he clutched the three-foot doll's face to his.

The monster who he now knew raped Sybil and murdered her father invaded his every waking moment. And the killer that worked for him *assassinated* his wife and six-year-old daughter. Because of *his own actions*. Because he championed The Lit's cause and got in the way of a bloody real estate deal!

At least Ty Leonov put Sybil's father out of his misery before the poor man suffered a lifetime of grief over his daughter's brutal rape and later, her murder.

But Greigh's profound grief only made him bitter and analytical. They would never bring these killers to justice by conventional means.

HE ALSO TORTURED HIMSELF FOR BEING SO EASILY deluded. They had been on the wrong track, looking for an angry poet as Sybil's killer with Voodoo as his method. But too many loose ends left them searching. That burned valuable time and cost Sango her life.

Then, they suspected one or both of the Donatis. But as tragic events unfolded, including Vince Donati's assassination, they learned Leonov was the mastermind, and Raspin his trigger. Men like that floated above the law. And to learn that Raspin *also* killed his own wife and daughter?

I can't change the past, but if we had solved this case sooner, dear Sango would still be alive. Even Vince didn't deserve to die like that, and right in front of poor Luca. I let the murders of my precious wife and daughter go unavenged for three bloody years. I put myself off the trail. **My selfish grief blinded me!**

Now, two more good people are dead and a good cop is off the job she loves. What else can't I see, even now?

Greigh recognized he was no murderer, even though he had killed in battle, and in the streets. But could he now let someone else do his killing for him since justice was as blind as he? More so? Greigh realized his bitterness tainted his ethics.

So personal for so long.

And now....

CHAPTER 83

Thursday, July 5th
    Flights of Fancy Gentlemen's Club
Chicago, Illinois
5:01 PM

SOMEONE SAT IN *his* SPOT. TEODOR RASPIN, A.K.A. Rasputin, approached the table, glared down at the wimp sitting in his seat with malevolence in his eyes until the pervert moved to another spot on the far side of the stage.

He told the boss they shouldn't be this predictable—every damn Thursday—but the heart wants what the heart wants, Leonov'd say. Besides, he wanted to celebrate America's Independence Day—belatedly—with a few fireworks of a personal nature.

Rasputin flagged his favorite server. He whispered in her ear as he slid a few folded hundreds onto her little drink tray.

"Any new girls this week, Andy?"

"Yeah, handsome. She's young and she's so black, she's almost blue. Plus, she's so new, she doesn't even have a dance routine yet. Name's Lindy. Want an intro, sweetie?"

"Sure, that'd be great. Thanks, Andy."

He slipped a few more hundreds to her. She smiled, but winced because as she walked away, the thug slapped her ass hard enough to hurt.

He knew he wasn't pretty. Didn't care. The obvious centerpiece of Rasputin's colossal head was his bulbous red and pock-marked nose. Too many buckets of vodka and fatty food. Too many nights living in trenches or shit-hole brothels surveilling shit-heels for clients in the old country before coming to work for Leonov.

Raspin always aligned all dozen of his black hairs by keeping them combed and waxed straight back. His neck hair, however, got real shaggy, like the Rasputin of old. The boss didn't care, as long as he produced results.

Two triple shots of vodka later, Andy sauntered over with a petite little *quadroon.* That's what the boss called 'em, but he didn't have a clue what that meant.

But do I ever know the boss's type.

Rasputin thought she looked about sixteen years old, and scared. Perfect. The boss is gonna love this one, for sure.

"Rasputin, this here is Lindy." She held out Lindy's reluctant hand for him to accept.

"Pleased to make your acquaintance, sir." Her twangy and muddled voice quivered. Took him several beats to parse what she had just said. Sounded like 'Plyzed-ta-mike-yah-kwyne-tinz-suh.' It all ran together.

She even sounds like a quadroon!

"Little lady, you're shaking like a leaf, and your tiny hand is ice cold. Hey, you got some world-class callouses."

"I ain't never done nuttin'' like dis before. Sir. I done work da fields afore comin' ta dis here city." She pushed her shy voice to be heard over the club noise.

Oh, man. The boss is gonna fantasize this girl is a slave!

"Well, don't you worry. You're about to become a very rich quad… young lady. Would you like to go for a ride in a very nice car?"

She peered at Andy with wide eyes, who offered her a slight nod of encouragement.

"Um, guess so."

THE PLACE REEKED OF MONEY. TY LEONOV'S PERSONAL suite on the twenty-seventh floor left little Lindy speechless. Round-eyed and slack-jawed, she looked up and around at all the chrome and gloss.

She said, "Oh, Lordy."

Aw, man, she's a fresh one, alright. The boss is gonna flip over this one.

TY SWAGGERED TOWARD HIS "GUESTS."

He wore a midnight-blue silk robe, a white silk ascot, suede slippers… not a synthetic fiber on his person. And he wore a huge smile when he saw Rasp with a little girl in tow. He wanted to ensure they saw every one of his too-white teeth.

"Rasp, you introduce me your friend?"

"Ty, this is Lindy. She's never done anything like this before, so she's feeling a little unsure of herself."

"Well, that's just okay. Lindy, I am pleasured to meet you. Let us to do this. I give you money—say, one thousand dollars. For that, I treat you like gentle lover for hour or two. Then, Rasp here, he give you ride wherever you wish to go. That help little? Lindy?"

The handsome man with bad grammar came close to drooling over this child-like waif in her translucent little dress and simple peasant sandals. He could see she wore no bra. Didn't need one. Authentic.

"Well, sir, I sure could use dat money. But, well, be it okay dat I ain't never done *nuttin'* like dis before? Sorry if I warn't clear on dat. I guess I'm willin' to larn, though."

Ty giggled.

Da, this will be night to remember.

"That's fine, child. I teach you. We have biggest fun together."

"Alright den, sir, yer terms be acceptable." She looked over at Rasp and said, "Andy from de club done tol' me ta say dat." She offered him a small smile. Rasp bobbed his head, chewed on his toothpick, and failed to suppress a smile as he glanced over at his boss, who just nodded his appreciation.

Rasp said, "Well, Lindy, I'll leave you in Ty's hands." He turned to leave, still smiling.

Still early. I'll go back to the club. Maybe talk to Andy some more. If she's not too busy.

Rasputin crossed the glossy lobby, nodded to the guard at his desk, waited for him to push the button, and shoved through the rotating doors to the street. Descended the dozen steps to his car awaiting him in the circle drive. He thought of Andy's ass and believed she liked him—or at least his money—well enough for a frolic.

A homeless man wandered near his car, either intending to steal it or looking for a handout. Rasputin's trained eye saw no thief here, just another poor sucker who didn't understand the rules of the jungle. If you weren't a predator, you were prey.

"Sorry, mister, you got a few credits to spare? I sure am hungry."

"Sure, why not? Here ya go." He reached into his pocket, came out with just his clenched fist. Delivered a vicious belly shot that doubled over the stinky indigent who fell to the ground. Rasputin sneered at him, and muttered, "Get a job, ya bum."

He turned to get into his car a few feet away when he heard the bum who was still down. He said, "Hey, you arrogant prick. Did I fail to mention I hate bullies?"

Bam, bam, bam, bam, bam, bam, click, click, click....

❧

LEONOV PURRED. HE PETTED THE GIRL'S SHORT AFRO LIKE he would a poodle. "Come, little one. You like glass of wine? Or something strong?"

"Yes, sir, whatever you gots. I could use some relaxin' right 'bout now. Whatever you havin'."

They both walked toward the bar just inside the windows that overlooked Lake Michigan. As Ty released her arm—it was so warm, and black, and creamy smooth—he turned away to pour their drinks.

He felt a pin-prick on the side of his neck and thought a bee had stung him. But there were no bees any more, not in the wild.

The next thing he knew, he and his quadroon were out enjoying the view of the darkening lake from his magnificent balcony. He had misplaced the last few minutes.

"Child, why we stand up here?"

It occurred to him he had a silly decision to make—to fall twenty-seven stories to his death or to fly away like the bee that had stung him.

He said over the noise of the gentle wind, "I choose to fly, yes?"

Tihomir Leonov, the wealthiest man in Chicago, the sixth richest person in America, President and CEO of Watchtower Inc., sensed more than heard this delightful child's voice whisper in his ear.

"Yes, evil one, you shall fly on wings granted you by the innocent souls you have murdered or defiled. This death is too easy. Die, you morally bankrupt fuck."

And with that, Ty drifted into the clouds, certain that he had misunderstood the little black angel at his side.

So young, but—

<h1 style="text-align:center">CHAPTER 84</h1>

The deaths of Tihomir Leonov and Teodor Raspin made both the local and national feeds. Greigh grinned. Life is precious, but....

The man who killed Mel, Clance, Sybil Thibodaux, Vince Donati—and probably countless others—plus the one who gave the kill orders, they both got better than they deserved.

Authorities called Leonov's death a suicide, although his autopsy revealed some exotic and unidentifiable substance in his bloodstream. Nobody needed the grief of giving *that* any visibility.

Raspin's shooting was deemed a mugging gone wrong.

On the same night.

A tragic coincidence.

GREIGH CALLED McQ. SOUNDING CHIPPER, HE SAID, "HEY there. I'm headed down to Sherwood to deliver the news to Zelda and Obeah Man. Care to join me?"

"Hi, Greigh. I'd love to. I'll meet you at your place in twenty."

"Minutes?"

"Shut up!"

Click.

He grew warm and fuzzy at the prospect of seeing Q again.

THEY GOT A FEW LOOKS. ENTERING THE LIT'S SECOND-floor hallway together, not dressed down, Greigh and McQ were greeted once more by thick air and the pungent buzz of humanity just getting along.

It seemed to Greigh this part of The Lit was... whole and good. People here seemed to help others and got to know each other more genuinely than elsewhere. Even while respecting each other's space. Most here had reduced life to its essentials.

And yes, there would always be malcontents.

They'd been here enough over the last two weeks that they even received a few friendly nods. Well, Greigh did. He even shook some hands when they were offered. Seemed nice to McQ. She now understood the appeal of this place like she never could have as a cop.

The Creole contingent from New Orleans had not moved. They still camped in the same spot in the same room across the hall from the second-floor stairwell. But now, others who had not been there before shared their space. The mood in the room seemed almost festive. But subdued. Maybe... reverent?

The three young men and one young woman with Obeah Man and Zelda looked more relaxed as they chatted with nearby campers, sitting in small circles.

But they came to attention when they saw McQ and Greigh approach. Greigh offered a friendly wave. The soft buzz in the spacious room descended into a near-hush.

They walked up to Zelda Zenaida Coincoin and Obeah Man—Clairvius Rincisse—who sat on their now-shared bedroll shoulder-to-shoulder. Sybil Thibodaux's estranged biological parents.

A wiry little woman with olive skin and hollow cheeks sat cross-legged just in front of them. She peered over her circular spectacles with reverence up into Zelda's eyes, but looked concerned as Greigh and McQ approached.

Zelda reached across and offered a reassuring pat on the young woman's scabbed knee. Greigh heard Zelda say, "We talks again, Indira. Blessings be upon ya, me dear."

The woman bobbed her head, held her hands in front of her for a moment as if she were praying, and rose to return to her own camp site nearby in the same room.

In her husky half-whisper, Zelda said, "Greigh, Miss Q, most welcome. Sit. Please."

Obeah Man smiled and nodded.

THEY SAT ON THE FLOOR, TOO. NOW ACROSS FROM THIS enigmatic couple, Greigh said, "We wanted to tell you ourselves. The man who attacked Sybil and killed her adoptive father four years ago, as well as the man who killed Sybil last month, are both dead. Justice has been served. You can take your daughter's body home in peace, now."

Both Zelda and Obeah Man began nodding their heads in slow synchrony as Greigh revealed the news.

Zelda purred, "We's thanks ya, Greigh, Miss Q. And our blessings be on you's, me dearies. We's understands de man dat kilt Sybil also kilt you's child and bride not so long gone. We's now lets our Sybil go, along wi' de anger 'n de pain 'n de shame. So must you's, too." She cast a meaningful glance, first at Greigh, then at McQ.

"How did you—?"

"Please accept deez humble gifts we's offers you's on behalf of de loa. Mebbe Bondye hisself."

Greigh knew the gris-gris they had conjured for him and for McQ represented a great honor. His face broadcast surprise and deference and appreciation. McQ had no clue, but she followed suit.

Zelda spoke while Obeah Man performed the honors of leaning forward to place the lanyard of each pouch around each of their necks with a few rumbled Creole words neither of them understood.

Zelda said, "Miss Q, we done conjured dis juju fer ya on behalf of de loa Erzulie, goddess a beauty 'n love. She's be all 'bout femininity 'n womanhood. Erzulie, she's represents de cosmic womb, mudder a de world. She 'n her family a loa, dey be called upon fer mudderhood 'n strong feminine sex'ality. Dis be blessings on you's as a woman, Miss Q."

"Thank you, Zelda. I am honored and grateful."

"You's so welcome, me dearie. And Greigh, fer you's, Damballah be a most important loa w' two sides, like you's, but you's knows dis." She paused to look into his soul through his eyes, like she knew every secret. There were many.

"Damballah, he's helps de god Bondye makes de cosmos, and he be keeper a knowledge, wisdom, an' healin' magic. Like us, you's now let go yer pain, ya? You's lose much. Dat past now. You's now heal and tink of Erzulie, 'n of tomorrow."

Zelda winked at Greigh, nodded toward McQ. They all smiled. Greigh said nothing, but a tear rolled down one cheek. He didn't need to say anything.

Zelda turned her attention back to McQ and said, "Oh, Missy, you's tanks you's friend Dani fer gettin' our little Lindy dat job where she work." Zelda cast a glance back over her shoulder at the little woman standing sentry with the three men behind them. "Lindy sends her tanks too, but she's says dancin' not fer her. She's maybe tries actin'. Says she's stayin' here fer a time in dis here place." She waved her arms to take in Sherwood.

"Of course. Sorry it didn't work out."

Greigh listened to this with interest before he spoke. "When—?"

McQ said, "I'll catch you up later."

CHAPTER 85

Rocko Bianchi reflected. Even though an influential lieutenant and muscle within Gaspari Copolla's organization, he had had a secret affair with Luca Donati once upon a time. Before Luca met and fell in love with Vince and secretly married him. Nobody's business but their own.

Aubrey Greigh said Sybil Thibodaux had seduced Vince to seek dirt on Ty Leonov. She had learned that Russian thug was the monster who raped her and killed her papá in Louisiana four years earlier. Vince must have blabbed to her about his collaboration with Leonov. He never could keep his mouth shut. No wonder she hunted that pig from Moscow and squeezed Vince for information.

Apparently, Leonov had Thibodaux eliminated, and set up an elaborate ruse to make it look like a Voodoo zombie killed her.

That's a real thing? Who knew? I bet Greigh did.

According to Greigh, despite the Voodoo smokescreen, Vince still wasn't able to convince Luca or The Lit's condo owners to sell. But then, his heart wasn't in it.

Little Vinnie could be convincing when he wanted to be.

Time must have been running out on Leonov's big stadium, hotel and casino project. He needed the land under The Lit and the

362

surrounding neighborhood. The Lit was now the *only* remaining property he still needed to acquire, according to Greigh and his own sources.

All out of options, Leonov escalated. Greigh said the Russian had Vince assassinated, hoping to put sufficient pressure on Luca to accept his purchase offer. That didn't work either. But then, thanks to information supplied by Greigh and that pretty redhead, Leonov and his trigger man, Teodor Raspin, ended up dead. A real shame. They were stupid enough to murder Vince, who was under Don Gaspari's protection.

Idiots. Serves 'em right.

Besides, Greigh was smart enough to realize they would never get Leonov or Raspin into a courtroom.

ROCKO ADMITTED HE'D GONE SOFT. THE CAPO CLOSEST TO Don Gaspari Copolla *still* held a spot in his heart for Luca Donati. Especially now that the lovable hotel entrepreneur's husband Vince was killed by Leonov's henchman.

Luca was all alone.

Not only that, but Luca's father, "Hard Tony," had known all along about Vince, Luca and himself. Even though their lifestyle was vietato —forbidden—in their culture, Tony had kept their secret, the saints rest his grumpy soul.

As far as Rocko was aware, only *he* knew that Tony and Don Gaspari himself once had a fling of their own in their reckless youth, so old Tony had understood.

NOW, THOUGH, THEY WERE ALL BETRAYED. THE OLD DON spoke out *publicly* against the "fancy" lifestyle. He forbad it within the Copolla family. Respectability had become Don Gaspari's top priority, above all else, even above the old loyalties, but within the old rules.

Now, Rocko—who had *always* been loyal to the old Don—felt betrayed by this hypocritical proclamation.

Despite his loyalty to the Don, Rocko could *not* do nothing.

Conflicted, he contacted his still-dear friend, Luca. Informed him that Don Gaspari had used them all to get rid of Leonov, his only competition for the land on which The Lit and the surrounding neighborhoods sat.

But with pressure from the Feds on his nationwide enterprises, Gaspari needed absolute innocence with respect to coercing property owners to sell. He would now just legally hijack Leonov's stadium/casino/hotel project targeting Chicago's Near Southwest Loop. But worst of all in Rocko's mind, despite his past sponsorship, like Leonov, **Gaspari, too, planned to demolish The Lit.**

That would destroy poor Luca!

ROCKO'S CALL CUT DEEP WHEN HE LEARNED FROM DEAR Rocko of this most personal betrayal. Though Luca had always enjoyed Don Gaspari's protection and personal affection, he too now felt not only betrayed but conflicted.

The Don would kick him out of his *home?* His and Vince's home? Luca was beside himself.

So many thoughts swirled through his brain.

I feel like my life is being flushed. I can't do this alone!

Greigh had vowed to help. After all, The Lit was his home, too. And the home of so many memories.

For both of them.

Luca called his friend Greigh

CHAPTER 86

The betrayal felt complete. All of this new input exponentially escalated Greigh's emotional turmoil, too.

They had just aided the Don in eliminating Leonov—his competition. How much of Leonov's plan had the old Don known about all along?

Now, according to Luca, Gaspari planned to execute those plans, *including the destruction of The Lit.* Instead of protecting it, the Don had been biding his time to acquire it and bulldoze it himself.

He is no better than Leonov. Worse. He used his so-called "friends."

GREIGH WRACKED HIS BRAIN. HOW MUST HE AVERT THIS catastrophe? With Zelda's and Obeah Man's Voodoo? Or the more practical approach—blackmail?

Brilliant, old bean. Blackmail one of the most powerful gangsters in America? That is nought but a death wish. Or... what if I can negotiate a compromise? What if his new friend Rocko would be willing to nudge the old man?

Greigh thought he might appeal to the Don's sense of honor, and out of respect for the son of the man who the Don was "once very close to." Greigh would be treading in shark-infested waters, and he would be the chum. But he, too, felt betrayed. First by Leonov, now by Copolla.

Greigh didn't give a damn about any property in the area except The Lit.

HE SHARED ALL OF THIS WITH McQ. NOW IT MADE SENSE to her. When they first learned that Vince and Luca were a couple, she wondered about the mob's uncharacteristic tolerance for their lifestyle. She now saw it was all a facade to achieve Gaspari Copolla's well-timed land-grab.

The man is a master of the long con. And dangerous. Greigh is going to negotiate with this guy? Nothin' but nuts!

Gaspari just laid in the weeds and let Leonov do all the dirty work of lining up his "urban re-gentrification project." Then, old Don just leveraged Greigh's and her information, along with the emotion of others, to get rid of Leonov without surfacing his true motive.

That damn Russian hadn't a clue what *re-gentrification* meant. Didn't matter. The Muscovite and his organization pressured owners into selling—for *years*—and almost succeeded. They led the slow and steady march to intimidate owners, to acquire deeds and permits while staving off political pressure.

Now that Leonov and his top lieutenant ate dirt, Gaspari could swoop in and pick up those deeds for pennies on the dollar.

Damn clever.

GASPARI CONGRATULATED HIMSELF. HE HAD HANDLED THIS affair masterfully. This project would advance his prestige within the community. He'd now demonstrate his own concern for "re-gentrification." Then his new friend, Greigh, called.

Of course, he would answer

CHAPTER 87

Greigh sat in his apartment once more. This call to Don Gaspari Copolla could end his life, or start a new one.

"Sir, allow me to get straight to the point. I've learned you assumed ownership of Leonov's stadium, casino and hotel project. And that it is your intention to demolish The Lit along with all the other buildings you acquired after Leonov timed out. Is that true? Sir?"

The prolonged silence that followed was not a good sign. Maybe the old Don was gathering his thoughts after being slapped in the face by an impertinent Scottish scribe. Then....

"Greigh, I know how much your apartment means to you. The memories... but I will offer you four times what it is worth. The same offer goes for all the other owners. And I will make Luca a wealthy man. He can then be a patron of the arts anywhere in the world, without all the worries. Now, is that not fair?"

Greigh gathered his next words with care. This could earn him a bullet in the head or a swan dive from his balcony. After five seconds of planning for a rough landing, he continued.

"Sir, you fail to understand that The Lit is more than property to those of us who live here. It is an ideal. It is a dream worth fighting for. *And* memories. Tearing it down for a casino and a hundred yards of green carpet tears apart hundreds of gentle souls.

"But I do not expect you to accept a mere altruistic ideal. I would like to propose a beneficial solution for *all* of us, including for the son of your *carissima*. Will you listen to an idea that I think you will like very much?"

Another prolonged silence. Could Greigh hear over the comms fingernails tapping furiously on a hard surface? Maybe that table next to the huge chair in front of the fireplace at Club Sicily?

"I will listen to your idea, Greigh. I owe you that much. But whatever you think you know, you will never use the word *carissima* again. Yes?"

Shit!

"Sorry, sir. Of course. Thank you. I wish to keep you as a friend, but also to enhance your station within this community *and across America*. This is now within your grasp.

"If your intent is to follow through on the original project that pig Leonov has been pushing—stadium, casino, hotel—I can help. I will advocate with Luca and all of our owners to support that project under your leadership. Let me explain why you will love this solution.

"I offer you a fresh perspective. The Lit comprises only five percent of your project's geographical area, including the area's vertical development potential. Build your project, sir, but adjust it so The Lit remains on its southern border. You then lay claim to modernizing the Near Southwest Loop *while preserving a pivotal piece of America's rich history*.

"Sir, you may or may not know Hotel Literati is already on Chicago's Historic Resources Survey because of its incredible French Beaux Arts style of architecture. Everything about it represents a pivotal period in our nation's history—from the 1920s when gangsters were revered members on the national stage, but nowhere more than in this community.

"Our building possesses unique historical and aesthetic value.

Demolishing her would be problematic for you legally, and perhaps politically with the city of Chicago. It would be viewed as a travesty by anyone passionate about significant historical sites. That's something that mongrel cur Leonov never understood. This historical designation is an enormous deal.

"*But,* with your blessing, and on your behalf as The Lit's new owner, I *also* would pursue getting The Lit added to the *National* Register of Historical Sites. You buy the building, the present owners keep their units, and perhaps you allow Hard Tony's son Luca to manage the property for you. That's *his* dream, and you reap the *very* public prestige of owning a *nationally* significant part of historic downtown Chicago, the greatest city in the world.

"*And* you *also* surround it with the most modern and profitable entertainment complex in the world, while providing hundreds, maybe thousands of locals good-paying jobs. Hell, you might even consider running for mayor with the accolades that will pile up at your front gate. I suggest this would be a monumental victory for all concerned, especially for you personally.

"What do you think, sir?"

"WHERE DID YOU GET YOUR INFORMATION, GREIGH?"

"It doesn't matter, sir. Like you, I have many friends. We all want what's best for your business *and* for our personal lives. It's that simple, sir. And I truly mean no disrespect."

Another pregnant pause, followed by a deep breath.

"Alright, Greigh. I will direct my people to adjust the project's parameters to accommodate your solution. And I look forward to working with you on achieving The Literati's enhanced status as a nationally recognized historical site. Thank you for seeking a solution we can all honorably live with. Once more, I am in your debt, Greigh."

Those last words sounded like they were hard for the old Don to utter, but he said them anyway.

"Sir, I appreciate working with honorable men, and you are a man of honor. Thank *you.*"

CHAPTER 88

A new day dawned. Greigh achieved some degree of emotional closure by saving The Lit *and* by seeing justice served, especially for his wife and daughter.

He no longer felt guilty over his growing feelings for a certain smart-arse lady detective. And he was more at peace professionally. It was time to begin developing fertile ideas for a new mystery series featuring a handful of Creole characters. With a smaller voice, he could carry on Sybil Thibodaux's work.

But instead of his darker stuff of late, which his publisher said wasn't selling like his earlier work, he planned to write some feel-good cozy mysteries. His publisher said he was sure to score a series of lucrative movie deals.

He also labored prodigiously to fulfill his commitment to the old Don. Besides, The Lit on the National Register of Historical Sites? That held great personal appeal. Partnering with Signore Copolla, now just Gaspari, they targeted specific but sweeping upgrades to The Lit necessary for prestigious sites of national significance. The old building received a badly needed facelift.

Greigh even committed to writing and publishing The Literati's historiography. This would be a factual account of its fascinating history, crafted within the proscribed principles, theories and methods of scholarly historical research and presentation. Such a study would elevate its heritage not only to a national level of prestige but also within a revered academic context.

Rumor had it that Signore Gaspari Copolla, patron of the arts *and* history, was thrilled.

Greigh settled into his writing routine once more. And that's when the University of Chicago offered him a teaching position as an honorary professor. He considered accepting that creative writing gig with a bent toward highlighting social issues, but only on his own timetable, of course.

McQ REMAINED ON ADMINISTRATIVE LEAVE. AT LEAST IT was with pay. But she was elated to have helped solve this high-profile case. She'd have to live with getting a civilian killed on her watch, but this job had never been without risk.

She had even convinced her sparring partner at the gym and exotic dancer extraordinaire, Dani, that her personal life wasn't as much of an emotional dumpster fire as previously presumed.

McQ remained on paid administrative leave for the time being for allowing Sango Mori's unfortunate demise during one of her rogue police operations. They told her it could take a while to sort out unless the department relented. Little chance of that. The department worried it could be held responsible for a wrongful death civil suit, even though McQ did nothing wrong.

Freaking optics.

She now harbored second thoughts about returning to the CED at all, even if cleared of all charges. She, too, felt betrayed. But she vowed to ask Greigh out, if for no other reason, to show her friend Dani that her personal life was not an emotional dumpster fire *at all*.

Oops, wrong reason, and not the real reason, *at all*.

McQ admitted to herself she had had more fun the last few weeks than during her entire career up to that point.

Is it wrong to want the job to be fun AND meaningful?

LUCA RE-EXAMINED HIS HEART. HE CONSIDERED GETTING back together with his old flame, Rocko, although he remembered they didn't have all that much in common. Besides, he wasn't yet over losing Vince. He might never be. But he so appreciated Rocko and Greigh saving their precious home with all its memories—bad and good.

With Don Gaspari buying The Lit and asking Luca to manage it for him, he continued living his dream, but without so many headaches and worries.

Now, he battled loneliness.

OBEAH MAN AND ZELDA VOWED TO KEEP IN TOUCH WITH Greigh as they returned to New Orleans with their daughter's body.

Greigh planned deeper research into Voodoo and Louisiana free Creoles of color for an upcoming manuscript that scaffolded on an old work in progress. He had become more fascinated than ever with the Louisiana Creole peoples during their colonial, antebellum and more contemporary evolutions of that ever-evolving culture.

Zelda invited him to St. John's Parish for a research trip, with a nod from the brooding Obeah Man. Clair still suffered from the loss of their daughter and the stain left by Jacques Memeaux, Voodoo mercenary. Zelda garnered a more spiritual perspective and seemed at peace.

At last. Even with her little Lindy Mansa Troisième Fillenée—third-born daughter—remaining in Chicago to pursue her budding acting career. People said she was very good, and that Lindy Mansa was a force with which to be reckoned.

They gots no idea, do dey? Dey will.

When Greigh visited, Zelda promised him a unique look into her healing world of Voodoo. But she warned him, "Be sure ta brings you's gris-gris. You's might needs dat juju, Greigh. I teach ya alla 'bout us forgotten peoples."

CHAPTER 89

M onday, July 21ˢᵗ
New Orleans, Louisiana
5:15 PM

Iᴛ ᴡᴀs ɢᴏᴏᴅ ᴛᴏ ʙᴇ ʜᴏᴍᴇ. Fᴏʀ ᴛʜᴇ ғɪʀsᴛ ᴛɪᴍᴇ ɪɴ ᴡᴇᴇᴋs, Doctor Jacques Memeaux, bokor for hire, breathed in the musky air of his shop in the alley off Rampart Street. He was happy to rinse the stink of Chicago and that whole Literati business out of his spirit. Not that losing that boy bothered him. Price of business.

The stench of those tunnels, though, lingered like the stank of an old brush fire soaks into hair and clothes.

The best of two worlds made him smile. He got the job done *and* the foreign mongrel who paid him—the old Russian—would cause no problems for his own future. That thug must have had a conscience he couldn't live with, the weakling. May Maman Brigitte usher him into the presence of Baron Samedi, the black rooster of Hell himself. At least his credits cleared.

He *had been* concerned that old fool—Clair Rincisse, who consorted with that witch, Zelda Zenaida—had seen and recognized him in that hotel's basement, but his little zombi had handled old Clair, right good.

Obeah Man, me bony ass.

That old man went down *hard.* Good riddance. Maybe that bitch Zelda will be a little less cocky now, if she'd even have the nerve to show back up in the Quarter or down the bayou.

Serves old Clair right for sticking his great black nose where it don't belong. Tru dat.

Then, Jacques issued a rare giggle of delight as he reflected. Without even knowing who Sybil Thibodaux was, he had been a party to the death of Zelda's very own daughter. The delicious irony was worth a damn sissy giggle.

He tossed his be-ribboned top hat that represented his signature attire onto the hat tree behind him, an old plantation piece he'd had for decades. Settled into his favorite armed straight chair of cypress carved with many charms—most of them protective. Leaned back on the chair's hind legs and lit his long-stemmed corn-cob pipe.

No sooner had he kicked his buckled jack-boots up onto the low counter in front of him piled here and there with the tools and arti-facts of his trade than the bell over his door tinkled a welcome to his first customer since returning to the city. Not the part for tourists, mind you, but old Storyville.

Jacques turned his attention from the half-assed flame in his pipe to the newcomer and looked surprised.

"You!"

It all happened so fast. Seconds later, Jacques expected Maman Brigitte to greet him, too.

Bam bam bam bam bam bam, click click click click….

CHAPTER 90

G reigh had travelled to Louisiana. After all, Zelda and Obeah Man invited him. Since McQ was still on leave from the CED, he had invited her along to the "Independent State of New Orleans." She never answered him. He went alone.

Predictable.

The weeks he had spent there gave him everything he needed.

He vowed to reconnect with McQ upon his return.

HE SUCCESSFULLY JUMPSTARTED NEW WORK. RESEARCH FOR yet another project took shape—the first book of his new series—fictional memoirs he'd call "Greigh Areas." The working title of the first in the series? "Voodoo Vendetta - A Literati Mystery." But that title could change.

Sango's friend from Sherwood, Jerry, would illustrate the project for him. The kid's talent would take him far. Plus, conversations with him about the death of their mutual friend proved to be more therapeutic than either would have guessed.

. . .

Two weeks later, McQ sat side-by-side with Greigh, so they could both enjoy the view.

They sipped a special concoction of sweet iced tea infused with his closet-grown mint leaves. A single huge candle with a trio of wicks flickered in the slight breeze of evening twilight as the city below them breathed and found its way to their settee, up on the tented dais.

The haze filtered through the trees and bushes that rimmed Greigh's covered balcony. He and McQ alternated between staring out at the city lights winking on and at the candle's flames dancing in front of them. They sat close, but weren't touching. Like two buddies.

McQ was still on administrative leave. At least until the insanity of the last six weeks could be sorted out. She visited Greigh's place for the second time in a week. Said she wanted to talk.

McQ said, "I'm not sure I even want to be a cop again. But I'm lying to myself. Can't imagine doing anything else."

Greigh said, "You didn't enjoy being a free-wheeling private dick with me?"

"Oh, don't get me wrong, big guy. I did, but you can't live forever on just desserts."

"Q, guys like Leonov and Raspin will always operate above the law. We would never have proven their guilt in court. You know that, right?"

"Yeah, I guess I do. The cop in me wishes that weren't so, but you're right. We helped get justice for Sybil, her father, Sango, and even Vince. By the way, did you hear that when Zelda and her entourage recovered Sybil's body at the nine-nine, they scanned everyone? Learned that the young woman with them, Lindy Mansa, is another of Zelda's daughters?"

"Yes, Zelda shared that with me during my visit."

McQ snapped her head to look Greigh in the eye. "She told you that and you chose not to share that with me?"

"I, ah, meant to do so, yes. What with all that's go—"

"My dear friend, Dani, told me she saw this Lindy leaving her club with Raspin the night Leonov died."

"That *is* a coincidence." Greigh swirled the wine in his glass as he prepared to enjoy its fruity bouquet.

"I'll remind you, Greigh, that was the same night a homeless man was reported in the vicinity. About the same time someone gunned down Raspin by his car in front of the Watchtower building. Almost exactly where we were parked the day we followed Vince Donati to his meeting with Leonov."

An uncomfortable pause preceded Greigh taking a deep breath that broadcast his exasperation. He set down his wine, scratched his neck and squinted as he swiveled to peer at McQ.

"All of that speculation and wondering and driving yourself crazy over something that is more solution than problem? What would you like to do with those factoids, Q?"

"I'm not sure, Greigh. No pun intended, but you live and think more in gray areas than me. A cop thinks in black and white. But we've seen where that gets us. Am I just over-thinking this?"

Greigh didn't hesitate in his response. "Do you think me selfish or immoral to celebrate the demise of four evil men? That Luca and The Literati—my home—will not only survive, but thrive with a new stadium, hotel and casino going up in my backyard? Close enough for a financial halo? Plus, old Don G—that is, Signore Copolla—is throwing money at us so we can make a big splash on the National Register? We needed justice served. She was. In full measure."

"*Four* evil men?"

"You hadn't heard that in addition to Leonov, Raspin and Bidok, someone gunned down Jacques Memeaux in his New Orleans shop?"

"Greigh, we *have* to work on your communications skills. When?"

"I heard about it while I was in town visiting Zelda and Clair.

She had nothing to say about that. But she did say, "Well, I struggle with this. I always will. But, bottom line, you're right." She was still conflicted, but for the greater good.... Unfortunate necessity.

Greigh picked up his glass again, stared straight ahead, and took a sip. "These days, Luca waffles between his grief over losing Vince and thrilled at seeing The Lit getting all dressed up for the dance.

"Q, too bad you can't afford to sublet Sybil's place down the hall. Or what if you could? I hear Professor Janssen will sublet cheap because his apartment was sullied by suffering the indignity of a heinous crime. You may have heard—that flat also features a dumbwaiter."

"Shut up, Greigh."

"Sure, Red."

For a playful moment, they leaned into each other's shoulders.

CHAPTER 91

He's never called me Red *before.*

But was a sublet at The Lit such a crazy idea? She could do worse than Greigh for a neighbor. With his endorsement…. She looked at this guy like she was seeing him for the first time. He seemed different.

I wonder….

"Greigh, I've been meaning to ask you about your life before you got married."

She was taking a risk, but not knowing gnawed at her unhealthy sense of curiosity. Besides, he seemed like a new man after the death of his wife's killer, along with the man who gave the order, and the monsters who killed his friend and neighbor. They had all been served a full measure of justice.

Or was it simple vengeance? Now, with his home once again secure, he seemed more self-assured than ever. That was saying something.

He didn't hesitate. "I was in the habit of indulging in two month-long retreats each year. I found them a source of boundless inspiration."

"Writer's retreats?"

"Most of my writing occurred after returning—between them."

"So, what did you do for a month at a time?"

"I performed sundry services for friends and acquaintances."

"Can you *possibly* be any more mysterious? C'mon, *we're* friends, too, aren't we? You still don't trust me?" She would not let this go.

He looked down his ski-slope nose at her, as if contemplating a speculative investment.

"Erstwhile Detective Chance Goodwyn McQuillan, you must understand I am bound by certain confidentiality agreements. Various foreign entities required my skills and discretion. Now and then, I was well-positioned to complete certain sensitive tasks—of my choosing, by the way. And part of that time, I also received specialized training. To share any more, well, you might find it all rather tedious. I've already said too much."

McQ's forehead grew more wrinkled as he spoke. The shape of her mouth spelled skepticism laced with doubt. Her lips quivered before she said, "You're either shining me on, or..." less doubt now, more incredulity, "you were a *spy*?"

His gravitas deepened as he rubbed his chin, then cradled his lowered forehead between a thumb and two fingers. Raised his head, looked her straight in the eye, and grinned, teeth and all.

Her eyes grew from slits to saucers, and back to pinched slits, all in a few seconds. "Oh, shut up! Greigh, sometimes you just piss me off!"

They both shared hearty laughter that lasted a little too long. He toasted their good health and to feeling like his old self again—after three long years.

He said, "I'll always live with loss, and cherish my family. Thanks for helping me get justice for them. Here's to moving on."

They clinked their glasses, antique Baccarat crystal, of course, as they peered into each other's eyes.

So if that was all BS, where did that freaking knighthood come from?

. . .

Butler's voice sounded urgent. "Greigh, I'm sorry to interrupt, but your debrief checkpoint is imminent. You are aware what happens if—"

"Yes, yes, Butler. Thank you." He looked embarrassed and said, "Sorry, Q. This is time-sensitive. I'd ask you to leave, but... I don't want to."

McQ set down her glass, uncrossed her legs, leaned forward, and prepared to leap into action, suddenly vigilant. But she had no idea why.

He leaned forward, too. Looked at his feet, tapped his temple, and said, "Check in." He waited two seconds for a connection, and whispered, "Alfa-dog-romeo-one-stroke-two-splat-zed, status green... Copy." And he double-tapped to disconnect.

An urgent and cryptic five second call? What the shit!

Her jaw had dropped and remained there. She noticed him watching her, and, what? Evaluating her reaction? Then, he said, "I'm re-starting those research trips again. If you're interested, you might consider joining me. With your CV and my hearty endorsement, getting clearances shouldn't be an issue, but that could take a few weeks.

"Q, I already know I can depend on your skill and courage under pressure. And sometimes a couple is less conspicuous than someone flying solo when battling boredom in exotic venues. What do you say, partner?"

"The hell?"

She jumped off the settee and almost screamed at him, "Whoa, mister! You don't get to ask me a question like that until you tell me what the hell just happened! So, what the hell just happened? 'Alfa, Dog, Romeo? For crissake, Greigh, *what is this?*"

He tamped his palms downward, imploring her to sit back down. His serene demeanor just pissed her off even more. She stood there and glowered down at him.

"I can't tell you how badly I've wanted to have this conversation with you. Advance Defense Regiment is a small and specialized covert arm of Interpol. I'm one of many independent contractors around the world that investigates sensitive cases. Our cover is our ordinary lives. I write my own ticket. I can say no more without your committing you to a rather rigid confidentiality contract. I repeat, what do you say, Q? Want to be a cop again?"

His coy smile drove her crazy.

*Oh, crap! Who **is** this guy?*

HE WASN'T JOKING! SHE PLOPPED BACK DOWN ONTO THE settee before she fell down. A wave of dizziness swept over her.

"I think I'm gonna puke."

After a full minute of deep breaths, she opened her throat and slammed down the rest of her wine. He just sat there, watching, with a straight face. Maddening!

She turned to peer into those icy-blue eyes she'd grown rather fond of and said, "You're recruiting me to be an International cop-slash-spy. *With you.*"

That was not a question.

The Beginning.

But of What?

APPENDIX A

CAST OF MAJOR CHARACTERS IN ALPHABETICAL ORDER

- **Gerard a.k.a. Rocko Bianchi**: Don Gaspari's most trusted capo—lieutenant and muscle.
- **Robin Bidok**: Disillusioned poet who lives in the Sherwood neighborhood within Hotel Literati, a.k.a. "The Lit."
- **Zelda Zenaida Coincoin**: New Orleans Voodoo sorceress of repute.
- **Gaspari Copolla**: Chicago's erstwhile top crime boss who craves respect and legitimacy.
- **Luca Donati**: Partner in ownership of Hotel Literati with brother, Vince.
- **Vincenzo a.k.a. Vince Donati**: Partner in ownership of Hotel Literati with brother, Luca.
- **Captain Lois Granger**: Detective McQuillan's boss at CED's ninety-ninth precinct in Chicago's Near SW Loop.
- **Aubrey Greigh:** Mystery writer, resident and owner of suite 7D, Hotel Literati.
- **Jerry**: Near-homeless visual artist who lives in the Sherwood neighborhood of The Lit.

- **Daniella a.k.a. Dani Kilby:** McQ's friend who is an exotic dancer at "Flights of Fancy" Gentlemen's Club.
- **Tihomir a.k.a. Ty Leonov:** Russian immigrant and Chicago billionaire.
- **Lindy Mansa:** A youthful member of Zelda Coincoin's entourage.
- **Officer Aidan a.k.a. Mac McKenzie:** Street cop and co-worker of McQ's at CED's ninety-ninth precinct.
- **Chance Goodwyn McQuillan, a.k.a. McQ, or Q:** Detective Lieutenant of the Chicago Enforcement Department, ninety-ninth precinct. Lead detective on the Sybil Thibodaux homicide.
- **Doctor Jacques Memeaux:** An unscrupulous Voodoo bokor (witch doctor)
- **Sango Mori:** Japanese poet, martial artist, and owner of apartment 7B at the Hotel Literati
- **Teodor Raspin a.k.a Rasputin:** Ty Leonov's muscle, assassin and procurer.
- **Clairvius Rincisse a.k.a. Obeah Man:** A revered Voodoo patriarch and close associate with Zelda Coincoin.
- **Sybil Thibodaux:** Creole inaugural poet laureate and murder victim.

APPENDIX B

Major Characters' Relationship Map

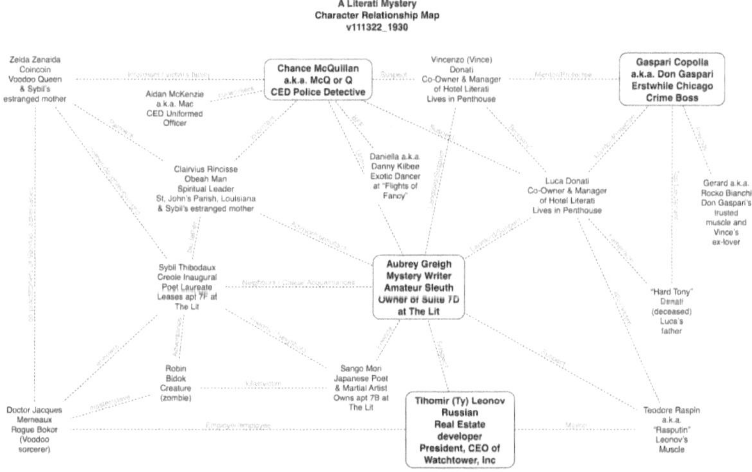

APPENDIX C

Greigh's Apartment Layout

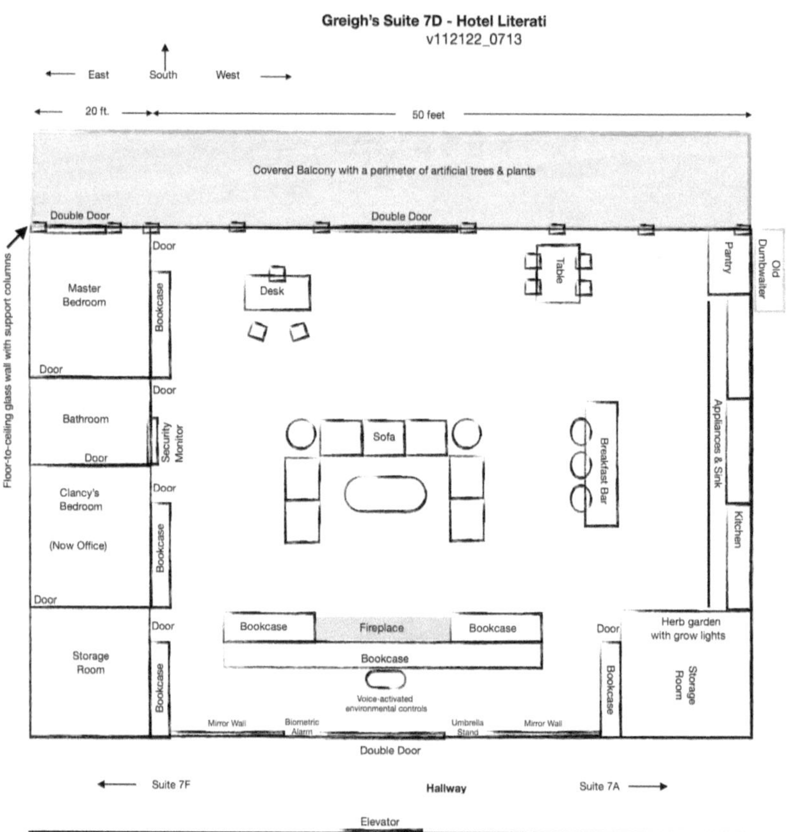
Greigh's Suite 7D - Hotel Literati
v112122_0713
East
South
West
20 ft.
50 feet
Covered Balcony with a perimeter of artificial trees & plants
Double Door
Door
Double Door
Pantry
Old Dumbwaiter
Floor-to-ceiling glass wall with support columns
Master Bedroom
Bookcase
Desk
Table
Door
Door
Bathroom
Security Monitor
Sofa
Breakfast Bar
Appliances & Sink
Door
Door
Clancy's Bedroom
(Now Office)
Bookcase
Kitchen
Door
Door
Bookcase
Fireplace
Bookcase
Door
Herb garden with grow lights
Storage Room
Bookcase
Bookcase
Voice-activated environmental controls
Bookcase
Storage Room
Mirror Wall
Biometric Alarm
Umbrella Stand
Mirror Wall
Double Door
Suite 7F
Hallway
Suite 7A
Elevator

APPENDIX D

Literati Floor Layout - Hidden Spaces

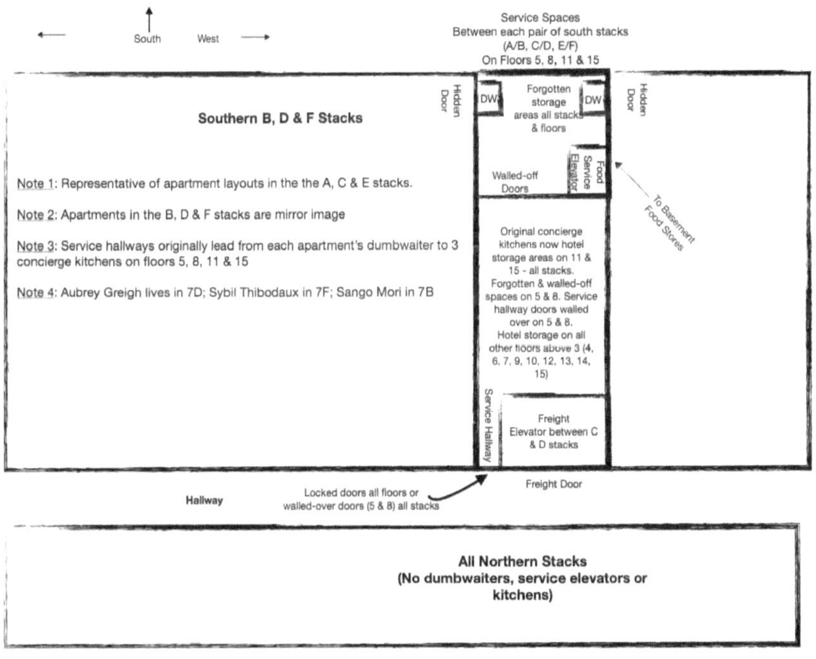

APPENDIX E

Hotel Literati - Concierge Floors
Floors 5, 8, 11 & 15

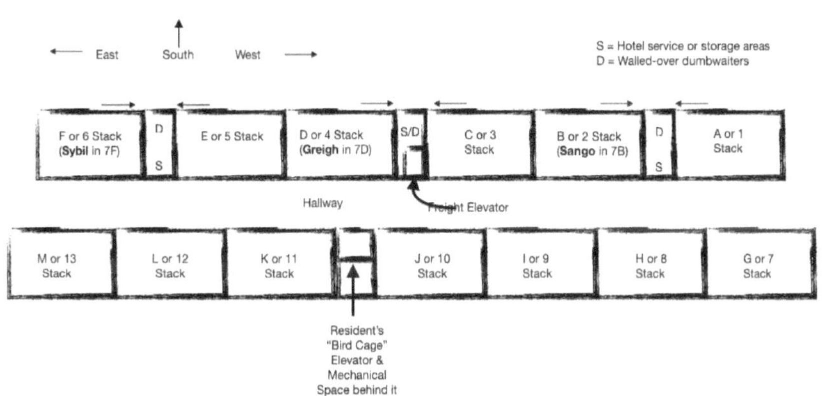

APPENDIX F

Key Locations

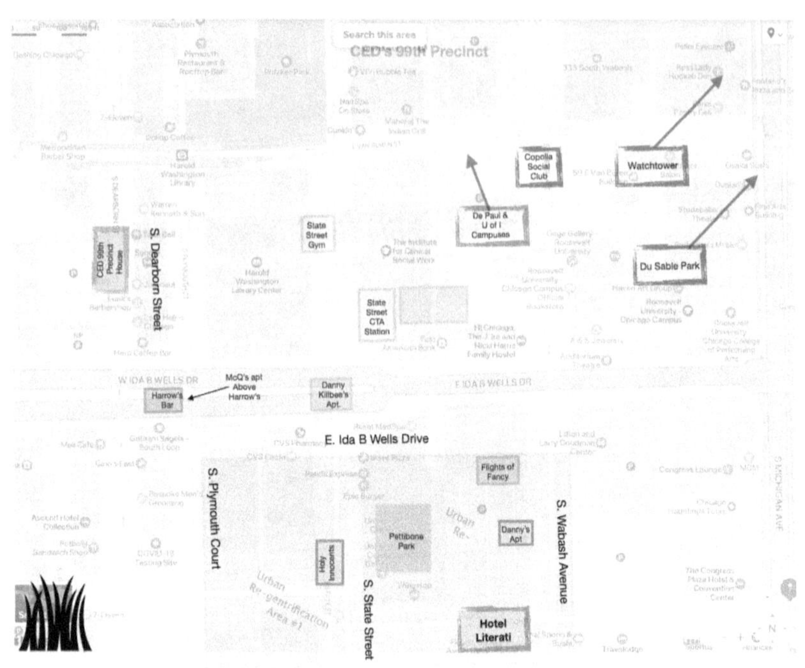

Search this area
CED's 99th Precinct
CED 99th Precinct House
S. Dearborn Street
State Street Gym
State Street CTA Station
Copolla Social Club
De Paul & U of I Campuses
Watchtower
Du Sable Park
W IDA B WELLS DR
E IDA B WELLS DR
McQ's apt Above Harrow's
Harrow's Bar
Danny Killbee's Apt.
E. Ida B Wells Drive
S. Plymouth Court
Flights of Fancy
S. Wabash Avenue
S MICHIGAN AVE
Pettibone Park
Danny's Apt
Holy Innocents
Urban Re-gentrification Area #1
S. State Street
Hotel Literati
Harrison Street

APPENDIX G

Watchtower's Location

Watchtower

120 North LaSalle
City Hall
DeVry University
Seven
LA Fitness
Staples
Primark
Remington's
Coyne College
Pancakes and Cafe
Jay Pritzker Pavilion
Millennium Park
Maggie Daley Park
41
Chicago Yacht Club
W MADISON ST
Cindy's
Target
The Gage
Watchtower Inc.
Chicago Stock Exchange Arch
E MONROE ST
W MONROE ST
The Library
Marquette Building
Palmer House a Hilton Hotel
Central Loop Hotel
2Twenty2 Tavern
The Art Institute of Chicago
S TOWER
W JACKSON BLVD
S CLARK ST
66
S STATE ST
DePaul University
Van Buren St
S COLUMBUS DR
E JACKSON DR
S JEAN BAPTISTE POINT DU SABLE LAKE SHORE DR
Harold Washington Library
Roosevelt University - Chicago Campus
W IDA B WELLS DR
LaSalle St Station
Urban Re-gentrification Area #1
Lillian and Larry Goodman Center
Grant Park
PRINTER'S ROW
S FRANKLIN ST
S FEDERAL ST
S DEARBORN ST
Jones College Prep
Warehouse Liquiors
E BALBO AVE
S LA SALLE ST
Harrison
Hilton
S WABASH AVE
Dearborn Station
East-West University
S WELLS ST
Lou Malnati's Pizzeria
Dearborn Park
E NINTH ST
Police Plaza
Showplace Icon Theatres
Eleven
Legal
41
N

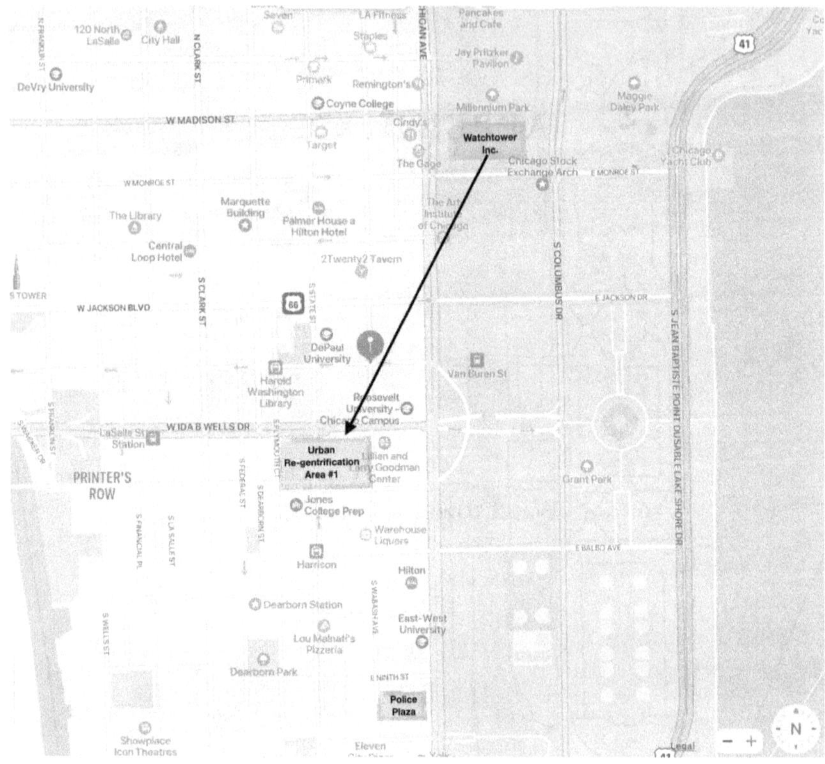

AUTHOR'S NOTE

Blended and varied cultures have always fascinated me.

As I explored my interest in such cultures, I combined that with my interest in how history and our interpretation of it sculpts our society, I felt this story filled a useful cultural niche.

I sincerely hope you found this tale fun, enjoyable and maybe even meaningful.

OTHER BOOKS BY GK JURRENS

Historical Fiction (Great Depression Era Crime)

- Black Blizzard: A Lyon County Adventure
- Murder in Purgatory: A Lyon County Mystery

Contemporary Fiction (Drama)

- Dangerous Dreams: Dream Runners: Book 1
- Fractured Dreams: Dream Runners: Book 2

Future Fiction (Paranormal Mystery Thrillers)

- Underground, Mayhem: Book 1
- Mean Streets, Mayhem: Book 2
- Post Earth, Mayhem: Book 3
- A Glimpse of Mayhem: Companion Guide to the Mayhem Trilogy

Non-fiction

- The Poetic Detective: Investigate Rhyme With Reason
- Why Write? Why Publish? Passion? Profit? Both?
- Moving a Boat and Her Crew
- Restoring a Boat and Her Crew

Mysteries

- **Secret Sword - A Literati Mystery** *Coming Fall 2023*

(turn the page to read an excerpt off "Secret Sword")

EXCERPT FROM SECRET SWORD

A LITERATI MYSTERY

More Than A Few Years From Now

August 31st
City Lux Executive Apartments
Suite 3-16
9 Tietgensgade
Copenhagen, Denmark

The open door placed Aubrey Greigh on instant alert. If he carried a gun, it would have led the way. He wasn't a master of mixed martial arts, but he could take care of himself better than most.

"Peter?" Nothing.

He would have expected Peter Fontera to have met him, if for no other reason than to show off his perfect face surrounding his blizzard-white dental implants. Not to mention his overall magnificent presence. Peter filled any room, but you still loved the guy.

Greigh had never been here before. As soon as he entered this suite—a rental—the portrait did not surprise him. It greeted him in the dim light—a framed head shot on the foyer's only table. Peter had placed it to catch the recessed spot overhead. Only the foyer was illuminated—by that one downward-facing light.

That portrait—was it an oil painting?—was small enough to fit into a suitcase, but large enough to broadcast professional vanity. It featured the tools of Peter's trade: a Botox'd face and perfectly coifed hair, implants and all, at the perfect oblique angle. All hovered over a flamboyant bow tie.

He was famous for those hideous ties. Even the characters he portrayed in every movie all wore them. The entertainment media loved to report that those ties were the subject of an ironclad provision in his every contract. Made him appear a tad wonky. Only Peter could pull it off.

Greigh didn't really care. Didn't know him, other than as a source. Most said Fontera was the nicest bloke ever. Not any more.

He allowed his set of ever-present antique brass knuckles gripped in his right hand and a small flashlight guide him. Now, however, Greigh couldn't help but track through the prodigious pool of blood that surrounded the international celebrity who lay at his feet, possibly deceased, certainly close to it. Unrecognizable except for that ridiculous bow tie.

Before tonight, everyone in the western hemisphere would have recognized Peter Fontera from stage and screen. His popularity had soared as the most prominent Windy City studios satisfied a sudden retro demand. A few years ago, the public hungered for human actors and real-world settings in their entertainment again, versus those that were computer generated or enhanced.

So handsome in life, he now seemed artificial. Peter was still alive, wasn't he? Or was that just incorrigible optimism? Though always repulsed by violent and messy death, Aubrey Greigh got to work.

All right, then. Apply compression to visible wounds—check. Mouth-to-mouth? Out of the question. Not much left of the poor bastard's face. Like that was one of the killer's targets. But no killing wound there. No chance for a controlled airway. Chest compressions, it is.

These high-velocity thoughts swirled like dust devils through

Greigh's parched consciousness. He started cracking Fontera's ribs a hundred times per minute until he soon realized it was all too little, too late.

No stranger to violence, he still abhorred it.

With Fontera's blood and other fluids everywhere, including all over his hands, arms, knees, and the soles of his sandals, too easy to leave fingerprints and distinctive tracks. Couldn't be helped. He had not worn gloves, much less, waders. Didn't expect to slog through a bloodbath and drop to his hands and knees into the thick of it. He mopped his sweaty brow. Most can't appreciate the exertion proper chest compressions require.

Did I just smear Peter's blood all over my forehead?

Earlier this evening, Fontera had contacted him. Said he had vital information to share. Too little, too late. Tonight's theme, apparently.

Greigh cursed himself for burning two precious minutes, administering useless chest compressions to a corpse. Even under less dismal conditions, he knew the average failure statistics behind CPR. Here and now, *far* worse than that. There was always room for hope until... there wasn't.

Well, then, right so! Face obliterated, chest wound still pumping, but... no defensive wounds? Unconscious, unresponsive. Shite be on the saints!

Time had gotten away from Greigh in a fog of futile optimism—his weakness. Now, the police couldn't be far. After failing to raise a pulse, Greigh got to his feet posthaste. Almost slipped and fell in the wet mess. Even his toes were now sticky and stinky.

Scrounged a kitchen towel to wipe his hands. But without water— the faucets didn't work—his hands just got stickier.

No water? Quite curious in such an opulent flat.

Time to beat a hasty retreat. The team would sort all the rest later. He turned to bolt out of the suite's door on the sixteenth floor of the ultra-contemporary City Lux condos. Just across the threshold, a gazillion-candlepower beam stunned him..

"Hænder, hvor jeg kan se dem. Nu!"

Bloody brilliant! Just what I need.

Greigh's working knowledge of Danish made it clear the copper had said, "Hands where I can see them. Now!"

He complied. No sudden moves. Not now. Street cops in any country made his left eye tick. The voice behind the light reported over comms. Translating in his head, "One in custody."

Four rough hands shoved him against the wall to his immediate right, in the hallway just outside the suite. Not his first rodeo, as the Yanks might say.

Three other tactical-clad human tanks slid by to clear the rest of the massive suite with their artillery at the ready.

Who had called them in? Were these concierge coppers? Nope, these boys were Tactical Squad—or whatever they called them here. Copenhagen's finest.

From deeper inside the apartment, one copper said, "Body!" And then three seconds later, a shout of, "Clear!" Then one more. A softer voice, likely the first human tank again, and almost inaudible from the hallway, the bloke spoke with, what? Horrific awe? "Holy Mother of God...."

Yup. That was the first one who discovered Peter's remains. Is that wanker now vomiting in this crime scene? Sure sounded like it. A tank with a sensitive gut? Bloody hell. Must be a rook. One of the Tacs? Isn't Chicago!

Before even being told to do so, Greigh piled both palms on top of his head, leaving two smeared hand prints on the wall.

Two hands—not his—turned out his pockets, while two more held a weapon to his left temple in a white-knuckled grip. They discovered his wallet, US passport, a few Danish and American bills clipped to a single credit card.

They dug deeper for some loose change, an A-bus pass, a folding knife, and a small flashlight. He winced. The officer manhandling him bruised the boys—the family jewels—exploring the depths of his jeans' front pockets for dangerous lint.

Greigh stared at his own shadow.

It stared back at him from the lavender wall, an inch from his nose.

The cop-strength body spot lit his backside with his hands still on his head. Not his best side for the official body cam recording, to be sure. His elbows gave his sharp-edged shadow a shape that reminded him of a bird of prey.

Someone sure enough preyed on poor Peter.

Greigh heard the cuffs clink as they snicked away from an equipment belt behind him. He anticipated the need to bring his right hand down to get hooked up. But not so soon or so fast that the arresting officer would think he was making an offensive move.

He swung his arm out to his side in a slow, wide arc, always keeping his hand open and visible, until it was low enough. With one hand now cuffed, he lowered his open left palm behind his back in the same fashion.

The cop grunted the Danish equivalent of an appreciative, "Huh," like it was a relief dealing with a professional. Textbook hook-up. But the poor fellow's breath broadcast yesterday's garlic. Caused Greigh's stomach to lurch. He'd bet this officer was likely into his second or third shift in a row. The guy could use a change of uniform and a shower, too. Bad breath and BO—the universal work language.

Exhausting, all this scurrying around. Most trying.

One officer read the Danish equivalent of Greigh's rights to him. Since Greigh had yet to utter a single word, they still assumed he was a local, despite the passport.

Hmmm… they're not as sharp as I thought. Or….

Another tactical tank escorted him out to a waiting paddy wagon, a high-security panel van out on Tietgensgade. Looked like they assumed he was a very dangerous guy—like an airborne F5 tornado biding its time to drop and strike without warning. If they only knew….

It was mighty uncomfortable to be so wet and sticky. He was a mess, face to feet, stinking like yesterday's sewage. Like he'd been rolling in the stuff. Not just blood, either. Smart cops. They'd thrown a plastic sheet over the seat toward which he was being guided in no uncertain terms. They forced him down onto a bench in the cage toward the rear door of the van on the driver's side.

After a while, old blood ripens and reeks before it scabs or scales. And that's just the blood. Even cop-calibre Naugahyde upholstery is not immune. Not even this snazzy Volvo EV van—high security law enforcement edition.

They seemed to have sent the first string—except for the projectile vomiter. Nothing but the best for the suspected killer of a celebrity vic.

Vultures were out in force.

By the time the human tanks had led Greigh out for his walk of shame, the night burned white-hot from all the spotlights out on Tietgensgade. Serious battery power pushed megawatts out there. Dappled the caravan of police cruisers and "his" van-slash-mobile cell in high contrast through the leaves of trees lining this exclusive neighborhood's sidewalks.

A veritable media circus had already set up behind the portable barricades beyond the Lux's circle drive. Somehow, the media always got the word, almost before the cops.

This would be a brilliant scene for a reality series called "Star Killer."

But the "Men in Black" surprised Greigh.

He spotted the pair of suits near the van. His sharp eyes sighted tiny lapel pins on these two well-tailored hulks. Each bore a white cross on a field of red with a gold border. Hard to miss on those custom-fit charcoal suit coats.

DDIS agents? Their international colleagues referred to them as the Danish Defence Intelligence Service. After all, who in Hell could pronounce their agency's real moniker in Danish—*Forsvarets Efterretningstjeneste*. Or who could remember what the acronym *FE* meant?

Greigh knew from researching a past manuscript for one of his earlier novels that DDIS responsibilities included collecting information about political, financial, scientific, and military interests.

So, why on Earth would DDIS be interested in a common homicide

—even a celebrity? What might they know that he didn't? Most curious. He'd ask Freya Ecklund, his handler.

Fontera had been in Copenhagen for the last three weeks on location for his starring role in "Dancing With Death." Although he clearly didn't foresee *this* scene as his finale.

And nobody had captured the murder on vid. That cold-hearted prig of a producer would no doubt lament that more than his star's violent demise.

Celebrity victims always nipped the best coverage—especially homicides with a salacious theme. And if that theme involved a bizarre modus operandi? Even juicier.

Was this personal vengeance, or something else?

Vultures have a job to do, too, I suppose. The same everywhere. Nobody recognizes me. So far, at least.

Greigh kept his head lowered, just the same.

If anyone did recognize him, he'd be famous for yet another reason. He chastised himself.

Bloody brilliant, this.

He could not afford this exposure. Inconsistent with the damn mission. He had screwed up. Stupid to attempt triage with that much blood loss. Had to try. He'd lost precious minutes needed to make his escape. A leopard can't change his stripes, as they say. Or some such rot.

American idioms!

There'd be Hell to pay, and he'd be the one paying. But these coppers were the least of his worries. He'd try not to think about all of this until after they cleaned him up. If he was lucky, they'd subject him to a good night's rest in a holding cell, and possibly even a state-sponsored breakfast. He hadn't eaten or slept since, what, yesterday? The day before?

Despite his best efforts not to do so, Greigh reflected during his bumpy van ride to Tärnby—he'd heard the driver chatting with his dispatcher. Not easy to switch off the mind of an investigator.

He imagined the dead guy's luxury rental suite before all the blood on the floor, walls, ceiling and furnishings, not to mention the contents of Peter's vacated bladder and colon.

Someone had rented that apartment almost a month ago for this star of stage and screen. It was every bit as spectacular as his famous high-rise on the *Mag Mile* back in Chicago. That's what the locals called it—Mag was short for Magnificent. They called it that or the *Miracle Mile*—a bunch of overpriced apartment buildings and concierge businesses inside the West Loop. That patch was once quite the tourist trap.

The best apartments boasted the most splendid lake views. But Fontera preferred the river side. They "re-gentrified" that entire area on the Chicago River about twenty years ago so they could justify the "exclusive"—that is, bloody inflated—prices for that rarified real estate.

These days, most stars and celebrities huddled near each other on Celebrity Row out at the southeastern shore of Lake Michigan. That portion of Chicago—the city now a regionplex—was recently part of Western Indiana before useless politicians redrew invisible lines. The lake now stunk like shite, but... it *was* lake shore.

Everyone said "The Row" made the Hollywood Hills look like a shantytown by comparison. They even featured their own mag-lev limo train from out there into all the major studio lots north of the Cicero district. And the rolling parties between The Row and Cicero were the stuff of legends.

No doubt Fontera's suite on the Mag Mile, as well as his mansion out on The Row, would fall to his heirs, if he had any.

Shite-for-brains idiots with money. I'm different, though... aren't I?

Fontera never had a chance.

In the few minutes Greigh had been in the celebrity's suite near Copenhagen's city central, he concluded the killer was not a professional. Too messy. Too personal.

It appeared the movie star had expired from exsanguination. Greigh's cop friend in Chicago—the lovely Chance McQuillan—would say he "bled out." A pro hitter would have delivered one or more decisive insurance wounds, just to make sure. Maybe a head shot. The killer's blade hit no vital organs. Sloppy, unless.... No, sloppy.

Greigh speculated Fontera might even have still been alive as the killer fled. *He'd* assumed so, hadn't he? It's possible he even interrupted the kill. And that would beg the question of how he missed the killer. No, this was not the work of a professional.

Further, Peter's door was open when Greigh arrived. No evidence of forced entry. And this high-end apartment featured a sophisticated security system with a vid monitor. Peter knew his killer and had let him or her in. He'd pass all this info on to Freya at his earliest opportunity. And possibly to the local police at the appropriate time.

They now sat in the Tårnby station.

The veteran street cop with the bad breath and body odor sat behind a small steel desk with chipped corners and dented sides. He stared at Greigh's passport. Still covered in drying blood—maybe that was by design—Greigh squirmed in the bolted-down guest chair with his right hand cuffed to its frame. The cop must have construed his squirming as post-homicidal jitters.

A smaller force here.

Tac guys double as intake processors? Interesting.

This squad room's ambience, though smaller, vibed very much like McQ's at the ninety-ninth precinct house back in Chicago. McQ's squad room before she was placed on administrative leave for getting a civilian killed, that is. Stunk of burnt coffee... and something foul.

He glanced up at the stained ceiling. Lots of dents, like this guy's desk, only smaller, and a lot more of them. Under his feet, most floor tiles had long ago defeated their underlying adhesive and lost their corners. Raucous dregs of humanity acted out minor flurries of boisterous drama all around them. Yup, much like the nine-nine.

Officer Halitosis said in lilting accented English loudly enough to be heard over the din, "So, Mr. Arthur Granby, is it? What kind of name is that?"

The very Scottish Aubrey Greigh said, "Irish, laddy. Grew up there. Now a naturalized American citizen, proud to say. Dual citizenship."

"So, Mr. Granby, why did you kill him? Mr. Fontera?"

"What say you just process me in, Officer? I'd be delighted to chat with your detectives."

"You'll then be spending the night in a holding cell, røvhul." Greigh knew that was the Danish version of smart-arse—paraphrased for polite company.

"'That'll be quite alright. What are your meal options down there, boyo?"

Even the Danes allowed those incarcerated one phone call.

"Freya, a complication in the mission plan, dear. I'm calling from Tårnby. Fontera is dead. It was personal, not a hit. I'm a suspect and in custody."

"Keep your mouth shut and sit tight."

He just adored her Danish accent.

And her black American ExpressCard.

Look for "Secret Sword - A Literati Mystery" in the Fall of 2023

ABOUT THE AUTHOR

~

GK Jurrens writes with undiluted passion, having published a dozen fiction and non-fiction titles to date including ten novels. He also teaches writing and publishing on the road.

More often than not, GK and his wife live and travel in a motorhome when they're not spending time at their condo in Southwest Florida. They wander their beloved North America as a source of endless inspiration.

After studying Liberal Arts and Electronics Engineering Technology, GK earned a Bachelor of Science degree in Business and a Master of Science degree in Management of Technology from the University of Minnesota, USA. He is the proud father of two adult children and the equally proud grandfather of three almost-adult grandchildren.

Six years of government service and a successful three-decade career in global high-technology preceded more than a few years of sailing America's waterways, the Florida Keys, and the Eastern Caribbean from the British Virgin Islands to Granada, near the coasts of Venezuela and Trinidad, with a brief foray sailing around the Greek Cyclades Islands in the Aegean Sea.

GK now pursues his life-long penchant for the creative arts: prose and poetry, painting (watercolor), traveling (North America), playing guitar (acoustic-electric) and his growing collection of Native American style flutes, some of which he crafted while living in the Arizona desert.

He enjoys quiet evenings reading and exploring movies, when not writing or sitting by a campfire alongside his copilot and soulmate of over half a century—'Admiral' Kay.

If you'd care to offer the author feedback, for which he'd be grateful, consider emailing **gjurrens@yahoo.com** or visit **GKJurrens.com** and subscribe.

facebook.com/genejurrens

instagram.com/gjurrens

linkedin.com/in/gkjurrens